I0668656

A CONSPIRACY TO MURDER, 1865

A CONSPIRACY TO MURDER, 1865

THE SYMBIONT TIME TRAVEL ADVENTURE SERIES, BOOK SIX

T.L.B. WOOD

Without limiting the rights under copyright(s) reserved below, no part of this publication may be reproduced, stored in or introduced into a retrieval system, or transmitted, in any form, or by any means (electronic, mechanical, photocopying, recording, or otherwise) without the prior permission of the publisher and the copyright owner.

This is a work of fiction. Names, characters, places, and incidents either are the product of the author's imagination or are used fictitiously, and any resemblance to actual persons, living or dead, business establishments, events or locales is entirely coincidental.

The scanning, uploading, and distributing of this book via the internet or via any other means without the permission of the publisher and copyright owner is illegal and punishable by law. Please purchase only authorized copies, and do not participate in or encourage piracy of copyrighted materials. Your support of the author's rights is appreciated.

Copyright © 2019 by Tara Brooks Wood. All rights reserved.

Book and cover design by eBook Prep
www.ebookprep.com

September, 2020
ISBN: 978-1-64457-030-2

ePublishing Works!
644 Shrewsbury Commons Ave
Ste 249
Shrewsbury PA 17361
United States of America

www.epublishingworks.com
Phone: 866-846-5123

ACKNOWLEDGMENTS

Numerous books have been written about the assassination of Abraham Lincoln, as well as his life in general, his wife, Mary, and his contemporaries. It is with great respect to historical figures that any work borrows from that history to create a fictional account or, one might say, revision of history. The author feels humility when tackling such a venture and, while conducting research of her own, begs permission to broadly rewrite certain events, places, and people in order to create a fictional account of the times. *A Conspiracy to Murder, 1865*, is a work of fiction and is a product of the author's imagination.

The author remains grateful to those who continue to encourage her to place pen to paper, so to speak. These include her husband, friends, and family as well as the publishing team at ePublishing Works.

For Nicholas

Waking or asleep
   Thou of death must deem
   Things more true and deep
   Than we mortals dream

TO A SKYLARK, *PERCY BYSSHE SHELLEY*

ONE

I may look human, but I am not and am apart from the throngs who, at times, surround me in blissful ignorance. And Kipp, my furry canine-appearing companion, is no dog. We are symbionts with a telepathic bond that enables us to travel back in time. Curiosity is one of the characteristics of my kind, and we like to solve mysteries of the past, which linger, unsolved, to modern days. And in my four-hundred-plus years on earth, I'd done just that, first with Tula and now with Kipp, who'd bonded with me during a journey to pre-recorded time from which faded paintings on rocks are the only remaining hint of humanity's struggle to survive. Kipp is unfettered by thousands of years of fragile genes and possesses all the natural attributes given to us by the creator and is the best, most solid partner any symbiont could desire. Because of the broad nature of his talents, partnering with him has been a growth experience for me, as well as for him. With all that being said, it seemed odd to me that my arm would be broken during one of our adventures. With the good fortune of relatively accident-free adventures, why now, I wondered? After all my experiences and mishaps during countless trips back in time, the fracture occurred during the pursuit of an entity known as Spring-heeled Jack who happened to terrorize

1

Victorian London on and off during the early 1800's. But I was thankful to be back home in contemporary times, recuperating.

It was early April in the piedmont of North Carolina; the daffodils were long since gone, their place in the rolling landscape taken by azaleas, which thrived in the softly filtered spring sunlight and the tantalizing breaths of warmth that preceded the summer that was yet to come. The change of seasons, with the sudden temperature spikes and lows, always made me hold my breath, hoping the flowers could withstand the rollercoaster ride of the unexpected. I smiled as I recalled the day that Kipp and I had planted the coral azalea, which blazed against the bright green of new grass, and the cool white one that memorialized my former partner, Tula. As much as I enjoyed the variation of seasons, I already looked longingly towards the future and the autumn that lay ahead. The musty smell of dying leaves, the bursts of chill in the air, a promise of winter to come, and the glorious flames of orange, red, and yellow...it was my personal favorite time of year. Glancing across the yard, I watched Kipp's posture as he became focused on something hidden in the early grass that begged to be mowed. The rainy season had caused nature to have an impressive growth spurt resulting in shaggy lawns and overenthusiastic hedges. The sunlight turned Kipp's ruddy coat of fur into a pool of molten copper that rippled when caught by the slight breeze; his plumed tail began to wag furiously. I had not thought of it before, but his coloration matched the fall palate of which I'd wistfully been dreaming.

"Petra," he called to me, using the telepathy of our kind, "I've found a baby bird!" Turning, he glanced at me. "What do I do with it?" He was clearly distressed.

"Back away, and let's see if mama shows up," I suggested, my advice not necessarily born of wisdom but more of practicality.

My traveling partner retreated several yards before crouching down in the grass, his long muzzle pressed down to the earth, as if he believed such a posture rendered him invisible. "I want to make sure he's okay," Kipp remarked, kind and thoughtful as was typical of him.

It was only a few moments later when the baby's mama arrived, chirping loudly from a branch overhead. I couldn't read the mind of a bird, but it took no special gifts to understand she was alarmed by the presence of Kipp, who, in fairness to the bird, appeared to be a large dog in search of a meal. The baby, who instinctively hunkered down in the grass when caught in Kipp's massive shadow, seemed to appreciate the motivational speech from his parent and, after a few failures, managed to whir clumsily to a low branch, his feathers looking like soft, downy fringe beating the air. He was off and running now, I thought with satisfaction. Maybe he'd have a chance since he was off of the ground, and his vulnerability to predators had decreased just a whit.

The heavy tree limbs overhead groaned as they scraped against one another, disturbed by a persistent wind from the northeast; lifting my head, I caught the scent of the azaleas, sweet and intoxicating. From somewhere in my quiet neighborhood, I heard a dog barking insistently. Kipp stared at me and shook his head. He, unlike me, had the ability to read the notions of many non-human creatures, but the dog was too far distant for a reading of the inner workings of his mind. The back door to my house opened, the loud squeak interrupting my peace. I'd meant to oil the hinges, but now was glad I'd let that go along with so many other things. The sound reminded me of the past and an old house I'd once occupied. That dwelling, beaten, neglected and sagging, had a wood framed screen door that protested mightily with the entry and departure of all visitors. It had seemed to me to be a happy noise. Shaking my head, I internally chided myself for my sentimental musings.

"What are you doing out here?" Fitzhugh used an economy of words, a quality I appreciated. There is something to be said for lacking subtle nuance.

Humans might speculate that telepaths communicate with ease with one another, but it is not always so. My kind are telepathically gifted but have, with our progression into modern times, devised all sorts of ways to not communicate in direct opposition to what was meant to be natural for us. Rules and regulations...and then more rules seemed to be the adaptation to the challenges posed to us by a human world. However, no matter what we do, we are not human, and to pretend to adopt their mores is ill-advised. Kipp was my blessing since he was straight out of the distant past and knew

3

nothing of being constrained by any hierarchy known to symbionts. He'd freed me in more ways than I could list.

"Just enjoying the breeze," I replied, smiling over my shoulder at Fitzhugh. I enjoyed the feel of my dark hair, captured in a braid that fell between my shoulders, slapping my back as I tossed my head; I felt sassy, the mood brought on by the spring weather as well as the healing of my broken limb. Since my health issues had been resolved, I could resume jogging with Kipp by my side. The crimp in my normal activity had left me sluggish and more than occasionally grumpy. And I needed no more reasons for my mood being low, irritable, and generally unsettled. A sequence of time-shifts had left me with unresolved issues and lingering moodiness that is not a good thing for one who makes her living by traveling to dangerous times and places.

"Well, don't be long. Peter, Elani, and Philo are coming by for you and Kipp to give the lowdown on your London adventure," he said, trying to sound gruff but failing. I knew him too well, and he could never be like the old Fitzhugh I once knew. "They managed to restrain themselves until now in kind consideration of your, uh, infirmity. And don't forget that I'm also waiting for your chronicled version for the library."

The break in my left humerus had not left me unable to entertain guests, but I'd used the issue to my advantage, not being particularly motivated to cook or clean. In the end, I'd managed a crockpot soup that required minimal effort along with a pan of cornbread—which, by the way, was one of my hallmark creations thanks to my mother and a few of her closely guarded culinary secrets that involved heating the oil and adding it back to the batter before pouring it into the hot pan. But I had not cleaned, with the exception of the guest bathroom, which was another holdover from my mother's rules of etiquette…clean sheets and a clean bathroom are a must at all times. As I followed Fitzhugh into the kitchen, I sniffed the air; my crockpot soup was filling every corner of the room with savory scents. Fitzhugh opened the door to the oven and removed a tray of brownies.

"For Elani?" I asked, knowing the answer.

He stared at me, not liking to be predictable but at the same time, enjoying the unexpected domestic tranquility we enjoyed. I'd known him for years, working in the library at Technicorps, where our collective of symbionts labored. Humans couldn't detect that we were not of their species due to our human-like appearance —the physical exception being our companions that looked like true, domesticated canines, as did Kipp—and we moved about as needed to disguise the fact we never seemed to age. Actually, we did, but at such a slow rate as to be unapparent. And then there was the question of our canine partners who never left our sides. Such a situation made moments exceeding difficult to manage, such as when Kipp and I were on board the *Titanic*. I know I missed a couple of fine dining experiences due to Kipp's doggy face and body, which prevented his crossing the threshold into the First Class Dining Room as I casually hobnobbed with the swells.

Kipp trailed reluctantly, not wanting to leave the yard but also not wishing to be far from my side. It was our way to create these bonds, humanoid with lupine, which enabled us to time-shift in search of adventures. But my bond with Kipp was unusually close, the usual guards that prevented telepathic intrusion having been abandoned, and Kipp was constantly in my head. One might think that sensation of total enmeshment would be unpleasant, but I'd come to embrace such as the natural intent and could not imagine life without Kipp's constancy.

My tendency was to be a bit of a slob, but as Kipp delicately sniffed my pants leg and raised a lupine eyebrow, I figured I needed a bath. Fitzhugh tried to hide his smile behind his mustache and gray beard that reached midway down his chest. I heard the ticking of claws against the wooden floor of the hallway, and a moment later, Juno stuck her head around the door frame; I could hear her tail thumping against the wall. She had arrived at my house with Fitzhugh, both in need of housing. Just as he, she was a valued elder. Unlike the disturbing trend among many human cultures to disregard elders as nonessential and a burden, symbionts still honored ours as the repository of knowledge and skills, and I hoped that never changed. Once a doggedly committed hermit except for Tula, I now shared my house with two lupines, Fitzhugh, and a striped feline named Lily who was snoozing in the rear of my closet in an empty shoebox that she'd claimed as her den. Her possession of the closet had proved problematic as she seemed motivated to attack my ankles every time I had to enter her inner sanctum. As I passed Juno, my hand drifted down to caress the soft, downy fur on top of her grizzled head. Juno was a treasure whose counsel I appreciated. She brought a measured balance to all discussions and rarely, if never, brought heat to a disagreement. Fitzhugh was another matter, and I'd had my eyebrows singed more than once over the years during an encounter with him.

Kipp followed me down the hallway to my room, which was in the rear of the house. For some reason, he found my need to take a bath amusing. After circling, he plopped down on a bath rug and casually began to clean his paws with the rough surface of his tongue.

"I'm always thankful when I see you having to douse yourself from head to toe with water, that I can just shake out my fur and, if I'm in the mood, give my paw a lick or two." Smiling, he rolled on his back and stared at me from an upside-down position which was never flattering, since his jowls hung loosely, and it gave him a goofy appearance.

"I wish you could see yourself," I replied, laughing. "The very image would wipe the smile right off your face."

The water felt good against my scalp and flesh, and by the time I finished, the small bathroom was filled with fog to the degree the image in the mirror was just a tantalizing shadow of my face. As I pulled the comb through my wet hair, I reflected upon my life. I'd not always been a loner and once upon a time was married with a child, having taken a vacation from traveling for a while. But that had ended, sadly, and all remaining of that time in my life was the occasional visit to my son's grave, which lay on the crest of a lonely hillside. After I resumed traveling, Tula and I encountered a disastrous moment for a bonded pair of time travelers when she was killed. Without the telepathic balance of a lupine partner, I was unable to travel and was going nowhere fast. If Kipp hadn't shown up, I'd still be sitting on a windswept hillock in the distant past, waiting for my lonely end. Kipp, with his endless curiosity, had sought me out, pinging like sonar to find me. Without him, I would have been trapped in time, unable to return home.

Kipp followed me into my bedroom and hopped up on my unmade bed. The room, as was most of my house, was furnished with pieces that had seen a fair amount of use, and the wear and tear showed on their scarred surfaces. The marring had never bothered me, and I viewed each piece as carrying history with it, just as did I. My four-hundred-plus years had left me with scars, too.

"You're kinda lazy," he observed, blinking his eyes as he waited for my response. With our mental bond, he'd been following my pensive thoughts and took the route of playfulness to restore my better humor.

"You could help around here more," I remarked.

"I lack thumbs, as you can see," he replied brightly, tilting his head to the side, as he gave his usual response.

"Your lack of thumbs doesn't seem to prevent you from doing anything you please." Glancing at him, I added, "I notice you finished the memoirs of Ulysses S. Grant last night on your Kindle."

"And it was a good read," Kipp replied, closing his eyes while he stretched, his large ears flattening against his head. "Interesting and extremely well written, too." His eyes opened. "I think even Mark Twain remarked about that fact."

I ignored him since he was clearly showing off. Never a fashion maven, I reached for a pair of sweat pants and a pullover that had seen better days. I reserved my moments for dressing nicely to travels when such attire would be mandatory. I hated corsets, crinolines, and enormous hats as well as pointy-toed shoes that compressed my feet to the point of pain and a stilted, wobbling gait. My one concession to beauty and elegance was the strand of pearls puddled on my dresser top, glowing softly in the ambient light. It would be incongruous to wear pearls with a sweatshirt, but I cared not. That particular adornment had been given to me by one William Harrow, a man I met while chasing—or more accurately, being chased by—Jack the Ripper during a trip to 1888 London.

Kipp's thoughts, tangled with mine, softened as he felt my chest squeeze painfully at the memories. "Does it hurt less with time?" he asked.

"Not really," I replied, feeling my mouth twist in a crooked smile.

I heard someone who pretended to be wise in the manners of the heart say that we didn't mourn a specific person but rather what that person and the relationship might represent. What hogwash, I thought. I missed William Harrow...his quiet, solid nature...his gentle kindness. With little effort, I conjured up the vision of his blue-gray eyes that reminded me of rain falling on a stormy day.

"Stop it," Kipp ordered. "You are only hurting yourself."

"We could go back and live there with him," I replied defiantly. "I know I could make him understand," I added, not sure that I really could. When we'd left him, he reluctantly understood that I was traveling through time. Still, he could only accept I managed such a remarkable feat through a machine of some sort like one out of the imagination of H.G. Wells. Would he feel love towards a non-human pretending to be a woman?

"Any time you want to return, Petra, I am yours and will follow wherever you go. Always," Kipp added, his amber gaze meeting mine. His eyes could be alarmingly intense and intimidating or soft with emotion...they were decidedly soft at that moment.

I knew he would, without question or complaint, do exactly that. But he was young, much younger than I, and his heart was filled with excitement to travel and be, well, a symbiont. Despite all Kipp's generous and well-intentioned protestations, he would not be content pretending to be my dog as I lingered at the side of a human man. Kipp was young, idealistic, and eager to stretch the boundaries of his enormous capabilities. I was imperfect and could be as selfish as any human on earth, but I wasn't quite selfish enough to impose a life of inertia upon my best friend.

"No, maybe one day, but not now," I replied neutrally. Glancing at the clock resting on the dresser top, I saw that my lack of need to primp for guests had served me well. I'd managed to wash, comb my hair, and dress in less than fifteen minutes. Feeling satisfied at the economy of my actions, I stared at the pearls, which seemed to glow as if lit by some internal, magical spark of life. Reaching for them, my fingers hesitated as they hovered over the strand. Could I leave them behind, just this once?

Kipp was staring at me from his comfortable spot on my bed. The sheets and quilt were tumbled, creating a soft nest for him. He always slept with me, his jaw resting comfortably upon my chest, my hand caught up in the heavy nap of fur encircling his thick neck. He'd introduced me to dream manipulation, a skill thought to be long extinct in our species. But I'd found I possessed the same talents in that area as did my Kipp. I often speculated, as did the small circle of friends who knew Kipp and I were privately stretching boundaries outside of the control of the governing body at Technicorps—also known as the Twelve—as to what our limits might be in terms of telepathic skills. That particular small, safe circle was about to congregate in my house for dinner, and it was a relief to not pretend to be something that Kipp and I were not. And we were definitely not a conventional duo of symbionts.

"Wear the pearls, Petra," Kipp said. "You're not ready to leave them—or him—behind, and it's okay." Kipp sighed, the sound soft in the confines of the room. "You may never wish to leave him behind, and that's okay, too." He tilted his head, looking dog-like as he did so. "And you look really pretty when you wear them."

Kipp did not yet understand the nuance of love and how it could bind us to one another. Yes, his love for me was intense and boundless, but it was the love of a friend, companion, and some-times that of a pup with his mother. I had no doubt he would die with me and for me just as I would for him. I'd tried to encourage him not to limit his love to just me. In fact, there was a lovely young female lupine, Elani, who would be arriving in just a few minutes. And there was no doubt that she was filled with the pining sort of love that caused one to ache interminably for my Kipp. In the symbiont world, he could join with her as a bonded couple, a marriage of lupines if you wish, and have a family, just as I'd once done. Smiling, I thought of Kipp with a room full of young pups biting at his legs and tugging at his large ears in rough play.

"Okay, don't go there," Kipp admonished me. "I'm not ready for that, and you know it, Petra."

"I'm sorry, Kipp. You know I'm not pushing you at all. It was your fault, anyway, bringing up Harrow again." I was seated at my dresser and staring at his reflection in the mirror. "I'm not ready to give up traveling, anyway, and I know you're not." Laughing, I remarked, "It's just fun to think of a room full of your kids, tearing up the place." Oddly, I felt like a potential grandmother, watching my adopted son, Kipp, create a family full of mischief and chaos, as I calmly imparted wisdom upon all. "And you will make a wonderful father one day."

"You're not that old, Petra," Kipp grumbled, tired of my bizarre musings. "And you're not that wise, either," he added, inserting a little mean spirited zing in the conversation.

"My arm makes me feel old," I replied, reaching up to gently touch the afflicted area. Yes, the cast was off, but it ached still, and often the throb intensified when the clouds were dark and heavy with moisture, and the rain was about to fall. I'd always attributed complaints about rainy weather affecting joints and such to an old wives' tale or peculiar superstition among humans, but it was a fact, I'd found, which applied in equal measure to symbionts.

"We need a vacation," Kipp opined, jumping down from the bed to the worn braided rug that for years had served as a barrier between my bare feet and the worn wooden floor of the bedroom.

Years, I thought. When would we be forced to leave this house, one which carried the imprint of my traveling as well as my persistently sentimental nature? I'd somehow managed to fill it with pieces of junk as well as some truly nice finds at flea markets and antique stores. There is no need to examine my propensity to select some little obscure object that would be overlooked by others...perhaps a cream pitcher with a chip in the porcelain that would make it an object to discard in favor of another which shone with perfection. And then there was the fact I'd also filled the house with fellow symbionts who mattered greatly to me—Fitzhugh and Juno—as well as one little cat who seemed to think that Kipp, much to his embarrassment, was her mother. My life with Tula had been more simple and carefree than now. But my life seemed to have more consequence, and I felt more content than ever.

"Yes, we do need a vacation," I replied. "How do you feel about a trip to the Smokies?"

Kipp hesitated, and I knew without reading his thoughts that he had something else in mind but would defer to me, as usual, just because he loved me. That quality was one I appreciated but had to fight against. Kipp was an equal partner in the relationship, and his needs also mattered.

"What were you considering?" I asked, trying to prompt him.

"Well, I was reading about this haunted steamboat that appears in a river in Alabama," he began.

I was thankfully spared a reply because a familiar tingle in the back of my mind told me that guests had arrived.

TWO

"What's for dinner?" Philo asked, never one for polite moments of murmuring how delightful it was to see one another and similar endearments. He gently squeezed my uninjured arm, and that would be about all I could expect, although sometimes I got a reckless kiss on the top of my head. Of course, he could skid by with such behavior since I'd known him longer than anyone else in the room, and our relationship might best be compared to that of brother and sister. I could become angrier at him than anyone I knew but take his side against all who would oppose him. Reluctantly, he'd become the leader of our oversight group and was now my boss, which could be interesting since I had the unfortunate tendency to oppose authority. Despite my irritable reaction to anything smacking of control, I was reasonable enough to recognize you couldn't have pairs of time travelers freewheeling in the past, meddling and manipulating history and changing the intended timeline of humanity. Some of my kind had done that sort of thing with disastrous results. We depended upon our elders and the careful recording of our history to keep us in check; Fitzhugh and his library was a critical part of that process.

Tall, slender, with graying hair and dark eyes that looked more shadowed of late, Philo was a couple of hundred years older than me—and that counted minimally for symbionts—but stress had aged him. I no longer mentioned the fact that Claire, his wife, was not at his side for events. He only talked about it rarely now, and I gave him the space needed. Philo was one of us who had never traveled, and he chose to bond early on with a humanoid symbiont. Their one son, Silas, had a history with Kipp and me, and I had no desire to discuss him. A shame, really, that Silas had failed to inherit his father's wonderful qualities. I'd tried to like Silas, for Philo's sake, but just couldn't bring myself to overlook his lack of ethics and selfishness. Philo and I just didn't "go there" anymore.

But something I did appreciate was that Philo frequently went off the grid, so to speak, and would allow Kipp and me to be debriefed without the noxious meddling of the Twelve. Of course, this was a violation of his job responsibilities, but he was wise enough to give us room to perform. The majority of the Twelve had never traveled and had no idea of the impact of their arbitrary and ignorant controls on those of us who did. When your life is on the line, as mine has been on many an occasion, you can't pause to reference the policy and procedure manual for the next step to be taken. There was a certain amount of going by the seat of one's pants that was involved in time-shifting.

It hadn't been that long ago when Philo approached me with a new task...one which I almost flatly refused before I was reminded that I worked for Technicorps and to do as I was told. But that task had turned out to be one that enriched my life, and I couldn't envision not having the young duo of Peter and Elani tagging along with the thought they'd one day be leading the way as I geared back to assume the role of wise elder. My only regret was that I lacked the ability to grow a long beard as did Fitzhugh; somehow, the hair threaded with gray cascading across his chest made him look the part. And what if I just grew older but failed to grow wiser? I tried not to linger on that disturbing notion.

The history of our kind had been that once we could bond with natural ease and travel. But the consequences of a relatively small number of us working to create more symbionts seemed to negatively impact that once prevalent ability. Now, young pairs had to be carefully selected for compatibility, and Peter and Elani had made the grade. The other fact was that many of us just didn't want to do something so dangerous as well as limiting the prospects for huddling around the hearth on a cold and blustery evening, reading bedtime stories to dewy-eyed youngsters. Traveling and family just didn't mix well. Peter was young enough to not care about such things, and Elani was in love with Kipp, so anytime she could be hovering in his charismatic orbit, she was happy. Kipp, gruffly but kindly, kept his distance from her emotionally, so as to spare her feelings. And despite my telepathic connection with him, I had no idea how he really felt about her. That was obviously concealed deep in a layer of his brain inaccessible to me. I'd learned to not tease him about Elani's feelings, an issue about which he had absolutely no sense of humor.

Peter, with his boyish mop of dark hair and brown eyes that sometimes peered out from behind tortoiseshell-rimmed glasses, could play a variety of parts during travel. His earnest expressions and partially honest naivety caused humans to effortlessly fall for his deceptions. In short, he seemed well-intentioned, and people naturally gravitated towards him. With the addition of a mustache and beard as needed, he could also appear older than his years. I grudgingly admit that he was moving faster in his career of traveler at the young age of fifty than I had, but in all honesty, I always have been remarkably lazy and not particularly smacking of ambition. But I was managing to keep up with the youngsters, and it was only after landing from a time-shift that I really felt my age. After all, at over 350 years older than Peter, I had a right to grumble from time to time.

At his side was Elani, one of the more lovely young lupines I'd ever seen. The colors in her coat, which was gray undershot with silver hairs, caused her to glow and shimmer when the lighting was just right. I could think, in my more speculative moments, that she was a creature based upon the imagination of a romantic author not bound by the usual rules of nature. Before Elani could stop herself, she glanced at Kipp, who was studiously examining a crack in the sheetrock of my ceiling. Yes, I'd seen that longing, aching heart expression before in my life...most recently staring back at me from my vanity mirror when deep in recollection about William

Harrow…and I felt for the youngster. Kipp wasn't ready for such romantic involvements and wanted to travel. A first crush is a difficult road to navigate.

My small dinette table in the kitchen looked as if it had survived a natural disaster, what with the battered vinyl top complete with a burn mark where someone had thoughtlessly set a hot pan. I sighed. The set was just another Petra rescue of some discarded item shoved in a dusty corner of an easily overlooked and crowded store that had weekly auctions to manage the bulging inventory. Fitzhugh and I began our mornings, now, playing peek-a-boo at one another across the top of that table. I became aware Kipp was staring at me.

"What?" I asked, using our private manner of communication that just included the two of us.

"You are getting very sentimental these days," he replied, pausing from his bowl of chicken and rice.

Trying to ignore him, I chased some vegetables around the bowl of soup I'd ladled and reached for another piece of cornbread, which I aimlessly crumbled on my plate. Fitzhugh and Philo were engaged in a rather high spirited argument about a proposed change to Fitzhugh's beloved library over which he felt ownership. I tried to ignore them, too. Glancing over at Juno, I saw she'd finished with her dinner, lacking the hearty appetite of the youngsters, Kipp and Elani. With a wink at me, she circled for a minute before plopping on the floor with a sigh and a soft thud. She had not eavesdropped on my dialog with Kipp, but I had a notion she sort of divined the issues that were left off the table. Juno was sensitive in that way, a gift of long life and gentle heart.

"I think I've figured out why," Kipp continued. I knew when he got like this the best action on my part was to not return fire. "You were alone, just you and Tula, for many years and got accustomed to that. Except for dealing with a few symbionts, you were isolated." I rolled my eyes at him, wishing he'd stop. "Your relationship with Fitzhugh was combative, and Philo has always been comfortable, like an old shoe. Now, Fitzhugh is like your family, as is Juno, and Peter and Elani are like family, too." Kipp tilted his head. "You enjoy this connectedness and sense of family even though you will deny it to the end."

"Why would I do that?" I replied.

"Because you're stubborn and sometimes kind of stupid."

"Are we boring you?" Philo took his turn staring at me. "I'm sure you and Kipp have some enormously important dialog in process. And as long as you're not discussing my rapidly graying hair, the dark circles under my eyes, or my concave backside, then I really don't care."

He, of course, was teasing me.

After we finished eating, I walked out on the narrow back porch to watch Kipp and Elani frolic as darkness approached; a stiff, slow Juno followed, enjoying observing, without envy or grief over lost days, the youngsters engaged in their rough play. She had once done such herself, but that was a long time past. Peter and Fitzhugh had volunteered for clean up duty, and I rushed outside before either could change his mind. Philo followed in a moment, and we stood there together, watching the sky change colors as twilight descended. It was that wonderful moment of utter stillness that covers the land as the sun drops from sight beneath the far horizon.

I knew I'd not been a good friend of late in terms of supporting him with his issues with Claire and the strain on their marriage. Quite honestly, after my return from a time-shift to the *Titanic*, I'd been so mired in processing my memories of that experience, that I'd not been very attentive to anyone. It was best for symbionts to limit their attachment to humans encountered in search of history's moments, and I found I had managed that quite nicely when a young and callow youth. I could lie with ease as I assumed my make-believe role and not bat an eyelash. As I aged, I found it progressively more difficult to maintain an artificial relationship with people who believed they were getting to know me. The fact was humans never got to know me, and I felt alone when in their presence. Kipp was right, I think. A convergence of events was softening me, and that was not a good thing for a symbiont. We were meant to be tough and analytical, if nothing else.

"I enjoyed our walk in Duke Forest," Philo began. It was obvious he was launching an opening meant to draw me in, and I would be forced to reply. With a sigh, he took a seat on the porch step. After a moment's hesitation, I joined him, our shoulders lightly touching. From the darkness, we heard Elani bark excitedly as Kipp flashed past her and into the halo of the backyard light, before disappearing again. Juno looked at me, her jaw-dropping in a lupine smile. The energy and silliness of youth, she was thinking.

"It was nice," I replied, my voice bland. Since the *Titanic*, I'd been plagued with nightmares and would awaken each morning at the time the *Titanic* slid past the surface of the cold Atlantic. Kipp knew, of course, and wanted to go into my mind and manipulate my dreams to happy ones, but I had prohibited such things. It didn't take a human analyst to tell me that I had issues I was working out. And Fitzhugh only had to look at the shadowed stains beneath my eyes each morning as we stared at one another across the dinette while sipping the morning brew of Earl Grey and waiting for a Pop-Tart to spring from the toaster.

"I have to think," Philo continued, undeterred, "that some of my best times have been spent with us walking along some over-grown path, the ferns and undergrowth brushing against my legs, as we try to get lost in the midst of someplace isolated and seldom trod." A dreamy, philosophic smile crossed his face. "And in the fall, when the leaves are almost blindingly bright as the sun highlights all the beautiful colors...I feel grateful and speechless." Philo's smile faded. "And then we all are forced to return to reality when we realize the leaves are in their death spiral and will soon fall to earth."

I glanced at him from the corners of my eyes, not sure what to say in response to his poetic dissertation. At that moment, I saw the corner of his mouth twitch and reached out to punch his arm with my fist.

"You're a booger, to use Elani's favorite term of describing Kipp," I cried.

"Just trying to lighten the mood," he said, grinning.

We sat watching the lupines, who had abandoned their play and shifted to mock predatory behavior. Kipp was fully capable of hunting prey as well as catching and devouring it, but with my supplying food, his hunting behavior was just for fun and to keep in practice. The lupines shared some qualities of canines in that they were hardwired to seek prey; their intellect, however, gave them choice. Their hearing, eyesight, and noses were vastly superior to their humanoid companions, enabling them with survival tools the rest of us lacked. And Kipp was correct in that he didn't have to take baths or wear a corset. I found myself feeling a mite jealous and wishing for more hair, big ears, and a longer nose.

"As your boss, I've been concerned over your preoccupation with some past time-shifts," Philo said, as he reached out to pluck a tiny twig that had fallen into my hair. "And as your friend, I'm even more worried." He began to twist the twig into a pretzel shape. "Maybe you need to back off traveling?" His voice was tentative, since he knew what such a statement would imply. Kipp was young and needed to travel but had the misfortune to be paired with me and all my current issues. But Kipp would not leave me, as he had adamantly stated on many occasions.

"I'm good," I replied tersely.

I was relieved when the back door squeaked on its hinges, and Peter's head stuck out the crack to announce that the *Fellowship of the Ring* movies were just beginning, and all three would run in consecutive order. What the heck, I thought, since it was a Friday night, and none of us were compelled to show up at work, bright-eyed and energetic the next morning. Philo seemed to want to stay, too, since Claire was out of town visiting Silas. During the *Two Towers*, I brought out blankets, a couple of sleeping bags, and pillows, and we ended up having an old fashioned sleepover. Fitzhugh was on the sofa, while the rest of us fashioned pallets on the floor. After squirming around to get all the wrinkles settled in my makeshift bed, I made myself comfortable with Kipp's broad flank as my pillow. Eventually, despite the sound from the television, the rhythm of his breathing combined with the warmth of his body eased me off to sleep. For the first time in quite a while, I had no nightmares and slept a dreamless sleep.

THREE

I felt somewhat disoriented and momentarily confused to find my living room filled with bodies --humanoid and lupine -- as well as one small cat who had parked her fuzzy body, which reverberated with purrs, between Kipp and me. As I opened one sleepy eye, the scene filled me with contentment. Aggravated, I realized Kipp was correct and that I'd become an old softie, filled with sentimental nonsense. Gently, I displaced Lily, who uttered a soft meow of protest; her body felt like a heated brick in my hands. Kipp thumped his tail, once, before stopping, since no one else was yet awake. Noiselessly, I tiptoed to the kitchen, so I could gaze out of the row of windows that ran the length of the room. It always made me feel I was outside, and I stared through the glass at the filtered sunlight that was breaking through the leaves in shimmering streams of pale gold. Elani appeared, and she and Kipp, who trailed behind, disappeared into the yard, making their rounds of the property. Philo was next, a lopsided smile on his face, enjoying a private moment alone with me before the room became crowded. Since I had not prepared to have guests for breakfast, it would be Pop-Tarts and cereal—at least I hoped the Cheerios still had a decent expiration date—for the humanoids, while I prepared chicken and rice for the lupines. After everyone finally assembled, straggling in waves, we supped; our appetites satiated, we crowded around the dinette for the story to unfold, which is why we'd gathered in the first place.

"Ok, tell us about Spring-heeled Jack." Philo rubbed a hand over his hair, which was already standing on end after a night spent on my floor. He nodded as I refilled his coffee cup.

There was always significant preparation so that one could assimilate and melt seamlessly into a crowd during a time-shift. I'd worked with Suzanne, who created wardrobes for travelers to match what was appropriate for the time as well as social class. In 1837 London, there was less physical segregation of the wealthy from the poor, and even in areas that would later become mainly populated by the poor, there was a mixture of the classes in the districts that bordered the city of London proper. Our destination was Battersea, which was located in the southern part of London. London was the central hub with the numerous districts ringing it much like small villages set in a country-like setting. Although my early years had been spent elsewhere in central Europe, my family led a nomadic life and migrated so as to not gain the curiosity of the populace. This sort of existence was true then of my species and still was in current times but to a lesser degree. And I'd been to England many times over the years in my travels, so this particular trip required little preparation for me to fit in with ease.

After a lackluster send-off party—and I admit, I had been a little disappointed since previous ones had been filled with humor and camaraderie—Kipp and I had made the time-shift sans Peter and Elani. Fitzhugh, actually, had proposed that we break apart our quartet for one shift so that Kipp and I could focus on our time together as a bonded duo. He didn't say so, but I suspected the residual trauma from our trip to the *Titanic* had something to do with his suggestion. The entire notion of traveling as two pairs simultaneously was rather novel in any case. We left in the fall so that our travels would roughly parallel our natural timeline.

A time-shift, for the uninitiated, is a rapid travel through time, backwards, and then a return to where one's life would have advanced in contemporary times, although that particular mark was negotiable. We were unable to travel as a duo into the future, although Kipp had moved forward in time, leaving his lonely past behind, when partnered with me. Kipp and I had covertly tried a real, honest-to-goodness trip into the future as a team and failed miserably. I have never been a good student of science or physics, but I guess our species has to have made a footprint in time to which to return, and that is the best explanation I can give. During the time-shift, the world becomes dark, and one feels as if one is diving off a high, narrow springboard into a black pool of water, immense and depthless. I've always thought my body was being stretched beyond its limits, almost painfully so, during a shift. Some natural protection exists in that we don't materialize inside of a solid object or in the midst of a cluster of humans. I liken it to fish that swim in large groups or a flock of birds turning and wheeling in concert while flying through a shadowed grove of trees.

This particular landing was rather hard for me, and I think it may have set the stage for the later fracture of my arm. When I regained my sensibilities, I was lying awkwardly on my left side, my arm twisted behind me, painfully so. Even though I tried to not complain, I guarded that injured arm until the day it was broken. But that story is yet to come. Reaching out with my right hand, my instinctive first move was to feel for Kipp, although I knew he was uninjured, and his typically jaunty attitude brimming with self-confidence filled my mind. He and Elani were the two most gifted and relaxed travelers I'd known.

"Watch yourself," he cautioned, his soft muzzle touching my cheek, leaving a damp imprint upon my flesh.

Glancing up, I was startled to see a man, who, although several feet away, was close enough to clearly have seen the two of us, Kipp and me, materialize out of nothing. His eyes darted downward, and I realized my skirt was up, almost to my waist, and my minimal undergarments were in full display. I was glad, in that instance, that some type of undergarment had just become in vogue for ladies since prior to that time, the style was to go commando. The man's mouth fell open as he began to stutter and point; a second later, he seemed to realize he was holding a liquor bottle in his hand. With a high pitched scream for one so heavily built as was he, the man threw the bottle, which shattered on a stone walkway, and began to run, his steps unsteady as he tottered along the dirt road that stretched off into the graying twilight. I caught a whiff of the cheap whiskey as it atomized into the air. Grimacing, I managed to unwind my arm from my back and gingerly pulled down my skirts. I needed a moment to catch my breath.

"Well, that hasn't happened in many years," I remarked. It was true that I'd rarely been seen, uh, magically appearing.

"Not my fault," Kipp sniffed. He clearly was not in the mood to assume any small bit of responsibility for the clumsiness of our landing.

Spring-heeled Jack made his first notable appearance in 1837, but after that, a similar character appeared over a time span that would seem to negate the possibility that he was mortal. This idea was reinforced when he continued to appear in North America up until the 1970s. But I'd personally never met Bigfoot or the Jersey Devil and remained a skeptic of such things. I had, however, met several ghosts, so perhaps I needed to remind myself to keep an open mind. But considering the ongoing reports of a Spring-heeled Jack figure, I considered the possibility of decades of copy cats. Some humans crave attention, I suppose.

Time-shifting for symbionts requires research as to the desired destination as well as acquired skill to land at the appropriate time and place. Since Kipp and I had made the journey to London previously, we only had to adjust our time trajectory. I add, with no false modesty, that we were very talented at our particular trade. After the man whom we'd startled with our impromptu arrival disappeared into the gloaming, I managed to stand, feeling a little dizzy. Fitzhugh warned me that as I made more and more shifts over the centuries, my ability to tolerate such trauma to my system as well as achieve a rapid recovery would lessen. Such physical limitations explained my slowness upon "landing" as opposed to the high energy and alertness possessed by my younger counterparts.

"No, you are not old by any means," Kipp remarked, looking up at me as his brushed tail began to wag. "You're still a young symbiont, but I just happen to be even younger. One day I'll feel just like you do today." He was trying to boost my mood, and I appreciated the effort, but I still felt pretty rough.

I winked at him before pausing to canvass our surroundings. Hearing the solid thud of footsteps, it was not difficult—and required no telepathy—to predict the arrival of a constable, summoned by the terrified voyeur. At least my skirt was back around my ankles where it belonged; my backpack, which carried an extra skirt and blouse and a few essential items, looked odd and out of place as it rested on the ground.

"Miss, are you alright?" the constable asked after glancing around the immediate area to try and determine how my appearance could have frightened a large, solidly built man.

Thinking quickly and lying adroitly is a very important skill for us, so without pausing, I created a little tale. "Yes, thank you, sir. There was a man here…I think perhaps he had imbibed some spirits…and when I walked past with my Kipp, he was startled and ran away." I blinked my eyes for good measure. "I didn't mean for us to scare him." Letting my hand deliberately drift down to lightly touch Kipp's broad back, I added, "Kipp is rather large, and I forget how people might react to him."

"Yes, right you are, miss," the constable replied, relief on his young face, which was lightly pocked with smallpox scars. He was tall, unusually so, built like a thin scarecrow that should be hovering in some wind rattled cornfield, attempting to frighten away insistent crows. "This is not a good place for you to be alone," he added with a gesture of his hands.

"So, what am I?" Kipp asked, his thoughts merging with mine. "Does the man not see me standing here, ready to rumble?"

"If you could show me to some respectable place where my Kipp and I might take a room, I would be grateful." I made no effort to change my diction and accent, and the man's thoughts betrayed he knew I was an American, perhaps some lost county bumpkin who needed all the help I could get.

The constable was happy to act as a chivalrous hero, even to carry my backpack, at which he had darted a puzzled look at its unusual style. As he led me down a street that was lightly traveled, I glanced curiously at my surroundings as one might expect of a visitor from out of town. We passed several storefronts, most of which were beginning to shutter for the evening. The area was poor, but as I knew from history, this district had extreme poverty cheek to jowl next to homes housing upper middle class as well as more wealthy people. Many of the laborers in the district worked for their wealthier neighbors, and a relatively peaceful coexistence prevailed. Social unrest as a result of poverty and working conditions was lurking on the cusp of society. The thick smells of chemicals and decay swirling past us had drifted to the area from the tanneries and slaughterhouses, which were not too far distant. Kipp wrinkled his long nose and looked up at me.

"Not sure how they stood it," he opined, trying not to cough. His keen sense of smell magnified what for me was extremely unpleasant.

"They didn't know anything else, so this was their normal," I replied.

"It's a stinky normal."

The constable stopped in front of a narrow building, squeezed in on either side by common walls from other businesses. The sign proclaimed that it was a dressmaker's shop. Grinning at me, the constable tapped lightly on the door. After a minute, a lit lantern from the back of the store appeared, and a petite, elderly woman opened the door, after having peered out cautiously through the window.

"Hello, Matthew," she said, beaming up at the constable.

"Good evening, Miss Logan," he replied. "I heard from one of your neighbors that your spare room became vacant." Turning, he gestured towards me. "I met this young lady tonight who needs a safe place and thought of you."

I stared up at him, a smile tugging at the corners of my mouth. "And how would you know I'd be a good tenant for Miss Logan?" I asked.

"I have a feel for people and pretty much can determine right up front their qualities, good and bad." He shrugged his shoulders. "It's a gift."

I laughed, reaching down to pat Kipp's head. Miss Logan was staring at him, and I was pleased that her thoughts were not negative. My huge companion was a little too large for some people, but not this tiny dressmaker. And although I was not particularly tall, standing next to her, I felt like a giant.

"What a lovely animal!" she said. "I just recently lost my little dog," she remarked, her chin quivering slightly as she spoke. "May I pet him?" Her hands were aching to feel his fur and touch him as she had her own companion.

"Kipp loves people," I replied.

Kipp eased up closer to her, careful to not be too rambunctious, and her small hands, which were mildly twisted by arthritis, gently rubbed the rufous fur on his back. He closed his eyes as she gently scratched along the crest of his spine.

"Why don't you scratch me there?" he asked, opening one eye to stare accusingly at me. "That's an exceptionally good spot, so please take note."

As Miss Logan continued to run her hand along Kipp's fur, I explained I would be in England for a few weeks and needed a room. "I'm a writer," I lied. "I'm here researching a story and will be out some in the evenings in search of some facts." I paused for a moment as we stood in the feeble light of a gas-lit lantern that shone nearby; a large moth beat its wings against the glass, trying to reach the tantalizing amber glow within. "I only tell you that so that you won't be disturbed by my comings and goings."

She stared at me, her eyes dropping to the modest jet brooch at my throat. Harrow's pearls were hidden beneath the high collar of my blouse. Her thoughts and that of the constable reflected their concern for me and more than a little disapprobation of my need to wander about the streets in an unsafe area without a male companion. Such activities were not particularly ladylike and definitely not a sign of intelligence or sound judgment, but as Miss Logan looked at Kipp, she smiled.

"I would normally not advise a lady to walk the streets unaccompanied, but I believe you have your escort," she said. "You may have a key and do as you wish."

As the constable left us, she escorted me into her establishment. The familiar fragrance of musty fabrics and candle tallow lingered heavily in the main room, which was a little dusty but neatly kept.

One wall had shelving containing fabrics on large rolls. A large cutting table was in the center, and there was a grouping of comfortable upholstered chairs to the side to accommodate waiting clients.

"I sew for many of the women in this district," Miss Logan remarked as she picked up a piece of tailor's chalk that had been left on a low side table. "Of course, many of the wealthy patrons seek out larger establishments in London, but I am content to ply my trade here. Fewer complaints and less arrogance, I've found," she added, smiling at me.

At the rear of the large room, there was a doorway that opened into a very small kitchen and another that led to Miss Logan's bedroom. The room I was to occupy was overhead, and a steep, dark, narrow staircase led to the second bedroom.

"I don't go up there much anymore," Miss Logan remarked, her tone a little wistful. "My hips are too stiff, and I'm afraid I'll take a tumble down the stairs." Lightly touching my shoulder, she said, "Why don't you go check out the room while I put on a kettle of water for us to have a cup of tea together? I was just about to prepare my nighttime cup when you arrived," she added hastily, so that I wouldn't protest over her extra labor to accommodate me.

With Kipp leading the way, and a candle in hand, I climbed the stairs, which opened out into a room that spanned the entire top floor. There was one large window overlooking the street, and a pair of faded brocade curtains hinting at a past elegance was drawn back with velvet ties snagged by bronze hooks. The walls were covered with aged wallpaper; some of the joined areas had lost their adhesion and buckled from the surfaces. The bed was ancient mahogany set with scratches marring the once polished surface, but the mattress was overstuffed and promised a soft, downy surface upon which to rest. I smiled at Kipp, who was wagging his tail, clearly pleased.

"What a neat room!" he exclaimed. I had to agree.

It took me less than sixty seconds to unpack my backpack, which usually was turned inside out upon my arrival to resemble a large carpet bag valise, but I'd not had the opportunity to do so due to the unexpected clumsiness of our landing. I guess I was initiating the early inhabitants of the area as to a new type of luggage that would show up in the next century. By the time we joined Miss Logan in the tiny kitchen area, she had a pot of tea steeping and had set her tiny round table with a sugar bowl and a small, chipped china plate that displayed a few tea cakes.

"Sugar?" the seamstress asked as she sat across from me. "Does Kipp like biscuits?"

Of course, Kipp's tail began to brush the floor where he sat since he had a sweet tooth and tended to like anything edible. As Miss Logan held out the broken half of a teacake, he approached slowly, extending his head to nab the treat carefully between his large teeth.

"Very well mannered," Miss Logan chuckled.

Kipp circled and plopped to the floor and began his reflexive deep dive into Miss Logan's vaulted memories that were inaccessible to me. While he sifted through her brain, I learned about her and the neighborhood the old fashioned way, through conversation.

"Yes, my clientele are not particularly well off, but I manage to keep quite busy," she was saying.

I studied her face. She'd once been pretty, with a perfect oval face and skin that hinted at having been milky and unblemished, even though it was now lined and had lost its tautness. Her blue eyes were faded, and I could detect what seemed to be a looming opacity, which would hamper her trade.

"What will happen to her when she can no longer work?" Kipp asked. He had a kind, compassionate heart.

"I don't know, Kipp," I replied truthfully. "But we will have few needs while we are here, and I plan on leaving all the money we brought behind."

We both knew that the Twelve asked for a full accounting of funds spent on a time-shift, but, hey, I was a symbiont –quite skilled —and I could lie like a rug. And since the members of the Twelve adhered to modern-day rules of non-intrusiveness into my thoughts, I could get away with pretty much anything. Between the coins hidden in the money collar Kipp wore, as well as mine, we could leave our hostess a modest endowment. Since she was too old to have offspring, I couldn't imagine my doing so would alter the natural timeline. I once worried more about such technicalities, but partnering with Kipp had caused me to view many things with a different eye.

Kipp sighed, satisfied at my response. His amber eyes drifted shut as he continued to search Miss Logan's past. "She was in love, once, when very young, and her heart was broken when he was killed. He was a warrior, a soldier I suppose, and died in another county. She never allowed herself to love another man after him." Kipp opened one eye to glance at Miss Logan, who had launched into a discussion about fabrics and current fashions with me. "She has a sweet nature, humble and thoughtful." His glance darted to me. "She's a keeper."

I knew I'd have to keep him focused on our purpose, lest he become mired in his worry and concern over the elderly seamstress. I, too, cared about her but had more experience than did Kipp in terms of leaving people behind. It was what we did…and there was no changing our nature.

I figured that Miss Logan could use a little help during the day, and Kipp and I would be prowling around the district after sunset, so I asked her if I could trade some assistance with cleaning, helping with customers and the like, for perhaps a blouse or two and some fresh undergarments. She immediately agreed. In any case, I cared not for idleness, and the activity would be good for my mental health.

"You can sew?" Kipp's eyes rounded.

"You know I was born a long time ago when there was no store-bought clothing, Kipp." I glanced at him.

"Yes, I know that. But can you sew?"

I knew he was picking at me, like an annoying sibling or child, and ignored him, turning my attention to helping Miss Logan rinse out our cups and stack everything neatly for the next morning.

"I will go shopping and procure some food items since Kipp and I will be your boarders," I remarked, not allowing her time to refuse. I could easily purchase food for Kipp from street vendors and then get fresh vegetables and fruits brought in from the country at a local market. The water access was at a pump behind her store that was shared with a few other tenants. Knowing the toting of water was difficult for her, I almost skipped out back carrying the large bucket she used for water, Kipp following. He giggled as I managed to clumsily slop water on my skirt, the liquid cold on my legs. After retrieving the water which would be ready for the following morning's needs and bidding her goodnight, Kipp and I climbed the narrow staircase that squeaked more than I would have liked, considering our proposed nocturnal comings and goings. Outside, I heard the rumble of thunder, and after stripping down to my chemise, I managed to find a firm enough spot in the soft bed so that I wouldn't sink down to the floor; the pillows and sheets smelled faintly of lavender with a sweet hint of jasmine, I thought. As a bolt of lightning flashed from between the narrow space where the curtains gaped, Kipp hopped up and managed a clumsy circle, as he tried to not get tangled in the soft mattress and coverings.

"I like her," Kipp mumbled, as he yawned in my face, trying to ward off the sleepiness that had infected us both. "We need to find her a dog," he added.

"Why don't we let her do as she wishes?" I asked.

"She wants a dog...it is screaming out in her thoughts every time she touches my fur." Kipp grunted softly. "I'll take care of it."

"Okay, boss," I replied, not interested in trying to oppose him. When he was in a determined mood, he was pretty much unstoppable.

FOUR

"So, where is the Clapham Churchyard?" Kipp asked, craning his large head to peer right and then left. It was a damp, dank moonless night, and the directions we'd been given would not have gained any applause from the makers of GPS systems. We'd been venturing out each night for the past week, but each trip required we familiarize ourselves with the topography when curtained by darkness. The moisture in the air felt clammy as I pushed back a curling tendril of hair that insisted upon drifting across my forehead.

"I think we will be close in a few more blocks." Pausing, I turned once to look behind me. I'd not bothered to detail our evening strolls with our landlady, since there was no reason for her to worry. She wouldn't understand that telepaths could pick up the thoughts of any potential attacker and avoid an encounter. And, well, Kipp's bulk was sufficient to keep most evil-doers away. A sinuous black cat curved around a building corner before being lost in the shadows.

"Good thing we're not superstitious," I said, letting go of my breath, which I'd unconsciously held. Even though I didn't fear for our safety per se, the suspense of waiting for Spring-heeled Jack was sort of like waiting for a balloon to pop…one is never truly ready.

The sidewalks, what little there were, were uneven; we were

lucky to occasionally step on flat stones set side by side. For the most part, the traveling surfaces were constructed of packed dirt decorated with the refuse that had blown to the base of the buildings and storefronts ahead of an unpredictable wind. The fog traveling from the Thames was as thick as a blanket, holding in the coal smoke from the numerous chimneys. The ripe smell of sewage caught in the back of my throat as I coughed and shook my head.

"I miss the fresh air of home," Kipp remarked, ducking his head under my hand. He was not usually wistful, and I tugged gently on his ear. A second later, I felt him tense as he gazed ahead, his eyes following the figure of a solitary woman who was walking rapidly along the road ahead. "Follow her," he ordered. "She's the one going to the churchyard." I realized his conclusion was formed from telepathy as well as intuition.

Yes, we arrived in London armed with the knowledge of what was supposed to happen and when, so our current activities were designed to place ourselves as close to the action as possible and observe. The exact date might be off a day or two, or even more, but we knew of an attack that occurred at the Clapham Commons churchyard in October, 1837. We'd come to this general area each night for the past week, and this was our best scent yet, proving we were on the right trail. I'd only taken a couple of steps when a man, poorly clad, stepped out from an alleyway to lightly grasp my arm. I'd been so occupied with Kipp and the woman ahead, I'd not bothered to scan the immediate area.

"Hey, missy. I need whatever money you might be carrying," he said, his voice deep and raspy. "Don't make me have to take it from you." The man's voice deepened with the second threat, and I tried not to giggle at his puffed-out chest. It was clear from his thoughts that he was a novice at such behavior.

"You really need to let me go," I replied calmly, staring boldly into his eyes.

Before he could speak again, Kipp stepped into the faint light and without making a sound, pulled back his lips to display his white teeth, which gleamed menacingly at the man. The would-be robber wisely pulled back his hand and stood, uncertain of his next move, while desperately wishing to disappear into the gloom. But he was terrified Kipp, like most dogs, would chase him down with the reflexive temptation to pursue any fleeting object.

"Don't go," I said, reaching out to touch the man's arm lightly. "Tell me why you need my money," I added, knowing the answer since I'd unraveled his desperate thoughts.

"It's my baby girl," he replied, his eyes meeting mine. "She's come down with fever, and I can't pay the doctor." As he spoke the words, he straightened his posture and pulled his dignity together along with his tattered coat, which was ill-fitted and too large for his thin frame.

"I will give you the money, but I won't let you take it," I replied. "Somehow, I don't think taking it by force is typical for you."

Kipp gazed up at me, and while I dug in my reticule for coins, we had our private dialog with one another.

"Are you changing his timeline or that of his daughter?" Kipp asked.

"I don't know…I guess there is a risk," I replied. "But also, in his true timeline, we wouldn't have been walking along this street, and maybe he would have rethought his plans in any case." Glancing at Kipp, I smiled at him. It had been my role to tutor him in terms of symbiont ethics, and here he was, giving me something important to think about. "You will be changing Miss Logan's timeline, too, if you insist on getting her a dog as a companion, as will I, if I leave her money." I sighed. "We always do cause a change, no matter how carefully we tread." It was true with symbionts as well as humans, that often the ones in authority could issue dictates without having fully considered all the implications. Had I inadvertently changed Harrow's timeline by his having fallen in love with me? There was no way to know for certain.

"I don't know what to say, Miss," the man stuttered, his face darkening with shame. "I don't deserve your kindness."

"And why are you doing it?" Kipp asked me, persistent in his thoughts.

"I guess I wanted him to have the opportunity of a do-over. All of us need a do-over at some point in our lives." Reaching down, I petted Kipp's head, thinking the man would relax if he thought Kipp was no longer going to eat him.

"Bless you." The man's voice was as soft as a whisper. Then he turned and disappeared up a narrow alley, fading into the darkness in a few seconds.

Our journey resumed, and fortunately, Kipp managed to pick up the scent left by the woman we believed was headed toward the Clapham cemetery. "She cooked with garlic today," Kipp grumbled, sneezing once. "I mean, really, could she have shown a little consideration for the rest of us?"

I shushed him, and after a couple of turns, we found ourselves at a church; the whitewashed wooden walls were sagging slightly, and the thin coat of paint was peeling off like dead skin. It was obvious the church family who supported the building were limited in funds. A massive oak, which had lost its leaves due to a slow death, loomed threateningly over the roof. When it fell, it would take out a large part of the church.

"She's over there," Kipp jerked his head while pulling his lips back from his teeth as he tried to suppress another sneeze.

We crossed the dirt road in front of the church and wound around the side to where an iron gate, rusted and hanging unevenly from its hinges, was open. Pausing, we saw a woman, dressed as a domestic, leaning over a grave with a handful of tied mums to place upon a favored grave. At first, she didn't see the figure which approached, weaving its way around the upright tombstones that stood like sentinels against the living world. But Kipp and I clearly saw him and began our work of trying to pick up the thoughts of the being who skulked with noiseless steps toward the woman. Just as I settled in, the woman looked up and screamed, her fear projecting out significantly enough that I lost my focus against her terror, which washed over us like a wave. The figure, dressed in black and wearing a large hat with a brim that shadowed his face, quickly turned away from her and ran towards the metal fence surrounding the cemetery. With one bound, he cleared an eight-foot fence! And if I hadn't seen it, I wouldn't have believed it. The woman, meantime, passed us, still screaming as she ran down the street, taking her scent of garlic with her.

"Well, it is a man and not some demon," Kipp began, making note of the obvious. "But he took off too fast for me to really latch on. All I got was his intent to terrorize her, and his amusement at her screams."

"How could a human jump over an eight-foot fence?" I asked, amazed at that nimble and athletic feat.

"Well, the later speculation was that he had springs in his boots," Kipp replied, knowing I'd read the same information as had he.

"I realize that, but it still seems unbelievable to me," I said. "I think we're left with more questions than when we arrived."

We returned to Miss Logan's, and I used my key to quietly enter; navigating the squeaky staircase was a challenge, but we must have done reasonably well because I heard no quavering voice asking after my well being. I fell into a dreamless sleep in record time, leaving Kipp to continue to process the few threads he'd picked up from the man in the graveyard. We'd have another chance...and soon.

October 1837 was a busy time for our prankster, and it was just a few days hence when we waited for the passage of Mary Stevens, who was a domestic servant at Lavender Hill. Per the records from interviews made at the time of the incident, she was returning from a visit to her parents and was to pass down a narrow row with the lovely and descriptive name of Cut-Throat Lane. After our previous encounter with the wannabe thief who was nothing more than a desperate father, Kipp and I had pretty much been left alone by the people prowling in the darkness who were up to no good. Kipp was his usual modest self, but his presence worked as an admirable guard against predators.

It was cooler that night, and the air felt fresher than it had during the duration of our stay to that point. Taking a chance, I inhaled deeply, enjoying the lack of sewer rot stink and the metallic taste one would get from being in close proximity to the slaughter pens; the latter was particularly noxious and tended to stick in the back of my throat for a long time. The evening was quiet, with a few dogs barking restlessly and the occasional laughter from small groups of people who gathered along the storefronts, their faces pale, nondescript images along the feebly lit walkways.

"It's odd to be here, realizing that Jack the Ripper won't start his dirty business for another fifty years," Kipp remarked, opening his mouth wide in a yawn. He'd been restless the night before, and I quickly had backed out of his dreams, which had surprisingly included Elani. With no wish to embarrass him, I made an effort to divert my thoughts, but he was too quick.

"Oh, yuk," he grimaced, lips pulled back in chagrin.

"Dreams are just that, and often make no sense," I replied, trying to reassure him. "I'll never tell," I added, suppressing my amusement at his reaction.

He looked away from me, and as I waited for him to speak, I became aware that his gaze was fixed on a woman walking towards us, her head down in thought. Her face wasn't visible due to the tilt of her head and the shadow cast from her hat.

"Mary Stevens," Kipp said, his words a whisper to me. As she walked past, we tried to look bored or busy and waited to follow at a discreet distance.

Her footsteps were but soft brushings along the packed dirt roadway, and I thought I recognized a vague tune she began to sing. She'd made this trip before and wasn't particularly fearful, although she knew the area to be dangerous. After all, she had nothing to steal, no money, no jewelry, and would be a disappointing target.

A moment later, we heard a scream and leaped into action, Kipp ahead of me, as usual, due to his natural four-wheel drive propulsion. As Kipp wheeled into the alley, I saw him take up an aggressive posture, and his frenzied barking echoed against the darkness. Arriving just a moment later, I was horrified to see a tall figure holding the young woman, Mary, kissing her exposed throat as his fingers stroked her shoulders. Despite the poor lighting, I could clearly see the flash of metal claws as the man ripped her bodice from her chest, exposing a flimsy chemise to cover her nakedness. He turned as Kipp continued to bark, and as he did so, his appearance was clearly visible to me. His face was covered by a mask that obviously was meant to make one think of the Devil; the eyes were large, oversized, and glowing. I could only think he used some type of phosphorescent paint to get that startling effect. As she screamed again, he pushed her away so that she fell towards us and began to run, gathering speed in a short distance before he made a flat-footed jump some ten feet in the air to land upon the roof of a low shed.

From there, he raced along the rooftops, his long, black coat flapping about his legs as he ran. Kipp, without hesitation, chased after the man; I followed as a couple of people arrived to assist the stricken young lady. Our goal was not confrontation but to get close enough for Kipp to really focus on the man's thoughts. But we lost him amongst the heavily populated area, where large numbers of people were jammed into a few square miles.

"I think I got a little more that time," Kipp said, panting, as he pulled up. "He obviously wants to make a name for himself, scaring people, hoping little children will to go to bed at night fearful that their bad behaviors will bring on the devil." After a moment, he added, "I don't think he lives in this area because he momentarily seemed confused about which escape route to take."

Kipp obtained more than had I, which was little to nothing. Our telepathy allows us to communicate as well as detect thoughts over short distances, but trying to latch on to the mind of a stranger when there were so many other divergent thoughts circulating was difficult. While on the *Titanic*, Kipp sorted through the crowds to locate an individual and did this with greatest success when that person was not a complete stranger to him.

Our next encounter followed soon after. The air was crisp, and my hopes for a relatively fog-free evening were granted so that visibility would be at the maximum possible. With some directions given by a couple of helpful, if slightly inebriated, workmen who were on their way home, we made our way to the location of Blackheath Fair, which was really no fair in the usual sense, and a place to stay clear of unless one was in search of trouble. I hadn't mentioned this particular excursion to Miss Logan, who would have been horrified, since no lady should go near the place, which was characterized by drunkenness and debauchery. As Kipp and I proceeded towards Shooter's Hill, we were passed by groups of young men who were drunk enough to call out vulgar remarks to me, none of which were particularly novel or creative.

"You know, in over four hundred years, the general tone of catcalls has not changed a bit, except for some of the actual wording," I remarked to Kipp. It was cool that evening, and I hugged my arms more closely to my body to preserve warmth. Overhead, the silvered disc of a fading moon was suspended against the blackened sky.

"Well, that last guy was a little over the top, and it took all my self-control to not bite him on the fanny," Kipp replied, grumbling over my admonishments that he not react to things he heard.

Laughing softly, I reached down and tousled the thick fur on his head, tweaking his right ear gently. "My hero," I replied affectionately.

We were actually on the outskirts of the fair when Kipp's head lifted. "I think I'm picking up on him," he said, holding his breath for a moment while he concentrated. "Let's move to the southeast." Kipp's abilities served him almost like radar would for humans, and he began to hone into the thoughts of the man, but there was still too much distance and chaos for him to latch on to anything of depth.

A trio of young women passed us, and my attention was drawn when I heard one refer to the middle girl as "Polly", since the attack would be made on a girl named Polly Adams. Without being overly conspicuous, we made a subtle loop around some large shrubs and began to follow at a distance. The road, which was a packed mixture of dirt and rock, led down a gentle incline before angling behind a copse of trees that seemed darker than the night itself. The women disappeared from our view when they took that path, the trees and underbrush concealing them. We heard a series of high pitched screams and darted forward, Kipp ahead of me as usual. The other two girls who'd been accompanying Polly almost knocked us down as they raced past, retreating in the direction from which they'd come. It was clear, in their terror, they had abandoned the girl to her fate. Then we saw Polly, who'd been accosted by the man, dressed as before in black. He was tall, much taller than was she, and he bent over her, using one arm to hold her while he used the other to tear at her blouse. Even though our purpose was not to interrupt the attacks, Kipp was caught up in his outrage over the mistreatment of a lady and gave a loud, involuntary bark. The man glanced up, and recognition of us flooded his thoughts.

We were caught in a deeply shadowed place, and I peered through the gloaming to try and better see his features, which were somewhat hidden under the brim of the hat he wore. I was convinced he wore a half mask on the top part of his face, leaving his mouth and chin uncovered. Spring-heeled Jack had been rumored to breathe blue fire, and I was waiting for such a display so that I could determine the mechanism, since it was clear this was a human man with no more powers than the rest of the species. As the man's eyes from behind the mask met mine, he put his hand up to his mouth, and a moment later, a flame of blue fire shot out, about a foot in length, only serving to terrify poor Polly even more, if possible, as she slumped in a swoon.

The man dropped her abruptly and roughly to the ground and began to run, with Kipp in hot pursuit, making it a foot race. There was a long, uninterrupted fence ahead, and the man took one amazing bound to clear the fence, as Kipp pulled up short with no route to follow. Dashing forward, I bent over poor Polly, who was babbling hysterically. As I helped her to her feet, she tried to pull together the remnants of her blouse, which had been shredded. The soft skin of her belly was scored as blood began to well along the cuts.

As others began to gather, drawn by the commotion, I quietly allowed myself to be absorbed by the crowd, and signaling Kipp, we faded into the darkness before a constable could arrive. I didn't need an interview of one Petra Goodgame to be recorded in the annals of history.

"He has a gas cylinder up his sleeve, attached to his forearm." In my mind, I formed a diagram so Kipp could follow my thoughts. "Then, he uses a fire starter with a flint to get a spark, and, whoosh, he creates the blue flame that we just saw." I felt satisfied I'd figured out the mechanics of one part of the theatre. Now we were left with the why behind it all.

FIVE

The sightings of Spring-heeled Jack were intermittent for a while, sometimes branching out from the southeastern districts beyond London's outer boundary into the rural countryside. Even with the contacts we'd made, Kipp was still a little stumped as to the workings of the man's mind. As talented as was my partner, he needed a moment of stillness so that he could focus and get past the superficial thoughts milling in the brain of the attacker. Once he established some degree of familiarity, the process opened up significantly. But there was another encounter on the horizon, and we remained quiet, not wanting our presence at every appearance to change the timeline and affect Jack's behaviors. The next highly recorded incident would not occur until February of 1838, so we spent our time helping Miss Logan in her shop. Although I hoped never to use a needle and thread again, she taught me some new skills as Kipp dozed in the corner of the room. Symbionts mark the passage of time differently from humans, and the waiting game was nothing new for me. I'd spent a couple of years in one past time-shift, so this interval was not impressive by my standards. However, I considered changing my return time so that I wouldn't be absent from Fitzhugh for so long but decided against such a move when Kipp began to analyze my motives.

"You're worried about him," Kipp observed, as I began to patiently rip out a line of seaming that I'd screwed up royally. "You don't want him to be alone."

I think it was Kipp's words that made me even more determined to wait out this particular adventure and be gone from home for the entire four months, despite the fact I could have returned the following day after my departure if I'd wished.

"And now you're gonna be stubborn and prove you don't care by staying gone the whole time," Kipp continued, yawning, as he stretched on his side.

Looking up from the pile of fabric, which seemed to stretch endlessly across my work table, I stared at him, trying to give him my most impressive stink eye in my expansive repertoire. Failing, I tightened my lips as I returned to my seam ripping. Kipp laughed softly and thumped his tail on the wooden floor of the shop.

"He'll be okay, you know," Kipp remarked with the wisdom of one so young. "Philo will look after him as well as Peter and Elani."

"Yeah, I know," I grumbled. "It's just…." I began, before letting my words drop off, unfinished.

"You miss the ritual of the morning tea," Kipp completed my thoughts.

"Yeah, I guess."

"And maybe the Pop-Tarts?"

"Yeah, I guess."

The time actually went by quickly, and I don't think I boast to say that our presence made Miss Logan's Christmas holiday a little more festive, since it was a busy time for her skills. We served as a mild distraction, and I helped her as much as possible, handicapped with my limited abilities. I even purchased some holly branches as well as cedar and created a festive display with some discarded ribbons along the sill of the front windows. The evergreen fragrance managed to override the strong smell of coal fire and tallow, providing a welcoming atmosphere to visitors.

There was one early, frigid morning when we ventured out, the frost-crusted street crunching beneath the soles of my boots, and brought home a holiday cake I'd purchased from a community bakery. Miss Logan was predictably delighted, since she had a bit of a sweet tooth, and promptly had cake for breakfast accompanied by a steaming pot of tea. I'd also, as a little present, purchased her some tins of more expensive tea blends, and she happily experimented each morning, to discover a new experience on the tip of her tongue.

Meanwhile, Kipp and I still kept to our nocturnal prowling but maintained more of a distance from some of the scattered sightings and followed after to see what we could glean from the reports of victims as well as the impressions Kipp gathered from the memories of the victims while fresh in their minds. I was determined we not scare away our prey from the very well documented February attack that was on the horizon. The winter that year was colder and harsher than usual, and we were content to spend time in the shop with Miss Logan, where Kipp would stretch out in front of her coal-burning stove, his eyes blinking sleepily. Our landlady had made him a comfortable nest of discarded fabrics to create a barrier between his body and the cold floor. The upstairs loft was not heated, and Kipp and I cuddled together with my body benefiting from his heavy warmth. In the early morning when it was still dark outside, and the sunrise was hesitant to arrive at such a cold world, the window to the room would be frosted over, and I could feel the ice fragments on my side of the glass, coating the panes with delicate patterns that resembled fine lace. Between Kipp, however, and the woolen undergarments I'd created with the tutoring of our hostess, I stayed relatively comfortable, except for my nose and ears.

One day, I heard the bell tinkle over the door to the shop while I was putting away some dishes in the tiny kitchen behind the main room. I could hear voices at a murmur, distorted by the wall. Being a telepath comes in handy, and I turned my head, although such was not necessary, but seemed natural somehow. Kipp, too, tilted his head to the side as might a curious dog.

"I don't like the sound of that," Kipp murmured, his thoughts escalating into a growl in my head.

Indeed, it seemed the man in the room was of the local society of hoods and criminals and was attempting to, uh, shakedown Miss Logan for some cash. She was bravely trying to send the man on his way when Kipp and I appeared in the doorway. The man, who was dirty, the smell of his unwashed body threatening to overwhelm the scent of the lavender candle I'd lit, stared at me first from red, bloodshot eyes; he'd been drinking and was more than a little intoxicated as he slurred his words, some of which were rude and definitely not appropriate in the setting. Kipp was and is a gentleman, first and foremost, and was predictably offended by the harshness of the language in the presence of ladies. As the man's eyes flickered downward, Kipp began a slow, prowling walk, and I realized the man thought he was about to be attacked by a wolf. Kipp played the moment well, pulling back his lips to expose a full rack of teeth, uppers and lowers, and that cinched the moment. The man backpedaled, falling over a pile of fabrics that were stacked by the work table. With a faint scream, he scrambled up, awkwardly, and stumbled for the door. He had the misfortune to almost fall into the arms of the local constable.

"I've been looking for you, mate," the constable exclaimed, as he yanked the traumatized man by the arm and began to prod him down the street, using his nightstick as a motivator.

"Thank you, Kipp," Miss Logan said, smiling at him as he approached and let her stroke his massive noggin. "What a fine dog you are!"

"Okay, that does it," Kipp said to me, rolling his eyes to stare at me from the corners. "We're going to find her a dog today!"

It was grievously cold, but Kipp managed to nag me into leaving the warmth of the workroom, where the heater blazed, the coals winking red behind the slats of the grate. Miss Logan had given me an old hat of hers that provided some warmth, and after bundling as best I could, Kipp and I hit the streets. After walking a few blocks, Kipp's head lifted with interest, and he led me down a narrow walkway where small, poor dwellings were nestled side by side. The curbs were littered with accumulated trash, and a narrow gully acted as the local open sewer. At the end of the lane, we stopped as a small party of men began to walk towards us, a crude stretcher being carried by two of them. The body it contained was covered, but it was obvious one of the residents had died. As they passed us, we watched a small dog follow the procession, whining, lost in the activity.

"She," Kipp said, looking at the dog, which sat shivering on the cold walkway, "lived there all her life with an old man. He died, and she is confused, not certain what to do."

The man obviously had no relations, and the neighbors were moving in and out of his tiny shack, removing items for their use. I shrugged, looking at Kipp. It could be seen as callous or just a smart way to enhance one's meager grasp on survival. A woman, who was walking past with a treasure trove of battered cooking pots, nodded at us.

"Poor little dog," she said, stopping to point at the dog, which looked like a mix of terrier and some other mystery breed. "My landlord won't let me have a dog, but I've always liked little Queenie and hate to see her live on the streets. I'm not sure she'd know how. She's not very old, that one." The woman chugged past, breathing out pursed lips that were slightly blue-tinged; she probably had heart failure herself.

"Call her," Kipp instructed me.

"Queenie," I crooned, stooping down in what I hoped was a welcoming posture. The little dog was really quite pretty, with a white coat covered in large, liver-colored patches. The dark eyes staring at me looked clear, and I surmised the animal was reasonably healthy. Her sides were well filled out, and I suspected the old man had shared his food regularly with her.

Kipp, using his dog whisperer mind meld, managed to help plant the idea in her dog brain that we were wonderful folks to know, and that she should just be happy to make our acquaintance. So, it took little effort for her to come bounding to my arms. She was heavier than she appeared, and I grunted a little when lifting her.

"Eating too many pasties," I remarked as Queenie began to vigorously lick my chin. It was obvious she enjoyed my serving as her transportation versus her paws having to touch the frosty, cold-hardened ground.

"Quit griping," Kipp replied. "This is the perfect companion for Miss Logan. She's not so young that she will be an annoying puppy but not too old that she will be dying off in a week or two. She's just right."

"Like Mama Bear," I observed.

"What does that mean?"

I knew that a full storytelling would be occupying our evening before we fell asleep since Kipp had not been introduced to the concept of fables and fairy tales. But Miss Logan was delighted, and Queenie, with the subtle telepathic work of Kipp, fell in love imme-diately, and the bond was cast. Even if we left London empty-handed in terms of learning more about Jack, we would leave behind one happy elderly seamstress and a pup which could have been left to grieve herself to death down a narrow lane where poverty ruled, and people—and dogs—either survived or failed.

Kipp and I attempted to make our paths coincide with Spring-heeled Jack on February 19th but to no avail. On February 20th, we returned to the general vicinity of Bearbinder Lane, which stretched between the villages of Bow and Old Ford in East London. It took little effort to locate the cottage where Jane Alsop and her family lived, and after hiding around the corner of a tumbledown shed across the narrow road, we tucked in to wait. A crescent moon split the night sky, which seemed vacant of any stars due to the cloud cover blocking large swaths of the view in thin wisps of pale gray that served as the veil on a dowager.

"He's close by." Kipp's words were a whisper in my mind, his breath warm on the back of my neck. It was still quite frigid, so anything to warm me was welcomed, even Kipp's breath, which was fragranced with garlic from a meat pasty he'd had earlier that day.

"I heard that, and my breath does not stink," he protested, clamping his mouth shut.

"I thought you didn't like garlic," I began but hushed as a figure came into view.

A tall, slender man wrapped in a long cloak that flapped halfway down his legs, paused at the small walkway that led to the front door of the cottage. With a movement that seemed preternatural, he turned, looking in the direction where we were concealed, but I managed to pull my head down just in time, and the man relaxed. Kipp, in a moment of stillness, could focus without the disruption of screaming women and general pandemonium.

"Well, I was wrong, I think. He does live in this general area and actually knows some of the people he's terrorized." Kipp turned his head slightly to better see the dark figure.

"So why does he do it?"

"He's a, uh, punk. He is a little man, inside I mean, who gets excitement from knowing that he has momentary power over others and then reads the paper to get the accounts afterward. He wants to be famous but has nothing to be famous for. So, he concocted this sad creature." Kipp nestled closer as I welcomed his warm body pressing against me. "Not much here."

I felt relatively philosophical about it. "Kipp, there have been some real punks with the ability to harm large numbers of people. Wars have started that way. At least this one man has limited ability to destroy populations and, although unfortunate, will only frighten a few people over the lifetime of his career."

"Yeah, but I don't like punks who pick on those who are weaker."

We waited for the predictable as I pulled Kipp a little closer to me because I thought he needed some grounding of a familiar and loving arm. The man, who hesitated at the doorway of the cottage, was dressed in different attire than previously. The clothing beneath the sweeping dark cape appeared to be white, and he wore less of a hat and more of a helmet. The witnesses had supposed he was wearing oilskin, but I couldn't make a determination about the fabric.

"The change in clothing is to help him not get burned when he does his fire breathing display," Kipp observed, closing his eyes for a minute as he sifted through memories. "He got burned last time he tried it." Kipp wanted to add "good" but held back.

Despite the cold in the air, I felt a bead of sweat trickle down my back. Even knowing in advance that the victim would survive the attack didn't seem to help as we crouched in the darkness. My calf muscles began to ache, and I moved just a little, worried a Charlie horse might cripple me and prevent a pursuit.

The man began to knock on the door, proclaiming himself to be a policeman, shouting he'd caught Spring-heeled Jack. A moment later, a young girl appeared, her graceful silhouette in the doorway highlighted by the soft interior lights within the dwelling. At the demand of the fake policeman, she brought a lit candle outside and had just crossed the threshold when the man attacked her, following the same pattern as before. The iron talons he wore began to tear at her blouse, pulling it from her pale shoulders. This time, he was more aggressive and began to score the soft flesh of her neck and arms with the weapons. Screaming, she tried to get away as he pulled a plug of hair from her head; I grimaced as her sensation of pain empathetically shuddered through me. As members of her family began to arrive, summoned by her screams, the man turned and ran, moving in our direction before veering off down an alley.

"Let's go!" Kipp ordered, and with a blur of auburn fur and toenails scratching on the dirt for a purchase, he was after the man, who began to zigzag when he realized he was being pursued.

I didn't like Kipp getting so far ahead but knew that the physical skills of Jack were greater than mine, and with his spring propulsion, he would be gone in a flash. I honed in on Jack's thoughts, and he was enjoying the chase, with the solid confidence that his cleverness and abilities were greater than ours. Consequently, he didn't take to the rooftops as quickly as before. Once, he looked over his shoulder, and I caught a glimpse of teeth and a broad smile as he teased us closer. Just as Kipp got within pouncing distance, I had my accident. A man pushing a heavy cart filled with firewood appeared from a side alley and crashed into my left side. I spun like a demented top and lost my balance, falling hard against a stone wall. The minute I hit, I felt the bone in my upper left arm snap; all I knew was that the pain was sudden, intense, and my vision almost went black. Kipp immediately stopped, feeling my agony run through his body in the physical symbiotic link we shared in response to a severe injury.

"Keep going," I panted, holding my arm and trying not to cry. It took the rest of my energy to reassure the old man who'd run into me to leave so that I didn't have to keep talking with him and depleting my waning strength.

"Don't be silly," Kipp replied. "I got enough on Jack, and we weren't gonna catch him anyway and change the timeline. It was just fun to give him a good run for his money and scare him a little."

I plopped down on an empty crate and sat there holding my arm, praying for the pain to subside. Instead, it came in nauseous waves. Gingerly, I pulled up my coat sleeve and then my blouse; thank goodness the bone wasn't sticking through the skin, I thought.

"We need to go home now," Kipp ordered, meaning a return to our contemporary home.

"I want to go back to Miss Logan's and leave her the money we brought." I felt my lip poke out with stubborn determination. Kipp glanced at me before shaking his head.

"You're irrational, but we'll do it your way," he said.

With my good hand curled into the fur of Kipp's neck, we slowly began the walk, which was about two miles, to Miss Logan's. Along the trip, I paused twice to throw up, trying to be discreet, in an alleyway. The locals didn't object, just thinking me to be another alcoholic who'd had too much rotgut whiskey that night.

Kipp, each time we'd stop for me to rest, would lick my face, his warm tongue acting to revive me. I knew I had to get back because if I passed out, there was no telling where I'd end up…or Kipp, for that matter. Failure was not an option, and that motivated my steps as I glanced down at my feet…one forward, then the other.

We knew Miss Logan would be sound asleep, so Kipp managed to convince Queenie, as I used my key, to not bark. After staring at us for a minute, her butt wiggling with the wagging of her tail, she turned and trotted off to resume her place of honor at the end of Miss Logan's bed. I was leaning on Kipp heavily by that point, as I wobbled up the narrow staircase. Once back in our room, I wrote a hasty note to our benefactor and told her that a family emergency had called us away. Taking all the money I had brought, along with the money concealed in Kipp's collar, which we always took along as a backup stash, I was leaving her a sizeable amount of money that in the economy of the day would last her for a very long time. Putting everything in my reticule, I had Kipp take it back downstairs to place it on Miss Logan's chair where she'd see it first thing in the morning.

Kipp returned to me, his toenails clicking softly against the wooden floor. I'd managed to climb on the bed, resting on my right side, cradling my fractured arm gently across my chest. The throbbing was no less, but at least I wasn't moving, and that helped some. And I hadn't vomited in the last twenty minutes, either.

"I remember when I was injured during our first trip together, you symbiotically shared my pain load so we could travel. You have to do that now, with me." Kipp stared at me; there was only minimal ambient light softly glowing from the large window over-looking the street, and that tiny point of light seemed caught like an insect in the amber of Kipp's eyes. One hates to bring pain to a friend, but there was no other choice, and I curled my right hand around Kipp's back, hearing him grunt as the wave of pain hit him, just as it had me. I was able to relax, just a bit, when the intensity of the agony lessened.

As we came in balance, I felt the familiar rush of a time-shift and knew we'd be home in a few seconds. My mind was so consumed with pain that I left everything in Kipp's capable paws, knowing he could pinpoint the time and place with no help from me. And he did just that.

"So, who was Spring-heeled Jack?" Philo asked.

During the course of the storytelling, we'd moved from kitchen to living room, and occasionally back again to snag a snack or two. The living room was a tumbled down mess with blankets and pillows still flung carelessly on the furniture and floor. We humanoids were enjoying a second pot of Earl Grey steeped at the experienced hands of Fitzhugh—and I never did figure out why his brew tasted so much better than mine—while the lupines finished off the rest of the brownies from the previous night. It was a good thing that lupines didn't share the issues of dogs where chocolate was concerned. And after a little pre-agreement I'd made with Kipp, we breezed past the fact we had left Miss Logan with a finan-cial endowment since I wasn't in the mood to have Philo frown at me and question my judgment which was driven by an unexpected sentimentality.

"I finally could pin him down that last night, as all was quiet and still as he approached the cottage," Kipp replied. He ignored the adoring glance tossed his way by Elani, who was discreetly using her paw to remove some fudge from her muzzle that made her nose look twice its normal size. "He was a local tradesman who, on the side, performed as a second class magician at parties and festivals… things like that. Like a lot of people who act out against others, he had built up a significant amount of anger over his childhood, which was not good. His father was brutal when he was not absent, and his mother spent most of her time drinking and bedridden. We can call him Jack, although his name was David, and scaring women, as well as men, fed some part of him that was in pain and enraged."

"So, a man with no voice obtained one by becoming infamous," Fitzhugh observed. "An all too frequent ailment of humanity."

"And you had a perfect score of no real accidents despite all your years of traveling," Philo said, careful to place his cup on a magazine versus the top of the coffee table. I cared not about such things, and the table already had enough rings to qualify as the Olympic symbol, if only they interlocked.

"I wish we could have gone with you." Peter quickly looked away, embarrassed by the wistful tone of his voice.

"Well, we needed you all to have some time to work on couple's skills, but now that you are back and Petra is finally healed, I think some rest and recreation is in order. And I want Peter and Elani to go with you since your arm probably can't handle the stress of driving for long distances yet." Philo smiled as I darted a quick glance at him, not sure where this was leading. "Kipp mentioned a haunted steamboat in Alabama…"

SIX

"I'm not sure if our timing will be the best," Kipp remarked as he munched on a saltine cracker from his vantage point in the rear of the SUV, "since some people have written that the *Eliza Battle* is most active during the late winter months, but we can always make a time-shift if needed to arrive at the appropriate time."

Oh, great, I thought to myself, while trying to quickly guard my thoughts from my intrusive companion. Not only were we on a ghost hunt once again, we might have to couple that with a time-shift.

"I heard that, Petra," Kipp interrupted my grumbling.

"Can I not have a moment for a private thought?" I replied, staring resolutely ahead at the interstate.

Peter was driving, which he enjoyed, and that suited me fine. Although I wouldn't say anything, my left arm had never quite healed properly and tended to ache from time to time when I couldn't move it freely. And hanging on to a steering wheel for hours was not preferable. Philo had commanded we leave town for a few days, and he actually moved in with Fitzhugh and Juno while we were gone, since he would be transporting the elder symbionts back and forth to work each day, he'd said. I knew that was bogus...

Claire was at home, as was Silas, and Philo needed to escape the tension created by a toxic family.

The trip to south Alabama could be managed in a day, of course, but we decided to break up the journey because the lupines tended to get very restless when cramped for too long. We stopped in Chattanooga for the night before rising the next morning to pick up I-59, which wound down through the lower Appalachians where the gentle ridge of mountains trailed as far south as Birmingham, below there to ease into a line of lovely rolling hills. Due to a cold front which had chased a spring storm, the early morning sky was cluttered with fog, the sun struggling to find the landscape through the low hanging clouds that obscured the tops of the mountains flanking either side of the interstate.

"So, since we have a long ride, Kipp, why don't you tell everyone about the *Eliza Battle*, so we will all be up to speed." I thought that would get him out of my brain for a minute or two. But he was happy to share knowledge and show off a little with a topic about which the rest of us were happily ignorant.

"The *Eliza Battle* was a steamboat—a side paddle wheeler—that was considered the finest of her type on the river. She ran on the Tombigbee River, when the weather would permit, and that was usually during the winter and early spring months, due to the condition of the water. Her departures and travels were a point of great excitement for the local communities along the river, as she went from Columbus, Mississippi to Mobile. A calliope had been installed, and there were musicians to entertain the passengers. There was dancing and general festivities while she made her way along the river. The boat was used to transport goods to the Gulf, mainly large amounts of cotton from the plantations. On her last trip, the water in the river was swollen from an exceptionally rainy season, and the pilot as well as the captain had difficulty visualizing the usual landmarks. The pilot struggled to find the main channel so that the boat would have enough clearance in the water.

"The actual date of the disaster remains disputed, but apparently there is at least one grave of a victim where the tombstone mentions March 1, 1858 as the correct date. And no one knows how the fire started. There is speculation that a couple of the roustabouts…" Kipp paused. "I like that word, by the way. Maybe I can be a roustabout during one of our time-shifts?"

I sighed deeply. It was going to be a long drive.

"Anyway, there was one story that a couple of the workers were trying to rob a stateroom and deliberately fired the room to cover their tracks. Another is that someone carelessly tossed a lit cigar which landed in the cotton, and the ship was carrying tons of cotton, so you'd think they might have banned things like cigars, pipes, and cigarettes…just common sense from my way of thinking. Or maybe a passing boat was throwing off sparks that managed to land in the cotton? The point is, no one knows."

Elani had some questions of her own. "With so many aspects of this event shrouded in mystery, why didn't you just time-shift back and explore it yourself?"

Kipp fell quiet, and I knew why. After our recent trip on the *Titanic*, he would not ask me to replicate anything close to a maritime disaster time-shift again, at least not anytime soon. And despite my love for Kipp and my desire for him to get all the experiences he could in his young and wonderful life, I had no desire to go aboard that ill-fated steamship to figure out what caused the fire. As it was, I knew I'd never get the screaming of the dying passengers on the *Titanic* out of my brain.

"Uh," Kipp stuttered, "I just wanted to see if we could pick up on the ghostly images this time," he answered awkwardly. "I thought it might be fun," he added, in case we'd missed the point.

Elani immediately realized her faux pas and became quiet, fearful she'd been insensitive of me, something of which I would never accuse her. She reminded me of what Juno must have been like in her prime…gentle, considerate, and bright. To reassure her, I turned in my seat, wincing a little when the seatbelt caught against my left shoulder. Smiling, I gave her a friendly wink to let her know all was okay.

Kipp pushed on. "The fire was discovered, and the crew was horrified to find that the water pumps on board didn't work. Then, as the captain tried to steer to shore, the tiller ropes, which had been burned through, were useless, and the boat was left to drift, uncontrolled, down the river. People began to jump off into the freezing water, some using cotton bales as rafts. Other people climbed to the tops of the submerged trees, hanging there, trying to escape the water. Many of them froze to death and others, who survived, were haunted for the rest of their days by the sounds of bodies hitting the water as people fell back into the river. There is no way to know exactly how many people died, and the accounts varied greatly."

As Kipp paused in his recitation, I signaled I needed a break. There was an exit at Springville, and Peter pulled off so that we could stretch and find something to eat. It was rather cool that day, and I pulled my jacket from the SUV as we walked around the parking lot and let the lupines caper about in the grassy verge. A wonderful aroma filled the air, drifting from one of the fast food joints that was busy frying up some chicken. I frowned at Peter, who was relishing the brisk weather in his short-sleeved shirt.

"What's wrong?" he asked, seeing the expression on my face.

"Aren't you cold?"

"No," he replied.

I'm not certain why, but his response made me feel grumpier. Where had my youthful zest gone, I wondered. Yes, I was the elder of this quartet, but I was a young symbiont, still. Humans might think me to be in my latter twenties, if that. Hunching my shoulders, I walked away, staring at the interstate and the cars racing to their destinations. Lots of humans seemed to have important business, I thought.

"You've had a series of hard time-shifts," Kipp responded to my private thoughts, as was his way. "Whitechapel devastated you. We followed with chasing the *General*, and that was physically a hard trip. And I don't even have to speculate about the *Titanic*. I know your arm still hurts at times, even though you won't say anything about it. When you feel that twinge, I feel it, too. You have good reason to want to huddle up, at home, with a good book, and not leave your chair for a few months," he added. "But I'm not going to let you stop traveling…not yet, in any case."

I glanced at him; he was standing in some early grass that was surprisingly overgrown due to the rainy spring. A wind was blowing from the west, and it caught his thick, ruddy fur, causing it to ripple, following the graceful patterns of the waving grass. My heart was soothed, and I knew he was right, of course. I was too young to give up my career, one which defined my very existence on earth. Symbionts were made to do just what Kipp and I were doing. Throwing up my hand in a little half wave, I signaled we were fine, as I took another sip of my coffee.

Back in the car, I turned on the radio, thinking the distraction of some music would be nice. I confess, I've always been a fan of classic rock from the 1960's and seventies and located a station that was playing Edwin Starr grinding out *War*. Elani had particular fun trying to master the lyrics, her thoughts echoing in my head in a deep, bass voice. The result was so funny that I couldn't help but laugh, enjoying her silliness, since she could be too serious at times. As we passed through Birmingham, Kipp's gaze was drawn out of the right side of the SUV.

"I'd really like to visit Sloss Furnace on the way back," he remarked wistfully.

"Don't you think we'd need some preparation for that?" I asked. "And I thought you were done with ghost business," I added, feeling a little mean.

"I am done with the Twelve mandating ghost hunting, but I admit, after our trip to Gettysburg, I thought about the experiences later." Kipp sighed, sticking his head up between the seats, his furry jaw resting on my shoulder. "I'm convinced there is more to be learned, but I'd just like to do it at my own speed...kind of like a hobby," he concluded.

I knew about Sloss Furnace, which was considered to be one of the most haunted places in the country. But to visit a place such as that required some type of sleight of hand to get the lupines past the gate.

"Philo took care of that, in the event we go," Kipp answered easily. "They've had so many ghost investigators over the years that our presentation would be novel: two canines who are sensitive to the paranormal. The management approved our visit."

"Well, how thoughtful of Philo and how nice you are informing the rest of us," I remarked sarcastically.

"I didn't know I had to get your permission," Kipp shot back.

The atmosphere in the car became suddenly tense; I glanced at

Peter who rolled his eyes at me before turning them back on the interstate. Elani coughed politely before circling and plopping down in the back.

Occasionally, humans and symbionts are gifted with insight, occasionally being the operative word. Who likes to admit when one is wrong and is being hard headed, obstinate and selfish? But I had my tiny epiphany at that moment, since Kipp had universally, up that point, followed my lead. I had a flush of pride as I realized he was moving apart as he matured and, for him, as well as us, that was important. Had I selfishly wanted to keep him under my wing for our entire partnership? Even I didn't know if I could honestly answer that question.

"I'm sorry," he began, licking the side of my face.

Despite the seat belt laws, I had to unclick mine so I could turn in my seat. "No, Kipp, don't do that," I replied. "You are right; you don't have to ask my permission, and I'm proud you are moving independently of me. I'm not the one to give you permission over your choices," I added.

He looked rather crestfallen, but at my words, his tail began to wag. Elani's head lifted as she realized we, in our clumsy way, were making up. Does anyone enjoy conflict? Maybe a few humans, but none of us in that car were happy over words spoken in anger. And even though we'd brushed past a little rough patch, I was glad when we approached our destination.

The original disaster had occurred during a stormy March, and it was now April, but there was no science involved that would force us to have to be present at the exact time the sinking had occurred. Our destination was the town of Naheola, Alabama, and Peter, after navigating past Tuscaloosa, looped further south until we picked up state road 114, which would eventually lead to Pennington. Naheola, just north of Pennington, was the town where, per the stories, the populace had raced out to the river's edge to try and assist the people who were stricken after the *Eliza Battle* began to burn. The highway crossed over the Tombigbee, and we thought that would be a good place to view the river and perhaps scramble to the banks to get closer if needed. The area through which we passed was no longer mountainous and became flatter as we drew nearer to the coastal plains. To either side of the road, fields stretched, some already deeply furrowed as farmers prepared the fertile land for crops to be grown.

The clouds on the far horizon had been building all day, dark and foreboding, and were heavy with moisture, so much so that the lower edges seemed to graze the feathered tops of tall pines. Spring was a notorious month for storms, but I had been monitoring the radio on and off, and thankfully, there were no tornadoes predicted. There was a corridor in Alabama that seemed tornado-prone, and our journey took us through that area.

"A stormy background might be helpful," Kipp remarked. "Many of the sightings have occurred during bad weather."

Of course, despite the weather, his ability to connect with things of the spirit world seemed solid, so if anyone could conjure the *Eliza Battle*, it would be Kipp. As the clouds crowded in to obstruct the once blue sky, we approached the bridge, which was our destination. Peter selected a place and stopped the SUV in a flurry of crunching gravel and dust. We jumped out and scrambled down the gentle incline leading to the bank, getting as close as possible to the water. The wind began to blow, bending the trees to and fro, and I could only hope the rain would hold off for a little longer. The Tombigbee stretched before us, its waters gray and beginning to show some choppiness due to the wind. A barge had just passed headed south towards the Gulf, leaving white foamed waves in its wake. The air smelled thick with the dankness of the river combined with the pending storm.

A few lonely cars passed, a couple tooting their horns, a surprisingly cheerful welcome to strangers, perhaps noting our North Carolina tags. Overhead, a dark wedge of birds veered to the southeast, fleeing the approaching storm. Kipp was next to me, his side brushing my leg; I could feel his warmth through the cotton of my jeans. He glanced up, and the excitement was evident in the fire I could see in his amber eyes. His tail wagged a time or two, just to let me know that all was good between us. Of course, it would always be good; nothing else would be acceptable.

"I'm seeing something!" Kipp exclaimed, with a quick, indrawn breath.

He encouraged us to enter his thoughts, and we could see the visions that only he, with his peculiar sensitivity, could truly experience. From beneath the surface of the turbulent, troubled waters of the river, there were lights that were visible, faded but growing in intensity. In a moment, the lights broke through the top of the water, and the form of a boat began to slowly rise to the surface, the water rolling from the superstructure as it bobbed into view, rocking gently from side to side as if righting itself. I could clearly see the name of the *Eliza Battle* scrawled across the side of the ship near the bow. It was an old fashioned paddle wheeler, magnificent and beautiful in form and design. The sounds of laughter echoed across the water; overhead, the clouds descended ominously, threatening to unleash a torrent upon us at any moment. I could clearly hear the sound of the calliope, as an unfamiliar tune played, perhaps one composed by the organist. A moment later, the laughter changed to cries of alarm escalating to screams from the phantom passengers, and the vision became brilliant, horrible, as fire began to consume the boat, tongues of orange and yellow lifting towards the sky. People, frantic to escape the heat, began jumping over the sides of the boat, and the sounds of bodies splashing into the dark water were clearly audible. The moment became so intense that I fancied I could feel the heat from the burning ship strike my face; without thinking, I took a step back to avoid the unpleasant sensation. At one point, I turned to Peter in astonishment, only to find him gazing at me, his mouth hanging open in surprise. Kipp's eyes were closed as his concentration intensified. We were so busy focusing our attention on Kipp, who was equally busy, that we failed to hear a car pull up and stop behind us.

"You folks okay?" A man's voice interrupted the experience.

It was a county sheriff's deputy, a young man, his face all serious beneath the stiff brimmed hat he was wearing. His intentions had been good, worry for us since the weather was about to break. But he had inadvertently disrupted the moment, and Kipp lost his grasp on the phantom, his legs almost buckling due to exhaustion. I put my hand firmly on the back of his neck, feeling the heat from his flesh; he was trembling. The burning *Eliza Battle* would not be recreated any time soon.

"I thought you might have car trouble," he added, smiling.

"We're fine," I replied, walking towards him. "We were just hoping to catch a glimpse of the *Eliza Battle*," I added mischievously.

The young deputy laughed, squinting a little as he glanced up at the sky. He had no desire to deal with the car accidents that usually accompanied bad weather.

"There are no ghost ships around here," he remarked. "Ghost hunters just made that up to scare people."

"I'm sure you're right," I replied, smiling.

We had just shut the doors to the SUV when the torrential rain began to fall. We sat there, on the side of the road, letting the SUV be pelted by the water. Peter had decided to wait until it let up just a little, before resuming the drive. Reaching forward, he turned on the windshield wipers, which began to slap lazily as they swung back and forth, the sound and movement hypnotic. It wouldn't take much more of that to put me to sleep.

"I know one thing," Kipp remarked. "I may have had enough visits to doomed ships for a while."

"That's good, Kipp. I was hoping you didn't want to visit the *Sultana* or the *Cyclops*," I replied, stifling a yawn.

"The *Sultana*…what's that?"

SEVEN

"I'm wondering if it is wise for you to continue dabbling about with this ghost business," Fitzhugh remarked as he brought the teapot to the dinette table. Kipp was in the back yard, making his usual rounds, and he'd left my mind for a while, leaving it surprisingly vacant. I paused to wonder if there really had been very little occupying my brain for most of my life.

"Why?" I replied, trying to focus my eyes. I'd awakened early and was relatively confident I would feel it all day.

"Kipp's ability to connect is so spot on and vivid in terms of the experience that it is, well, too real. It places a psychological burden on all of you who share, besides the toll it takes on Kipp." Fitzhugh poured my tea, almost carelessly, so that a tiny drop missed the cup and landed upon the tabletop. Such an occurrence was rare for one with his skill level. "Oops," he remarked, smiling at me. Was it my self-indulgent imagination, or was Fitzhugh happier and more content than before? Of course, I'd never bothered to really get to know what made him tick until lately.

"Well, you know Kipp's level of curiosity," I replied with a yawn. The tea was too hot, so I studied the steam rising off of the cup for a minute before hazarding a sip. Changing the subject, I remarked, "Elani proposed a possible time-shift during our ride home."

Fitzhugh raised his eyebrows and smiled. "That was only waiting for the right moment, I suspect. Elani is no meek flower, and I predict she will become very dominant as she grows older and more confident."

"Yeah, I can't wait until she decides to take on Kipp after her crush wears off." I laughed. "Right now, she is too infatuated." I sipped at the tea, managing to burn my tongue in the process. Hastily, I placed the cup back on the table to wait a little longer. "She wants to put together a trip to the time of Lincoln's assassination to determine the guilt or innocence of Mary Surratt."

Fitzhugh's expression became sober, and his playful tone changed. "It would be a challenging trip in more ways than I can enumerate."

"Well, I would think so," I replied. "To get close to her would put a traveler smack in the middle of the web of conspirators pulled together by John Wilkes Booth. Also, Mary Surratt was a known Confederate sympathizer in a town where the federal government was operating. Any people associated with her could be lumped in when the assassination occurred, and people were being hauled off to jail with very little cause and no due process. There was a fair amount of unlawful activity at the time in terms of the government and how citizens were treated."

"Yes. It seems desperate times called for extreme measures. The suspension of habeas corpus was debated at the time and still is by constitutional scholars and historians. But you have to admit it would be fascinating," Fitzhugh said. He paused to add a little more honey to his tea, having acquired my habit. Once, he'd been a purist where tea was concerned, so I suppose I had corrupted him. "The subject of her guilt or innocence died when she was hanged, and only she knew for certain. Of course, she protested her innocence, but so have legions of others who are condemned."

"If Elani wants to do the research and approach the Twelve, it's fine with me." I was ready to move on. "She and Peter can make that trip and then report back to the rest of us." I almost sniffed to show my lack of interest. Almost.

Fitzhugh parked his thin elbows on the tabletop. He'd not combed his hair yet, and the long strands hung down past his collar.

His beard, too, had not been trimmed in a while, and he looked like some wizard who'd been holed up in a dark cave for years. I thought for a minute he was irritated at my casual disinterest before I realized he was curious…and concerned.

"Petra, what would you like to do?" Picking up the teapot, he topped off my barely touched cup; the fragrance of bergamot filled the room. The sun took that moment to brighten, as the clouds that had been hovering between the earth and sky shifted to the east, and the kitchen filled with light and warmth. It spoke of our evolved relationship that he didn't have to elaborate or clarify his query.

"I'm not sure," I replied. "Somehow, I've lost my focus, and I guess it is due to many things." My eyes met his. "I can think of a time when I would have jumped at a trip such as this, but now I just seem to be, well, cautious." I laughed. "You would never, in the past, called me overly cautious, would you?"

"If you will permit," he said, smiling, the expression in his eyes softening. "You had a very, very difficult time-shift with Tula during which she was lost. The death of a bonded symbiont is one of the most traumatic things that can happen to one of us. Since then, everything has been in a rush…developing your relationship with Kipp and subsequent challenging time-shifts. Then, the Twelve decided you need to become a teacher and have you working in a quartet, something unheard of with our kind." Fitzhugh crumbled the end off of a cold Pop-Tart. The store had run out of his favorite strawberry, but he didn't complain about the blueberry substitute I'd nabbed. "I think you have the right to be just a little tired and maybe feel a little lost, too."

I think symbionts, just as do humans, take others and situations for granted, much too easily. I'd known Fitzhugh for years and thought of him as a cantankerous old codger, using his years of wisdom as a cudgel with which to batter me with criticism. In that moment, as the light illuminated the kitchen—highlighting all the dust and accumulated lupine hairs on the floor—I had my moment of revelation that perhaps all things do have a purpose and that Fitzhugh and I had come full circle. Philo and I shared honesty bred from friendship; Fitzhugh and I shared something else that evolved from being former combatants to allies in the present. He was giving me the benefit of his wisdom, finally, and I was no longer guarded and defensive; I soaked it up like a sponge. It felt good.

"I think I've been foolish for many years," I remarked with a lopsided grin.

"How so?"

"I wanted to fight you instead of listening to you."

He raised his eyebrows. "Well, I'm glad you finally realize the folly of your hardheadedness."

I had to laugh. Kipp was at the back door, pressing his damp nose against the window, ready to come in. I realized he'd politely stayed out of my head while Fitzhugh and I chatted. He brushed past me as I opened the door, his nails clicking on the floor.

"I was trying to give you two plenty of time, but there was a horsefly out there that just would not leave me alone," Kipp whined, rolling his eyes. "You know how I feel about them," he added. With a big grunt like dogs might make, he circled and plopped on the kitchen floor in one of the bright patches of sunlight. I saw a cloud of dust and hair fly up when he hit the floor.

Kipp didn't fare well when there was little happening in his world; in other words, he became easily bored. Although his default choice would be to nestle at my side like peas and carrots, his mind was too active, the world too full of challenges to sit quietly and wait for me to lead. We started out with such an arrangement, but he had outgrown such childish nonsense. I was proud of his evolution to maturity. And all of this was why I would not just escape back in time to be with William Harrow…at least not now.

Since the weather was nice, Kipp and I began the two-mile trek to Technicorps, passing the landscapes that were so familiar that I felt I could walk with my eyes closed and safely make the journey. I'd resided at my little house in North Carolina for quite a long time in the world of contemporary symbionts. I lived with the mild anxiety that at any moment I could receive the call to come to the big front office and receive my marching orders. There had been some gossip suggesting the poor, declining collective in Alpharetta, Georgia, where we'd met Tristan and Meko, was targeted for a major refurbishing, which would include new staff. The buildings as well as the campus seemed sadly neglected to my critical eye. I had no wish to go there, where the overgrown shrubs crowded the doorways and plucked nervously at my sleeves as I passed.

A squirrel scolded us from the low branches of a young maple tree, flicking its tail in agitation as we passed. Kipp craned his neck back to eye the creature before giving a loud bark, at which the squirrel darted to a higher perch. Kipp's thick tail began to wag; he always appreciated a little game of challenge with other creatures since he typically would win due to his intellect concealed in the body of a canine. He naturally possessed an unfair advantage.

"Remember what Philo said," Kipp remarked, his eyes meeting mine. For a moment, the filtered sunlight was captured and caught fire, and his eyes turned red before the flames subsided, and the familiar amber returned. "He will work something out so that he, Fitzhugh, and Juno will be with us. And I bet he will include Peter and Elani, too."

I wasn't aware until that moment that I'd been consciously thinking about moving on in life, but obviously I had. Reaching down, I comforted myself by stroking the top of Kipp's broad head; the fur was warm and soft beneath my fingertips. He pushed a little closer until his sides were grazing my legs. It was good to be back in a familiar routine, despite the fact a stack of manuscripts needing translation awaited my arrival. My non-traveling job was tedious beyond description.

"But you are very good," Kipp said, wagging his tail in an affirmation of my translation skills that was not needed but nice to hear, I suppose.

A mid-sized SUV rolled past us before slowing with a little toot on the horn. It seemed Peter had a new ride, and as he rolled down the window to give a cheery hello, I approached so that he could dutifully brag on the new vehicle. Like any young guy, he was proud of the acquisition. Fitzhugh was riding shotgun; it had evolved that Peter pretty much took Fitzhugh and Juno to work every day, unless the weather was horrible, and then I crowded my elders along with Kipp into my tiny, battered car. Maybe I needed to stop that considering how much more room they would have with Peter. Grinding my teeth, I recalled Peter had even bought a canine ramp to accommodate Juno. He'd thought of everything while I thought of nothing.

"Or you could get a nice, new vehicle like Peter," Kipp observed. "You just don't like change of any sort," he concluded. "And that ramp!" Kipp softly whistled in the back of my brain working overtime to provoke me.

Ignoring him, I leaned in to inspect the interior. Juno gave me a lupine kiss on the side of my face. Inhaling, I appreciated the lingering new car smell. I didn't like to think of the smells in my car, which had aged over time like some type of noxious, moldy cheese.

"I got to choose the color," Elani remarked with excitement and pleasure.

"And it's lovely," I replied. The color was a rich, tobacco brown that had a bronze cast in the light. It reminded me of the color of fall leaves that had just passed their peak of color and had begun to wane but remained beautiful nonetheless. Trying not to smile, I saw Fitzhugh carefully replace his metal "go cup" that obviously contained his morning tea in the convenient cup holder on the molded dash. Since he would not have purchased any such thing for himself, I knew that Peter had thoughtfully obtained it for the elder's comfort. Peter caught my glance and winked at me.

I waved them on. Peter enjoyed driving so much that he would appreciate the new car, complete with pristine exterior. My bet was that he would wash it every weekend. Of course, one ride with the lupines and the hair would take over, but that was a part of our relationship with our partners.

"Like you don't have hair," Kipp said, staring at me. "The other day I turned over in bed and realized I had one of your long hairs in my mouth. It was disgusting."

Reaching down, I made an exaggerated brush of my jeans with my hand, opening my eyes wide as I did so. "And I am simply covered with your tufts of hair, no matter what I do, big boy."

Kipp playfully began to chase me as I ran, jogging lightly. Of course, it took no effort on his part, and he ran me down in less than five seconds and deployed his teeth to give me a pretty uncomfortable nip on the calf of my left leg.

"Ouch!" I cried. "You are way too rough with the teeth!" I

began to vigorously rub my leg, unhappy with Kipp's natural arma-
ment and his use of it unfairly. "What is it with you and the teeth?"
I whined, staring at him.

Growling, he got down on his elbows and began to run in little
circles around me, leaning in, acting as if he was going to bite me
again. I was acting affronted and serious but inwardly was happy he
was feeling so good and having fun. He and Elani needed a play
date; he could be rough with her with no consequences since she
was as tough as was he.

A car slowed, and a man called out. "Are you okay?"

I looked over, and a middle-aged human man was staring, horrified, at the spectacle of Kipp assaulting me. His cell phone was in
his hand, and I realized he was about to call the police.

"Kipp, heel!" I barked, and Kipp immediately complied, flattening his ears and pretending to be submissive. I cheerfully thanked
the good citizen for his concern and waved him on.

"Just wait and see what I've got in store later on today," Kipp
threatened. "But I'll play good for now." His amber eyes had a
disturbing glow, and I had a brief moment of worry as to his intent.

Technicorps loomed ahead, the building outlined stark white
against a vivid blue April sky that was cloudless; the day was already
heating up, and I predicted a hotter than usual summer ahead. The
carefully maintained gardens stretched to either side and around the
back where a towering tulip poplar loomed over a concrete bench
discolored by lichens and stains from tree sap. I'd spent many hours
beneath that particular tree pondering the mysteries of the universe.
Yes, I could move on and had done so many times in my life, but I
was comfortable and oddly settled.

Kipp and I separated; he was headed to his classroom where the
young lupines waited. I guess it was a mark of his genius that in a
relatively short time, he'd evolved from a primitive world to become
a mainstay in our contemporary collective. He and Juno taught the
youngsters English, and his highly popular ethics class was open to
all. I'd thought about dropping in but feared my presence might
make him nervous. I took the stairs to the basement where Fitzhugh
waited, having beat me to work since he had ridden in splendor
conveyed by Peter's golden chariot. The fragrance of brewing

coffee hit me square on, which meant Mark Elliott was already busy.

"Good morning," Mark's voice rang out.

I'd been prepared not to like him when he first arrived to work as Fitzhugh's assistant, drawing an unfairly hasty conclusion that he might just think he was Mr. Wonderful. With wavy hair the color of a wheat field, eyes so blue that one was reminded of the warm waters of the Gulf, and teeth that were suspiciously white, I found his perfection to be a bit much. But he actually was a nice guy and head over heels in love with Suzanne. And all of that suited me just fine.

"I'm glad you're back and ready to go at it," Mark commented, thoughtfully setting a mug of coffee on my work desk.

The mug was one that had found its way from someone's kitchen, as a discard, to our little kitchenette. There was a floral design with a black cat arching his way up the side of the mug, the cat's tail forming the handle. It was pretty awful, and I understood why someone covertly disposed of it, probably in the dark of the night. The scent of the coffee was inviting; Mark had added a splash of cream thinking the brew was a little too strong.

"That German translation is kicking my butt," he confessed, laughing. "I think those folks just created a new language and didn't bother to tell the rest of us."

We'd found that there were some jobs at which he was superior and others at which I had mastery. Fortunately, neither of us developed a big ego about being the "best" and we just tossed off manuscripts back and forth until we figured them out. I'd actually never had a work partner who turned out to be as easy going as Mark. As it turned out, I'd been wrong on just about every count where he was concerned. And easy going was a good quality in someone who spent hours translating the exploits of former travelers into modern-day parlance that could be scanned into a computer system for posterity. This was my job between travels and one which made me frequently swear softly beneath my breath.

A few hours into the morning, he paused at my desk and raised his eyebrows, pointing at the vacant chair nearby. "Can I have a moment?" he asked, as he began to sit. There was no good way for me to say no, so I nodded.

"I've been seeing Suzanne," he began, his eyes meeting mine before quickly darting away to stare at the far wall. I stayed quiet, waiting for him as his eyes examined the paint scheme that Fitzhugh had mandated. Most of the walls at Technicorps were painted in the traditional way of most large companies and were a bland, nondescript, pale, putty color that made one ache for some diversity. In the library, however, the walls vibrated with the deep richness of Victorian hues. I privately applauded Fitzhugh for taking a stand for individuality.

"It's become kind of serious and, well…" his voice drifted off.

I knew he needed help and was gratified he must have felt some safety to seek counsel at my advice counter. "I've been married," I began, hoping that was a good opening.

"Yeah, Fitzhugh mentioned that one day," Mark replied. I was pleased he didn't give the obligatory regrets for my loss; I didn't need it from him. "I actually would like to, uh, pop the question to Suzanne and wanted a female opinion on what I had in mind."

"Okay," I said, trying to sound neutral. Actually, I was curious and couldn't wait.

"Suzanne loves hiking, and we go to Duke Forest as well as some other places nearby. I thought I might ask her while we are out walking, somewhere in nature…the places I know she likes." He frowned. "But I'm afraid it won't seem romantic enough, and maybe I ought to take her to dinner or something more formal."

I laughed softly. "Take her somewhere she enjoys, and if that is hiking, it will be the perfect spot. I think it's a very romantic idea."

His face lightened. I had validated his first instinct, and that was all he needed. "Thanks, Petra."

"So, will you guys stay here or ask for a move?" I asked.

"Actually, I've been approached by the Alpharetta collective; they are working to refurbish and re-energize the whole complex. I'd be made the head of the research and collections division, like Fitzhugh is here." He shrugged his shoulders good-naturedly. "You and I both know that Fitzhugh won't give up control any time soon."

"Well, that is true. But I would miss you two," I remarked honestly. Susanne's loss would be the bigger of the two for Technicorps, because she was so skilled. But it was not my issue to solve and would fall on Philo's overburdened plate. And it seemed that at some point there would be a new assistant for Fitzhugh, and that always was interesting.

EIGHT

"Hey, help me pull this limb to the street," I called out.

It was a workday, unbelievably hot, and I knew I probably smelled...and not like the sweet, alluring fragrance of a tea rose. One glance at the smirk on Kipp's expressive face told me I was correct. There was a flowing rush of darkness as a cloud shifted position overhead before it moved on and the sun emerged brighter than ever. My eyes squinted half shut as I monitored the atmospheric conditions. Hot, humid days such as this could quickly produce thunderstorms with little to no warning.

"The guy who took Suzanne's place is the rudest, most caustic being I've ever known," Philo remarked as he joined me to drag the downed limb to the curb. Kipp followed, pulling another limb, involuntarily growling as he jerked on the debris. Elani danced at the edge of the limb, obviously fighting the temptation to grab the other end and pull against him; the determined look on his face stopped her momentum to play tug.

My yard was a mess, the result of a mid-summer hurricane season that had been active and seemed to target the Carolinas more than was fair in one summer. Peter, Elani, and Philo had arrived to help me do general clean up. Fitzhugh was occupied painting the front door to the house after I let him select the color, which was a nice, deep green. It didn't pop but was soothing, and I liked it. And when one is recruiting free labor, it does not do well to be overly dictatorial as to the efforts and results.

"Worse than Fitzhugh?" I replied, grinning at Fitzhugh, who raised his eyebrows in response. I noticed his forehead was damp with sweat and paused on my way to the rear of my house to check on him. "Do you need a break?"

"Don't hover," he replied, frowning at me.

A brimming glass of iced tea, the condensation beading up to trickle slowly down the sides of the glass, rested on the porch step, so he had plenty of hydration. He knew his limits…at least I thought he did, and I forced my thoughts away from his past cardiac issues. On the other side of the glass storm door, Lily dragged her striped body and back and forth as she meowed at Fitzhugh. Next to Kipp, he was her current favorite. I'd always thought cats to be rather fickle with their affections, but she was remarkably consistent. I knew I was only needed for bodily warmth, so I accepted my low status in the household. Rejoining Philo, I walked towards Peter, who was using a chain saw he'd borrowed from a friend. I'd wondered, when he first arrived with the saw in hand, if I needed to keep a phone in my pocket to call 911 when he managed to cut off a leg. But he'd proved to be extremely competent with the machine and made fast work of some very long branches that had fallen. I was impressed but didn't want him to get cocky and careless, so I kept my applause silent.

"You know that in all these recent transfers between collectives, some traveling pairs were sent our way since we are down in our quota," Philo said, stopping to pull out a bandana and wipe his face. "So just when we need Suzanne the most since she is the best in the business, they send Karl, who perpetually seems to have an attitude and wants to argue with everything proposed." He frowned. "I've been called down to the workshop ten times in the past two weeks to mitigate conflict resolution." Tucking the bandana back in his rear pocket, he glanced at me. "But he is very competent if you can put up with his personality."

Philo was at heart a peacemaker and a gentle soul, usually only allowing himself to be irritable with me. His nature explained his current rift with Claire and Silas, since he lacked the oomph for a serious confrontation. He just didn't like to fight. Smiling, I put my hand on his arm, which was sweaty and covered in sawdust.

"What?" he asked.

"Nothing," I replied. Inwardly I was happy he had at least one individual with whom he could let go, from time to time. We all need a friend like that. As I leaned forward to pull another limb loose from Peter's growing pile of debris, I thought, with some satisfaction, that I had Kipp and Fitzhugh, as well as Philo, to serve as my safe sounding boards. I was doing well in that category, for once in my life.

"In any case, I have a meeting with him Monday. I can't allow Karl to run off our new talent." Philo reached down to a small table that held a pitcher of tea and poured a glass. The sweat rolled off his face as he almost drained the beverage in one swallow. "The new pairs are not as experienced as you and Kipp but definitely have several important trips under their collective belts."

"Yeah, I've met them, although briefly, when they toured the library. And what's the latest on a new assistant for Fitzhugh?" I glanced at the old symbiont, who paused, paintbrush hovering in the air, as he waited for Philo's reply.

"Well, the word has gotten around about him and it makes it difficult," Philo replied, deadpan.

"Good!" Fitzhugh exclaimed. "I don't need any help. Petra and I are doing fine, just as is."

Well, we weren't, and the work was piling up at an alarming rate. Once Peter had been the assistant in training but now was engaged in other things. Then there was Margaret Shelton followed by Mark. No matter how Fitzhugh felt about the situation, things would change, and probably soon. I glanced at Juno, who was resting in a cool patch of dark shade cast by an oak tree. She had fallen into a deep sleep, her sides rising and falling in a hypnotic rhythm. Her hind legs kicked a little, ruffling the grass bed on which she lay, and gently I peeked inside her thoughts so as not to disturb her. Yes, I know I was being intrusive, but I was starting to do things automatically, just like Kipp. He, with his libertine approach to life, was a corrupting presence, steering me away from all the rules and regulations that had defined all I'd known to be truths. Juno's dreaming mind was reliving a moment in her early childhood, running with her siblings along the side of a flowing river. The sunlight seemed captured by the water and reflected off of the fluid surface much like a wind chime made of dangling crystals, a kaleidoscope flashing on the sloping banks. It was a happy dream, full of color and movement. Carefully I withdrew; Kipp caught my eye and winked, since he knew what I'd been up to. If your best friend isn't a safe place for secrets, I don't know who is.

It was getting late in the day, and the shadows began to lengthen. Although I was not a big fan of hot summers, there was this time, as the afternoon began to wane, when the sounds of chirping, clicking insects intensified, and the birds escalated their activities before becoming still as darkness fell. It seemed to me there was something special about the quietness that preceded twilight. I ushered everyone inside one at a time for a shower; both Philo and Peter had brought changes of clothing. Then, before I hit the shower, I called and ordered several pizzas. TCM had a scheduled showing of *North by Northwest*, and it would make for a fun evening.

Later, as Cary Grant tried to elude assassins while galloping over Mount Rushmore and dangling off George Washington's left nostril, I noted that Philo had nodded off, his chin bobbing on his chest. Fitzhugh followed my gaze and his lips tightened. Unexpectedly, and without invitation, his thoughts entered my head.

"We'll take care of him," he said. The thought flowed as did Kipp's, becoming a natural part of my mind.

My eyes opened wide in surprise at Fitzhugh's breach of symbiont protocol and manners, since he'd failed to politely knock at my proverbial door before coming inside, uninvited. He smiled in response. Kipp, from his vantage point on the floor, was a part of the triangle, since he'd registered Fitzhugh's thoughts, too.

The movie ended, and Peter and Elani, after whispered good-byes, quietly exited, their SUV purring quietly down the street, its tail lights glowing red in the black of night. Gently, I touched Philo's shoulder; if he kept at it, his neck would have a crick for a week.

"What?" His eyes opened suddenly, his face momentarily confused.

"The good guys won." I smiled. "You are welcome to the sofa," I began.

"No, I have to get home." His voice sounded empty.

I knew there was more and walked him out to his car, which only looked a notch better than my battered jalopy. There was a full moon and some bright object next to it that I could only surmise was one of the planets; for a brief moment, I despised my laziness, since it would have been simple to figure out that pretty, winking object, and I'd not bothered to name something worth of recognition. A few lightning bugs were flashing their tails among the low hanging branches of the trees. Philo leaned up against his car and stared up at the moon, not speaking for several seconds. His eyes met mine, caught in the shadows.

"Silas has been relocated from the west coast to the Alpharetta collective," he began, sighing. "Vashti has announced her intent to separate from him, and he will no longer travel." Philo paused for that to sink in, since the dissolution of the traveling symbiont bond was unusual and almost unheard of. "I'm trying to get her to come here and let me find her a new partner." He smiled. "I always liked her, and in some ways, she is like a daughter to me." Crossing his arms across his chest, he added, "She really has no other immediate family."

"I like her, too."

"But not Silas," he remarked, the corners of his mouth turning down.

"We had a disagreement about ethics," I replied. "You will need to ask him."

"Oh, I did. I'm disappointed in him and also in Claire, who will go over the cliff with him rowing as fast as possible. The only one with any integrity is poor Vashti." Extending his hand, he held still while a lighting bug rested upon his outstretched index finger, the flashing of its body illuminating Philo's flesh in yellow strobes. Resting against the car, he crossed his long legs and gazed up at the night sky again. "I've known Claire since I was a youngster, and we've been married more years than I can count. Funny, though, as much as I'd like to say her exit leaves me empty, it doesn't. We've been distant for so long that it feels, well, like nothing."

"You sound depressed," I remarked cautiously.

"Not really, Petra. I'm tired. But I'm ready to get untired," he said, smiling faintly. "I have a good job, wonderful friends, and I'm ready to move forward."

The lightning bug became interested in something other than Philo's finger and took off, hovering, before beginning a zigzag pattern of flight, following its friends to a gathering place beneath the outstretched limbs of an oak tree. Philo pushed away from the car and pulled me into a familiar hug. Observers might wonder if he needed more than just friendship from me, but it had never been so and wasn't then. I was a safe friend and happy to be just that. More would have been like getting intimate with my brother, and the yuk factor there was immense. Philo's lips grazed the top of my head, and he ducked his tall body down into the front seat of the car. "See ya," he said bravely.

Fitzhugh was waiting inside, clearly concerned. "Is he alright?"

"Yeah, I think so," I replied.

We walked to the kitchen to let Kipp and Juno venture out to the back yard before retiring. Fitzhugh took a seat at the dinette while I camped out at the door.

"It is hard for us to terminate relationships," Fitzhugh remarked. "Our genetic makeup almost mandates we stay connected to the end."

"Two relationships will end with this—Vashti and Silas as well as Philo and Claire. Oh, and I think Vashti might come here, which would be nice. She could, at the beginning, live with Philo and that would give him some companionship. She's a dear, wonderful lupine and will help him heal."

"Glad to hear that," Fitzhugh murmured.

"And while it's just the two of us, what was that little stunt you pulled by barging into my head earlier today, Mr. Rules and Regulations?"

His face turned pink before he coughed delicately as he considered his reply. "You are a terrible influence upon me, you and Kipp both. Your freewheeling ways have corrupted me."

I laughed. Outside, Kipp re-emerged from the darkness, politely escorting a slow-moving Juno back into the light. I hovered at the door, waiting for them. Kipp's eyes caught mine through the glass as his tail wagged.

Later, in bed, I reflected upon the day. Symbionts, it seemed, share some things with humans. We have the ability to love, to have that love broken, grieve, and start over again. We also have the unfortunate ability to totally give up and not fight for things that matter. Philo would not be allowed to do the latter. Kipp's muzzle pressed hard against my breast bone.

"Hey, turn the page," he demanded.

"Where's your stylus?" I asked, grumbling but not really minding. I held his Kindle as he scanned the page he was reading.

"Just being lazy," he replied. "I'm trying to wrap my head around this book."

I'd read most of the classics, including *Wuthering Heights,* and unlike many modern books, I found the nuances of language and cultural references caused me to focus more intensely. I figured humans struggled even more considering they hadn't lived in those past times and I had!

"I mean, what's with Cathy and Heathcliff? It was obvious she loved him but she married someone else. Why would she do that?" Kipp turned his face towards mine and was so close that his eyes almost crossed as he tried to focus on me.

"Love is complicated," I replied, not feeling energetic enough to mount a dissertation.

"Not for me," he huffed. "I love you, and that's all there is to it."

"Well, there are different types of love." I wiggled my shoulders into the pillow to get more comfortable. It must have been close to midnight, and I had no idea why neither of us had already fallen asleep except there was no pressing need to be up at the crack of dawn. Outside, I heard the first drops of promised rain begin to strike the roof. The sound would serve to ease us off to the land of nod in no time.

"Kipp, you've never told me about your father," I began, my tone tentative. We'd been dealing with Philo and his family issues of late, and I wondered if Kipp's lack of a living family of origin was working on his heart.

He sighed and moved his heavy body closer to me. It was clear he'd lost interest in Heathcliff for the night—which was fine by me, since reading about the toxic type of love between the protagonists was fatiguing—and I put the Kindle on the side table. The rain began to fall in earnest, and rumbles of thunder began to roll from the skies, causing the base of the bedside lamp to tremble against the wood tabletop. Lily, who'd probably been napping in the front parlor room—whoops, that was a slip from old times, since no modern individual probably refers to a room as a parlor—hopped up at the end of the bed, her eyes glowing from the ambient light edged around the bathroom door. With a soft meow, she joined us, curling up against Kipp's warmth. I guess the thunder drove her to seek safety in our nest versus her closet hidey hole. I rubbed my thumb against her little noggin as she tilted her head, allowing my caress to cover more square footage.

"My mama said that he went hunting for us shortly after I was born, and he never came back." He glanced at me, his profile a shadow in the darkness. "The world was savage, full of danger..." He let his thoughts drift away, unfinished.

"What was he like?"

"Mama said I looked just like him," Kipp replied. I could hear pride as well as yearning in his voice. "She said he was kind, noble and fearless to a fault." He sighed. "Sometimes, I'd see her glance off into the distance, where the hills were hidden by the early morning fog, and I realized she was always waiting for him to return...maybe the fog would break and she'd see him in the distance. She seemed sad, I think." His chest rose and fell again, as Lily gave a contented chirp and snuggled closer. "Petra?"

"Yes?"

"Is it normal that I have trouble remembering things about my mother?"

"Yes, Kipp, it is. As time passes, we can't recall the sound of someone's voice or even the scent of their body. I used to love to press my nose against George's body after his bath, inhaling that sweet, clean baby scent. I don't know what that is like any more and can't conjure it up, no matter how hard I try."

As he fell quiet, I wondered how the wheels had come off the bus, and we had become mired in depressing talk of long lost loved ones and the experience of grief. After all, we'd started with an analysis of a classic tome and ended somewhere far distant from that perusal. Maybe he needed not to read the dark, dense classics, many of which spoke of sadness and desperation. I thought of *The Good Earth* and *David Copperfield*, trying not to clench my teeth.

"Kipp?"

"Yes?"

"I'm not going anywhere," I said.

"I know. Me neither."

"And you know, Philo will be okay," I added. "He's tough enough to withstand the hurt and loss."

"Well, that may be true, but in any case, like Fitzhugh said, we'll take care of him."

NINE

"I really have no interest in this trip," I began. It seemed I was saying that more and more frequently, as I paused to consider the limited alternatives. If I retired from traveling, then Kipp would have no partner, so that was out. And if I even broached the subject of trying to find him a new partner, he'd refuse, so that was equally a nonstarter. Besides, if I retired, they'd stick me in the library until I became as old and gray as Fitzhugh, and I'd die of boredom. At the fire flashing in Philo's eyes at my words, I cleared my throat. "Sorry, that was hasty of me. Let me hear more about the proposal."

Kipp's eyes opened wide since hearing "sorry" from me in any form or fashion was far and few between. His large ears flattened as his sense of humor pushed forward. "I bet that was hard," he smirked.

"Yeah, you'll never know," I replied, laughing softly, my words part of our private exchange.

Kipp and I had been called to Philo's office, and there were no dewy-eyed, hopeful youngsters underfoot, waiting with bated breath on our decision. I did appreciate the fact he was talking to us, just us, before making any announcements or pushing us to do something we'd despise. I'd been in that office many times under the previous managers, usually to be corrected for something I'd done that was met with disapprobation. So one would think I hated that room, but the contrary was true. There was a wonderful set of windows overlooking the pretty garden, which was well kept but managed to maintain a natural, almost wild appeal. Since it was late summer, only the crape myrtles were in bloom, dusting the ground beneath the tulip poplar with discarded blossoms. On the far horizon, the afternoon clouds were gathering for the usual storm that seemed to take place every day at sunset as the sun was dropping from view.

"The trip proposal and research was done by Elani, who did an excellent job. And she and Peter didn't ask for you to, uh, accompany them. But this is such a fragile time period that we cannot take any chance that their involvement will change history. Novices with only two consequential trips are usually assigned to something less complex, Petra. You know that." Philo left the chair and perched on the side of his desk; almost idly, he began to gently swing his leg. It had been weeks since Claire left to join her baby boy, I thought sarcastically, in Alpharetta. On the floor near Kipp, our old friend Vashti relaxed, since she'd become the new companion to Philo. Her arrival had caused some discomfort for Elani, who was horrified to see Kipp's affectionate demeanor towards her. I finally had to take Elani aside and privately reassure her that Kipp bore no romantic love for Vashti, and she was somewhat mollified.

I glanced at Vashti, who opened one brown eye at me and thumped her tail on the carpeted floor. It was not difficult to recall the first time I saw her in Whitechapel, chained to a post, bruised from abuse and harsh treatment, neglected and starved...her coat a tangled, filthy mess. Now, as the sun shone through the windows, the light rested on her mottled gray fur which had waves rippling through the thick hairs. It was nice to see her looking so good, her natural vitality restored. Since it was in the nature of the minds of curious beings to speculate, I wondered, for a brief moment, if Philo might reconsider his choice to have never traveled. There was the possibility that he and Vashti could forge the needed bond. True, the initiation of traveling was typically for the young, but there was no reason he couldn't try. I had an even wilder, more hysterical thought. What if Philo and Vashti could bond, then Fitzhugh and

Juno could, also? We could have four pairs of traveling symbionts creating havoc in the universe. Now we're talking, I thought, enjoying the prospect of it all. Of course, such a notion was impossible, and I reigned in my wild musings.

It was with effort I returned my focus to the matter at hand. "So, in other words, President Lincoln must die on April 15, 1865," I said, my voice flat.

"Yes, it must happen as it was meant to be."

Odd, I'd never thought of it until that moment, but the doomed *Titanic* struck the iceberg on April 14, 1912, and she sank on April 15. Lincoln was shot on April 14, 1865 and died the following morning on April 15. To heck with the ides of March…the middle of April seemed a little more consequential. And so that I'd not forget—as if I could—the *General* was abducted on April 12, 1862. Yes, April was a happening month, historically speaking.

Kipp's interest was immense, since he'd read multiple books about the Civil War period and the personalities of the day. I shared that interest, and it was sort of a specialty of mine, that era. I'd met the Union generals Grant, Sherman, and Hancock as well as the Confederates, Hood, Stonewall Jackson and Longstreet. Personally, I found Sherman to be the most fascinating. He'd been considered to be mentally unstable, and it was due to Grant's belief in him that his career was resurrected. It led to a loyalty between the two that was remarkable. Besides, Sherman was a brilliant man and following the twists and turns of his brain had been a challenge. But he was a focused and ruthless combatant, as the residents of Georgia were to discover to their everlasting dismay. I thought Longstreet, who was pretty much hated in the South after he turned Republican and tried to mend fences after the war, was regarded unfairly by the people for whom he'd gone to battle. His competency and skills as a general were easily forgotten. He'd tried to get Lee to avoid Gettysburg but failed. When Lee got the battle fever raging hot, there was little one could do to make him take another path. I'd made previous trips to that period before Kipp entered my life and then we, along with Peter and Elani, made the trip to observe the abduction of the *General* as we followed along in pursuit on a swaying, charging *Texas*.

"You know, it could get a little awkward my hanging around Washington during that time period," I began, trying not to whine. "Grant might recognize me."

"And I'm certain, as clever as you are, you can figure out a solution to that minor problem," Philo replied. With a sigh, he rose from his chair and went to the window overlooking the garden. I saw his mouth twitch in a smile, and for a fleeting moment, I thought of entering his thoughts naturally, as Kipp and I did constantly with one another, but held back. Fitzhugh managed to break protocol, but he was, at his age, blazing new trails. As well as I knew Philo, I wasn't sure he was ready.

"There's a couple of birds out there, beneath a shrub, having a territorial dispute," Philo remarked, laughing. His posture relaxed as his shoulders dropped. "Humans and symbionts aren't the only species who can't manage to get along."

"Do you mind if Kipp and I take Elani's proposal and review it and then, maybe, get with Peter and Elani, since it is their trip? You realize that they might not want us tagging along," I began, trying to keep my tone from sounding hopeful.

"I've already told them they can't go alone. They are waiting on your decision."

"Well thanks," I said, feeling the heat rush to my face. "If we say no, we are in the proverbial dog house. And if we say yes, we will be thrust into one of the most tragic and pivotal times in the history of the United States."

"And I would think you, who likes to think of yourself as a historian, would love this opportunity," Philo replied smoothly, his tone dismissive, signaling the conversation was at an end. Our closeness as friends didn't seem to impede his authoritarian position as my manager.

The following morning, which was a Saturday, found me nursing a cup of coffee while sitting at my battered dinette table as the early sunrise was just starting to illuminate the kitchen. Kipp and I were planning a run before the day began to heat up, and I was enjoying the quiet. Juno had met us, restless after an interrupted night of sleep, and she and Kipp were out back, prowling. The dew was wet on the grass, and I smiled as I watched Juno pick her paws up high, fastidiously, to keep them from becoming soaked.

"You're up early," Fitzhugh commented as he walked behind me, giving my shoulder an affectionate squeeze as he passed. The water poured into the kettle as he began the morning tea ritual.

"Yeah, couldn't sleep," I replied, stifling a yawn.

"What's bothering you?"

I sighed deeply. "Philo has Kipp and me looking at a time-shift."

"And you are ambivalent?"

"It's this trip that Elani has proposed to look into the Mary Surratt affair. We talked about it," I added, trying to keep the irritability from my voice. Fitzhugh took his seat across from me, as he waited for the water to heat. "Can you imagine?" My eyes met his.

"I've always considered that had Lincoln lived, reconstruction would have been handled very differently," Fitzhugh replied. "He wanted reconciliation, not punishment, and perhaps some of the antipathy that remained for countless generations would have been avoided, or, at least, lessened." He smiled at me. "And history has been critical of Andrew Johnson for many reasons. In that day and time, a southern Democrat following in the footsteps of a Republican president made for a situation filled with potential pitfalls. Johnson found himself on the opposite side of the radical Republicans. We have to leave such moments in time for human historians since we can only speculate about the what ifs.

"Lincoln was a fascinating figure with his lack of formal education and innate drive to learn. And he managed to keep learning, studying battle tactics so that he could direct and discuss with his generals, a point of which seemed to enrage General McClellan. I think he referred to Lincoln as the "original gorilla" or something equally unflattering." Fitzhugh rose to rescue the whistling kettle and pour the water into the waiting teapot. Almost immediately, I detected the bergamot fragrance wafting through the air, the scent helping to clear the lingering sleep-induced fog from my brain.

Kipp's moist nose made a print on the window of the kitchen door as he stared at us. Clearly, he and Juno were finished and ready to come in. Fitzhugh opened the door and a second later, the kitchen floor was covered with damp, slightly muddy paw prints.

"Sorry," Juno said, glancing up at me, her large ears drooping in chagrin.

"No problem, sweetheart," I replied. "Kipp can mop later," I added, feeling mean. When humanoids cohabited with lupines, there was just going to be a lot of hair and paw prints, and that's a fact.

Kipp, in response, huffed, and, after circling, plopped on the floor.

Fitzhugh brought the tea service to the table and, at my nod, poured me a cup of amber tea. I was feeling lazy and obviously feeling entitled to being served.

"I think it would be a limited trip, and you could avoid the notable personalities of the day, focusing your attention only on the Surratt household and the comings and goings of John Wilkes Booth and his gang," Fitzhugh began. He sat back in the chair and crossed his long legs at the ankles. "If it is a question of determining her guilt or innocence, it would be a matter of sifting through her thoughts, something any of you could easily manage over a short distance, or you could rely upon Kipp for the greater challenges." He winked at Kipp, who thumped his tail at the complimentary remark concerning his abilities. "And you wouldn't have to go in the heat of the summer, when Washington was almost unbearable."

"Why's that?" Kipp asked, finally interested in our conversation.

"Washington was built adjacent to a swamp. There was more than one waterway, and, as the population swelled during wartime, those were used for general sewage disposal. The heat, combined with insects and the matter of disease due to poor sanitation, made the summers unpleasant. The Lincoln family would retreat from the White House, due to its proximity to the swampy lowland, and go to the Soldiers' Home, which was a few miles away, and remain there from mid-summer until November." Fitzhugh took a delicate sip of his tea; with a napkin, he dabbed at his mustache. "Lincoln's son, Willie, died of the fever that was so prevalent."

"What is it with humans and the lack of common sense about sanitation?" Kipp began to groom his paws, his pink tongue removing the moisture from the early morning dew-coated grass. "I mean, even animals know not to soil their immediate living area with poo."

"People didn't know about bacteria, germs, or organisms that are not seen by the human eye until relatively recently in history," Fitzhugh said. "We learned about it when I was young, and that was a very long time ago, when a traveler informed us."

Kipp, who was brighter than most, had as much trouble wrapping his head around the notion that even though we thought our time was current, we could just be existing in the past and some traveler from perhaps a hundred years in the future could come back to visit us. The reason that such things were discouraged was due to the chaos it created.

"When you think about it, Kipp, during your time-shift to the time of the *General*, those people perceived you and your companions as being their contemporaries. In fact, all those people had been dead for many years by the time you arrived." Fitzhugh smiled. "It makes me dizzy when I think about it, too," he added comfortingly, not wanting Kipp to fret over being lost in the maze. "It's kind of like trying to figure out when time began…you just can't do it."

Kipp shook his head and began to lick his paws with more vigor. It was good to not linger on such notions, I thought.

I rousted my partner up out of his blue funk and, after donning my running clothes, we set out for a trot into the countryside. It had been a while since we'd gone to the cemetery to visit my George's resting place, and I was feeling sentimental. After studiously avoiding any situations or stimuli that might make me sad, Kipp had shoved all of it in my face and I found, to my delight, that his bossiness helped me to heal. I really didn't feel sad when visiting George's little plot on the hillside, surrounded by other departed souls; instead, I felt comfortable and reflective in a positive way.

In a short time, my feet were thudding out the comforting rhythm of a slow jog. I was not a speed demon and cared not what others, who had more skin in the game of running, thought of my meandering trot. It really just felt good to be outside, and the running caused me to breathe deeper, and the result cleared my head remarkably. Kipp was quiet, his thoughts withdrawn from mine, as we ran as a pair, separate for a change. As if he realized the separation, he angled a little closer, so that his furry flank was brushing my right leg as we ran. He had no need to comfort me as I knew he would never stray far from my mind and heart.

The habitation thinned, and we drew close to the cemetery. As we passed under the arching iron entrance, I glanced up at the sky, when the hillside before us was unexpectedly shrouded in a wave of darkness. But I had no need to fear; there was no impending storm brewing. Instead, a white, perfect cloud, which looked like a mound of whipped cream, had moved to block the sun momentarily. In the next second, the cloud shifted, and a sudden burst of brightness overwhelmed the green hill, illuminating the granite markers standing starkly upright, their pale coolness a contrast to the organic greens and browns upon which they rested.

It was not seeming to run across the graves, so I slowed to a walk, carefully zigzagging while enjoying the sensation of the deceleration of my heartbeat in response. My hand drifted down to stroke Kipp's head. Just beneath the crest of the hill, I found George's place, the grass thick, only slightly withered due to the summer's heat. After checking the ground for ant beds, I plopped down, while Kipp angled up next to me, sitting so that I could drape my arm over his back. It was a good place from which to view the world. My hand, across his broad chest, could feel the solid thump of his heart against my palm.

"Peter and Elani are coming by this evening so that she can present the idea of the time-shift," Kipp remarked. Overhead, a solitary crow flew to the southwest, cawing loudly as he passed overhead. His head twisted slightly as if he was watching us, no doubt wondering what we had planned as we rested amongst the granite tombstones. We must have seemed to be suspicious characters to him.

"Okay," I replied noncommittally.

"You know, it could be a very interesting trip and yield some valuable historical information," Kipp continued. He turned his massive head so that I could scratch between his upright ears. The sunlight pulled all the deep reds and gold tones from his glorious coat; his eyes sparked fiery amber in the light.

"You have decided you want to go," I replied, trying to keep the dullness from my voice.

"No, I really haven't. But I am eager to hear Elani's presentation, and if she has managed to do the research, we would be silly not to consider the pros and cons." He exhaled, and I realized he'd been careful in his words.

Pulling him closer, I said, "Kipp, you don't need to be so cautious with me. Remember, it's healthy and good for us to disagree and argue, if needed." His face was so close to mine that his nose looked three times its actual size. "I promise I haven't thrown out the idea and will consider it fairly."

"I thought you didn't want to be around during the time of Lincoln's assassination?" he asked.

I paused while a late summer bee droned overhead. Kipp resisted the urge to snap at the insect, which was annoying but harmless. Following Kipp's thoughts, he realized the little bee was another fellow creature, just being about his business. Since he meant us no harm, no harm should come to him. For a big, rough, kind of scary looking lupine, Kipp had the heart of a pussy cat.

"I didn't...don't," I replied hesitantly. "But I recall many past trips Tula and I made that were not number one on my favorite list. This is our occupation, after all." It had taken me a while, but I thought, at that moment, that I'd come home. It was time to embrace my nature or forever run from it.

We had obviously talked it out, and it was time to leave. Finally, I roused myself into a slow jog, and when we arrived at the house, I was a sweaty mess, and Kipp was panting like a bellows. I looked forward to a shower and retreat to my room to read. Kipp had finally finished *Wuthering Heights*, thank goodness, and I was curious to see what he planned next in his classics line up. It seemed a good way to spend a lazy day, since my yard work was caught up, and perhaps even doze a little before Peter and Elani—who promised to bring Chinese takeout—arrived later that evening.

After closing the plantation blinds and shrouding the room in darkness, I clicked on the ceiling fan and climbed into bed, my hair still damp from the shower. Kipp was waiting for me; he'd dropped the Kindle on my pillow, and I powered it up.

"Well, what will it be?" I asked, checking the library that Peter had carefully assembled.

"I ran across a book called *The Last of the Mohicans*, and I liked the title. I thought it might be fun to read it together."

That happened to be one of my favorites, but it had been a while. The overhead fan was making a hypnotic, whirring noise, buzzing softly against the dimness of the room. I tried not to yawn as I turned the electronic page and read the first line aloud, while Kipp lazily closed his eyes.

"Hey, I thought you were gonna read this," I whined, not really upset but just fussing for the fun of it.

"I like to hear your voice," he replied, opening his mouth in a loud yawn.

I'm not sure when we both fell asleep, but it was somewhere in the middle of chapter two, I think.

TEN

The fragrance from the Chinese food hung pleasantly in my small kitchen, as Fitzhugh, Philo, Peter, and I gathered around my dinette that fortunately accommodated four people, if we huddled close and kept our elbows politely tucked to our sides. Philo had been a last minute add on, bringing Vashti, who was busy with the other lupines, scarfing down chicken and vegetables on a bed of rice. She was momentarily fascinated by the tiny pieces of corn before crunching on one, allowing herself to savor the flavor and texture before nodding. I smiled, thinking of how she'd looked when we rescued her compared to the present, when her health and vitality was fully restored. I was happy to not see her ribs straining against her fur. Of course, the memory also conjured up a snapshot in my head of that moment, the first time I met William Harrow. My hand drifted up to my throat, and I allowed myself the luxury of letting my fingertips graze over the cool strand of pearls. Kipp's head went up, his eyes meeting mine, his tail thumping the sheetrock in support. Surprisingly, Fitzhugh made another unauthorized quick dive into my head as he noticed my touch of the pearls, a much welcomed mental hug. I realized he was enjoying his newly permitted behaviors that mimicked Kipp's and in his advanced years was becoming more, uh, natural. I smiled at him. It was a private moment in a room filled with telepaths.

"I know what you mean about Karl," Peter was saying, as I snapped to attention. "I met him today, Philo, and he just about took my head off for no good reason. His lips are all pinched like he's sucked a lemon," Peter added, demonstrating for good measure.

Philo rolled his eyes, knowing he shouldn't talk about personnel issues but happy all secrets stayed within the boundaries of our group. He couldn't talk to Claire anymore, since she'd left, and Vashti was still pretty new on the scene. As I watched them, I wondered if she would want to pair off again to travel or if she was content just padding around at Philo's side. The trip during which Kipp and I had rescued her had been a tough one, and her relationship with the unethical Silas had been gravely disappointing. She was older than Kipp but still a young symbiont with plenty of traveling years remaining. What an odd group we made, I thought…a couple of elders on the far end of the spectrum, youngsters hovering expectantly on the cusp of adventure, and some in the middle who were trying to not become jaded by life.

"We will be interviewing a new assistant for you, Fitzhugh," Philo began, anticipating the negative response.

"I've told you I really don't need anyone," Fitzhugh sputtered, dabbing at his mustache with a napkin.

"And if you'd keep from running everyone off," Philo responded, not meaning it. "you'll still have Petra in between time-shifts," he added, his voice soothing. "But the work is piling up, and you know it." After hesitating, he added, "I've been talking to Peter, Kipp, and Elani and will soon be making some staffing announcements."

Fitzhugh raised his shaggy eyebrows, crossing his arms at his chest. It was not an inviting posture.

"Peter has agreed to return to the library to help, in between other assignments." Philo glanced at Fitzhugh, who was noncommittal. "Elani is going to take over Kipp's English class for the young lupines; Kipp will keep his ethics class as well as assume more of a management role over all the activities that involve the education and training of the lupines."

My mouth fell open in a smile. Kipp had concealed this news from me, so I was as surprised as the others. I was proud of Kipp and his rapid ascension to a position of authority. I glanced at him, meeting his eyes; his ears flattened as I registered his fundamental sense of humility. He would never be one to seek out advancement but could take on the load with ease and a grateful heart. And for a symbiont of Elani's youth to be given such responsibility was a compliment to her intelligence and grace.

"Well, I suppose that is acceptable," Fitzhugh remarked, his voice gruff. "At least I won't have to break in a newbie. Peter knows how I operate."

"And how!" Peter replied, before he could exercise good judgment and keep his mouth shut. The rest of us had to laugh and even Fitzhugh smirked, just a little, his lips tightening.

"Any plans for Vashti?" I asked.

Philo exchanged a guarded look with her. "She and I are also talking, and at this time, she will stay with me and get accustomed to our collective, making connections as well as friendships. Who knows?" he added, cryptically.

The table fell quiet, and Elani demonstrated her excellent sense of timing. "I'm ready, if you all are, to begin."

"Yes, let's do that," I responded, my voice a little too loud. I felt perhaps I'd broached a topic that was a little too raw in terms of Vashti and was ready to plow forward with a different subject.

While Fitzhugh made the ubiquitous pot of Earl Grey, I cleared the table and let the lupines out the back door for a quick dash through the yard. Juno, since we'd started giving her some turmeric with the glucosamine, was noticeably spryer, and she managed the back steps with a little more spring to her walk. I took a moment to walk out on my narrow back porch, enjoying the darkness, never able to decide if I enjoyed sunrise or twilight more. There was a soft breeze threading through the trees; the leaves rustled gently against one another, the sound soothing as I closed my eyes to focus. I caught a vague fragrance of some blooming flower that brought a sweet taste to the back of my tongue. A full moon hovered overhead, highlighting the trees and shrubs in the yard; shadows cast gave promise to the hidden mysteries of nature. Down the street, somebody's dog was barking; a car door slammed and an engine started. Smiling, I thought of the uniqueness of our position. I lived amongst humans, and they never grew suspicious of my true origin. Around me, they went about their lives, happy and confident that they understood the essence of the universe swirling around them. We could never make ourselves known; it would be destabilizing, to say the least. The temptation of humans to use our skills, even in the pursuit of good, would be too overwhelming, and corruption would be the outcome.

In the yard, I was pleased to see that Elani had relaxed her tense posture with Vashti, who had engaged in the game of chase that Elani and Kipp had perfected. If anything, she was almost a little better at it, using her natural predatory instincts in a more calculating manner than just running willly nilly back and forth as fast as possible. She managed to barrel into Kipp and sent him flying, not an easy task considering his solid bulk, and he landed hard, with a grunt. Juno laughed so hard, eclipsing the usual lupine style laugh where the jaw hung open, that she began to wheeze a little.

"Okay, guys, before someone gets hurt," I mildly reprimanded the trio.

Panting, they touched noses, the lupine equivalent of a fist bump and a signal that there were no hard feelings. As they passed me to come inside, Vashti glanced up and slowly closed one eye in a conspiratorial wink over her assault on Kipp, who was trying not to show that he was slightly limping. I shook my head in mock reproof. "You're a bad girl," I whispered to her.

"Here is how I have planned the time-shift," Elani began, once we all settled. Peter brought a plate full of cookies he'd dumped from a box, and Fitzhugh's tea had been served.

We were in my front room. Silver waves of moonlight broke through the large windows to puddle on the worn, wooden plank floor. It was a comfortable house but not a tidy one, and the collected junk from the ages lent wisdom to it, if that was possible. Could inanimate objects bring a presence with them? It often felt so. As I sampled a cookie, I wondered what the expiration date had been on the box. The morsel seemed a little stale, and I quickly washed it down with a gulp of scalding tea. I wasn't sure which was worse: the taste of the cookie or the lingering burn on the roof of my mouth from the tea.

Elani's presentation was just a rough run-through, since all trips had to be approved by the Twelve, who were notoriously nit picky. Of course, in all fairness, that was their job. Who knows, when I grew much older, would I be asked to be a part of such a group, monitoring the activities of youngsters? I didn't think so. My natural opposition to authority would resign me to another fate.

"May I ask something before you begin?" Fitzhugh's voice was soft and polite. Odd, he had rarely been that careful with me when I was younger. At Elani's nod, he said, "Why are you interested in this particular event?"

"Many people believe that the facts around Lincoln's assassination are a certainty. For instance, John Wilkes Booth's involvement is without question. The attack by Lewis Powell on Secretary of State Seward also was well documented. But Mary Surratt claimed her innocence up until the moment she was executed. I just find it interesting. Was the government anxious to assure security and stability by wrapping up the case despite possible evidence to the contrary? Powell, to the end, claimed that Mary Surratt was innocent. Why would he have cared, if she was equally guilty, and he faced execution no matter what? And what about the last-minute appeal to President Johnson? He claimed later he never saw it." Elani shrugged in the manner of lupines.

"And why do you think the determination of her guilt or innocence at this point would matter?" Fitzhugh placed his teacup on the table and leaned forward, rubbing his hands together as if to generate warmth, even though the temperature in the room was comfortable.

"An innocent woman may have been killed," Elani replied, her dark eyes glancing around at the rest of us. "Isn't that enough?"

"Many innocent humans have died since time began," Fitzhugh replied, sighing. "You will need to prove that this death is consequential enough to validate the need for a time-shift."

Elani, to her credit, was not put off by Fitzhugh, even if she huffed softly. After a moment of thought, she replied.

"I think the drama of the times, the hysteria in the government, which was threatened with instability due to the assassination of the president, and the question if justice was rushed just to put a period on history…all those things make this a worthy trip. True, we won't be able to investigate the motives of all the players, but the fact the government prosecuted Mary Surratt and executed her is significant. Was there sufficient evidence or was it based on emotion and other political considerations?"

Fitzhugh shrugged his thin shoulders, nodding. "I only ask because the Twelve will be careful on this one due to the need not to have any inadvertent impact on the timeline. The assassination of Lincoln was an immense trauma to the nation, but it must happen."

"How does it lay out in your mind?" Philo asked, sipping cautiously on his hot tea. He sniffed as the steam tickled his nose.

"Well, I had to do some extra research, since Petra visited those times in the past and has met Ulysses Grant. There is the possibility she might encounter him again." Elani settled in, shifting her hindquarters to get more comfortable. "Fitzhugh helped me find her documented account in the library." She looked over at him and wagged her tail as he winked in reply. "Petra and Tula made a time-shift to follow the activities of a group of female Confederate spies who were traveling back and forth across the lines, gathering information for the Confederate government."

"You never told me about that," Kipp remarked, looking slightly hurt.

"And you don't know everything, Mr. Wizard," I replied, ruffling the fur on the top of his head. I had moved to the floor to join him, his body curled around my legs and his jaw resting on my thigh.

"Anyway, she met General Grant who allowed her to travel freely in search of her missing husband," Elani added, giving Kipp a rather stern look since he interrupted her flow.

"What was he like?" Peter asked, pushing up his glasses, which had slid down the bridge of his nose. With his free hand, he shoved away the heavy mop of unruly hair that fell across his forehead.

"Interesting," I replied. "He was a humble man who had faced serious failures many times in his life. He never quit, but would accept the failure and look for another way to create a life for him and his family." I smiled in recollection. "He was deeply in love with his wife, Julia, and was a committed family man. The times he drank were when he was separated from her." The smile faded. "Grant was a very fierce commander and never considered withdrawal to be acceptable. He kept pushing forward until he achieved his goal. That quality was what Lincoln liked, a man who would engage without hesitation. However, Grant did face criticism for the large number of losses of soldiers during his engagements. Historians either thought the losses were acceptable considering the final outcome or that Grant was a butcher."

Peter nodded his head and dug his hand into the bowl of pretzels he'd brought to the living room and which proved more popular than the cookies which languished on the chipped Fiesta ware plate...another vintage find of mine. Vashti begged a pretzel and began to crunch as pieces of salt fell to the floor. She looked over at me, apologetically, and I waved away her concern. Lily, having awakened from her nap in the depths of my closet, joined us and was crossing back and forth across Vashti's paws, as she was trying to eat. Cats have that intuitive notion of how to be annoying but subtle.

"So how would you explain Petra's appearance to Grant if she comes into contact?" Philo asked, wanting to see if Elani had considered all angles.

"Petra traveled as the wife of a man who went missing during the campaign in Chattanooga in the fall of 1863. At that time, Grant was in charge of the western armies of the Union and had moved forward to break the lines held by the Confederate army. Her guise was that of a traveler from eastern Tennessee, where there were strong Union sympathies. Her husband had joined a militia supporting the Union and was involved in the Chattanooga campaign." Elani paused for a minute, for questions. "Her name was Petra Holmes, by the way."

"Why Holmes?" Philo asked, cutting his eyes towards me.

"I was reading *The Sign of the Four* at the time," I replied, smiling.

Kipp's tail began to wag since he enjoyed all things Sherlock Holmes.

"Were you able to gather information about the spies?" Peter asked, his brown eyes meeting mine. He looked way too young to be involved in our dangerous business, I thought, although he'd done well, I admitted grudgingly. I'd made many more careless boo-boos during my tenure than had Peter to date. The thought made me feel irritable.

"Read the documents," Fitzhugh grumbled, agitated that Peter might want an easy out as well as his diverting the attention off of Elani's recitation.

"Anyway, Grant was sympathetic for whatever reasons he might have had, and allowed her safe passage." Elani looked at me. "He will probably remember you if you happen to run across his path again."

"And how will you control for that?" Philo had been quiet, contemplative, during much of the story.

"I thought we could state that her husband had been killed, and she now is traveling with her brother, Peter Keaton."

"And why is Peter not in the army since there was a draft?" Philo asked.

"Peter has been abroad, working as a correspondent for The Times while in London." Elani looked around the room, hoping to see positive nods to her thought processes.

Kipp seemed remarkably quiet for one who often had a strong opinion and never hesitated to make it known. In our manner of private speech, I gave him a little mental tickle of inquiry. He didn't respond with his mind, but his ears flattened as his tail lightly brushed the floor, so I knew he was okay. I figured he was trying to be considerate of my cautious approach by letting Elani's story evolve.

"In terms of how we get access to Mary Surratt," Elani continued, "that will be more difficult. And the only way it will work is if we can establish some sort of base close enough to her townhouse that we can monitor her thoughts. Kipp, especially, will be critical. My plan was that we would present ourselves at her home, inquiring about local housing options. We will not want to be in residence in her home, considering that will affect the historical trajectory of several people following the assassination. While we are conversing with her, we will become familiar with her thought patterns so that we can access them later, as needed. We will need to do the same with some of the other notables, most specifically John Wilkes Booth." She paused to glance around the room in order to monitor our reactions.

"What do you know specifically about her?" Kipp asked. He consumed history with a hunger seldom matched but was not up to speed on Mrs. Surratt. When we left for our time-shift, he would be, I knew without a doubt.

"She was from Maryland, which at the time was a conflicted state in terms of the issue of slavery, and she was clearly pro-confederate in her sympathies. She and her husband owned land south of Washington where they operated a tavern. Her husband later bought a rooming house in Washington and let out the rooms for income. Despite her husband's acquisition of properties and generation of income for the family, he fell into financial difficulties and began to drink alcohol excessively. He died, and the problems continued to worsen. She finally moved into the city and lived in the townhouse her husband had bought, leasing the tavern to an acquaintance. She practiced the Catholic religion, had three children, and although it is documented she allowed confederate sympathizers to congregate at her townhouse, there was questionable proof about her involvement in the assassination of Lincoln." Elani paused before saying, "She was in her early forties when she was hanged."

Philo stood, stretching his back slightly, before moving over to the front window. He stood silently watching as a car moved past, its muffler annoyingly loud, to disappear into the darkness. Crossing his arms across his chest, he turned, his eyes meeting mine, the expression guarded.

"I think the trip has merit," he began, breaking his gaze at me. "Of course, the final decision is not mine and will have to be submitted to the Twelve. However, considering the exceptionally delicate balance of history, I think it is unlikely that they will condone a very young team who has not traveled solo to go on such a trip." Philo looked tired. "And, yes, I know that in the past such things were not considered with such care and teams traveled all the time with no supervision. But some bad things happened, too, and maybe we are evolving and trying to show more responsibility as a species. Remember, the dominant species on earth is human, not symbiont. We have to compliment what humanity does, not add to the chaos."

"Petra, what do you think?" Elani's soft words echoed in my head for a moment. She was a wonderful symbiont, and I figured one day the literature would be full of her exploits. Elani balanced Peter's rashness and was a thoughtful, deliberate lupine. As I reflected, I realized how much she and Peter had added to my rather plodding and sometimes predictable existence.

"I think it sounds like we are going to take a trip," I replied. "If Kipp is game," I added, knowing the answer.

"I was born game," Kipp said.

A truer statement was never made.

ELEVEN

"You don't want to wear the standard, established clothing of the times but yet you travel. Can you explain that line of reasoning which, if you will pardon my saying so, is rather irrational?"

Karl and I had gotten off to a rocky start, and I took a deep breath. And I'd made a special effort to be good, I really had. Since Suzanne, who knew all my peccadilloes, had departed in marital bliss to Alpharetta, Georgia, I would have to figure out how to communicate with this critical, but difficult, new player. Ignoring his remark, I tried another tactic.

"I hear you're an expert on the antebellum period and will rely upon you to help me be able to move within that society," I began, smiling. I only hoped I didn't show too many teeth while doing so.

"Don't play me," Karl replied, pursing his lips.

Recalling Peter's spot on mimicking of Karl, I ducked my head, trying not to laugh. Kipp, at my feet, didn't help matters by glancing up at me, his face all filled with lupine innocence, as he laughed uproariously in the back of my brain.

"Oh, I'd never do that," I said, my eyes wide and guileless.

"You simply must wear undergarments under your skirt that

reflect the styles of the times," Karl went on, breathing deeply and obviously trying to stay patient.

He was a middle-aged symbiont, apparently unattached, not bad looking when he wasn't pursing his lips. His dark hair was thinning on the crown, and I noticed he brushed the other hairs over the spot to cover the patch. Karl, it seemed, had a little vanity, but didn't we all? His eyes were very dark, almost black, making his pupils disappear into the pools of darkness.

"It's the hoops that get me, Karl," I began, trying to explain. "I can't move quickly in an emergency, so you see it is really a safety concern." Actually, there was some validity to my remark in addition to the fact I didn't like my skirts swinging like a bell in the tower of Notre Dame.

"Well, I guess I can see your point," he began grudgingly. "I think I can construct a stiff layer of petticoats that will be softer and more malleable." Karl glanced up at me. "Will that meet your expectations?" he asked, pursing his lips again. It was clear he disapproved and considered my renegade notions to be an obstacle to his finding perfection in his work.

"Yes, thank you," I smiled, pulling my lips over my teeth that time in case he saw exposed teeth as an aggressive challenge.

Kipp had found a pile of discarded fabric on the floor of Karl's workshop and, after circling and tromping down the wool, made a bed. The multitudes of fabrics created a musty funk in the room; Kipp suppressed a sneeze in the back of his throat. He would only need his usual money collar that was indispensable in the event of an emergency. True, he hated any constriction around his neck, but if I had to wear stiff petticoats, I didn't want to hear any of his griping. The door to the workshop opened as Peter and Elani arrived for their consultation with Karl.

"How'd class go this morning?" Kipp asked Elani. She was fresh off her first solo English class with the young lupines. All of them could only wish to travel one day, following her example.

"Fine," she replied, joining him on his pile of fabric, careful not to nestle too close. "A couple are having difficulty with conjugating verbs, but other than that, they are all doing well."

"If you need any help…" he began, glancing at her from the corners of his eyes.

"No, I'm good," she replied, staring straight ahead.

There was a little awkwardness between the two of them, and Kipp shrugged off the question mark I posed in his head. It occurred to me that the odd feeling hovering in the room was not due to Elani's perpetual love struck feelings for Kipp but rather the fact that Kipp was now technically her manager. He was trying out his new wings as a boss and that changed the dynamic between them. Better him than me, I thought. Kipp's ears flattened as he met my eyes. I smiled, encouragingly, while wondering if he'd find management was not his thing.

"Hi," Peter said, joining me. His cheeks were shadowed from the facial hair he was cultivating, another nod to the fashions of the times to which we'd journey. He hopped up on one of the high stools that jutted up to the elevated work table. He must have been feeling good, because he began to gently swing his right leg back and forth as he softly whistled. His fun stopped when Karl narrowed his reptilian eyes at him.

"I have your garments hanging in the dressing room for a fitting," Karl said to Peter before returning his attention to me. "I'm hesitant to give you any period jewelry to wear. Yes, I heard about your losing the valuable stickpin during a previous journey." He cocked his head to the side. "These pieces are a valuable part of history and not to be taken lightly."

Kipp began to giggle in my head. There had been a time when I would have fired back, not willing to take such a talking to from someone who had no idea what traveling entailed. As I considered my reply options, I wondered if I'd softened too much. As it happened, I'd rather liked the fiery Petra, and my new, milquetoast self seemed rather bland and uninspiring.

"You realize there is a strategy in not fighting, too, don't you?" Kipp remarked privately.

"When did you get to be so smart?" I replied.

"When I became a manager. Philo told me all about it and said he often uses that strategy with people like you." Kipp settled more firmly in the wool. "I think it works." He leaned forward to lick his paw for good measure. "I completed my first online module on management skills," he added, tilting his head as if he expected applause.

"Are you listening to me?" Karl asked. I noticed his voice took on a distinct whine when he became agitated.

"Yes, of course," I replied brightly. If he had been anything like Suzanne, he would have offered me coffee by now.

Peter emerged from the dressing room, thankfully pulling Karl's laser focus from me for a few minutes. Idly, I walked over to a stack of fabrics, letting my fingers graze the surfaces, noting the soft wool as well as cool feel of silk. This trip would be like the others in that we would complement our wardrobes once we arrived. Peter had a backpack, much like mine, in which he would carry the essentials; upon arrival, we reversed those backpacks, which were obviously not in vogue in past times, and create a carpetbag type valise that would not draw attention.

"Since you are arriving when the weather will be cold, you'll need an overcoat and warmth in your undergarments." Karl droned on about his plans while I glanced at Kipp, who looked asleep. The lupines had it made, I thought darkly.

I was happy to leave there and return to the library, accompanied by Peter, where Fitzhugh was struggling with the computer. "You know I hate these contraptions," Fitzhugh glanced up at us, a strand of long, gray hair tumbled over his forehead into his eyes.

Peter laughed and made an exaggerated display of cracking his knuckles and flexing his fingers before taking over the keyboard. Before he'd begun to travel, he managed most of the scanning and uploading of our translations into the computerized system of saving our history. I admit I was only slightly better at those matters than was Fitzhugh and was happy to leave all things involving the computer to Peter or whoever his successor might be.

"How did the meeting go with Karl?" Fitzhugh was obviously curious.

As Peter began his pursed lips impression, I scooted back to the kitchen to look for something to eat. Someone had brought in a tin of butter cookies, and there were still a few left in the bottom. Tea and cookies sounded good as I put on the kettle. Leaning against the edge of the counter, I glanced around the small room. The countertop really needed to be replaced, having been scarred over the years by the thoughtless placing of hot dishes from the microwave as well as the kettle on the surface. I guess it was easy, when one was not at home, to have no concern for the property of others. With that in mind, I pulled off a paper towel from the roll and began to wipe down the surface, hoping that a mild cleaning would indicate my good citizenship. Shortly, the kettle began to whistle as the water roiled, and I poured the hot water over the loose tea, which was in a diffuser. Just to establish my mark of individuality, I had chosen a spicy Chai tea that Peter had found at a tiny, out of the way market. Fitzhugh arrived, no doubt thinking I needed help.

"No Earl Grey?" His shaggy eyebrows rose.

"I decided to be bold and shake up the establishment," I replied, laughing.

"Smells delightful," he commented, nodding his head in approval.

Fitzhugh hovered, tut-tutting at me as I set out three cups from his antique tea service and placed the few remaining cookies on a small plate. I even placed some napkins in a fan pattern, thinking it would impress Peter. Fitzhugh never bothered this much at home with me, so I wondered what was going on with him. He seemed a little over-involved.

"What's up with you?" I finally asked, trying to keep my tone light.

"I don't know what you mean," he replied gruffly, shaking his head at me. But he continued to hang at my elbow, seeming unsettled. Reaching toward the tray I was preparing, he broke off half of a butter cookie and held it between his fingers, not eating it.

"Fitzhugh?"

"Well, it's just I was thinking that traveling is very dangerous business, as I know from my years with Lydea." He was almost stammering. "And I wonder at what point will you and Kipp choose to settle down and stay home, permanently?"

He was worried about me and wouldn't say so straight out, that much was clear. As I carefully considered my reply, I realized that our living situation had changed him as well as me. He'd grown a sense of affection, an almost fatherly type of love for me. I knew I'd need to proceed cautiously with my reply, and it seemed honesty was the best route to take.

"Fitzhugh, after Whitechapel, I have had doubts about traveling." I looked up at him, registering his features, which had once seemed so foreboding and rigid and now seemed compassionate and caring. How was it, I wondered, I'd never seen that quality in the past? Humans were guilty of the same oversight with one another... not bothering to delve past the superficial and discover the complexities of one another. "I've had past trips that left me feeling sad, uneasy, and generally bad due to connections with the humans I got to know and left behind to their future. Especially if I knew their future to be a grim one, it hurts."

Fitzhugh nodded. He'd once confessed to me he'd fallen in love with a woman he met while traveling. As much as Philo cared about me as a friend, he could never understand the personal toll taken on one's soul by traveling.

"But Harrow, well..." My voice faltered. "He broke my heart." I felt the tears come to my eyes but blinked them away. "And then *Titanic*. Oh, Fitzhugh, that was terrible. When I think about it, I still get cold and begin to shake, as if I were there again."

"You were very hesitant about that time-shift, and perhaps I should have advised you more wisely," he said, tilting his head to the side.

"No, everyone was right about that time-shift except for me. This is what we do, right?" I boldly reached out and put my hand on top of his, which was resting on the counter. For a moment, I saw what that long distant human woman had seen in him to fall in love. Despite his crusty exterior, he had a strength based on compassion and wisdom that was intoxicating. He turned his hand, so my palm touched his.

"Fitzhugh, I will retire one day, of course. But Kipp needs this right now so he can maximize his capabilities. I don't even think we've touched the surface in terms of what he can do." I laughed. "I was bugging him recently about finding a mate because I was feeling grandmotherly and wanted a room full of his pups bringing chaos to order."

Fitzhugh laughed, too, as he conjured the image in his mind.

"But it's not time for me to quit, yet. As much as I have grown to appreciate working here," I said, spreading my free hand to indicate the library, "this is not my destiny. I actually don't know what I'd do with myself if I weren't complaining about another time-shift. I've never wanted to do anything else."

He broke his half of butter cookie into a quarter and held out the piece to me. "I understand completely. I felt the same way for most of my earlier life and was only forced to stop traveling when I lost my focus and the motivation to take such risks had disappeared." Then he did something unexpected. He pulled me close and let me rest my head on his chest. Since Fitzhugh was tall, my head naturally tucked beneath his chin; it was a comfortable place from which to view the world. I could hear the steady beat of his heart from that vantage point and probably could have stayed like that for a while, except Peter, who had the most unfortunate timing of any symbiont known to existence, bumbled in, looking for tea and cookies.

"Whoops!" he blurted out, as if he'd caught us in the act of illicit behavior.

"It's okay," I said, withdrawing from Fitzhugh's arms. "I needed a hug."

"And, unless you find this impossible to believe, so did I," Fitzhugh added.

"What if I need one?" Peter asked, lifting his eyebrows.

"Well, you won't get it from me," Fitzhugh huffed, breaking the spell he'd cast.

Karl, I have to admit, was a much more efficient worker than was Suzanne and finished our wardrobes under the time frame allowed by the Twelve. He had to work us in, balancing the needs of one of the new pairs of travelers we'd inherited with the fruit basket turnover that had resulted in Suzanne and Mark's departure, along with some others I'd known for years. Once again, I bit back any lingering anxiety that my predictable environment would be disrupted and focused on the issue at hand.

Elani had completed the presentation of the proposed time-shift to the Twelve with no complications whatsoever. I was proud for her but wondered why, over the years, I'd had to fight tooth and nail for every trip I proposed. Was it just something about me, I wondered?

"Yes, it is you," Kipp replied to the questions rolling around in my often empty skull. "They sense your combativeness and the fact you want to argue every point to tedium with them. As much as they appreciate your skills, they don't like working with you or managing your business."

"Well, thanks, Kipp," I replied, blinking my eyes.

"You asked."

"Not really," I replied. I liked to think of myself as open to feedback but found the positive feedback was much nicer than the alternative. Honestly, who enjoys a shellacking about one's character? Oh, yes, humans ask for honest impressions, but I don't think they really want to hear the negative ones. They just say that so they will appear open, earnest, and willing to adapt and conform. Changing one's character is no easy feat.

It was the third week of October, and Philo and Vashti invited us to go for a nice ramble through Duke Forest, one of the places over the years that had been a private refuge for me and Philo. It had, in many ways, become our place to think and process all things impacting our worlds.

"I appreciate you and Vashti moving in with Fitzhugh and Juno," I began, pausing to pick up a leaf with unusual coloration. Looking up at the canopy above us, the leaves were fully into their change due to an early fall that brought a crisp coolness to the mornings, stretching on until mid-day when the sun hovered directly overhead. There was a mild breeze that caused the leaves to stir, and occasionally one would float downwards to join the others which formed a carpet beneath our feet as we shuffled noisily through the debris.

Philo smiled and took my hand as we walked. "It works good for me, too. Closer to work and someone to fuss with about who is gonna fix the coffee."

"You mean tea, right?" I laughed. "And I will have clean sheets on the bed and make sure my bathroom is acceptable," I added.

"Petra, your house always looks so nice and clean," Vashti remarked. A stray ray of sunlight was caught up in her fur, bringing out an extra dimension of color I'd not seen before.

"Ha!" Kipp snorted derisively.

"You forget, I lived with Silas," Vashti said, "and he was a slob."

At the mention of Silas, we all felt Philo withdraw just a bit from the pleasure we shared. Vashti's ears drooped as she thought she'd been a little careless with her comments.

"Okay, guys," Philo spoke up, his voice a little louder than was needed. Overhead, a wedge of crows cawed noisily as they migrated through the trees, threading a flawless patch through the outstretched limbs. "No one needs to tread carefully around me anymore. Here is the reality going forward. I had a wife, Claire, who is no longer my wife. We had a good many years but have gone in different directions. I wish her well. I have a son, Silas, with whom I disagree about his life choices. I wish him well, too. And now, I have a daughter, Vashti, and we are enjoying our time together." His hand reached down to gently caress her head, finishing with a gentle tug on her left ear. "You all don't need to be so tentative."

I sort of knew what he meant. After I lost my husband and son, my co-workers and friends were afraid to mention their family members for fear it would provoke a sad memory. Actually, I enjoyed hearing of their exploits and happiness, and all my thoughts about my lost relationships were good ones. There was no sadness in terms of the actual core of those connections to me. Yes, I experienced the grieving process that symbionts and humans, as well as some other creatures that walk the earth, have, and for too long would not display pictures of George in my home. Now, thanks to Kipp, my son's smiling face met me every morning, resting from behind a piece of glass on my bureau.

Kipp nudged close to me, pushing his shoulder against my leg. His thoughts became an embrace, a veritable love bomb. Reaching down, I tangled my fingertips in the warm fur of his neck. Humans would never understand the bond between symbionts, both physical and mental, since it was unique in its qualities. We were separate, but then we were not.

"I see you and Karl managed to work past your difficulties," Philo said, clearly ready to move on past sentimental notions.

"Yes," I replied. Spying another pretty leaf, I leaned forward to retrieve it from the ground. It was from a sweet gum tree and was still bright green in the center, with orange tips on all five prongs, looking as if someone had dipped it in paint. "I had to put my foot down in terms of actual hoops and sensible shoes, and he finally heard me. Since he's not traveled, he doesn't seem to realize there is often a lot of walking involved, and I have no wish for blisters." Closing my eyes, I recalled the moccasin-like footwear I'd worn while living with the pre-historic tribe when Kipp first met me. Those were sweet.

"Juno will assume Elani's English class in her absence, while Vashti is taking on Kipp's ethics class," Philo mentioned idly as I nodded my head in response.

We'd drawn near a familiar narrow waterway, and the sounds of the water rushing around a deep curve were soothing to my soul. The gurgling was sufficiently hypnotic that I could have easily stretched out and taken a nap. In fact, I'd done so many times in the past in that particular spot. The smell of the rotting vegetation of nature combined with the mustiness of the dying leaves piling on top of an already crowded forest floor made for a fragrance unique to autumn. I inhaled deeply, welcoming the familiar sensations.

"What?" Philo asked, stopping to look at me.

"I never thought you'd be a manager," I replied. "And here you are making staffing decisions."

Philo must have noticed his shoulders were slumping because he straightened his posture, twisting his neck slightly as he did so. "You need some new shoes," he remarked critically, staring at my feet.

"When I get back," I replied.

TWELVE

The leaving party was memorable, and I welcomed that playful energy after the lackluster one that preceded our trip to the *Titanic*. Peter's mother, Evelyn, brought her genteel self and had finally decided she must capitulate with Peter's choice to travel or risk a permanent fracture of her relationship with her only son. As a nod to his ancestors who traveled, too, he wore his grandfather's pocket watch. This time, Evelyn didn't take me aside to secure a promise to bring Peter safely home. It was nice to believe that perhaps she had developed some trust in me but even more importantly in Peter, whose abilities were starting to expand and solidify.

Our friends who attended the leaving party had departed, leaving my house curiously empty. Often those parties more closely resembled a roast, and I had frequently been the main topic of discussion with my past embarrassments being brought to light. I was happy, since Peter was developing a history of his own, to find he was the focus of a few less than charitable remarks, one of which left his face burning red. Evelyn was predictably horrified but showed restraint in keeping her thoughts carefully guarded from the rest of us.

"It's just part of the magic of traveling," I reassured him.

"But why us and not Kipp or Elani?" he asked. "I didn't hear any humorous comments about either of them."

"We are perfect," Kipp replied, wagging his tail. "You two are goof-ups."

I forced Peter to help me clean up the mountain of dishes. I'm not sure when the post-party clean up had evolved into the actual travelers having to do all the work, but it had. Maybe it helped distract us and decreased anxiety over the upcoming travel. There was no actual history on that, and I knew since I'd researched the topic previously after I'd spent three hours washing dishes. My thoughts were particularly dark that day. Fitzhugh, Juno, and Lily were all that remained other than us. Fitzhugh was sitting at the dinette, quiet and contemplative, while Peter and I labored at the sink. I had taken a cloth and was struggling with a stain of tomato sauce on the counter that proved to be particularly vexing.

"When will you replace that?" Peter inquired, nodding at the chipped tile countertop.

Glancing over my shoulder, I saw Fitzhugh quickly suppress a smile. He knew the answer in the back of my mind...never, if I had my druthers.

"It's still serviceable," I replied, my tone more defensive than I'd wished.

"Yeah, but it looks awful. They have this new composite stuff that looks like granite," Peter began before noticing the expression of intransigence on my face.

Was I that stubborn? Probably. I shuttered the thought before Kipp could weigh in with his opinion.

Walking to the back door, I went outside, enjoying the burst of cool air on my heated face. Kipp and Elani moved in the shadows, following the trail of a long-departed field mouse, their noses busy, pressed against the crisp stalks of grass which would be covered in frost by the morning.

As I stood in the darkness, I reflected upon the preparation for this time-shift. I was surprisingly content with Karl's clothing designs, which were based upon a functional skirt and blouse with a little, fitted jacket over my blouse. He'd actually let me chose the colors, something unheard of in Suzanne's workshop. I'd gone with a nice, deep brown for a change. We'd decided to keep our clothing very simple for several reasons. One was that we wanted to project an image of people who were far from wealthy, hoping to mingle and disappear amongst the masses. Also, the war had resulted in issues with import and export and procuring fabrics was iffy at best. So plain was good. I actually liked Karl's planning. He had me wearing three skirts, the navy one beneath the brown, the green one beneath the navy, two pairs of undergarments as well as a fairly adaptable hat with extra ribbons I could add to match my clothing. Suzanne had never shown that foresight. In my backpack, I had four extra blouses, nightwear and a robe, tights, and other assorted items. I'd definitely not feel the push to gather clothing as quickly as I had in the past. I wore a nicely tailored coat of wool, geared for warmth, which fell just below my knees. Karl thoughtfully added a woven muffler for my neck as well as some gloves. I was beginning to like him. He remained rather stingy about jewelry but did allow for a couple of less valuable brooches that I could wear at my collar. Of course, Harrow's pearls were always with me, hidden, cool, and smooth against my flesh. Peter and I delightfully compared our loot.

"Check this out!" Peter exclaimed, holding up a third pair of pants. "Karl came through, big time." He put on his hat and strutted in front of the mirror, swinging the walking stick Karl had included.

"Put in a monocle, and you'll look like Mr. Peanut," I observed dryly.

"Who's that?" Kipp asked in his eternally curious manner.

As I conjured up the image of the character, Kipp began to giggle, as did Elani, who let her loyalty to Peter falter for just a moment.

We had decided, since it was Elani's trip, it was fitting she should plot our journey. The ability to hone in on a particular destination was inherent in our species and accuracy was enhanced by either having been to the locale previously—so I knew for a fact I could materialize in Harrow's drawing room without breaking a sweat— or studying maps that depicted the topography and other features. So, we had left it to Elani to do the homework, with Kipp's collabo- ration. She would lead the time-shift, and Kipp could help make any minor corrections as needed. He naturally possessed more talents with all things involved with time-shifting, which came to him like a reflex versus the contemporary process of plotting and deliberation.

Kipp's head lifted from his pursuit of the lingering mouse trail as his eyes met mine across the dimly lit back yard. For an instant, his amber eyes caught the light from my back porch as they glowed like those of a beast in the forest. Our lupine brothers and sisters could have traveled a primitive, elemental route in their development but chose to stay at our sides, evolving as did we into what we'd become in the present day.

"I love you." Kipp's thoughts floated across the yard.

"Back at you, kiddo," I replied, waving at him.

As much as I didn't want to return to the kitchen, I finally forced myself to go back inside, the heat of the room hitting my face like a blast furnace. Peter turned, staring at me a minute, and I knew he wanted to ask if I planned on helping him but kept his words bitten off. I picked up the drying towel and began to put away things as quickly as possible. I was ready to move on.

Kipp and Elani finished their excursion and begged to be let in, their noses making damp spots on the glass of the storm door. Kipp's fur was standing on end from static, and he looked like a big red puffball as he walked over to a reclining Juno, who was comfortably curled in front of the infrared heater churning out warmth from the corner of the kitchen. She raised her head, wagging her tail at Kipp, who leaned forward to gently touch her gray muzzle with his. I knew that was their goodbye.

"Come help me," I ordered Peter. My bed had to be made with fresh linens for Philo, and I was too lazy to dart back and forth to each side to pull and tuck. We made short work of that job, and the bed made, I shooed Peter out so that I could get prepared. Kipp joined me in my room as I began to don the layers of clothing I'd need, while Peter and Elani used Fitzhugh's room.

"The idea of three skirts is clever, but I feel like the Pillsbury doughboy," I whined.

"Well, I have to wear my money collar," Kipp groused, showing his teeth. "You know I don't like things around my neck."

I was sitting, as best I could manage with all the padding, at my dresser, trying to loop my hair in a fashion that would be acceptable for the times. To set the atmosphere as well as create a pleasant scent, I'd lit a candle that Fitzhugh had picked up for me as a thoughtful gesture. Warm fragrances of maple and pumpkin were threatening to ignite my latent appetite for something decadent to eat. A soft knock on my door interrupted my concentration. At my reply, the door cracked open and Fitzhugh peeked in.

"Are you decent?"

"Yes."

He entered, Juno with him. "I thought we'd keep you company while you finish up," he said, smiling. Fitzhugh must have been feeling pretty comfortable, because he took a seat on the edge of my bed. "You know, I'm not an invalid, and Philo really doesn't need to stay here with us," he began.

"Me neither," Juno chimed in, wagging her tail.

My eyes met Fitzhugh's in the mirror. "I'm not really doing it for you two," I replied. "I thought it would be good for Philo."

"Oh, well, then," Fitzhugh sputtered.

We were quiet, all four of us, as I tried twisting my hair into a roll that kept poofing out oddly on one side. The flame of the candle, snagged by an invisible wind current, began to shimmy, causing shadows to dance on the darkened walls of my room. The plantation blinds were shuttered, and the candle, along with the ambient light from the bathroom, was all that gave illumination to the space.

"And there's the convenience, since Peter isn't gonna be around to take you back and forth to work." I tried not to curse as my hair would not cooperate.

"Okay, I get it," Fitzhugh replied, somewhat irritably. "Just part that mess down the middle and pin it in the back," he advised. "You're going to be wearing a hat, anyway, so who cares."

I widened my eyes, staring at him. "Who cares?" Laughing softly, I said, "I'll remember you said that one day in the future."

He ducked his head, laughing, too. "I think I'm getting old," he said, shrugging his shoulders.

"No, not you!" I said, making a face of amazement.

I took his advice, and using the comb made a relatively straight center part. Then I pulled it back, creating a neat chignon, and began to pin the hair in place. Not a contemporary style, but with the hat, it would pass.

"You know, Petra, I was giving thought to all the possible mysteries to unravel that surround the assassination of Lincoln. It's rather a shame this visit has to be brief and focused, even though I understand the rationale." Fitzhugh sighed, the sound soft in the room.

Symbionts had, historically, made some seriously deep dives into the past. It had been easier, when we were less enmeshed with humanity, to disappear for years at a time to embed oneself into a particularly sensitive locale. Now, it seemed, if a longer time-shift was indicated, the result was the pair would be relocated to a new collective and begin life anew upon return. We'd had pairs embedded in the courts of Julius Caesar, Cleopatra, and even in the administration of George Washington. I, when much younger, was sent to scout out some lingering questions around Napoleon. I must say, I didn't care for him or that trip. Neither did Tula. Napoleon was a distinctly narcissistic fellow, and his court was filled with enough intrigue to make one's head ache. If the collective ever decided another trip to that location was needed, they would need to find another pair of symbionts to make the trip.

"I remember Arnie and Tig made a trip to investigate the truth behind the disappearance of Edward V and his brother who were confined to the Tower of London by their uncle, Richard III." I frowned as the memories flooded back. Leaning forward, I put my elbows on my dresser and stared at Fitzhugh's dark eyes in the mirror. "They never spoke of it, but their stories made it to the chronicles and were required reading for those prospective travelers who might be too faint of heart for the rigors involved." My eyes glanced down to the mirrored reflection of Harrow's pearls, which would go with me, hidden beneath the fabric of my blouse. "That trip changed them, and they never felt quite the same about traveling."

Fitzhugh nodded his head as Kipp stared at me. I knew Kipp wanted to pose a question but hesitated, not wanting to appear to be morbidly interested. But why should he be any different than legions of historians?

"Fitzhugh can pull it up, Kipp, if you want to study the accounts." I sighed. "It is an exceedingly difficult read...or at least I found it to be so."

"Do I need to know?" Kipp looked at me, trust in his heart. He would follow my lead.

"I can't make that decision for you," I replied. "I'd like to shelter you from some horrible things, but it's not my job to decide how much your shoulders can bear."

Kipp settled down; his mind became calm, like a pool of still water before a storm. He couldn't remain quiescent for long. It just wasn't in his nature.

"Considering the fact that the Confederacy was operating spy rings all throughout Washington, the political leanings of the locals, questions about the loyalty of some of Lincoln's top officials..." Fitzhugh paused. "Why was Booth allowed to pass the Navy Yard Bridge and escape that night? Yes, I know what the record says, but wasn't the fact that he'd be allowed passage rather ironic?"

Kipp resumed grooming his right paw, wanting to look his best upon our arrival. He'd even had me vigorously brush his coat until it gleamed. He stopped and glanced up at Fitzhugh. "It will be tempting to go past our mandate and delve further. But we really can't unless we plan on somehow being a part of the action for all the years of Lincoln's presidency."

Fitzhugh shrugged his shoulders. "It is Elani's plan, and I think she wisely recognizes her limitations as well as Peter's. They are not ready to be gone for years, having to stay in character for an extended period. It requires a discipline that is acquired through experience. And neither Elani nor Peter would want to be absent from home base for any length of time, that much is true."

I knew he didn't mean it as a criticism but as a fact. I'd not made my deep dive until I'd been traveling for years. It was a place one worked up to after many time-shifts. And I no longer wished to do it, either. Home had become more relevant as I grew older.

"But all truths gained are important, are they not?" Kipp asked. He tilted his big head to the side, taking in all three of us in turn.

"You are right," Juno answered. "Even the smallest moment of truth in a conflicted history is important. It's not always the flashing lights and the shiny objects that matter."

The room fell quiet. Fitzhugh wanted to say goodbye and wish us good luck but was hesitating. Juno looked from him to me, her grizzled, graying muzzle still, only her eyes moving back and forth.

"Uh, we will use the front room," I began, stammering, trying to break the spell of silence that hovered awkwardly.

Fitzhugh stood, turning to brush out the wrinkles he'd made by sitting on my neatly made bed. "Of course, it's time for you to go." His face was guarded, his eyes shadowed. "Good luck." For some reason, he'd retreated into himself. And because of our modern constraints against the natural ebb and flow of telepathy, I didn't follow him.

"Come here, you old thing!" I exclaimed, pulling him towards me into a hug. "Don't forget to pay the power bill which is due in a week," I admonished him. "I left my checkbook on the desk. And I figure by now you know how to copy my signature," I added, lifting my eyebrow.

Fitzhugh laughed. "I promise." He gently extricated himself from my arms. "Be careful."

"You know I always am careful."

"Well, no, you haven't been, and that's why I worry." Fitzhugh smiled at me.

Juno managed to stand after a tiny struggle; Kipp was at her side and would have given her an assist if possible but, as it were, could only lend his emotional support. They touched muzzles. In my connection with Kipp, I could follow their flow of thoughts and the love that had developed between the two. Juno never had children and thought of Kipp as a son. She had the proud feelings towards his accomplishments as if he'd been her own.

"Be good," she said, her dark eyes meeting mine.

"You know I always am," I said, parroting my earlier remark.

"Well, no, you haven't always been, and that's why I worry," she replied cleverly.

THIRTEEN

The time-shift was one of the better ones I have managed over the many years I've done such a thing. I'm not sure, but I highly suspect Kipp did something, perhaps a skill from his almost magical toolkit, to cushion my landing after the disastrous events we encountered during our examination of the Spring-heeled Jack phenomenon. I guess Kipp didn't want any more broken arms, although he bore no responsibility for that particular mishap. Actually, after the initial dive off into oblivion, I felt as if I floated down, as gently as a flower blossom upon a pond of still water, to land, my legs tucked neatly beneath my torso, in a pile of fragrant, crispy straw. During the initial few moments of disorientation, I took a deep breath and registered the smell of large animals, perhaps horses, and the earthy, organic richness of manure. Hopefully, I was not sitting in a pile of the latter. A soft, familiar sound confirmed the presence of horses as a soft whinny echoed against the walls of the enclosure. Kipp, his recovery faster than mine, threw out his sonar to see if there were any humans close-by. After a second or two, he gave an all-clear.

"I think we are good," he grunted with satisfaction. He was pressed close to me, the bulk of his body heavy against my right thigh. Kipp's head rose as he gazed about the building in which we'd materialized. It was clearly a barn, with several stalls filled with horses; their heads bobbed in surprise at the inexplicable appearance of four beings in their midst. A couple raised their heads, their nostrils blowing, as they tried to pick up our scents. A moment later, they relaxed, figuring we were of no consequence -- couple of people with their dogs, perhaps, even though they recognized the lupines were not really dogs, but something fairly close in their estimation. Bored with us now, one chestnut-colored mare began to pull straw, munching loudly.

Elani, tucked in next to Peter, was yawning. She gave the appearance of nonchalance, almost seeming to be sleepy and bored. She was a natural for this sort of thing, her relaxed attitude in direct opposition to Kipp, who was alert, almost agitated in his busy canvassing upon his arrivals. Elani stood, shook herself vigorously to rid herself of the clinging wisps of straw, and then stretched to and fro, almost dancing on tippy-toes as she worked out any muscle kinks. Peter was sitting, his legs crossed, his hat slightly askew with a piece of straw clinging to his beard. He managed a cheery wave of his hand at me.

It was then we heard a soft cough that obviously had a human origin. I don't know why, because it sounds silly, but I involuntarily ducked, as if doing so could make me invisible. Kipp stalked towards the sound, his body low; in the next second, his tail began to wag.

"There's a man over there lying in the straw, sleeping. He smells funny—not sure what that is—but he seems, well, drugged or something." Kipp frowned, mentally. "I don't know why I didn't pick him up?"

"Probably had too much to drink, and he wasn't dreaming, so there were no active thought patterns for you to snag," I responded. "Let's get out of here."

With speed born of practice, I quickly unpacked my backpack and reversed the receptacle into the carpetbag that would be less conspicuous. Then I transferred the contents to the carpetbag, not minding the straw that managed to find its way there, too. I could deal with that problem later. Peter finished just a moment behind me, and the four of us quietly made our way to the smaller side door that led to an alley. We paused in the dimly lit narrow brick-lined space to view our surroundings. I craned my neck back to gaze at the moonless sky, which was cluttered by clouds, making the alley dark as a bottomless pit. A couple of men, laughing loudly, passed the entrance of the alley but did not look in our direction.

"Just a minute," Peter said. "Turn around." He then gave my backside a serious brushing off with his hand. "You've got straw everywhere."

I glanced at Kipp, who smirked in response. We had, indeed, arrived, if Peter felt emboldened to manhandle me in such a fashion. He'd once been way too fastidious to touch me at all. However, since Kipp couldn't make me look presentable, and Peter had actual hands with which to work, I was grateful for all the help I could get. I responded in kind by doing the same to him, finishing with an adjustment of his hat.

The alley stank of old urine and stale, rotting food. It was probable that the stable worker used the alley as his latrine as well as lunch break room. Elani rolled her eyes as she coughed politely, blinking her eyes. Against the far wall, a pair of eyes glowing red stared at us; a moment later, a large rat scurried away, alarmed by our presence and seeking safety somewhere else.

"I have no idea why humans soil the area where they eat," she began. "Animals know not to do that."

"I suspect, sweetheart, that the people who use this alley are probably doing so after having consumed a large amount of liquor," I replied, ruffling the soft, dense fur on her head. She would always be a favorite, somehow managing to combine Kipp's best qualities with those of the sober-minded and grounded Juno. Elani was family, now.

Having made ourselves presentable, we stepped out of the stinky alley and onto the street, which was only marginally better. I'd actually not been to Washington in my previous travels, but knew the times, in general, and expected pretty much what I saw. The completion of an aqueduct had ensured the availability of clean drinking water, although the rivers remained polluted from human waste. As a consequence of war, too many humans had crowded into a space not designed for so many bodies and the waste they generated. While some of the streets were covered in a macadam covering, many were composed of packed dirt combined with rock, and the result was a lot of mud everywhere. This was especially true since the streets were used to herd cattle and other livestock back and forth as needed for the Union effort of supplying meat to the troops. Washington was one of the staging grounds for supplies, with cavernous storehouses situated near the rivers. Karl kept some of this in mind and had made my skirts just an inch shorter than might be otherwise indicated, to allow for the mud and trash. I hoped I didn't look like some bumpkin with pants way too short, white socks showing as I traipsed along the byways.

A couple of men approached, laughing at some private joke. I saw their eyes shift towards us before dropping down to behold the enormous lupines who were natural attention-getters. There was nothing nefarious in their thoughts, merely curiosity. We'd paused beneath the halo of a ,streetlamp; a fine mist that was turning to sleet was falling. I figured one of our first purchases might be umbrellas.

"Sirs, beg pardon," Peter intoned, stepping forward and tipping the edge of his hat for a good measure of politeness. "We are looking for H Street and wonder if you might give directions."

The men tipped their hats, too, nodding respectfully in my direction. The larger of the two could have passed for a young Santa Claus, with a large belly and cheerful face partially hidden behind a snowy white beard. What I could see of his face was youthful, and his white hair was obviously premature. He was warmly dressed, as was his companion, in a wool overcoat that fell below his knees. A scarf of some soft material was knotted at his throat. I was envious of that scarf, given the cold breeze that hit me in the face.

"Young man, you are on First Street," Santa replied. "If you will go to your left until you meet G Street, turn left again and you will walk a few blocks until you get to 6th Street where you will turn again, right this time. You will find yourselves on H Street." The man beamed at us, obviously pleased with himself that he could assist strangers.

"Thank you very much," Peter replied, touching his fingertips to the brim of his hat. "May I ask you the date, please?" Peter laughed self-consciously. "We've become a bit disoriented due to our travels."

"Why it is December 14th," the man replied. "And of course, you know the year is 1864," he added, laughing, exchanging a glance with his companion, who was smiling and winked in reply.

As we walked away, Peter laughed softly. "Now I know what is causing that horrible stink." He glanced at me. "We are near the Tiber Creek, which was badly polluted with human waste after Washington grew too fast." He had obviously made it one of his initiatives to familiarize himself with the streets and landmarks, which actually was a pretty smart thing to do.

"Oh, yuk." Kipp managed to look disgusted as he inhaled deeply and caught a whiff of the waterway.

Fortunately, Elani had actually listened to the directions and memorized them. Well, that was as it should be since it was her trip by design. I confess I'd been too busy staring at the storefronts and other buildings and was lazy enough to hope someone else was paying attention. Maybe this supervision thing was pretty sweet, I thought to myself. I could go along for the ride but not have to prepare. It fit the growing lack of motivation that seemed to define my life. Kipp, who was following the progression of my thoughts like a terrier after a rat, ducked under my hand and gently bumped my thigh.

I wasn't certain of the time, but it had the feel of pending daybreak. My main gauge was the growing activity I noted on the narrow street. There was a small, bob-tailed wagon loaded with coal making deliveries, as well as another large wagon with wooden crates stacked precipitously on the back section. A scruffy mutt of a dog barked ferociously at Kipp and Elani from his vantage point on the hard board seat of the coal wagon.

"Yeah, come and get some," Kipp said, snarling at the little dog. Of course, Kipp was just playing, but I saw the dog's eyes widen in response.

"Kipp, try and not terrorize the locals," I admonished him. "And, please, no more movie-style dialog."

"Okay, boss," he said, his tone cocky. His fur was brushed from cold, almost snapping with electricity and vitality.

It was only a short time when we passed the jail, which had the sad, hopeless appearance of many such buildings. The front was lit by flickering lanterns, which cast moving shadows on the rough brick walls. As we turned on G Street, I saw the sun peek over the eastern horizon, the light cascading softly over my shoulder to touch my cheek. I hoped with the rising of the sun that the miserable sleet would move on and remain a thing of darkness.

We kept to the sidewalks, where they existed, and otherwise hugged the side of the road, since the streets were becoming more congested. Unfortunately, the curbs were a collecting place for trash and dead leaves, and we had to watch our footsteps. Reaching into my coat pocket, I retrieved a handkerchief; I could feel my nose running and knew I probably looked a mess. The cold was damp and bitter, and I was feeling it despite my warm undergarments and the three skirts I was wearing. I'd be glad to rid myself of two skirts, since I felt over-stuffed and awkward. I preferred a little more fluidity in my movements and had needed the ability to move quickly more than once in my past adventures.

"Your face has turned a color I've not seen before," Kipp remarked. "And your lips are blue," he added. "Petra, we must get you somewhere warm." His voice in my head was urgent with concern.

I knew my limits and was certain I was okay, despite the frigid air. I grudgingly admitted that something warm to drink would be nice, and Peter rushed ahead to scout out a street vendor who was nursing a large receptacle of coffee simmering over an open fire pit. He obviously had a good business with everyday laborers who sought out a cup of something hot before they began their daily grind. Peter returned with a couple of tin cups brimming with coffee, the steam rising in the morning air. I figured the brew would be raw...cowboy coffee, they called it in modern times when it was served up in fancy bistros to courageous patrons who pretended to have stomachs made of iron. After pausing, I caught the encouraging expression in Kipp's eyes and hazarded a sip. The brew lit a fire in my mouth before sliding heavily down my throat, scalding it along the way, until it hit my stomach with a thud and a mini explosion. As bad as it was, it did the trick, and I began to regain feeling in my extremities. Peter obviously had a similar reaction, if the expression on his face was any gauge.

"Better?" Kipp asked, tilting his head to the side.

"Yes, as long as this stuff doesn't eat a hole in my stomach," I replied with a grim smile.

Reinvigorated, we began to walk again. Elani had been conspicuously silent, so I glanced her way to be met with a wagging tail. I raised an eyebrow.

"Just a little nervous," she replied honestly.

"Me, too," I said. "I always feel like I have butterflies," I added, laughing as her thoughts tangled with mine as she sought out the meaning of a new expression.

We stopped in front of a four-story gray brick building on the corner of H Street. I swallowed hard, recognizing the place from pictures that had stared back at me from history books. It was here that one of the most infamous killers in history met with his co-conspirators as he hatched his plans to bring down a government through the simultaneous assassination of key officials. Even though I routinely examined famous points in history, this moment had an unexpectedly surreal feel to it, as if I were viewing things from a distance, just a passive voyeur and not part of the action. I glanced at Peter and was surprised to see myself comforted by the confidence he exuded. No, he wasn't cocky, just ready for action. Kipp nuzzled my hand, angling his head beneath, begging for a scratch.

"Petra, it's time," Peter said, reaching out to touch my shoulder, his hand somehow managing to convey warmth through the fabric of my coat.

Thankfully, I was somewhat rejuvenated by the bitter coffee and nodded at him. It was his turn to take the lead. We waited for a team of oxen, straining against a wooden yoke, pulling a heavily laden wagon carrying lumber, to rumble pass, the wheels causing the street to tremble, before crossing. Research told us the street-level door led to the dining room and kitchen, so we dutifully climbed the stairs to the second level landing, where Peter used the door knocker to summon an inhabitant. During the short wait, I occupied myself by staring down the street, looking for landmarks and becoming familiar with the area. There was a row of similar dwellings that did not give the impression of wealth but more of middle-class comfort, if such a thing existed. I knew Mary Surratt advertised for only gentleman boarders. All the houses seemed well maintained, and the street was relatively free of any sort of refuse. Even as I had that thought, a man walked past, pushing a large receptacle on wheels, picking up trash that might have been the result of late-night littering.

The door opened, and I was a little surprised to see Mary Surratt gazing at us, having expected that maybe a housekeeper or other worker would be given the task to greet strangers. She was taller than I, with a broad, square-shaped face and a jaw that was strong and well defined, but not unpleasantly so. Her facial features were evenly balanced, her nose straight, her eyes deep-set and direct beneath arching dark brows. Her hair was parted in the middle and swept back in rolls on either side in the contemporary fashion of the day, one which I'd never favored. Gold earbobs dangled delicately, the type of jewelry a lady would wear...not too much, but just enough. As Mary Surratt's gaze swept over our odd group in a rapid assessment, an expression of curiosity crossed her face.

"Yes?" she asked, allowing herself a polite smile while clasping her hands at her waist.

"Are you Mrs. Surratt?" Peter asked, removing his hat. Elani decided to sit, since she was trying to appear well behaved. A second later, Kipp's backside hit the cold brick of the porch landing.

"I hope I don't have to sit here too long," he grumbled. "This is cold on my fanny."

"Shut up," I replied. "Peter is trying to focus." It was an ongoing job to keep Kipp reined in.

"Yes," Mary Surratt replied, nodding her head.

"I am Peter Keaton, ma'am, and this is my sister Petra Holmes. Please forgive the earliness of the hour, ma'am. We were sent to you by an acquaintance in the hope you can be of assistance to us." Somehow, he had managed a skillful blending of dialects that would make his origin hard to pin down. Peter had done that on purpose so that he could move more easily in a deeply divided society.

"It's rather brisk out here," she replied, glancing up at the gray sky which promised a cold, freezing rain turning to snow as darkness fell. "If you would like to come into the parlor," she began. Staring at Kipp and Elani, she hesitated for a moment, uncertain of protocol and manners in an unusual situation.

"Brother, I will be glad to stay out here with the dogs," I offered, taking my handkerchief and giving my nose a vigorous rub just to demonstrate how blasted cold it was. I'd read her correctly, and her sense of gentility would not let her chat with Peter in the comfort of her parlor while I froze on her porch step. "I would not wish to incommode Mrs. Surratt," I added, just to push the envelope.

"No, please come in," she said, backing away from the door and gesturing with her hand. Her lips tightened; she was not keen on Kipp and Elani tracking wet paw prints on her floor but would tolerate it for the sake of good manners.

"I don't care for the dog reference," Kipp said airily. "And my feet are not muddy."

"Me neither, Kipp," Elani remarked, joining his attitude.

"Can it, both of you," I hissed. Peter gave me a grateful nod as I tried to manage the rambunctious nature of the lupines.

We followed Mary Surratt into the parlor, which was a nicely appointed room; a fire blazed on the grate, and I felt somewhat cheered that I might get warm again. Trying to not appear too rude and ill mannered, I surreptitiously glanced around the walls at the pictures and along the mantle where framed pictures as well as the typical objects one has sitting around a home for decoration rested. She obviously had good taste and assembled just the right balance of items to make the room welcoming without seeming cluttered.

A young woman, maybe only in her late teens, entered the doorway, pausing for instructions. She was obviously the household servant, a thin, narrow-shouldered girl with pock scars on her pale skin. Her dress was plain and a full-length apron covered the front of the garment. The girl's eyes met mine for a brief flash, the expression rather blank and dull. Her life would be filled with toil at the direction of others...or at least, that was how she viewed the world. There were those who had and those who worked for those who had. It was as simple as that in her experience.

"Maureen, please bring us some tea," Mrs. Surratt requested, her tone mild and not unpleasant as she directed the girl. Mary's eyes returned to us. "And how may I be of assistance, Mr. Keaton?"

FOURTEEN

As Maureen scuttled off to the kitchen, which was one level below where we sat, Mrs. Surratt saw to our comfort.

"Are you close enough to the fire, Mrs. Holmes?" she asked, a slight frown settling upon her smooth brow. In her early forties, she had aged well for the times and could have passed for a younger woman.

"Yes, thank you," I replied. She had adroitly picked up on the fact Peter and I had different last names and assumed I was a married woman.

She settled her skirts, which was an ongoing issue with women of past times. I'd settled many a skirt in my days and was happy to wear sweat pants and jeans in contemporary times. Just thinking of a pair of nice, broken-in jeans made me a little home-sick. My own condition, with three skirts bunched under my back-side, was uncomfortable, and I tried not to squirm against the padded fabric beneath me. I felt like a toddler in a booster seat. Mary's gaze flicked almost imperceptibly towards the lupines, who were trying to appear bored and well behaved. No, she wasn't overly fond of dogs in her home, but her innate need to be cour-teous won the day. She would have been an amazing poker player with her calm façade and deliberate manner, and I was grateful to be a telepath who could read her mind instead of her facial expressions.

I glanced at Kipp, who was doing his deep dive into her mind, sifting through her memories that had been laid down over the years. I was somewhat startled to realize that Elani was attempting the same thing, straining a bit. Well, good for her. She needed to flex her muscles, and if Kipp was pushing his abilities, why shouldn't she? Maybe Kipp's skills were not so unique after all but just had been lost over years of convincing ourselves as a species that some things were just not to be done? But there did seem to be a factual basis that his primitive origin gave him more strength and agility in his talents.

"My sister and I are looking for some lodging for the short term," Peter began. "I know that you take gentlemen only, but we were hoping you could refer us to someone who could accommodate us." Peter was really good at that sort of inquiry since he had that heartfelt, puppy dog kind of expression that people just believed. He, generally, was likeable, while I believe I usually served as an irritant...or at least I'd been told that on many an occasion. "We need rooms in a respectable part of town where we will be around fine people, such as yourself," he added for good measure.

Mrs. Surratt obviously liked his latter comment and preened just a tiny bit. She did view herself as a lady, and although not of wealth, she managed a business that was keeping the family fed and clothed. The dialog paused as Maureen returned with a loaded tray carrying a teapot, cups, and a plate with some crusty biscuits. Mrs. Surratt waved the girl away and did the chore of serving us herself. The steam rising off the surface of my cup of tea tickled my nose; I curled my palm around the delicate china and was happy to note I finally had feeling returning to my stiff fingers.

"Well, I think it may be difficult to find a place that can accommodate your needs," Mary Surratt replied delicately, her gaze encompassing the lupines.

Kipp glanced at me. "She knows of a place but doesn't think it is necessarily appropriate for a female," he remarked.

"Push her, Kipp." My glance at him was veiled as I took a sip of the tea, which was quite good, although an uninspiring blend. I felt an unexpected twist of my heart as I thought of Fitzhugh, back home, probably preparing tea at that very moment. In my mind, I conjured the fragrance of Earl Grey steeping.

Elani glanced at me, narrowing her eyes. It was rare I asked Kipp to manipulate the thoughts of a human, since it really was not an ethical behavior. But it was necessary we have lodgings near the Surratt home where we could monitor Mary's thoughts and those of prospective visitors. History indicated that John Wilkes Booth was introduced to John Surratt on December 23rd. Our timing was good, giving us the opportunity to set up a listening post nearby.

Kipp began to casually lick his paws as he concentrated, once again, on Mary. He glanced up at me and wagged his tail. It was obvious he enjoyed doing things that were natural for him versus following symbiont codes that were set down for reasons that might be good but also might not be. It was as effortless for him to enter her mind and plant suggestions as it was for Fitzhugh to brew an excellent pot of tea.

I glanced at the windows that overlooked the street. The sounds filtering past the glass suggested that commerce and trade were escalating as the day progressed. The noise of wagon wheels creaking and the occasional whinny of a horse, along with the murmur of human voices, entered the warm, cozy room, muted but evident. Unexpectedly, there was a sound of something crashing to the floor on the level below us; Mary Surratt allowed a frown to flash across her face before resuming her remarkable poker face.

"And how are you finding our city, Mrs. Holmes?" Mary Surratt was acting as a proper hostess to pull me into the dialog.

"We only just arrived," I answered. "It seems very busy," I added with a deliberately self-conscious laugh. "I'm accustomed to a little slower pace."

"And where is your home?" Mary Surratt was curious in the context of a war-torn nation.

"I'm from Tennessee," I replied. Through my years of traveling I'd managed to acquire a nice tool kit of languages and dialogs and chose, during this trip, to speak with a softly rounded type of accent, not deeply southern but not really anything else. I, like Peter, didn't want to stick out amongst the population.

"Oh, how nice," Mary murmured, relaxing her guard some-what. "I've never traveled there myself, but hear that parts of it are lovely." The fact I was from the south brought her comfort due to her pro-Confederate leanings, and she almost uttered a sigh of relief. She assumed I would have the same types of thoughts about the war as would she. As she rose to warm up our tea, a sweet fragrance of some floral scent wafted through the air as she bent over my cup. Jasmine, perhaps? Walking to the stairway, which led to the kitchen below, she called for Maureen. The girl appeared quickly, no doubt not wanting to be chastised for lagging.

"Maureen, I want you to go fetch Mr. Paul Garland," Mary said. "Don't forget your coat and hat, child."

I personally hated for Maureen to have to go out into the cold but kept my mouth shut. We had to let this household function as would be normal. From the few murmured words she'd uttered, I realized from her speech that Maureen was an Irish immigrant, many of whom were put to use serving in the army as well as in homes as servants and laborers. I cut my eyes at Kipp, who had relaxed now that his manipulation of Mrs. Surratt was complete.

"Nicely done, Kipp," I murmured, watching his tail thump the floor in response to my compliment.

"Mr. Garland is a gentleman I know who has a property on this street, actually on the diagonal across that way," Mary said, pointing vaguely out the window. "He purchased it with the intent of trans-forming the street level into a tea room, while he will convert the other levels into rooms to be let out to borders." She folded her hands on her lap as her lips tightened slightly. "The previous owner let the property decline, and there is extensive work to be done in order to make it habitable. Mr. Garland has had to delay his plans for renovation due to difficulties getting materials and workman in place as long as this war continues." Her face clouded for a moment and she looked at her hands, forcing them to be still in her lap. "But I believe portions of the building are habitable, if you don't object to less than sterling conditions."

"That sounds perfect for us, Mrs. Surratt. Perhaps the presence of our dogs won't be an issue," Peter added, laughing politely.

"Actually, Mr. Garland has worried over the property being

vacant, concerned that vandals might try and enter the building."
Her grave eyes met mine. "This town is full of riff-raff due to the
war," she added as her lips turned down at the corners.

I didn't interrupt Kipp, who had returned to his deep dive into
her mind. As we sat there, I let my thoughts turn to Elani for a
moment. It was clear that she was motivated by Kipp's talents to
challenge her own limits, maybe privately or perhaps with our
support. We knew, from symbiont history, that lupines once had the
ability to enter the minds of others and control their actions. Kipp
possessed this, but I knew of no contemporary lupine with that skill.
Was it there, in Elani, dormant, waiting to emerge? For all my time
spent to date with Elani, she remained a lovely mystery.

With effort, I returned to the subject at hand. It was clear that
Mary Surratt had strong feelings about the war, and my canvassing
of her surface thoughts immediately revealed her Confederate leaning. I also caught a twinge of worry about her son, John, as that
thought flickered across the tablet of her mind. She nursed an
ongoing concern that he would be in trouble due to his connection
with the Confederate government. But her thoughts stopped there,
as they should. John Surratt would not meet John Wilkes Booth until
later in the month of December. I did clearly pick up that she
suspected her son worked as a spy for the Confederate government,
even though he wouldn't admit it to her. There was a profound
fondness for her youngest son, her baby, and maybe her greatest
affection was for him over her other son and daughter, Anna. I
thought of how he refused to return to aid her when he knew she
would be executed. Apparently, although his mother would protect
him, he had no such feelings of responsibility to defend her if he
thought she was innocent. He alone possibly had possessed the
ability to save her life if he'd spoken on her behalf.

We heard the front door open, and the blurred sounds of chaos
from the busy street flooded into the foyer. I saw the slim figure of
Maureen bustle past before she silently disappeared down the stairs
to the kitchen; her relief at returning to a warm house was evident
in her posture as well as her thoughts. A moment later, a tall,
middle-aged man with a face red from the cool air stepped into the
parlor, sweeping his hat from his head as he did so. His graying hair

was combed over a balding spot on top, and a pair of bright blue eyes formed the focal point of an altogether pleasing countenance. As Mrs. Surratt rose to see to his comfort and Peter stood to shake his hand as greetings were exchanged, Mr. Garland took a seat, leaning forward in an inviting posture, curious as to why he'd been summoned.

"Mr. Garland," Peter began, "my sister and I are going to be in Washington for a brief period of time and are in need of lodging. We travel with our beloved dogs and that poses an issue with most establishments." Peter smiled, the beguiling face of an honest, earnest young fellow. "Because of my dear sister," he continued, gesturing at me, "we need to be in a respectable area, so that further compounds our difficulties."

Mr. Garland glanced at me and sat up a little straighter in his chair. He ran a hand across his balding pate, concerned that the removal of his hat had left his thinning hair disturbed. Kipp giggled in the back of my head, while faking innocence as he snored softly.

"And Mrs. Surratt told you of the townhouse I own on this street," Mr. Garland said, smiling. He glanced at the lupines, who continued to play as if they were snoozing. It was evident he liked dogs; a smile crossed his face and one didn't even need to bother reading his thoughts. "I'd like to be able to accommodate you, but the townhouse is not in the best condition," he began.

I started to ask Kipp to get the man to reconsider any negative thoughts but held back. We'd let Peter test his ability to lie his way through this discussion and manipulation. Elani's tail twitched, just for a second, in agreement.

"Well, sir, Mrs. Surratt has told us that. But your building is on a good street, and until you begin work on the improvements, you would have paying tenants. And our dogs are amazing watchdogs and would help protect the property from any nefarious individuals." Peter paused. "We only need the rooms until mid-April," he added, trying not to sound too eager and breathless.

Mr. Garland took a deep breath. "There are no servants in the house," he began. "The kitchen is on the lower level, much like this townhouse, with a parlor on the second level and rooms on the third." He glanced at Mrs. Surratt. "The top level has damage due

to a failing roof, which I am replacing before I begin any other reno-
vations."

"As I said, this would be only temporary, and we would be good
tenants." Peter started to add it would be a "win win" but then
decided that might be an expression that seemed out of place in
1864. "I can pay for the entire stay upfront, as they say," he added,
smiling.

"Well, there are advantages in not having a vacant building,"
Mr. Garland conceded. "But I feel, in good conscience, that I need
to show you the townhouse so that you will not be disappointed. It is
truly in need of major work, young man."

"Sir, if it gives us protection from this weather, we will be
grateful." I spoke up, knowing my words would sway him in the
right direction. "I'm not accustomed to such cold," I added,
widening my eyes. To appeal to his unconscious mind, I lightly
wrapped my arms about my lower chest as if I were chilled from
the elements.

He smiled in return. "The stoves are the things that are in good
order," he said. "It will be no problem to have coal and wood delivered so that you can be warm, Mrs. Holmes."

Yes, I'd appealed to the chivalrous side of his nature as I knew I
would. Some humans might think our natural manipulation of their
kind to be shameless and deceitful, but it was just what we did. How
else is a species such as ours, which co-habits a crowded planet, to
remain under the radar of humans while trying to exist within the
definition given to us by the Creator? I occasionally felt guilt but
tried not to linger in that place of bad feelings.

"I will be glad to show you the property, Mr. Keaton," Garland
said. "I'm actually on my way to my office, and we can go to the
townhouse now, if you wish."

"Excellent," Peter replied.

As we stood and murmured our thanks to Mrs. Surratt, I intensified my intrusion into her mind, while privately encouraging Peter
and Elani to do the same. Her patterns of thoughts would need to
be sufficiently familiar to us that we would be able to pick her out
amongst many from our spy hole across the street.

"What amazing dogs!" Mr. Garland exclaimed as he replaced

his hat. "I don't think I've seen any to match them in size and appearance."

I had always told humans that Kipp was a red-crested Chinese mastiff, and he had complained every time over my made-up breed type. I'd never quite understood his dislike over something that reeked of exotic, but thinking quickly, I tried to piece together a new name.

"Mr. Garland, Kipp and Elani are both from a breed that was and is still used in Siberia to herd and protect livestock as well as hunt. They are truly very adaptable." I stumbled, trying to think of a clever name. "And these particular dogs are extremely hardy and courageous," I added, still thinking.

"How about Siberian Tiger dog?" Kipp asked, liking the name.

"Or Silver Siberian mastiff?" Elani suggested, using her coloration to create a name, ignoring Kipp's glare.

"They are Siberian Deerstalkers," I finally stuttered, hoping Kipp would approve the deerstalker part since he liked Sherlock Holmes.

"Oh, cool!" Kipp exclaimed, happy over the hastily improvised moniker.

"Siberian Deerstalkers?" Mr. Garland looked momentarily puzzled before he smiled. "Just another example of how large is our world, and there are so many places of which we only have a cursory knowledge." He stood, hat in hand. "If you are ready to accompany me," he said invitingly.

I was ready to go at that point, because I wanted an opportunity for Kipp to assemble his thoughts and share in a place where we didn't have to be simultaneously dealing with humans. In other words, I wanted us symbionts to have time together to process events, people, and impressions. As we were saying our goodbyes to Mary Surratt, I realized again what a remarkably controlled woman she was in terms of guarding her thoughts. She had obviously learned, during wartime, to monitor what words left her lips in front of strangers. And even though there was some lingering fondness and friendship for Mr. Garland, he was not in her safe circle of friends, and she limited her sharing to him of superficial matters.

"Please come back and visit me, Mrs. Holmes," Mary

murmured softly, her hand pressing mine. Her hands were large and strong, and given her height advantage, I glanced up at her face. Reading her thoughts, I was surprised to see that she was being genuine with me and not simply being polite as custom dictated. Mary Surratt spent her time running her household, seeing to the needs of her boarders and worrying about her children, especially young John. She had no close female friends and was basically lonely. She'd moved to Washington from the tavern her husband had managed in the countryside, and the main social connections she had made were through her church.

"I will do that, Mrs. Surratt." I smiled. "And perhaps if we establish a modest household so close by, you can come and have tea with me one day."

"And of course Kipp and Elani are welcome here, since they are so well behaved,'" Mary added with a soft, ladylike laugh. "And you, too, Mr. Keaton," she said in a rush, her cheeks coloring faintly as she feared she'd been rude. It takes a lot to be rude to a symbiont, but of course she didn't know that.

As she walked us to the door, her hand dropped down to lightly touch the top of Elani's head. I wondered if she'd find the funny little point on Elani's noggin, and she did, after a moment's search through the dense fur, locate and caress that spot. She smiled, glancing at me.

"Growing up, I was not around dogs very much. And then I was sent off to school where there were no dogs. I think I can see why people value them…they have a comforting presence."

"Yes, they do indeed, Mrs. Surratt."

FIFTEEN

The townhouse, set on a diagonal from Mary Surratt's home, was almost identical in form, at least from the street level. Mr. Garland acted as our guide, discreetly taking my elbow with a feather's touch to lead me to safety across the busy street. Upon closer inspection, it was obvious there was significant deterioration and neglect, with paint peeling from the door that led into the street-level kitchen and dining room, as well as a couple of windows that had been boarded up as result of broken panes of glass. Mr. Garland turned to us as he pushed the key into the door lock. The door frame must have been slightly warped because he had to push hard against the door a couple of times before the wood popped free. As he opened the door, a whoosh of air smacked me in the face; it smelt stale, vaguely unpleasant, and I could clearly detect the scent of old food, perhaps something that had rotted and been left behind by a workman or previous inhabitant.

"I warned you that it is in need of many repairs," he said apologetically, his skin blushing soft pink.

I walked forward, moving to the far counter; there was a pump, and I almost shouted with joy. We wouldn't have to tote water, slopping it on ourselves, from some public outlet. There was a small recessed area covered by a full-length curtain, and as I peeked behind the fabric I found a metal hip bath. We could at least stay relatively clean, unlike some of my past trips when bathing was rare. But then I had lived through times when bathing yearly was the norm. These arrangements seemed more than adequate.

"It seems to be a solid structure," Peter replied. Although his voice was calm and appraising, he was clearly excited. Privately, to us, he was pleased. "Petra, this is perfect. We'll be close enough to monitor the transactions in the Surratt household. I mean, all of us can do it, not just Kipp."

I'm not sure why, but even though he didn't mean it to sound dismissive, it did, and I saw Kipp's ears flatten. Elani darted a quick look at Kipp, her tail wagging feebly. Peter, to his credit, showed some sensitivity and caught his error.

"Kipp, that came out wrong," he began, stumbling with mending fences with Kipp while simultaneously examining the kitchen level with Mr. Garland. "You have long-distance skills the rest of us clearly don't, and I guess I was just excited that for once, I could do things on my own." Peter stretched out his hand. "It was selfish of me."

Kipp angled next to him, as Peter ran his hand down Kipp's broad back. "No, it wasn't, Peter. Maybe I'm just a little too proud of my uniqueness, and that's not a good thing." Kipp fell silent after that remark, and I knew we'd revisit it, just he and I, later that evening.

The parlor landing was filled with sunlight, which rested on the dusty floor in a checkerboard pattern matching the window frames. The few pieces of furniture scattered about the room would be functional for our needs. We didn't go to the fourth floor, which was reportedly in shambles. Apparently, the inadequate roof, which gave minimal protection, had allowed water to do extensive damage to the ceiling and woodwork on that upper level. Mr. Garland had made some emergency repairs, but the entire roof and some of the supporting beams needed replacement. That was first on his to-do list.

"I actually have the work arranged, but it won't begin until after this winter passes," he said. "If you and Mrs. Holmes are willing to stay here, of course the rent will be negligible." Mr. Garland had been excited over the thought he could make money off of a dormant property, but upon walking through it with us, he became embarrassed that he'd try to rent the hulk to anyone, but especially with a lady in residence. Despite the cold in the room, he had a fine sheen of perspiration on his face. I wasn't sure how that was possible, considering the chill.

"Mr. Garland, this will fully meet our needs," I spoke up, concerned he might back out. "I think if we can use the kitchen and this second level, since there are two small rooms in the back of the parlor to serve as bedrooms, it will be more than sufficient. We will have no reason to go to the third or fourth levels at all." Smiling at him, I willed the circulation to return to my fingers, hoping to generate some warmth. I looked forward to curling up against Kipp that night; he was better than sleeping with a heater.

"The stoves," Garland said, indicating a large one in the parlor and referencing the one in the kitchen, "are functional and will supply heat." He glanced at me, and of course since I was monitoring his thoughts, it was apparent he found me to be an attractive female and felt kindly towards me. I looked away, catching Peter in mid-smirk; I narrowed my eyes with a nonverbal expression that clearly expressed my displeasure. Before he could be seen by Mr. Garland, he managed to wipe the expression off his face. Kipp started to tease me, too, before I warned him to carefully consider his other options. Elani sighed deeply. She was disgusted with the boys and their questionable sense of humor.

Mr. Garland looked around the parlor again. The old furniture was covered with sheets, resembling ghostly apparitions scattered across the room. Fortunately, the front windows of the parlor were mainly intact and gave us a visual of the entrance to Mary Surratt's home. Seemingly embarrassed by the sweat on his brow, Mr. Garland discreetly dabbed at his skin with an embroidered handkerchief. As the cloth fluttered, I caught a whiff of some manly fragrance.

While Peter and Mr. Garland chatted, I wandered to the rear of the parlor level and poked my head in one of the two small rooms. Tiny, but fine from my perspective. I'd lived in some horrible places while shifting, so this seemed very nice…cold, but nice.

"Don't worry," Kipp said. "I'll keep you warm at night." He ducked his head under my hand as my fingers tunneled into the thick fur on his neck. "Mmm…that feels good," he murmured.

"So, because I can't wait until later, what was that exchange you had with Peter?" There was a narrow bed pushed against the side of the wall, and I sat on it tentatively, hoping it was sound and that I wouldn't crash through to land on the floor in a tangled heap. Kipp sat, too, after quickly assessing the floor surface for debris. The bed was so low to the floor that Kipp was at eye level with me. It didn't take long to view the room; other than the bed, there was a battered bureau, a straight-backed chair that looked predictably uncomfortable, and a mirror on the wall that promised a distorted reflection of oneself, like one of those trick mirrors at a carnival or sideshow. The wallpaper, which had faded so much the pattern on its surface was unrecognizable, was peeling away from the wall. There was no window, and the room felt like a tomb. There was an oil-burning lamp on a small corner table, so at least I wouldn't have to grope in the darkness.

"Is there something called false pride?" Kipp asked, turning his head slightly.

"Yes, I suppose so."

"Well, it's not a good quality, and I think I have it."

"What do you mean, Kipp?"

"When Peter said those words, I immediately realized that I take pride in being special and didn't want give that up." His ears drooped. "I felt ashamed of myself."

I sat quietly, not sure how to respond in such a way to allow him the growth space he needed as well as be a good friend. After a deep breath, I made an attempt. "Kipp, you are one of the most humble symbionts I know, if not the most humble. Most symbionts and humans, too, for that matter, like to have some recognition for a good quality they possess. It could be something minor or something big." I gave him a moment to process my words. "If you pretended not to notice your unique qualities, then that would be a lie and false humility."

He edged a little closer and put his muzzle on my knee. His eyes closed as I stroked his head and gently tugged at his large ears.

"I'm not able to do some of things you can do, Kipp, and that's a fact. But you can't do some things that are inherent gifts given to me. It is the same way with humans. Not everyone can be a rocket scientist. Some don't possess the intellect, while others come from backgrounds where they've been deprived of education or haven't had the nurturing needed to believe in themselves." I sighed. "It's okay and honest to realize you have some acceleration in your skillset as long as you don't think you are better than the rest of us."

"I don't think that at all, Petra!" he exclaimed, his eyes opening wide. "Peter is amazing on this trip, taking command of the dialog and moving the process along. He's showing maturity and self confidence that's very encouraging for his future as a traveling symbiont. Elani did almost all of the planning and led us to a flawless landing." He swallowed hard. "And you're wonderful."

I laughed softly. "I'm not particularly wonderful, but I'm really happy that you believe I am, since it feeds my ego and makes me feel good."

Kipp's tail began to wag, brushing a semi-circle of clean on the floor.

"Are we good?" I asked.

"Always," he replied.

We reluctantly rejoined the others in the parlor. I liked the fact it was a sunny room, and we would benefit to some degree from the natural heating as the rays broke through the dirty panes, which needed a good cleaning, to rest upon the floor. And the sunlight was refreshing after the darkness of the bedroom.

Mr. Garland, having been persuaded by Peter that despite the condition of the townhouse, it was perfect for our needs, said he would send a couple of his household staff over to clean the kitchen and parlor levels as well as have coal and wood delivered. He also promised some fresh linens for the beds, which was not necessary but considerate. As he rushed off to see to those things, we were left alone.

"Peter, you did a great job," Elani said, clearly proud of her partner.

I was in agreement with both Kipp and Elani: the young symbiont had grown since our *General* time-shift. He really loved this sort of life, maybe even more than I had when much younger. Peter's face flushed with pleasure over the praise.

"See, Kipp," I said privately. "Peter enjoys being told good things about himself. We all do."

Symbionts possess an adaptive quality since time-shifts can put us in positions of being greatly deprived for extended periods of time. When our bodies are put under significant stress, our metabolism slows and nutritional requirements lessen. But it was a fact we did require nourishment, and I wasn't keen on us trying to prepare food in the kitchen, although I knew how to cook on an 1860 era stove—which was no crockpot—and the effort required would challenge my inherent laziness. I'd noted the kitchen stove used wood, while the parlor heater relied upon coal. At least, thanks to the operational water pump in the kitchen, we wouldn't have to journey forth to obtain water. We gathered around a large round table in the area just outside of the kitchen. It was planning time to get set for the next few months. I decided to relax and let the youngsters do the work. Maybe this team time-shifting was no so bad after all, I mused as I observed the energy of youth at play.

"I think our first need is to procure a regular food source," Peter began.

"And how!" Kipp exclaimed. "I'm already hungry."

Peter cleared his throat, and drummed his fingers on the table. Lifting his dark brows, he stared at Kipp for a moment before resuming. "I think we will go to a market and obtain some canned goods, maybe some dried meat for the lupines, but that we also engage a local establishment to deliver us regular meals. We happen to be close to several hotels that probably serve meals to guests as well as visitors. So, I will try to arrange a catering agreement."

"As long as I have food," Kipp said, clearly trying to annoy Peter much like the playful antics of a nagging brother. "I'd hate to have to start hunting the alleyways. Peoples' dogs and cats might start disappearing," he threatened, narrowing his amber eyes. Of course, he was kidding and wouldn't take out any domesticated pets, but in truth he was a skilled hunter by nature.

Elani shook her head, rolling her eyes. She knew, as did I, that the best way to deal with a rambunctious Kipp was to ignore him.

"And Petra, you and I can look at our clothing and see what additional needs we will have. I realize Karl supplied more than the usual, but we will be here for a few months, after all." Peter was way ahead of me, thankfully.

"I thought of asking Mary Surratt if she knows of a woman locally who takes in laundry and such," I remarked, feeling the need to try and offer some contribution.

"Good idea," Peter said, his face brightening. "I still can't believe our good fortune in snagging a place so close by." It was a fact, plain and simple, that successful time-shifting combined skill, knowledge, ability with just plain old good luck at times.

We separated at that point, taking time to unpack our meager belongings and put the items away in our adjoining rooms, which shared a common wall. Peter let me choose, but since the bedrooms were equally horrible, I didn't see where there was a great decision to be made. I also used the time to remove two of the three skirts I was wearing and felt so liberated that I managed a clumsy pirouette across the floor of the parlor. It was only a short time later that a couple of workers from Mr. Garland's employ showed up to complete a cleaning of the habitable spaces. It seemed to be the opportunity for us to take care of the food issue. I almost hated to go outside but reassured myself that with the rising of the sun coupled with the disappearance of sleet, it would be more tolerable. I was pleasantly surprised to find the day progressing to a surprising level of mildness, considering the harsh beginning we'd experienced earlier.

Hugging the side of the street to avoid horses, carts, wagons, and such, we picked up 6th Street and walked south several blocks, arriving at the National Hotel. The five-story white building was enormous, stretching along 6th Street; the entrance was on Pennsylvania Avenue. I turned to see the unfinished dome of the capitol in the distance silhouetted against the blue sky.

"Even though I know we're here, it seems unreal, doesn't it?" Peter smiled at me. The knot of his tie was slightly askew, so I reached up to straighten it, patting his chest with satisfaction. Peter, in turn, did me the favor of adjusting my hat, which always seemed to be drifting to an odd angle on my head.

"Yes, that never changes," I replied.

We stopped outside the front entrance, deliberating, and after a moment, Peter went inside to see if he could negotiate a catering arrangement. I moved slightly away from the doorway, so as not to impede traffic, Elani and Kipp flanking me. Suddenly, Elani took a deep, shuddering breath, and her thoughts of surprised recognition flooded my mind. Glancing up, I made direct eye contact with John Wilkes Booth, who was exiting the hotel, which was his home base while in Washington. He was as handsome as the descriptions, immediately recognizable from the photographs which followed his infamy. He was not overly tall, of slender build, with black hair and piercing dark eyes that seemed as black as his hair. A smile pulled at the corners of his mouth as he registered my bold stare, and he removed his hat in a courteous, sweeping, and graceful gesture. I bet he'd practiced that maneuver to perfection while standing in front of a mirror, studying his reflection from different angles. He wore a black frock coat, black trousers, and highly polished, gleaming brown boots that came to his knees.

"What magnificent dogs!" he exclaimed, glancing briefly at Elani and Kipp before returning his gaze to my face. John Wilkes Booth was widely known to be a flirtatious admirer of the opposite sex and had countless affairs in the various cities he visited as part of his acting career. He viewed women as conquests, part of his right as a well-known figure. Instinctively, Kipp pushed closer against my leg, and he barely managed to suppress a growl.

"Thank you, sir," I replied. I found it was a little surprising that I felt distinctly nervous, an unusual state for me. The realization that I was just inches away from a notorious killer was unsettling, and this is an admission from a symbiont who pursued Jack the Ripper up and down the crowded and fog-filled streets of London. "Elani and Kipp are wonderful companions."

John Wilkes Booth must have felt emboldened by my friendly reply because he stepped closer and leaned in to ruffle the fur on Elani's broad, silver head. "I'm John Wilkes Booth," he added, hoping I'd heard of him, wanting me to stroke his massive ego.

"Are you the actor?" I asked, widening my eyes. I was forced to engage with him, although I would have greatly preferred that a meeting not take place this early in our trip. The thought nagged me that this encounter could lead to awkwardness later on during our stay.

"Why, yes, the very same. And you are…?" he asked, smiling.

"Mrs. Petra Holmes," I replied.

He blinked for a second, not sure how to proceed before landing squarely on his feet. "And is Mr. Holmes accompanying you?" Booth pretended to look up and down the sidewalk before his black eyes returned to my face.

"Mr. Booth, I am a widow," I replied. "My brother is inside the hotel and should rejoin me in a moment."

He made a fake sad face but was privately happy that I was unmarried. In actuality, he had his hands currently full with a woman he was courting, but he was always interested in who else might be available.

Kipp was canvassing the man's thoughts, his eyes half closed in contemplation. But on the other hand, something had happened that disturbed Elani; I was not accessing her actual thoughts but felt currents, much like electricity, running through her. We'd have something to discuss when I could manage to shoo JWB along on his merry way.

"I simply can't leave you alone here and will wait with you until your brother returns," Booth declared. "There are certain individuals whose coarseness is intolerable in the presence of ladies," he added for good measure, almost rocking back on his heels.

I am no slouch at telepathy, although I'm no Kipp, and knew that Booth did nothing out of goodness' sake. He was a calculating man, that much was immediately clear, and he was trying to score points with another human being. His personality toolkit included all the machinations available to sociopaths, and at that moment he was, indeed, charming. I could see why people fell under his spell and the degree to which he could manipulate others. Booth had an innate charisma that served him well in his acting trade. At some point in our exchange, he'd reached out to gently take my hand, and I noticed his were small, almost feminine in appearance, smooth as would be the case in a man who didn't know physical labor. He wore a gold ring on one finger that winked at me as the metal was caught in the sunlight.

Despite our immediate good fortune in finding a townhouse near Mary Surratt's home, this meeting was ill-timed and could lead to difficulties later on when Booth began to visit that dwelling. Yes, Peter and I could try and conceal our appearances from Booth through disguises, but the lupines would make us stand out, no matter what we might do. I wanted to sigh and roll my eyes, wishing desperately Booth would let go of his false chivalry and move on, but he wouldn't, so I was stuck making idle chit chat with the man.

"Petra, it's good," Kipp nudged me with his shoulder. "I'm getting to know what makes him tick and will be able to recognize him easily from a distance."

However, Elani still seemed ruffled and unsettled, moving her paws about, shifting her weight against the cold street surface.

"Are you okay?" I asked her, while simultaneously deflecting another Booth question about my personal affairs.

"Later," she replied, her eyes clouded and disturbed.

"Hello?" Peter arrived and was trying not to look too startled to see Booth nestled cozily at my side. I made the introductions and allowed the two of them to do what society and convention called for.

"Well, now that I see your escort has returned, I will be on my way," Booth intoned, his lips pulling back in a smile, perfect teeth revealed. "I hope, perhaps, you can catch one of my performances while you are in Washington," he said his eyes on my face. "And of course, you also, Mr. Keaton," he added hastily. With the grace of a performer, he replaced his dark hat on his head, managing to achieve the perfect tilt so that it dramatically swept over his fore-head. I almost giggled as I thought of Carly Simon singing "You're So Vain".

We watched him move amongst the crowd, his agile, graceful body disappearing in less than a minute. I turned to Elani again, concerned. She'd managed to close herself off and seemed unusually distant from us.

"Let's go back to the townhouse," I suggested. "We need to talk and debrief."

SIXTEEN

The appearance of the interior of the townhouse, by the time we arrived back on H Street, was greatly improved. The dust-covers had been removed, the floors were swept, and the meager pieces of furniture cluttering the wide board flooring had been polished so that the scratched, marred surfaces shone where the sunlight fell upon the wood in splashes of golden warmth. The room smelled of beeswax and lemon, the latter of which overpowered the previous staleness that hung suspended like a fog. Our original plans to visit a dry goods store were postponed because I felt a good debriefing was more important. Something had happened to shake the normally imperturbable Elani, and I needed to investigate.

"I arranged, with the management at the National, a catered hot meal daily," Peter began. "It's a little costly, but unless one of us wants to cook all the time, it is the best I can figure. One of their busboys will bring it around noon time."

"Don't look at me to be the chef," I replied, satisfied with the arrangement and not concerned with the money. "We will still go to a dry goods store and get some items we can use to supplement or prepare here," I added, soothing his worry. He'd done fine, and we could always change the arrangement with the National at any time.

It was important to get the essentials, such as food, lodging and clothing, taken care of up front so that one's mind would be clear for the work of telepathy and sleuthing.

"I'm interested in everyone's impressions of John Wilkes Booth," I began. We were in the front parlor of the townhouse; I was perched on the edge of a worn loveseat that had seen better days. There was a broken spring or something else equally annoying digging into my backside; I shifted slightly, trying to get comfortable. "Peter?"

"He struck me, from my brief impression, as aggressively projecting the image he wants people to see. All humans do that to some degree but even more so in him." Peter was sitting across from me in a chair that didn't look any more comfortable than my loveseat, and his spine was crammed against a high, unyielding, wooden back. He'd turned the chair to benefit from the warmth of the stove, which the workers had thoughtfully ignited before they left. "He is calculating, vain, preening, and I got an impression of an underlying lack of true self confidence."

I'd removed my hat, glad to be free of it, placing it on a side table. Glancing up, I noticed, with satisfaction, that the parlor's front windows had also been cleaned. From outside came the loud voices of some people in the midst of a dispute. It was easy, without discipline, to become distracted by so many human minds, but the ability to tune unneeded thoughts out was one of our necessary skills.

"Yes, I felt the same," I remarked. "His surface thoughts were consumed with wanting to be seen as a chivalrous man to me, thinking I was a woman he wanted to impress." I turned to Kipp. It was obvious to me Elani was not ready to talk.

"He is interesting, not too difficult to unpack, and what I found was unpleasant," Kipp began. "Booth has a great amount of built-up anger and resentment, much of it focused on his family. His father and brother eclipse him in their fame, and he has convinced himself that he is the superior actor who has yet to be recognized adequately by the public." Kipp sighed deeply. "I suppose that is preferable to his realizing he might be the second-rate actor in the family." He was comfortably placed just close enough to the stove to be warmed but far enough away to not get overly hot. He glanced at me and wagged his tail, needing a smile from me, which I gave. "Then, there is the part of him that, with his anger, has become twisted. He is consumed with hatred of people who have dark skin. Booth thinks he is superior to them for reasons that are unclear." Kipp looked up at me, confused. "I don't understand that problem with humans, since all people are, well, people."

"Kipp, humanity, as far back as can be traced, is full of tribalism and separations between humans due to issues with culture, race, religious beliefs and other markers. We don't have those types of issues amongst symbionts," I remarked, "so it is difficult for us to comprehend."

Kipp managed a lupine shrug of his massive shoulders. "He feels people with dark skin are less human, and his agitation is almost uncontrollable at this point. He manages to mask it with his courtly behavior to most people and only reveals his true feelings to a small, safe circle of like-minded associates." Kipp paused a moment before asking, "Do you think his basic feelings of insecurity and competitiveness within his family have fueled his need to think he is superior to another group of humans?"

"That would be very hard to unravel, Kipp," I replied. "But it is a logical conclusion to draw and not a unique dilemma for the human species." I was increasingly concerned with Elani, who seemed withdrawn, preoccupied, even brooding, and such a state was uncommon in my lupine brethren, but especially so with her.

As if she was peeking in on the workings of my brain, which she wasn't, she perceived my worried thoughts directed at her. I attributed that to her sensitivity in general as well as familiarity bred from time spent in adventures and adversity. Elani raised her massive head, her dark eyes meeting mine across the narrow expanse of the parlor. For a moment, the sunlight faltered as a cloud passed across its trajectory, only to reignite a moment later, brighter and more golden than before, the rays filtering through the fine particles of dust that floated in the air.

"I'm okay, Petra," she began.

"What's wrong?" Peter asked, his words coming out in a rush. His query was immediately followed with chagrin and worry that he'd missed something critical with his partner. After all, he should have been more tuned into her than would I. Kipp also seemed momentarily confused, a rare position for him to occupy.

"Elani?" I asked. After all, it was her job to discuss her feelings and experiences, not mine to explain them for her.

She sighed deeply, stood, stretched to and fro, before resettling herself a little closer to the heater. The warmth from the coal fire radiated out into the parlor; the ripples in the waves of light were clearly visible as the heat shifted through the different levels of air in the room. I heard loud voices outside the front window as some men engaged in an altercation, but I was too concerned with Elani to pay them any mind.

"I had an odd experience that left me feeling disturbed," she began. Elani looked at Peter, who was wearing an expression of remorse, clearly upset he'd not been paying attention to her thoughts. "And it's okay, Peter. I'm actually glad you weren't hovering in my thoughts since I needed space to process what happened."

"What did happen, Elani?" Kipp asked. "We are a safe place, you know." He was not speaking as her supervisor but as a friend. It might have been my imagination, but I think his eyes softened a little as he watched her.

"When John Wilkes Booth reached out and stroked the top of my head, I had a flash of complete understanding of him. His feelings, thoughts…all the elements that made him who he is, rushed through me." She searched for words. "I had no control over it, and his bad, angry, evil thoughts almost overwhelmed me." Elani's eyes met mine. "If I'd been humanoid, I would have cried."

"So, it was conveyed through his touch?" I asked. "You weren't making any effort, such as the one Kipp was engaging, to read his thoughts?"

"No, I wasn't at all." Her distress was palpable, filling the room with feelings of anxiety and tentativeness. "I didn't like it because I couldn't stop it."

Kipp was unusually quiet, and I felt him retreat from me as his brain began to make calculations, firing on all cylinders. Peter, meantime, was silent, too, still trying to decide if he'd failed her in some enormous way.

"Do you remember when we went to contemporary Atlanta in our preparatory trip to locate the original setting of the train depot from which the *General* would depart?" Kipp asked, looking around at all of us before settling on Elani. She nodded her head. "You had an odd experience where, when you made contact with the ground, you had flashes of the people who'd lived there, walked on that earth, in the past." Elani nodded her head again.

"What are you thinking, Kipp?" I asked.

"Maybe there is some ability in symbionts—perhaps in only the lupine tree—to obtain the information I get from my deep dive into thoughts from physical contact." Kipp looked at me. "There has to be, or else how do you explain this skill that Elani seems to have? I know I don't have it to her degree and can only minimally pick up impressions from a locale, so perhaps it is genetic, passed down through her family line."

"Would that be normal?" Elani stared at Kipp. "Or is there something…wrong with me?"

"No, Elani. It would mean that we continue to discover talents of our species that have been hidden due to all the rules and regulations placed to constrain us in the modern world." Kipp looked up, his eyes passively examining the cracks in the ceiling overhead, as he searched for an analogy. "Are there not humans who seem to have talents that vary from the norm, and historically those humans were set apart because others felt their talents were aberrant or even demonic in nature? And there may be incidents in the recorded history of our kind, but it just hasn't been shared because no one asked."

Elani looked away from us, obviously hesitating, not sure if she should share what was lingering in her tangled thoughts. I shook off Peter's glance, warning him to let her make her way carefully.

"This wasn't the first time," Elani finally said, letting out a deep breath she'd been holding. "It has happened to me since I was a pup, but my mother told me to never say anything about it. She was afraid that I'd be in trouble with the collective."

"Have you had it with us…me?" I asked.

"Yes, it starts, but I learned to block it with symbionts when I was a youngster. I don't allow it to proceed because, well, I wasn't sure that it was acceptable. It almost gives me an unfair advantage over others." Her dark eyes met mine. "And especially with symbionts, since it would be intrusive and perceived as an aggressive act."

"Did anyone else in your family have such a skill?" Peter asked what to him seemed to be a safe question.

"My parents and siblings, no, but my mother told me that her mother had the skill. She said her mother, who I never knew, said she could feel the life force in others by her touch. It must have caused a great deal of trouble for the family because my mother was very guarded about it." She hesitated, her eyes clouded momentarily with the memory. "When I pressed her, she became angry, so I would stop asking questions. The only thing she ever said was that her mother had referred to the experience as the kaleidoscope." She answered the unasked question. "For me, it's almost like flashes of light, sensations, and impressions that are constantly moving before they fall into order and make sense."

"Elani, are you willing to experiment a little with this while we are on this time-shift?" I asked. "Since, as Kipp says, we are safe, this would be a good time to determine the limits of your abilities."

She glanced at Peter, who was still trying to process what had taken place. "Peter, you are my partner. What do you think?"

He cleared his throat, delaying for a moment as he considered how to reply. Lifting his hand, he ran his fingers through the dark mop of hair that tended to fall down over his eyes, combing it into place. The gold watch chain that was secured to his grandfather's pocket watch stretched across his lower chest, the bright links catching the light from the windows. I noticed he'd, over time, developed an endearing habit of lightly fingering the chain, much as I did Harrow's beloved strand of pearls. The touch of my fingers against the pearls was soothing, and I figured Peter obtained the same sense of grounding and security when he was connected to his family of origin through a cherished object.

"Elani, I trust you implicitly," he replied. "I think if you have some ability that is rare but natural for you, it would be important to explore it…that is, if you wish."

"I would like to, but I think I need to learn how to control it," Elani replied, after a moment of deliberation.

"Are you willing to explore it now?" Kipp asked.

"Yes." Her dark eyes met his.

I was curious as to what Kipp had in mind. With Kipp, I could never be sure.

"Petra, I want you to caress Elani's head, just as did Booth, and let her see if she has a flood of impressions." Kipp was all manager at that point, directing the action. But I trusted him and Elani and was willing to follow where he led.

Elani was warm, her body huddled in front of the heater; I rose and went to her, crouching at her side. Leaning in, I rested my hands on her broad head. The warmth from her fur was wonderful against my fingers, which seemed to be taking a long time to regain any feeling after our early morning arrival.

"You're like a little warm brick," I said, grinning at her. Her tail wagged in response.

"Don't force it," Kipp directed.

"I've got this," Elani replied, her tone a little sharp as she glared at Kipp.

We stayed like that, my fingers enjoying the warmth of her fur, for a minute. Finally, she sighed.

"I'd like to say I'm surprised by you, Petra, but I'm not. You're the same symbiont I've grown to know and love."

It was an odd sensation for me. I'd had fellow symbionts intrude aggressively in my mind, and I knew the sting of that sort of violation which was considered obscene in our world. What had evolved in contemporary times was a flow of surface thoughts between telepaths, asking for permission to go deeper...the exception being my relationship with Kipp, which had no boundaries. But when I touched Elani, I felt no such sensation of her burrowing into my being, and instead it was as if I melted, relaxed, and she was like a gentle wind blowing against my flesh, subtle and cooling. There is nothing else in my experience that compared to that moment. And then it ended.

"What did you get?" I had to know.

"I saw your childhood...your love for your parents was like

sunshine, all warmth and safety. And there were impressions of you running across a pasture thick with green grass; you were laughing and playing with another one of your age. It was a happy moment. I even got the sensation of how the grass felt against your bare feet, cool, damp, organic. Then there was your son…" her voice drifted off. "I tried not to linger there." She turned her large, gray head and glanced away as she collected her thoughts. "So, from viewing the kaleidoscope of your experiences, both good and bad, it all fell into place, and I believe I understand your core."

Kipp rose and walked over to her, then took up position at her side. "Me next."

Elani's dark eyes widened, but she kept her expression composed. I understood immediately what she felt…the notion of her beloved one lying close and touching her was pretty intoxicating. It was with effort I focused on the moment, not allowing myself to recall being in Harrow's arms. But since we were in the middle of a quasi-scientific experiment, Elani tried to remain business-like. Kipp gently rested his muzzle along her shoulder, and they stayed like that, breathing in concert, for a minute. Her eyes drifted shut as she relaxed. As the heater cranked out waves of warmth to drift across the parlor, I watched the two of them, one with a ruddy, auburn coat, almost mingled with the pixie dust ethereal gray of the other, completely at ease with one another for once, as the tension of uncertainty disappeared. After a couple of minutes, Elani raised her head as Kipp gently edged away from her body. I lifted my eyebrows in query.

"I gathered distinct impressions of when Kipp was a puppy and how he felt about his mother, his pain and, well, fear, when she died and left him alone. He always yearns for her, on some level, as well as his father. After his father went missing, he felt responsible to be strong and brave for his mother. And his amazement as well as relief upon finding you, Petra, his utter loyalty and love for you is like no other I've seen." Elani paused. "It was harder with Kipp, and I'm not sure if that is because he is a fellow lupine or due to his personality construction."

Or because you are in love with him, I thought to myself, glad that Kipp, momentarily, was not actively monitoring my brain. "I doubt you need to repeat this with Peter," I remarked. "With the amount of contact you've had in bonding, you would have reflexively had to explore him."

Elani nodded, and the room fell quiet, the only noise coming from the streets. There was an escalation of the sounds, and Peter walked to the window to view the street below.

"There are drovers herding cattle," he remarked almost offhandedly. "Going to the mall to be held for the war effort." Peter laughed softly. "The beasts escaped from the main herd, and the men have been after them, going up and down side streets trying to get them back in control. To say they are unhappy is an understatement."

I knew he was trying to change the tone of the room, but there was business to be settled. "Let's talk about the ethics of this, Elani. Your ability, in my view, is no more of a potential violation of another than is our telepathy. I have experienced the intrusive, violent type of telepathy that was inflicted upon me where another symbiont went into my mind and tore my thoughts from me." I glanced at Kipp, who nodded his head. "Fortunately, Kipp was there to block that process and rescue me."

"When did this happen?" Elani asked.

"During a trip to Tombstone," I replied. "But I've experienced other unethical intrusions in my lifetime, too. Such occurences are partially why symbionts are required to gain permission to access one another's thoughts. It's almost like knocking on a door before entering."

"You and Kipp don't do that with one another," she replied. "You are constantly in each other's thoughts."

"Yes, because we made a decision to follow the actions that would be normal for Kipp. And now I can't imagine him not having complete access to my mind. When he removes himself, I feel as if part of my soul is missing." As I spoke, I realized the truth of what I said and how integral Kipp had become to my life. As great as had been my love for my former partner, Tula, my relationship with Kipp was different in that it eclipsed love and trust to go even further to a place difficult to define. "But Elani, if you think about it, you've had the self-control to block this intrusion with your peers, so it is no different than if I choose to not, let's say, force myself into the hidden thoughts of Philo. You've been doing the, uh, right thing, all along."

She visibly relaxed at my words, and almost as if she wanted to reassure us that she was okay, she began to groom her forepaws with a pink tongue. That didn't last long because another issue was growing in her mind. "Peter, I think we will make a stronger team if we work to develop the type of relationship that Kipp and Petra have with each other." Her eyes met his across the room. "It follows what is natural for us as a species, and I think if we make the choice to be bonded and travel and engage in dangerous work, we need all the talents available to us."

I was still hunched on the floor and had, in a rather unladylike move considering the times, pulled my knees up to my chest and wrapped my arms about them. It was so warm in that parlor that I had the thought we might be better off to leave our small, unheated bedrooms and sleep on the parlor floor. But then, there was Kipp, my own personal heat source.

Peter looked older as he contemplated her words. The facial hair drove some of that impression, but it was more: Peter was rapidly maturing in his thoughts and behaviors. His fingers drifted down to the watch chain again as his fingertips found the cold metal. "Elani, I'd like that, too," he replied simply.

SEVENTEEN

The next day, we prepared to finish settling in, and a trip to a dry goods store was first on our agenda. We'd gathered in the street-level kitchen where Peter and the lupines ate the remains of the previous afternoon's delivered food from the kitchen of the National Hotel. I nibbled on some bread and cheese that'd accompanied the meal, which had consisted of a great deal of meat. True, I could eat meat, but made other choices when my survival was not at stake.

It had actually not been too bad temperature-wise, lying in the tiny room with Kipp, who did keep me warm. But the room had the feel of a closet, and I awoke, more than once, in confusion, thinking the walls were closing in to collapse upon me. Kipp would press his muzzle against my cheek or neck, his nose moist against my flesh, to give me comfort and help me drift off again into a dreamless sleep.

We ventured out, the early morning chill striking me rather harshly, contrasted against the relative warmth of the townhouse, thanks to Mr. Garland's coal and wood-burning stoves. The sky above was a bright, cloudless blue, and I was grateful for the absence of falling moisture, thinking of the sleet and rain that had met us upon our arrival. Peter asked a passing gentleman for directions to a store that might serve our needs, and we were told to go to New York

Avenue, where we would find more than one place to shop. I was delighted, since I'd read about a famous toy shop owned by Joseph Stuntz that was on the north side of that street. The avenues of Washington were crowded, even more so with the influx of people due to the war. Thousands of former slaves flocked to the city seeking protection and refuge as well as employment, since many of the men were skilled laborers, and the women were highly sought-after for their valuable domestic skills. I'd read of Mary Keckley, who was one of the most talented seamstresses in Washington, fashioning gowns for the elite women of the day. She became Mary Todd Lincoln's almost constant companion and nursed her through the loss of Willie, who died in 1862. Mary Keckley learned to read and write and purchased her own freedom, no doubt a woman to command respect. Also, the capitol was filled to the brim with people who served the war industry. In addition to the actual soldiers, there were the contractors and the others who made certain there was food, clothing, ammunition, and housing, as well as overseeing all the other hundreds of moving parts. A line of soldiers marched past, their arms swinging in rhythm to their footsteps, their jaunty kepi hats bobbing in unison. Their minds were easy to unravel...thoughts of loved ones, home, returning to a previous life that seemed almost out of reach... sad thoughts mingled with notions of hope. One young man—little more than a boy—glanced at our odd party, which was an attention-getter due to the lupines, and a crooked smile twisted his face before he assumed the rigid mask of the soldier in formation. I did pick up the soft tune of someone humming *Lorena*, the sound drifting across the crowded street to the corner where we waited to cross.

"What makes people willing to fight against other humans?" Elani asked. After she'd made her physical empathetic connection with me, something had changed between us, and I felt a closeness that I'd not felt before. We were totally at ease with one another. For a flash, I wondered how she and Kipp were proceeding with their relationship since she'd also had the same exercise with him.

"Some of these men are conscripted and are forced to fight." Peter lifted his head and gazed at the column, which was disap-pearing from view. "New immigrants were sometimes met fresh off the boat and told that as an exchange for citizenship, they would have to join the army. And then there were many who fought due to their conscience, feeling they had a responsibility to defend their county."

"I know the historical reasons, Peter," Elani responded, her tone patient, "but that is not my question. How does one actually take an action that can end the life of another human?"

I reached down, finding the hidden topknot of her skull underneath the fur covering her head, my fingers curling around to scratch the underside of her jaw. "Elani, sometimes people are put in a situation where they must act, or their life is forfeit. They don't have a choice. But humans I've known who have to do such things, find it a sobering event and one they don't take lightly. It sometimes haunts them for the rest of their lives."

Thinking that Elani was getting caught in the quicksand-like mire of the human condition, I drew her attention to the toy store that was famous in its day. We'd made it to New York Avenue, and the windows of the two-story Stuntz house were filled with the delightful handmade toys about which I'd read. Drawing closer, Kipp seemed mesmerized by a porcelain doll that beckoned to him from the street-level window. His breath, from his mouth and nostrils, began to cast a foggy circle on the glass. I almost had to physically drag him away, so captivated was he, so that we could make our way to the general goods store that was another block distant.

A bell tinkled brightly as we entered, and the lupines were quick to drop to the floor next to the door, making themselves into as small a couple of bundles of fur as was possible. The storekeeper, a middle-aged man wearing a white apron stretched across his barrel chest, frowned and opened his mouth to protest, but Peter bounded across to the counter and announced we needed to pick up a significant number of items and needed his assistance. The man's expression immediately changed, proving, once again, that money is the great equalizer. While Peter grazed throughout the men's ready wear section, I picked out a dressing gown, another chemise, a couple of plain blouses, and a few other items. For some reason, I'd left home without a hairbrush, so I got that, too, as well as a wide-toothed comb so I could groom the lupines.

As Peter was negotiating some canned goods and dried meats, I made the circuit of the kitchen goods and found a pretty tea set. Unfamiliar with the pattern, I traced with my fingertip a trail of tiny daffodils that danced around the potbelly of the teapot, noticing the little flowers wound their way into the bottom of the delicate cups, to rest there, staring up at me with their happy faces. Biting my lip, I pulled away, but Kipp's head lifted as he watched me. Before I knew it, Peter had added the tea set to the growing pile of goods, as well as a kettle we could use to heat water on the kitchen stove. It was a little embarrassing to be found coveting the tea set, but it reminded me of home and the wonderful ritual of tea with Fitzhugh.

"It's okay, Petra," Kipp said. "Let's get the tea set. It'll bring you happiness during what could be a difficult time."

"And I like tea, too," Peter said, his face flushing at my startled glance over what had been a simply nice deed between two symbiont collaborators. He casually asked the shop keeper to add a tin of his best tea blend to our bill.

After giving the shop keeper our address to have the items delivered later in the day, we decided to continue walking. The weather, though cool, was tempered by a bright sun hanging overhead that warmed the fur on the lupine's backs. Kipp and Elani had become restless due to a lack of action, and a long walk seemed in order.

"I'd really like to see the White House," Elani announced. She sounded, in that moment, like an out of town tourist ready to see the sights.

Since she was never one to be pushy, I wanted to accommodate her, and the walk would do us all good. We continued on New York Avenue, heading roughly southwest, dodging overburdened wagons, men in military uniforms, and everyday laborers about their business. The street was fortunately constructed of macadam, and we were spared some of the muddiness that had seemed to plague our journey to date. The sky above remained cloudless, the dome of blue arching from horizon to horizon with only the slightest breath of wind on the air. As a miniscule breeze curved around my face, a tendril of hair fell across my forehead. I tried, in vain, to tuck the hair back up under my hat, but it persisted in tickling my brow as if someone was teasing my flesh with a bird's feather.

"Look!" Peter exclaimed, literally stopping in his tracks while raising his arm to point ahead. Directly in our path was the White House, similar in form to the contemporary one but without all the fences, barriers, and other modern necessities. I wondered if the lawn would have any hope of being green in the summer, so trampled had it become by the ongoing flood of visitors and supplicants. Even now, there were numbers of people standing outside waiting, their feet restlessly shuffling as they waited, I suppose, for an audience with someone important.

I glanced to my right to mark the spot of the Seward house where the ghastly attack upon the then secretary of state would occur simultaneously with Lincoln's assassination. It was quiet, the windows shuttered, as opposed to the bustle of activity at the White House. We decided to make a tight loop and begin walking back towards our new home, since curiosity had brought us, and we had no need to linger. Unexpectedly, I saw a boy—a young boy—running across the lawn of the White House, leading a black and white goat on a tether. The goat didn't look too excited to be pulled around but followed reluctantly, jarring along with a stiff, reluctant gait. The boy's dark head lifted as he caught view of the lupines, who couldn't be inconspicuous if they tried. He began to run, chasing after us, since we'd pretended to not see him.

"Hey, stop!" he cried, running in front of us, goat at his side.

This was another unfortunate moment, and I wondered if our current time-shift was destined for us to unexpectedly collide with the notables of the day. First was John Wilkes Booth. And now, blocking our path was Thomas Lincoln, known as Tad, youngest son of Abraham Lincoln.

"Well, this is great," I muttered to my companions.

"I like your dogs," Tad continued.

"And I like your goat," I replied, feeling the need to engage him since the moment had happened, and we couldn't make it disappear. He was a child, after all.

"I'm Tad," he said, tilting his head as he squinted his eyes half shut against the brightness of the sun. "You're pretty," he added, smiling.

"I'm Petra," I answered. "And you are very handsome."

He laughed again, clearly delighted with my words of praise. History told us that Tad was impulsive, never disciplined, wreaking havoc in the White House, disturbing Cabinet meetings and the like. He wasn't mean spirited, just kind of wild. The loss of his brother, Willie, had deeply disrupted the family, and no doubt Tad suffered from the endless grief of his parents, who indulged his fancies. The few words he'd spoken were not clearly articulated, and it was clear he had some type of speech impediment.

Without asking permission, he boldly stepped forward to touch Kipp's broad head after handing me the goat's tether. Yes, that pretty much fit what had been written about the boy. He was neatly dressed in a black suit with long pants, since it was winter, but I could see him in a pair of knee pants quite easily. I wondered where was the little Union soldier's uniform he was rumored to wear at times.

Reading the mind of Tad was pretty easy for all of us, since he didn't have the quantity of memories set down in his brain as would an adult, as well as his thought processes being less complex. But his mind was surprisingly filled with trauma, mostly due to the death of his brother, and the subsequent havoc that event raised. His mother, Mary, summoned mediums to the White House to try and conjure the spirits of her two dead children; Tad was disturbed by this and terrified by what might be happening behind the closed door during a séance. The fire in the White House stable that had killed his and Willie's ponies was particularly vivid in the thoughts of the boy. Willie's pony was a physical link to the brother he'd lost, and now the little horse was gone, too. It was clear he felt great love for his mother and father, and despite Mary Lincoln's erratic moods and behaviors, she was a doting mother. I couldn't fault Tad for his lack of discipline since his grieving parents gave him little structure. What did one expect from a curious and lively twelve-year-old? On the other hand, I could understand how parents who had lost two children out of four might be less likely to be harsh with the surviving ones. Despite the fact I was supposed to remain detached and analytical, I felt my heart squeeze just a little as I watched the boy.

Tad moved from Kipp to Elani; her dark eyes closed as she concentrated on his physical contact with her. She was engaging in her newly revealed ability to gather impressions as his hands ran over her head and neck. Well, I wasn't sure how the rest of this time-shift would proceed, but it was already proving life-changing for one beautiful lupine named Elani.

"Wait here," Tad ordered, his childish voice sounding a mite imperious. "I'm gonna go get Papa so he can see your dogs." He darted away, leaving me holding the goat's tether.

"Let's get out of here," I said, alarmed. It could disrupt our entire trip if we were to get entangled with people so early on. There was a nearby sapling, so I secured the unhappy goat, and we beat a hasty departure.

We decided to flee along G Street, since it would be less heavily traveled, we figured, than Pennsylvania Avenue. After a hurried dash for three blocks, we paused for a breather. I was accustomed to jogging, but racing along in my heavy skirt was different than in my running clothes, and I admit I was breathless for a few moments.

"Just grateful I'm not wearing a corset," I said, rolling my eyes at Peter, who was likewise trying to breathe at a normal rate.

"Me, too," he responded.

We walked back to our new digs on H Street, and just moments after letting ourselves in through the kitchen-level door, a delivery boy arrived driving a small cart led by an old mule that looked as if it was ready for retirement in a green field full of fragrant clover. As the boy brought the packages inside, I eagerly looked for my tea set and had it unpacked and sitting on the table in short order. It was prettier than I recalled. Now that I had a few items assembled, I glanced at my companions.

"I'll be back in a flash," I said. Kipp started to follow but stopped at the door, his head tilted to one side. It was one of the rare moments he was not plastered at my side.

I grabbed the new woolen shawl I'd picked up at the general store, wrapping it securely about my shoulders. The garment, though lightweight, added immediate warmth to me, and I felt like a baby swaddled in a snuggie of some sort. Elani had selected the color, though the choices were limited, and it was an earthy green which complemented my hazel eyes, or so she said. Dodging a man who was driving a gaggle of geese along the street, using a long stick to prod them along by taking advantage of their natural tendency to move as a group, I crossed over to Mary Surratt's townhouse and climbed the brick staircase to the parlor landing. After making a feeble attempt to straighten my hat, I lifted the door knocker and gave a couple of ladylike taps. Maureen must have been close by, because she almost immediately opened the door, her face showing recognition of me.

"Hello, ma'am," she said, bending her knees in a little curtsey.

"Could you tell Mrs. Surratt I would like to speak with her a moment?" I asked, smiling at the thin girl.

Maureen, after seeing me into the warm parlor, darted away. I looked around the room, contrasting it to the hulk in which I currently resided. It was a rather shocking contrast, but of course our goal was not to impress the neighbors but to establish a spy nook, and that we'd done. We only had a short time before Booth would meet Mary's son for the first time and then the activity in her townhouse would escalate.

Mary Surratt walked into the room, the fresh scent of lavender wafting across the air currents as she moved. Her clothes must have been stored with sachets of crushed flowers or perhaps she was wearing some perfume; my bet was on the sachets, since that was a common practice, and it was wartime, limiting the availability of what might be thought of as luxury items. She smiled, but her face, as before, was guarded.

"Why, Mrs. Holmes, how nice to see you," she breathed, uttering the expected greeting. Her thoughts were not negative, but she was distracted and disturbed, and it only took me a moment of sifting through her mind to discover why. Her son, John, had returned and was in residence upstairs. There had been an altercation between the two that morning, and she still felt the sting of agitation, although she was trying to tamp it down. By her nature, she was not an overly emotional woman and high spirited arguments did not fit with her character. I wish I'd brought Kipp, but it was too late to have that worry. He was still in my head, but it would have been fortuitous for him to be there with me.

Mary and I murmured polite comments back and forth before I got to the point. "Mrs. Surratt, I realize my home is very humble in comparison to yours, but I would like to invite you for tea," I finally managed to say.

"Why, how kind," she replied.

Odd, she actually meant it. From our earlier impressions, we'd gathered she really had few female friends and spent her time with her family as well as managing her business.

"And I'd love for you to bring your daughter, if she is available," I added. Of course, I wasn't being polite. We needed to become familiar with Anna, too.

As Mrs. Surratt asked after our new accommodations and the like, I searched the house telepathically until I located John Surratt, who was in his room upstairs. Kipp, who occupied his typical cozy spot in my head, gave me a thumbs-up as he used me as a bridge to do his own quick survey that would help both of us to recognize the man in the future. I felt a beading of sweat dampen my forehead, such was the effort for me to canvass that dwelling to locate one man amongst others.

After Mary agreed to visit me on the following day for late morning tea, since she had obligations in the afternoon, I begged to take my leave. Thankfully the geese were gone, although they'd left their, uh, mark upon the street, and I had to pull up my skirts a little higher to avoid dancing upon the landmines. Perhaps there would be more rain that night to cleanse the area.

"You should have had me with you," Kipp greeted me, as I breezed through the doorway. "John Surratt is there, and I could have started work." He actually was pouting a little.

"Kipp, I know Mrs. Surratt is not keen on having dogs in her house. I was trying to not push it. But if we can get her and her daughter over here, in our house, we will have an opportunity to get more information." I mock glared at him, hands on my hips. "Okay?"

"Well, I guess so," he grumbled. "I don't like being left out."

Elani seemed to know how to get him out of his moods, and she hopped up from her place in front of the stove and, after biting him rather fiercely upon his left haunch, took off up the stairs, Kipp in hot pursuit. Peter and I exchanged looks as we heard the heavy footsteps tromping on the worn flooring above us; I grimaced when I heard something crash to the floor with a heavy thump.

I raised my eyebrows at Peter. "Kids."

EIGHTEEN

ven though my ego did not need to be stroked by having a
parlor as well-appointed as the one of Mary Surratt, I did put
Peter to work moving the sparse furnishings to best compliment the
beaten, weathered room. I wanted it to look nice, I suppose, and
perhaps that reflected a personal vanity. He even lit a candle that
managed to fill the room with the soft scent of juniper, which
diverted one's attention from the otherwise funky smell of rotting
timber and mildew. While Kipp and I planned on entertaining and
simultaneously sifting through the minds of our neighbors, Peter
and Elani would travel to Pumphrey's stable, which was located on a
diagonal across from The National Hotel. We still had time to
explore the city and surrounding countryside, waiting, as it were,
until December 23rd. Peter endeavored to hire a carriage for us so
that we could get clear of the congestion of Washington and,
perhaps, find a nice piece of land upon which the lupines could
stretch their legs. Kipp, particularly, was feeling too confined. His
heavily muscled body needed regular exercise and playing tag with
Elani in the townhouse wasn't sufficient. With no effort, I could feel
his built-up tension mounting.

I'd decided to wear one of my new readymade blouses, which
had a softly rounded collar upon which Harrow's pearls could rest

for all eyes to see. They were a lovely strand and added an elegant touch to the blouse, which was beyond plain. Kipp confessed to feeling a mite anxious, a very rare occurrence for him, so I tried to soothe him by combing him and smoothing his thick fur coat. He finally found a patch of sunlight cascading in through the parlor windows and, after trampling down a bed of imaginary leaves, circled and plopped to the floor with a big sigh. There was a tap on the front door.

"It's go time," Kipp said, opening one amber eye to stare at me.

"Where on earth did you hear that?" I asked.

"A movie I was watching," Kipp replied, stretching his jaws wide with a big yawn. I fancied I could see halfway down to his stomach.

Mrs. Surratt, looking cool and composed as she had before, stood at my doorway, her daughter, Anna, at her side. Anna was a pretty young lady, and although I could see her mother's features in her face, they were softer, more feminine, and her chin had a fetching little dimple. As I ushered them past the threshold, they both cast discreetly curious glances about the foyer as well as the parlor as we entered. Following their thoughts, I recognized their shock at how shabby was the dwelling and some degree of horror that I'd made it my home. But none of this was evident on their faces.

"Why, Mrs. Holmes," Mrs. Surratt purred, "I see you have been at work." She smiled, and after surreptitiously checking the surface of the loveseat, sat and folded her hands in her lap. She was wearing the dark clothes of a widow, although she was past the requisite time for mourning, I thought. Maybe dark was simply her choice.

"Yes," I replied. "The furnishings, which are not ours, of course, are terribly worn, but the rooms we occupy are clean, and Mr. Garland keeps us supplied with plenty of coal and wood, so it is delightfully warm."

Anna had to bite back her tongue as something that would have been rude almost made it past her full, well-shaped lips. She wasn't an ill mannered girl, but the poor condition of the townhouse was startling to her. Veiling my eyes, I allowed myself to inspect her. Anna had dark hair like her mother, and the thick mass was intricately coiled and twisted to the back of her head. She was wearing a pert little hat that was more for decoration than any utilitarian purpose of which I could think. She glanced across the room and almost gave a start when she saw the enormous form of Kipp lying in the patch of golden sunlight.

"Oh, my," she said. "He is a large dog, isn't he?"

Mary gave her a withering look, no doubt having worked for years to teach the girl the value of deferential manners and polite discourse. It would be, no doubt, seen as impertinent to remark upon anything found in the house of a host unless invited to do so.

Kipp, just to show off, took that opportunity to stand and make a big production of stretching and yawning—all teeth exposed— before assuming his position on the floor again. Somehow, he managed to make his bunched-up shoulder muscles ripple in the filtered sunlight for an additional exhibition of his wonderfulness. "Do you think she liked that?" he murmured to me. "I've got more if she wants to be impressed."

I suppressed a laugh with a big hiccup, and covering my mouth I excused myself to race downstairs for my daffodil tea service. It was good to momentarily get away from Kipp, who appeared to want to make me break concentration, and, besides, I was oddly excited to be able to show off the pretty set of patterned daffodil china. As I balanced everything and began the trek back up the narrow stair-case, the steps of which groaned and creaked under my feet, I hoped I wouldn't do a classic Petra clumsy whoops and end up at the bottom of the stairs with the broken pieces of the tea set on the floor, the remains of a tea cup resting gently upon my head like a little porcelain beret.

"Don't fall," Kipp called to me. He was needling me for some reason.

"Oh, Mrs. Holmes, what a lovely tea service!" Mary Surratt cried, meaning it, as I set the tray on the pitiful table that acted as a centerpiece of the room. Peter had shoved a little piece of wood beneath one of the legs so the table wouldn't wobble so badly.

"Thank you, Mrs. Surratt," I replied. "My brother insisted that we purchase it so that I could be surrounded by a few of the finer things." I smiled, trying not to show my teeth. Deliberately I patted the pearls at my neck, making it appear to be an unconscious gesture.

"Oh, have mercy!" Kipp groaned, rolling his eyes.

As I served tea to Mary and Anna, Kipp was busy at work, and he and I were exchanging thoughts with the rapid back and forth to which we were accustomed. And as I communicated with the humans in my midst, I simultaneously spoke with Kipp as we traded off impressions. Kipp's ability to go deeper than the surface was critical, and I was just thankful he was my partner.

"Mary and her son, John, had a huge argument this morning, and the vibrations of that argument still resonate within her." Kipp took a deep breath. "Mary's husband, John's father, made poor financial decisions and also was one of those humans who value alcohol over other things. He died, and Mary feels she has done the best she could to secure safety and security for her family. But John is engaged in things she fears, even though she believes the Confederacy has the right to leave the Union."

Indeed, her thoughts, feeling the sting of what must have been a loud and unpleasant fight, were easily apparent to me, and I was barely making an effort. It was tempting for me to be lazy with Kipp around to do the heavy lifting. But it was clear she was furious at John for putting himself and the entire family in jeopardy…he was a spy working for the Confederacy, that much she had determined. But he kept many things from her in the event she was questioned. So, while she wanted the South to be successful in its attempt to form a new nation, she didn't want her son taking risks to make that happen. Mary Surratt would prefer the burden fall upon other loyalists and leave her family untouched.

"I wonder why she supports the Confederacy?" I mused.

"I guess everyone was being forced to take a stand, and she and her husband were Confederate sympathizers and entertained like-minded people at their tavern before she became a widow and moved to Washington," Kipp replied. "She was born in Maryland, which although Union had a great division amongst its people over the war, and she was educated in Virginia. Beyond just going along with what she grew up being told and what she experienced, I don't know that I can ferret out a particular causative moment."

Not wanting him to get mired in the shifting quicksand of human thoughts looking for something that really didn't matter, since we were dealing with the here and now of Mary Surratt and not what necessarily brought her to this place, I gave him a mental hug and told him to move on.

"Anna feels less strongly and actually has some feelings of resentment that her mother seems so attached to John. For her part, Anna is angry at John and worries his activities will bring emotional pain to her mother." Kipp turned his head, his amber eyes finding mine. "Jealousy is a powerful human driver, isn't it?"

"Yes, Kipp. But while there are many human emotions we truly don't understand, symbionts are not immune to jealousy and must guard against it, just as must humans." I wasn't trying to be preachy, just stating my opinion. Kipp wasn't jealous of anyone or anything, so I had no worries there. If anything, I needed to be more concerned over my own potential fall from grace.

"It's good they came, however, because just by following their thoughts and examining their memories, I think I can identify John Surratt easily. He has become familiar to me through them." Kipp laid his head down, resting his chin on his forepaws. Even though his eyes closed and his body was still, his mind was alert, unclouded with worry, and following all the transactions, both spoken and unspoken.

"Do you have any pastimes that you enjoy?" Mary was truly curious about me, that much was evident. She seemed to sense my oddness in world where the role of women was predictable.

"I like to read, and I've been known to do a little needlepoint," I replied with a self-conscious laugh.

She smiled, nodding. "I will send over a lovely piece I'd begun but will never finish. Perhaps you'll enjoy having it to work on during these dreary winter days."

"Needlepoint!" Kipp exclaimed. "What in the world is that?" As I formed a picture in my mind, he almost snorted a laugh. "You! Ha, ha!"

Ignoring Kipp was becoming a challenge. With great effort, I redirected my attention to Mary Surratt. "How very thoughtful, Mrs. Surratt. I will enjoy having something with which to occupy myself. Idle hands are the Devil's workshop, are they not?" Following her thoughts, I recognized her concern over her failing eyesight, which was the reason she had been unable to finish the piece. So the historical references about her poor vision had a factual basis, after all.

It was clear Anna was bored and ready to move on. No, she was not in any way rude, but she kept shifting positions and staring out the front window. She was young, and listening to us prattle on about teacups and needlepoint was pretty dull. Mary, no doubt, deciphered her daughter's body language and began wrapping up the visit.

"May I beg one favor of you?" I asked, as the three of us stood. When Mary nodded her head, I said, "Do you know of a local woman who takes in laundry and such?"

"My house girl—Maureen—well, her mother does laundry and other services for many people on this street. I'll be delighted to ask Maureen to stop by on her way home and let you make the needed inquiries." Mary Surratt smiled, pleased with her ability to help me.

As the front door shut behind them, I returned to the parlor window, which overlooked the street, and watched them walk back to their townhouse, their hats bobbing along amongst the people who were in transit. Kipp thumped his tail, clearly trying to make up after his, uh, needling me about the needlepoint.

"I forget, Petra, how old you are," he began before stuttering to a stop. "No, wait, that came out wrong. I meant to say that with your age, you have experienced a lot of things that the rest of us haven't."

Somehow, that clarifying remark didn't help my feelings, and I waved my hands in his face, picked up the tea service, and carefully navigated the narrow stairs, Kipp following closely. We'd just made it to the ground level kitchen when Peter and Elani burst through the doorway, fortunately making it inside before the rain arrived as if dropped by a bucket. Peter shrugged off his coat and threw his hat on the table, while Elani shook off the few raindrops that had found their way to her dense coat. The cold air from outside had chased them inside, fighting with the warmth of the stove for supremacy. The kettle was still hot, so after motioning Peter to take a seat, I started on another pot of tea.

"You guys will never believe who we saw at Pumphrey's stable," Peter began, his eyes almost bugging out of his head with excitement. "We were making arrangements for a carriage, when in walked Lewis Powell! We immediately recognized him from the pictures taken while he was being held prior to his execution." He paused for a second. "Of course, we made ourselves inconspicuous, and I acted like I was examining a horse, so he paid us no attention."

"Considering the brutality of what he does to William Seward, it felt odd standing close to him, listening to him exchange pleasantries with the stable hand," Elani said. "Powell had to have a vicious nature based upon his later actions."

I was hoping the two of them did more than just register amazement and a moment later was ashamed of my thoughts, which had given them no credit for thinking proactively. Peter's face had a glow, and I'd seen that before when he was feeling pretty good about himself. Once upon a time, I'd seen that glow on my face, too.

"We both concentrated on his thoughts and will be able to identify him when he makes his way to Surratt's boarding house." Peter nodded and the glow intensified. He was waiting for something.

"Great work," Kipp said, wagging his tail. "We have a good start on being able to piece together some of these fragments when the people start to converge." He stared hard at me, wondering why I was not being more supportive of the young duo. "We have met John Wilkes Booth, Mary Surratt, Anna Surratt, Lewis Powell, and I think I have a handle on John Surratt."

"Don't forget Tad Lincoln," I added, feeling cantankerous for no particular reason.

Kipp stared at me again. Sighing, I smiled at Peter. "Some of the best moments in our line of work are just coincidence, and it does really help our ongoing effort that you could mark Powell." I avoided saying "good job" since I felt no need to hand out treat biscuits every time Peter did what was expected of him.

"What the heck is wrong with you?" Kipp asked me privately. With effort he suppressed a soft growl as he stared at me.

"I'm old, remember, and with that comes the privilege of being irritable, grumpy and just plain old cantankerous," I replied airily. "I've decided to take a page from Fitzhugh's playbook," I added, just to put a period on the point I was making.

We talked again, but it wasn't until later that night, as Kipp and I had retired to our narrow bed in the tiny bedroom. I'd blown out the flame from the oil lamp, and the acrid smell of the smoke and the lingering odor from the oil floated in the air, filling the small room. Kipp snuggled closer than usual, partially due to the size of the bed and also because he seemed to think I needed something from him.

"What's wrong?" he asked again.

I wanted to avoid his question and desperately wanted to go to sleep. But I knew he would stay in my brain, burrowing like a tick until I talked with him.

"I just don't want to run around after Peter and Elani telling them what a great job they are doing all the time," I answered, the words sounding churlish and unkind even as I spoke them. But there was no way to sugar coat things, since Kipp was in my head and knew the honesty of my thoughts. There was no way to lie to him. That is either a downside of being a telepath or an advantage, depending upon the day of the week.

He fell quiet, his muzzle stretched across my chest. Idly, my fingers found his neck, and I began to massage the thick muscles, which seemed a little tense. Had I caused him to worry? Outside, a loud roll of thunder rumbled, and I heard the rain intensify. If this carried on through tomorrow, it would be a good day to camp out, monitor the Surratt's from across the street, and do little to nothing. Maybe drink a couple of pots of hot tea? I wish we could have brought the Monopoly or Clue set with us. The days could prove to be long, and close confinement could worry away at one's otherwise good intentions.

"But that's not really what's bothering you, is it?" Kipp asked, his words soft in my mind. He was being unusually tentative.

"What could it be?"

"You worry, on some level, that you will become irrelevant," he finally said, stumbling over his words. "Here you are, with a young team who have barely traveled, and they are mastering things at a quicker pace than you did when you were their age. What will be left for you to teach?" He obviously reflected back to our discussion about jealousy. "You aren't jealous and are proud of them, but you wonder what it means to you as an older symbiont…and no, you're not old, Petra, so I was just kidding about the needlepoint thing. But you are older than Peter and have been questioning how much longer you want to travel for some time." He pushed his chin harder against my chest. "It probably gets irritating to have him running around, all excited, bright-eyed and bushy-tailed."

I admit it was startling to have it laid out in just that matter-of-fact manner, and the truth stung. But it was true, and when I examined myself at that moment, what I found wasn't pretty. I felt my lips turn down as I considered that I was being selfish, a quality I didn't appreciate in others, and even less so in myself.

"I don't think you are selfish," Kipp said hurriedly. "I think you are struggling with your job as a mentor, wondering what more will there be for you to share once Peter and Elani have learned what there is to learn." He paused. "Actually, I've had similar thoughts."

"Really?" I asked, turning my face towards his in the darkness. His breath was warm on my flesh, and I felt the hair curling along my cheek stir.

"Yes, and I'm not just saying that to make you feel better. Elani has a novel skill that will make her unique and needing me to do my deep, mental dives may become obsolete." Kipp sighed. "I know I'm not old, but sometimes I feel it, compared to her." Actually, if one considered that he was born in prehistoric times, he was older than any living symbiont, but that fact seemed an irrelevant technicality.

I hugged him tightly. "Our challenge, my friend, is to figure out how to evolve as our young team eclipses us with their energy, drive, and, yes, even skill level with many things. Although, Kipp, no symbiont will ever match or exceed your skills, and that's a fact."

He bowed his head modestly. "That remains to be seen," he replied cryptically.

"Can I sleep now?" I asked.

"Yup," he replied.

A crack of thunder sounded outside, causing the glass base of the oil lamp to tremble upon the tabletop. It was good Mr. Garland had made emergency repairs to the roof, since I had no desire to wake up in a puddle of water from rain that had managed to cascade down from the upper levels. Yes, tomorrow would be a good day to huddle and monitor activity.

NINETEEN

Peter made one purchase during our shopping spree, and I'd not paid attention to the wrapped package until we gathered in the parlor the next day. The rain was coming down outside in opaque sheets of gray, intermittently obscuring our view of Mary Surratt's home, which loomed darkly like an abandoned hulk across the way. And while we didn't venture outside, the four of us kept our radar tuned for any action, but it appeared the Surratt household was as reluctant to venture forth as were we. The thoughts of the occupants were quiescent, still as a pool of calm water. On the well-used table in the weathered parlor set a chess set, Peter's surprise acquisition.

"What's this?" Elani asked, walking over to touch the white rook with her nose, nostrils flaring.

"I knew we didn't have any other games with us, so I thought it would be a good time for the lupines to learn chess. Petra, you know how to play, don't you?" Peter's face had that worried expression he sometimes wore when he wasn't certain of an answer as he waited for my response.

"Yes, although I'm barely adequate." I responded.

"I'm pretty good," Peter said modestly, although I suspected he was better than that. "I thought we could teach Kipp and Elani and let them play with us moving the pieces and collaborating."

Kipp looked at me. "If you are barely adequate, and Peter is pretty good, do I get to choose my partner?" He was clearly being a stinker.

"I think we have plenty of time to trade off," I replied airily. "And how do you know I don't prefer Elani anyway? After all, girls rule!"

"You got that right," Elani huffed, breathing hard, glaring at Kipp.

"Actually, trading off is a good thing," Peter inserted smoothly with a surprising diplomatic turn that I'd not seen before. "That way, Kipp and Elani can learn from both of us and then develop their own unique approaches to the game."

I felt mildly vexed I'd not thought of that myself, but it was too late, and if I tried to say anything as a recovery statement, I'd look immature and defensive. There was a distinct part of me that longed for a cup of Earl Grey to share with Fitzhugh. He'd become an unexpectedly solid confidant. Maybe his age gave him that ability, since he'd lived long enough to see and hear it all and rarely could surprise creep up upon him, like a stealthy cat stalking prey.

I prepared the tea service for Peter and me and loaded the tray with tea cakes, freshly baked courtesy of Maureen's mother, thinking the lupines would enjoy a snack, too. Peter kindly offered to carry the tray, which was a plus since he didn't have to navigate the creaky stairs while tugging on the edge of a long skirt. As I followed him up, I could hear the soft wheek wheek sound of his woolen britches. I hoped he didn't plan on any covert operations where silence was a must. He pulled two chairs to the table and took two pawns, one white and one black, and held his hands behind his back.

"Choose," Peter said, smiling.

I tapped his right arm and was rewarded with the black pawn. Despite our earlier exchanges, Kipp reflexively came to my side while Elani went to Peter. Then, Peter and I took turns explaining the various moves of the pieces. Of course, being telepaths, we were honor bound to not peek at each other's thoughts as to gain an unfair advantage. And it was probably good Kipp was my partner, because we quickly found that Peter was actually very good, and I was not even adequate. I enjoyed chess, and always had, but played like a child, just making impulsive moves because I liked to see my pieces soar dramatically across the board. Peter played with the needed calculation and ability to see what would transpire three or four moves in advance. In addition, he was my superior in terms of competitiveness, since I'd lost that quality a couple of hundred years ago. So, during the first game, Kipp and I got our butts whipped. Elani looked up at me, her chocolate eyes brimming with sensitivity and emotion. I knew she wanted to apologize, but I just winked at her. She didn't have the heart of a shark.

"Do you want to play with Peter this time?" I asked Kipp, knowing his competitive nature.

"No, you and I are gonna master this," he replied, his voice confident and sounding a little tough. He was probably channeling the inner, primitive Kipp who once hunted the prehistoric tundra on the continual search for survival. That particular Kipp was relatively unbeatable.

I wonder if all those who play chess enjoy certain pieces. As I observed my companions, I noticed Elani seemed to have a fondness for the bishop, while Kipp liked the intricate move patterns of the knight, which had the surprise attack quality of a ninja. Simple symbiont that I am, I liked the rook, which reminded me of an old-fashioned ashtray as it blundered along in a straight, unimaginative line. Peter was talented enough to use all the pieces to the utmost, even the little pawn.

Kipp and I were on our way to victory—with me leaning heavily on an aggressive Kipp—when a tap sounded on the down-stairs street-level door. Peter raced down, his footsteps loud and echoing on the staircase, and a minute later shouted that the delivered lunch had arrived. The lupines began to salivate as the fragrance of the food drifted up a level to the parlor. So, we paused for all to convene in the delightfully warm kitchen, which had an intimacy lacking in the well-lit parlor room.

"What is this?" Kipp asked, his eyes widening at a hunk of meat that had been seared and was covered in tiny potatoes and carrots.

He'd eaten beef before, but this was marinated in red wine and had a distinctive scent.

"Beef roast," I answered, trying not to laugh at the expression on his face. I hoped the chef had not used too much wine since an inebriated Kipp could prove to be difficult to handle.

Kipp and Elani, single-handedly, polished off three quarters of the roast, leaving a little wedge for Peter. I stuck to my vegetables as usual, enjoying some sliced fresh-baked bread, also courtesy of Maureen Fitzgerald's mother. She'd become a valuable player for us, with her availability to do our laundry and also supplementing our diets. We'd not even asked her about cooking for us; she was simply a smart entrepreneur and offered, tempting us first with some wonderful fresh-baked goods. And we paid her very hand-somely, so she appreciated us in kind.

The torrential rain continued, and as the temperature hovered around freezing and occasionally dipped below, the precipitation would occasionally turn to sleet and even snow, the latter of which always fascinated Kipp. So, we lingered in the townhouse, seduced by the warmth from the stoves as well as keeping our bellies full with food. We napped and played chess, and I grew so lazy that it was rather embarrassing. And it was easy to lose track of time, but we didn't and realized that the fateful meeting between John Wilkes Booth and John Surratt was less than a week away. When that occurred, my laziness would have to transform into action, I reminded myself sternly.

We awoke to find the skies blue once again, and the temperature outside was tolerable, with a bright sun that had finally broken free on the eastern horizon. The three days of being confined with one another had led to the lupines becoming restless, and Peter and I grew irritated with the small things, such as how he sipped his tea and how I ate the homemade bread supplied by Mrs. Fitzgerald. I'm not sure why pulling the bread apart with my fingers and studying each morsel from different angles before popping it into my mouth agitated him, but it clearly did.

"If I don't get outside and run around some, I'm gonna explode," Kipp finally admitted. "Being stuck here, waiting, is driving me nuts."

Since the rest of us felt the same, there were no apologies needed or given, and Peter put on his coat and hat. "I'm going to rent us a horse and buggy for the day," he said. "We'll ride out in the country and enjoy the land as well as get some exercise."

"Do you know how to drive a horse and buggy?" I asked, hoping there was at least one thing over which I would be his master.

"Well, to prepare for this trip, I went to a local stable in Durham and took riding lessons as well as learning how to drive a horse pulling a trap. So, yes, I think I'll manage," he replied, his tone just a smidgen sharp.

Kipp stared at me, turning his head slightly, watching my face. After our talk about my becoming irrelevant, he knew my thoughts without having to pry. Kipp was waiting for me, I knew.

"Peter, that's great," I finally replied, somewhat surprised to find that I actually meant it. "Preparing for all eventualities is important to what we do, and I'm glad to see you were thinking ahead."

With a pleased flush on his cheeks, he grabbed his hat and disappeared out the front door, Elani at his side, her tail wagging with pleasure. As his bonded companion, she was rightly proud of his accomplishments and growth.

"So, how was that for you?" Kipp asked, making his way to the kitchen stove where he circled and plopped to the floor where the wooden planks were warmed by the lingering fire. With a soft sigh, he rested his big head on his outstretched paws.

"Okay," I replied, sitting at the table. "I think our talk about how I was feeling helped me, Kipp. And I actually thought about past mentors when I was just learning and how they encouraged me, even when I was surpassing what their abilities allowed. I realized it was selfish of me to worry about my need to gear back a little while Peter is in such a growth phase."

"Well, if you listen to me more often, issues such as this can be easily managed," he replied smugly, licking his forepaws as if to put a period on the discussion.

Peter actually proved to be a very competent driver, threading a narrow path through the congested streets, as we headed north on Vermont Avenue, which, we all knew, lead to the Soldiers' Home. It was only a brief interval before the bustle and congestion of Washington dropped away, and we were in the countryside on a dirt road that smacked of rural America. The thick, noxious air of the city dissipated, and I inhaled deeply, smelling the scent of cedars and woodlands. The woods stretched across the softly rolling hillsides, and when one gazed off into the distance, the trees, which had shed their leaves, faded into a blurred wash of gray, with the deep green of pines and cedars jutting out of the ominous darkness of the forest. Occasionally, I would spy an American Beech, which was a favorite of mine. Their leaves, dead from the change of seasons, still clung to the long, low hanging branches where they trembled in the breeze, the colors shifting as the leaves twisted and turned from weathered silver to dull tan. As a gentle wind from the northeast stirred those pale leaves, they began to chatter, speaking to us as dead things animated to life against an otherwise silent fringe of trees. We saw movement along the edge of the woods as a small group of whitetail deer dashed for the deeper areas of brush, their tails flashing like signal flags as they fled. It was cold that day, and I edged over on the seat of the buggy to link my arm with Peter's. He glanced at me and a tentative smile crossed his face.

"A little brisk," he remarked, lifting a dark eyebrow.

Peter gently eased the mare that was pulling our buggy to a stop so that the lupines could stretch their legs and run, unopposed. I decided to descend also, allowing Peter to take my arm and assist so that my skirts wouldn't cause me to stumble and go flying to the ground. Pulling my woolen shawl closely around my shoulders, I wandered onto the grassy verge, glancing around with curiosity at the flora and fauna, such that it was, that inhabited the area in 1864. So much of the surrounding territory had been damaged by the war that it was nice to walk on land that remained natural and untouched. Off in the distance, Kipp and Elani were racing along the tree line, his ruddy auburn coat a sharp contrast to the dead foliage, while Elani's ethereal gray blended so well that she seemed to vanish at times. Overhead, a cloud crossed the path of the sun, causing an unexpected darkness to fall across the land before being chased rapidly to disappear beyond the tree line.

Peter grasped my arm, pointing ahead. A man on horseback

approached. He was distant still but coming towards us as a brisk trot. It was clear he would reach us before we could recall the lupines. Peter and I exchanged glances, and I shrugged. We'd just say howdy-do and the man would move on. But as he came closer, I felt a creeping anxiety, almost like a hand clutching my throat. Not again, I thought. Yes, there was a figure dressed in black, wearing a tall, classic stovepipe hat. And his posture on the horse suggested he was a man of great height. As the man pulled his horse to a halt, he stared down at us before seeming to recognize it was ill-mannered to not recognize a lady in his presence.

His face was unmistakable, the face possibly one of the most recognizable in history. As he dismounted from his horse, I marveled over how someone so tall could descend with such grace. It was easy to forget he'd been raised in a home where hard, physical labor was demanded of him and led to a lifetime of strength and agility.

"Well, hello," Abraham Lincoln said, pausing to sweep the tall hat off his head. "It's not often I encounter travelers on this road," he added, smiling. His voice was surprisingly high pitched.

Peter and I exchanged glances and decided to play stupid. "Hello to you, sir," Peter replied, pulling his hat off his head almost as an afterthought. "I'm Peter Keaton, and this is my sister, Petra Holmes." He lifted his arm, pointing to the edge of the woods where the lupines were racing. "We brought our dogs out from the city so they could run a bit."

A breeze ruffled Lincoln's dark hair, which he wore a little long that day, the ends drifting over his collar. I had the idle thought wondering if his wife, Mary, trimmed it for him, betting she did. Wrinkles were set deeply in his flesh, making his complexion uneven. His eyes were gray and direct as he assessed us in his measured, deliberate way. After a brief moment, he turned toward where the lupines stood, gazing back at us. Kipp and Elani were clearly astonished and beat a hasty return to our sides. In my head, I could hear Kipp muttering, "Oh boy, oh boy, oh boy."

"I'm Lincoln," he said, using his preference of being called by his last name. "And you must be the people with the amazing dogs," he added, laughing. "My son, Tad, told me about meeting you." He thrust his hands in the pockets of his frock coat, which was rumpled and looked as if he might have slept in it. I noticed he wore no greatcoat, despite the chill in the air.

Kipp arrived and, after wagging his tail at Lincoln, began his deep dive into the mind of the man. Elani, after a glance at Peter as if gaining his approval, moved close to Lincoln, allowing him to pet her head and thump her sides. Both lupines would share their observations with us at a later time.

"You've caused me a bit of trouble, young man," Lincoln said, laughing again, wagging his finger playfully at Peter. "Tad has bothered me since that day, demanding I find him a puppy." He gazed at Kipp. "I don't think I've seen dogs like these." I watched his long, slender fingers tunnel into Elani's silver-gray fur as he massaged her flesh and gently pulled at her large, upright ears.

"They are Siberian Deerstalkers," I replied, smiling. "Rather rare here, I think."

"Well, I think Tad would be happy with any sort of mongrel," Lincoln remarked. "The goat has not been a sufficient diversion for him." He sighed, and I followed his thoughts to the tragic burning of the White House stable when both Tad and Willie's ponies had been killed. Lincoln was no more able to heal Tad's pain than he was that of his wife. The scars of the burdens were carved into his face, his shoulders carrying both the stress from the ongoing war as well as the injuries to his household.

It became clear that Lincoln was an affable man who liked to, well, chat. His days were filled with conflict, agonizing decisions, and stress, so merely chewing the fat with a couple of strangers was pleasing to him. He was a practiced storyteller, enjoying the expressions on the faces of his audience. His horse, which was pretty unremarkable, seemed to enjoy the rest, too, and leaned its body weight against Lincoln until the man moved. I noticed the horse, a clever beast, moved, too, shifting its weight again against its master.

"And where do you hail from?" Lincoln asked, staring down at me. He was at least a foot taller than was I.

"From Tennessee, sir," I answered. He'd not mentioned he was the president, and I decided to keep my address of him neutral.

"Ah, Tennessee. A beautiful part of the country," he murmured, smiling, but his thoughts were sad when he considered all the scars that had been inflicted due to the war. Lincoln rocked back on his heels, stretching his back slightly.

"And you, young man?" He directed his gray eyes towards Peter, who was trying not to be star struck.

"I just returned fairly recently from London where I worked for the Times," Peter said, lying adroitly. "My sister was in need of companionship, and we hope to make our way out west, perhaps to California."

"I've not been that far west myself, but I hear from people I know"—and he was thinking of Grant as well as Sherman—"that the western coastal areas are quite lovely. There is lots of land to be had for the taking," he added. "However, it is a difficult journey and not for the faint of heart." His head turned, as did ours, as another rider approached from the road he'd just traveled. It was not long before that rider, an unkempt looking man wearing a slouch hat, his coat only half buttoned against his chest, pulled up his horse.

"Mr. President," the man began. "I've asked you to wait for me," he said, almost whining.

"All is well, John," Lincoln answered the man, waving his hand in an irritated gesture. He glanced back at us and raised his shoulders in an almost sheepish gesture and with no explanations.

"That man is John Parker," Peter hissed to me privately, having done his own little detective work.

I immediately took a dislike to the man, since it was due to his neglect on the night of the assassination that Booth had such easy entry to the presidential box at Ford's theater. Later investigations cleared him of any part in the conspiracy, but the timing had been uniquely opportunistic, and if he'd been at his post instead of drinking ale at Taltavul's Star Saloon, there would have been a likely different outcome on that fateful night. The other bodyguard, William Crook, shared my low opinion of Parker, who stared first at Peter then at me with his tiny, red-rimmed, rheumy eyes. He'd already hit the bottle that morning, too, unbeknownst to Lincoln, who seemed to have a neutral opinion of the man.

"Mrs. Lincoln is planning a trip to New York City to shop for gewgaws and other such things, and she has it in her head to take Tad with her. But I might just hatch a little plan of my own, with the help of you two and your pretty doggies," Lincoln said, pursing his lips as he thought. "Tad is awfully recalcitrant in terms of his studies and has made more than one tutor throw up his hands in surrender. I was thinking you, young man, since you are a man of letters," he said, nodding at Peter, "could spend some time with him on his reading and ciphers, the lure being your nice doggies." His gray eyes were drawn upward as a flock of geese flew overhead in a perfect V formation; his lips twitched in a smile as he followed them until they were lost over the wood line. His mind filled with an almost poetic admiration of their freedom and effortless ability to escape the war and all its tribulations.

Peter stared at me, not sure what to do. We'd just had an unexpected curve ball lobbed in our direction and had to take care, lest we alter history in some measurable way. For all our studies, I'd not paid attention to whether or not Tad went with his mother on her grand tour, and it could have gone either way, although I suspected he'd gone. We'd already affected the timeline from our very presence as well as this unfortunate meeting. Kipp and I exchanged glances, and he could have nodded, but he held back.

"Your turn to decide," Kipp said to me. "This is a decision for an experienced traveler, and that's you, Petra."

Of course, I trusted Kipp completely and knew he was not coddling me or giving me a false positive comment just to boost my ego, which seemed to be fragile of late. He spoke from his heart. The temptation to spend some time with Lincoln was overwhelming and none of us would, in our lifetimes, get another chance such as this. But we'd have to be careful, very careful.

I nodded my head at Peter. It seemed we were committed.

TWENTY

"Lincoln is a complicated man," Kipp began.

We were back in the townhouse trying to process what the lupines had gathered from their contact with the man as well as examine our best path to proceed forward. We couldn't allow ourselves to become diverted from our primary focus of this trip, and that was to examine the motives and actions of one Mary Surratt.

"Mary Lincoln is consumed with consulting spiritualists and mediums," Kipp continued, "the like of which bother him, since he is a man of reason. But that being said, there is a degree to which he believes in the prophecy of dreams and portents. There are issues from his childhood which he carries on a daily basis. There is, after all these years, still a nagging resentment and dislike of his father, which he tried unsuccessfully to leave behind. He also has lingering depression over the death of his mother despite the affection he had for his stepmother, who cherished him and encouraged his love of learning."

Kipp rose, walked over to the stove in the parlor and, after circling, plopped down again. He glanced at the front windows, which were covered in early morning frost that spread like fine lace over the rippled, imperfect glass. "For all his gregarious nature, and

he likes people, he has the ability to be calculating in his relationships as well as manipulative. His folksy approach is part genuine
and part something else, I think." Kipp sighed. "His mind is brilliant, and he occasionally is frustrated at those around him who
can't match the way his mind works." He glanced at Elani, wanting
her impressions from her physical fact-gathering abilities.

Elani was stretched out in a faded patch of light that managed
to draw forth the depth of colors hidden in the gray. As I gazed at
her, I fancied I could see some blues, purples, and even pinks lurking
amongst the hairs of her dense pelt. She caught me looking and
wagged her tail. I knew I wasn't half as nice in appearance as she
gazed at my face. She was a pretty girl, while I'd been told on more
than one occasion over my four hundred plus years that my nose
was too big and made my face seem unbalanced. Harrow had liked
it, I recalled, almost with a sniff of disdain at all the others who
hadn't. It was nice to find a man who had cherished the imperfect
and somehow made it perfect in his mind. Love did that sort of
thing.

"He is a good man, wanting to do the right thing for his family
and others," she opined. "I felt this rush of endless curiosity, the
busyness of an eternally questing mind, and, hidden beneath, the
concern that maybe he could fail." She glanced at me. "And there is
a surge of grief, loneliness that is the underpinning of it all. Despite
his being surrounded by others, he has always felt lonely and has a
very small circle of people who he considers to be friends. The spiritual side of his nature is conflicted, too, and he has questions about
what happens after this life."

Reaching to the table, I picked up my daffodil teacup and took a
sip of the rapidly cooling brew. There was the broken half of one of
Mrs. Fitzgerald's wonderful tea cakes, and I crumbled the edge and
took a bite, savoring the gentle wash of sweetness on my tongue.
Peter gestured at the teapot, signaling he could refill my cup, but I
brushed off his gesture. Although we were committed to engage
with Lincoln to some degree, the process worried me.

"I agreed to this because the thought of spending time with such
an important historical figure was simply too compelling to refuse.
But we all must concede this is dangerous territory, and for many

reasons. First, we cannot do anything that will affect the timeline, so our footprint must be cautious, deliberate, and light. And we must remind ourselves that our mandate for this trip is to follow the thoughts and behaviors of Mary Surratt. For all we might like to get diverted, Lincoln is merely a player in this drama." I felt my forehead crumple in a frown. I'd agreed to this potential mess as the elder—allegedly wiser due to my experience—and now had second thoughts.

"Well, I think we did the right thing by telling him that I would be willing to meet with Tad at the Soldiers' Home a few times per week," Peter began. "The White House would be much too visible a place, and we will be less likely to encounter Booth or any of his confederates if we are out of town. True, there was the time when Booth tried to kidnap Lincoln on his way to and from the Soldiers' Home, but there is no evidence that he stalked the actual residence there, and we can try to come and go unseen."

I felt restless and stood, brushing out the wrinkles in my skirt with my hands. "Let's go for a walk," I suggested. "I'd like to see Ford's Theatre."

It was cold, but the sky was clear as we set out. Maybe because the weather was nice and the roads were not their usual muddy selves, there seemed to be an escalation in activity, and people bustled almost shoulder to shoulder to be about their business. We paused as an overloaded wagon passed us carrying fresh-cut pine trees; the scent of pine sap lingered, making a nice contrast to the other less pleasant smells of too many people and animals crowded in too small a place. Thankfully, a weather front had passed through Washington, taking with it the usual pungent odors from the polluted rivers; that smell tended to hover, captured if as within a dome by the low hanging clouds, magnified exponentially when it was raining. The wagon was pulled by a team of draft horses that seemed almost bored with the challenge, their docked tails flicking against their rumps in annoyance. It only took a few minutes before we paused to face the theatre that would house infamy. I lifted my hands to my cheeks, feeling them flush with unexpected emotion. The building had been rebuilt after a fire destroyed the original in 1862. Although it was still early in the day, the taverns which flanked the playhouse on either side—Taltavul's Star Saloon and Greenback Saloon—were already engaged in robust business, and I heard voices fueled by inebriation.

I probably shouldn't have been surprised to see John Wilkes Booth emerge from the theatre, a sheaf of papers in his hands. He was known to collect his mail which was delivered to Ford's, where he was a well-known figure. His head lifted as he saw us, a smile crossing his face in recognition as his eyes met mine.

"Is this coincidence or bad luck?" Peter asked. "We seem to be stumbling over people all the time."

"It's a small town," I replied, shrugging my shoulders while stepping into my role.

"Why, Mrs. Holmes and Mr. Keaton," Booth said, crossing the street to approach us, strolling gracefully. Knowing the rules of the day, he whipped off his hat in respect of my presence. "Such a lovely day made even nicer by meeting the both of you again." Booth's charm offensive was in full display as he leaned forward to grasp Peter's hand in a firm, but not too firm, handshake. It was just the correct pressure expected in conventional society, another sign of a well-practiced man. Booth turned to me and took my hand gently, bowing over it; as he did so, I caught the light fragrance of the pomade in his black hair. I hoped he wouldn't kiss the back of it, and he didn't. I felt myself gently exhale the breath I was holding.

"He's good," Kipp murmured, moving closer to my side. Kipp had a natural protectiveness of me that couldn't be overridden by logic or reason. It was clear he didn't care for Booth as did none of the rest of us. There wasn't much there to like. He was an angry, manipulative man filled with rage and calculation. About the best I could manage would be to feel badly about such a twisted soul and wonder about the loneliness of such a journey in life.

Elani, however, showed what being a symbiont is all about, as she angled next to Booth so she could entice him to stroke her fur. I admired her for sticking to our business. The idea of his hands on me gave me the creeps. Booth, of course, couldn't help himself as he laid his hand lightly upon Elani's soft head and caressed her ears. I watched her eyes drift shut in concentration. Maybe there was one thing positive to say about Booth…he apparently liked dogs.

"May I offer to be of assistance on this beautiful day?" Booth was taking it a bit over the top before I realized why he was so freaking happy. He had received communication from Dr. Mudd and was excited over his anticipated meeting with John Surratt. From his perspective, pieces of the puzzle of his life were quickly falling into place. It was with effort I kept my lips from turning down in a frown.

"Thank you, Mr. Booth, but we have an engagement and chose to walk rather than ride, since the weather is so lovely," Peter smoothly responded.

"Well, you are looking at a fine theatre," Booth remarked, sweeping his hand to indicate Ford's. "I often play here," he said, adding, "I hope to excellent reviews." He laughed with pretend modesty, but it was all an act. At that point in his life, almost every interaction, other than those which reflected his anger at the political situation in the country, was a manipulative effort to be seen as a charming man. But the roiling hatred within him almost wafted off his body as a stench, and it was all I could do not to recoil. Being a telepath in the presence of such people can be a difficult business.

Kipp looked up at him, tilting his head to the side like a curious dog might do. "I still don't get why a person would let his mind get mired in such evil thoughts," he said. "I can't stay with him for long because it makes me feel bad."

I agreed, my hand reaching down to soothe Kipp, running my hand along his broad back. "Don't do it then," I cautioned him. "We probably will only make brief visits to determine his intent and then let him stew." Glancing down at Kipp, I added, "I can't imagine his existence is a happy one. He has no control over the world which, from his perspective, needs attention. His perspective, however, is based on warped and evil notions, so all he can do is spin helplessly, filled with rage."

We were to go to the Soldiers' Home late that afternoon, where Lincoln planned on having Tad brought so that Peter could try and engage the impulsive lad. Mary Lincoln had departed for New York for her shopping spree, and John Wilkes Booth's meeting with John Surratt was a couple of days away. So I felt we were on sound footing to continue as planned. There was a risk we'd be spotted going to and from the home, but the Confederate spies typically would be watching for Lincoln's comings and goings, and we were nobodies. The only stirrings we'd felt from the Surratt household were minor disturbances when Mary and John would argue over his involvement in surreptitious activities for the Confederate government. But all of that was known to us, and John Surratt was not engaged in any active plots involving Booth at that time.

So, as the day began to wind down, we hopped in the hired carriage, and Peter led the horse out of the city, north, for the three-mile trek to the Soldiers' Home. A steady breeze from the north was chilling, and I noticed clouds gathering on the horizon that seemed heavy with the threat of rain. As we moved along, the clouds seemed to dip lower until they clung to the tops of the darkening tree line, the almost black evergreens looking like tent poles holding up the canopy.

The Soldiers' Home was a huge campus comprised of extensive acreage where buildings were in use to house injured soldiers as well as veterans needing care. One building, quaintly called a cottage, had become Lincoln's home away from home and served as the White House during the months when Washington, due to its proximity to a swamp, was unbearable. A man met us at the door, and he introduced himself as John Hay, one of Lincoln's secretaries; he looked like a teenager, his handsome face smooth and unlined, despite the stress of his job and his constant worry over the well being of Lincoln. He was irritated he'd had to bring Tad, feeling like being a baby sitter for the boy was not in his job description. But such was his love for Lincoln as well as his loyalty, that he bit back any arguments and brought the rambunctious boy to the cottage. As we exchanged introductions, I walked into the cottage, amazed that it would be called such. Mary Lincoln had extensively renovated the fourteen rooms, and the pretty, feminine wallpaper was fresh, the paintings on the wall in fashionably good taste. The ceilings were high enough that the rooms felt open, and I realized what a pleasant contrast the rooms were to the White House where the halls and corridors were crowded and often chaotic with people hovering for an audience.

"The President will be along later this evening," Hay said,

fingering his hat, clearly itching to leave. Society was different then, and Lincoln had immediately trusted his judgment and was fine with leaving his son with a couple of strangers. I watched Hay flee in relief as he galloped his horse down the road we'd traveled, the animal's hooves throwing up clods of dirt in its haste.

Tad, from his perspective, was delighted to see us and spent the first hour romping on the hillsides with Kipp and Elani. I figured if we exhausted some of that boundless energy, which got caught up in mischievous acts, the boy would be more amenable to learning. As I watched from the window, however, I wondered if Tad would outlast the lupines. Kipp was looking a mite fatigued as he chased the ball for the umpteenth time. I tried not to laugh as I followed his grumbling thoughts about why humans thought it was so amusing to throw a ball for a dog to chase to the point of utter exhaustion.

Lincoln had asked Hay to bring some supplies so that Peter could have a makeshift classroom. While Peter looked for a suitable room, I shamelessly wandered, poking my nose where it didn't belong. Actually, dust covers were in place, the exceptions being the room that served as a library and one bedroom, which Lincoln probably occupied when he slept over, seeking refuge from the White House, which was no home to the man. Hay had a worker start a fire in the large fireplace in the library, and a selection of cold foods was set out on a small buffet table. Lincoln, who was known to eat a single egg for breakfast, was a notoriously light eater who picked over his meals. I tried not to laugh as Peter began to bargain with Tad, who seemed to be an expert at getting his way. Yes, he could play with Elani while he learned his alphabet and practiced writing the letters. I wasn't sure that child-rearing was in Peter's wheelhouse, but then he'd had no experience, and I had to applaud his gameness.

Kipp, exhausted, joined me in the library as I perused the bookshelf, fascinated, as always, by an expansive selection of books, many of which were no longer in print. Reaching up, I found a bound collection of some of Shakespeare's tragic plays. Well, that would make for some light reading, I thought, my mouth twisting with humor.

"That Tad is a hot mess," Kipp said, flopping on the floor, his sides heaving with his breaths. "His mind is completely undisciplined, darting from one thing to another, no focus at all!"

"Remember he is a child, Kipp," I reminded my friend gently.

"Count me out for fatherhood, then," Kipp replied grimly. "I don't think I'm cut out for it."

While Peter and Elani were stuck with Tad, I selected the most comfortable chair in the room and began to read. The air held the scent of lemon furniture polish and a subtle hint of old, sweet cigar smoke, perhaps from past gatherings Lincoln had held in the room. Of course, it was not long before I dozed off, warmed by the gentle flames in the fireplace, the bound volume of Shakespeare heavy in my lap. Kipp, too, had fallen into a deep sleep, snoring softly. I awoke with a start, as a hand gently touched my shoulder.

"I didn't mean to alarm you," a now-familiar voice said. "But I didn't want you to awaken and see me sitting here, unannounced," Lincoln said.

I sat up in the chair, massaging my neck, which had a serious crick after I'd slept, my head tilted, for who knows how long. Please, I thought, don't let there be a slobber of drool on my face.

"No, you're okay," Kipp said, acting as my wingman.

Glancing towards the windows, I realized darkness had fallen in the rapid, unexpected way of short winter days. I started to stand, but Lincoln waved me back, smiling.

"You look very comfortable, Mrs. Holmes," he said. "May I get you something?" Lincoln walked over to the table, and I realized that when he arrived, someone must have quietly refreshed the offerings, because a crockery pitcher, its sides glistening with moisture, was now on the table. "I have a hankering for buttermilk and finds it helps the digestion," Lincoln remarked, turning to smile again at me.

"I actually love buttermilk." I bit off my next words which would have been confusing to the man, since I started to add it was difficult to find the real thing in my modern world. In his world, all buttermilk was the real thing.

It would be something to be remembered in my old age, being served a glass of buttermilk by Abraham Lincoln, who then took a chair opposite mine, stretching his feet towards the fireplace. I recalled he suffered with cold hands and feet and figured if I gave him permission, he'd do what was natural for him.

"Sir, will you think me terribly ill-mannered if I remove my shoes and pull my chair a little closer to the fender?" I asked. "My feet tend to get terribly cold during the winter months." Of course, it was uncouth and not ladylike, but Lincoln was one man who really cared not about such things.

"Mrs. Holmes, I won't think you ill-mannered if you don't think badly of me if I follow your lead."

We giggled like children as we pulled off our shoes and scooted our chairs closer to the fender of the fireplace. And I'm grateful that Kipp was an honest witness, because I wouldn't have thought Abraham Lincoln could giggle, but he did, and when it happened, I saw a glimpse of his long lost childhood and the boy he might have been if only he'd not found grief at such a young age. As I stretched out my feet towards the fire, the warmth felt good on my toes and had a cascading effect on the rest of my body. Kipp watched, having tucked himself in a tight knot, his eyes taking in the activity, his mind curiously calm and distant from mine. I realized he wanted to let the interchange flow naturally between me and Lincoln. I relaxed; the ball was in my court as Lincoln asked me about the play I'd been reading.

"*Hamlet*," he remarked. "A dark tale if there ever was one. Of course, many tragic stories revolve around death and despair, do they not?"

As he spoke, I realized the irony of his words. During his presidency, he had received numerous death threats and still did, on an alarmingly frequent basis. He spoke brave words in response, acting casual about the threats, but in his mind swirled the notion that he would not live long. On some level, he expected to die while still a relatively young man. As I reflected, it also seemed strange that as we spoke of Shakespeare, his were some of the plays in which John Wilkes Booth had acted. And his brother, Edwin, had acted in *Hamlet*, seen by Lincoln. The universe seemed small when I considered all the intersecting parts.

Kipp was engaged in following the intricate patterns and laid down memories in Lincoln's mind. I felt him shudder as he encountered the impressions stored when Lincoln's two sons died. He'd been a remote, detached father with his eldest son but had become an involved father with his younger children. Kipp sighed deeply as he sort of got stuck, like in quicksand, in the depth of Lincoln's melancholy that hung over him like a dark cloud.

"Kipp, move on," I said, my words stern in his mind.

He sighed again and then, with great effort, moved past the depression which was almost like a roadblock. "I've not felt anyone with this much grief before," Kipp remarked. "It is as if he has stored this from the time he was a child and lost his mother. Each subsequent loss just piles on the sadness in his heart. It's one reason he indulges Tad as he does, as well as Mary. He worries about her, understanding she is not stable. But despite all her mood variability and erratic behaviors, he loves her and thinks it is his job to provide her with a calm, predictable relationship. He is utterly committed to her." Kipp glanced at me. "Is commitment a choice, do you think?"

I knew he was asking, thinking of his own relationship with me. "Kipp, move on," I said again, my eyes meeting his amber ones, which reflected the sparks of red and orange from the fireplace.

Peter, thankfully, took that opportunity to emerge, exhausted, from his session with Tad, who jumped with delight into his father's lap. The boy tugged gently on his father's beard, laughing as he did so.

"You look like my billy goat," he said, giggling.

"And I've been called worse," Lincoln responded with a smile, as he patted Tad's leg.

Peter dutifully gave a report, and it seemed, with the attractive lure of Elani, the boy had actually applied himself and had agreed to do homework! Peter, with no skills as a parent or a teacher, had managed to do something that had confounded other tutors who threw up their hands in surrender to the willful lad.

"If this time-shifting gig doesn't work out, you have a great future as a teacher," I remarked privately to Peter, who narrowed his eyes in response.

We said our goodbyes, leaving the two of them standing in the doorway, waving, as we departed, the horse's hooves thudding against the hard-packed road. I asked both the lupines, with their superior radar, to search for potential spies who might be watching for Lincoln's comings and goings. If they were present, they would most likely report our odd appearance, and the word could find its way back to Booth. If that happened, we'd have to deal with it in some creative way, although I hadn't worked out that solution in my mind. Maybe we'd be lucky, for once.

TWENTY-ONE

"I've found a carriage that has an enclosed back section," Peter mentioned as we lingered over breakfast the next day. The rain had returned, casting a pall over Washington and forcing people to hover under porches, dashing from cover to cover, and we spent our free time engaged in chess, where I found I had more success when partnered with Elani. The fact was, with the game of chess, I needed all the help I could get, and both the lupines were quick studies, but where Kipp was overbearing, Elani was patient, and I didn't grimace when making a bone-headed move.

"Well, that's good," I replied. "The lupines can be concealed, and it will make any quick identification of us to Booth by others who may be watching the roads a little more difficult."

To also help confuse spies, we planned to vary our times we went to the Soldiers' Home, and since it was such an erratic pattern, it would throw them off. Sometimes we might see Lincoln; other times, he would have a staff member bring Tad. And it was not daily in any case, so that worked to our advantage. A knock on the kitchen-level door interrupted my musings. It seemed I was rehearsing all events over and over in my mind, a sign of my disquiet over how things had occurred to date. I would have been much happier if we never had met John Wilkes Booth or Abraham

Lincoln. But we had to deal with both events, now, and minimize disruptions to the natural flow of history.

The visitor was Maureen, who hurried inside as a roll of thunder concluded with a flash of lightening that illuminated the gloom outside. After a quick bob of her head, she smiled at me, rather shyly I thought. We'd had a few contacts with her in our dealings with her mother. Both were fine, hardworking folks with good hearts and no ill will over their less than optimal situations in life.

"May I get you something hot to drink?" I asked Maureen, whose eyes widened with surprise.

"Oh, no ma'am," she breathed, horrified. "Mrs. Surratt sent me over to invite you to an afternoon tea tomorrow." Maureen rolled her eyes up, trying to recall the exact words she had recited. "She wants to return the kind invitation you extended to her and her daughter." Maureen finished in a rush, rocking back on her heels as she relaxed her knees, pleased she had remembered the words verbatim. "And she said to please bring your doggy, too," she added with an impish grin.

I glanced at Peter, since he'd planned to go to the Soldier's Home at that time. But as he nodded at me, we realized this worked even better, since if there happened to be people watching the road, the pattern of two adults traveling with their two enormous dogs would be changed.

"Yes, Maureen, please tell Mrs. Surratt that I appreciate her kindness." Any opportunity to get into the household was one we couldn't miss due to her son's involvement with the Confederate government. Soon, spies and collaborators would begin to use the Surratt house as a gathering place for strategic planning. And when that happened, we'd be watching from our hidey-hole across the street.

After Maureen left, timing her dash across the street when the lightening had been absent for a few seconds, I returned to the table to pick over the remains of my meal. Peter and Kipp resumed their spirited debate over some point in history that seemed to consume their interests...quite honestly, I'd not paid attention to their exchanges. Elani was stretched on the floor before the stove, yawning, her eyes blinking sleepily.

"I worry we are a little off pace," I blurted out. As the others snapped to alertness, I glanced at each of my companions in turn. "We really have no grasp on anything we've been searching for, and I'm concerned we've gotten sidetracked by all the other things that seem to occupy our time and interest," I added.

"In what way?" Elani asked. This was her trip her design, after all, and any thoughts I might have directly impacted her.

"Our focus should be Mary Surratt, and I almost feel like I am a tourist, a sightseer, occupied by visiting historical sites and meeting famous and infamous people. My engagement with Mary Surratt is not what it needs to be." I felt my shoulders lift with tension, pulling them up almost to my ears, it seemed; rolling my head from side to side, I tried to stretch out the tightness in my neck. The kettle of water was simmering on the stovetop, and I walked over to prepare a pot of tea, feeling as if I needed to occupy my idle hands with something constructive. Kipp had withdrawn his busy thoughts from my head, allowing me space to think without his presence.

"What do you think we should be doing differently?" Peter asked. Without his horn-rimmed glasses, he looked younger, almost like a teenager with a full beard of dark hair. He swept his hair from his forehead with his fingers before gently stroking his beard to smooth the stray hairs.

"I think we may need to separate more, making occasional visits to some of the haunts mentioned in history, hopefully encountering some of the other players in this grisly drama. My hope would be that we can gather thoughts from some of the men involved that might implicate or exonerate Mary Surratt. So far, all we gather is that she knows her son is involved with the Confederate spy ring, and she is worried for his safety." I brought the steeping teapot to the table and pushed my half-eaten plate of food aside.

Elani gave a deep, shuddering lupine sigh as she considered my words. Even though I was the elder whom she respected, it was, as I'd pointed out, her time-shift. She was in the position to consider how to proceed. Kipp, meanwhile, closed his eyes, and although he was not asleep, he gave an excellent imitation of the desert-bound Sphinx resting in the depthless sand of Egypt, his legs tucked beneath his powerful body. He reminded me of a house cat pretending to fit in a meatloaf pan.

"I realize it is seductive for us to want to spend time with Lincoln, since his days are so short," Elani began. "And I'd like to see some of that continue but very limited." Elani paused and might have hummed if she'd had the ability. "I think Peter can continue to work with Tad but following the plan of a schedule that varies the routine so that any spies might be less likely to associate him with Lincoln, per se. And, Peter," she said, glancing at her partner, who sat up straighter in his chair, "you need to think of a very good story in case you are stopped by spies." She glanced at me. "There may be valuable information we can gain from any potential Confederate agents who are monitoring the roads."

I actually hadn't considered that point, but it was a sound one. Picking up one of the fragile daffodil-patterned teacups, I turned it in my hands, marveling at the artistry and delicacy of the china. Holding it up to the light, I noticed through the translucence of the china a sweet, diffuse glow of amber, which would signify the teacup to be of good quality. Squinting, I examined the hallmark on the base. Sighing, I stood, replacing the cup on the table. It was time to get to work.

"Today is December 23rd, so I recommend we covertly stake out The National Hotel and attempt to eavesdrop on the initial meeting of Booth, Dr. Mudd, and John Surratt." I glanced around the room. "Everything that follows begins to come together, to be set in motion, with this meeting today."

"They will be traveling on 7th Street," Kipp remarked, having fallen out of his stupor. "So we can set up two posts, perhaps one on C Street and the other on Pennsylvania Avenue. Of course, Elani and I will make it difficult to blend in, so we will have to remain hidden as best we can."

Being stirred into action was the best way I could think of to reignite our focus, so we took turns watching the front entrance of Surratt's boarding house, ready to follow John Surratt when he left on his way to meet Dr. Mudd and Booth. A friend of Surratt's and fellow boarder, Louis Weichmann, was said to have accompanied him. And although he had been trusted by the Surratts, he would later give up information that would implicate the family with the conspiracy against Lincoln. I guess he was covering his own behind so that he, too, wouldn't face an accusation and imprisonment.

Waiting is just part of what symbionts do, and I admit I began to doze in the bright patch of sunlight that found its way mid-afternoon to the center of the parlor floor. I jerked awake as Kipp's thoughts shouted into my brain as well as that of Peter and Elani. It was time!

Grabbing our heavy coats and hats, we dashed down the stairs and exited through the kitchen door. I glanced up at the sky, which was thankfully free of threatening clouds. The streets were a muddy mess from the almost constant rain, and I puddle jumped as best I could so as not to completely ruin the hem of my skirt. John Surratt's slender, slight figure was disappearing down the street as he walked west, Weichmann at his side. Surratt had a unique rolling gait, making him distinctive in the crowd, so it was easy to keep them in sight, and fortunately the road and sidewalks were busy with people, thus helping us to vanish, lost in the sea of humanity. As the two men turned south on 7th Street, we slowed, knowing that at some point, Booth and Samuel Mudd would encounter the two and return to Booth's hotel room to conspire.

Kipp closed his eyes in rapt concentration before he looked up at me and nodded. The first meeting had taken place as the four men made the necessary introductions. Kipp, as he'd done before, almost acted like a collector of the distant thoughts, focusing in on them and feeding them to the rest of us who had some similar skills, but not to his level. Oh, yes, the men were all pleased to meet one another. I looked at Peter, my mouth twisting. Without saying anything, he grasped my upper arm, giving it a squeeze, before he and Elani struck out on their own, their destination Pennsylvania Avenue. I watched Peter's dark hat bobbing along as he wove a path amongst the people who were traveling at that time of day; Elani moved with a sinuous grace at his side. It was only a couple of minutes before they disappeared from view, as well as my thoughts.

"Let's go," Kipp urged me, using his long nose to poke me in the thigh.

"Okay," I replied, and we cut over one block to then travel south along 6th Street, slowing our pace so that we wouldn't inadvertently run into Booth before the four men got inside the hotel. Our path seemed clear, and we turned on C Street, traveling a half a block before we claimed a spot near a haberdashery that must have catered to upper-class gentlemen, if the clientele was any clue. Half shutting my eyes against the sunlight, I realized that the sun had passed its zenith and was beginning to descend in the west. Already, the sky had lost the brilliant blue of midday and was beginning to soften with the muted, lavender grays of twilight. Kipp jumped back as an overweight man almost trod on his toes.

"Watch it," Kipp grumbled, growling involuntarily. The heavy gentleman, hearing the ominous rumbling sound, turned, became alarmed when he saw the oversized Kipp glaring at him, and hurried away, swinging his walking stick vigorously.

"Try and contain yourself," I warned Kipp. "We don't want any attention drawn to ourselves."

Although humanity teemed around us, Kipp turned his remarkable ability to search and focus, and it was only a few seconds later when he looked up at me, pleased. "I found him," he said, breathing a deep sigh of relief.

I actually could follow his thoughts and linked my mind with his, almost as if we were holding hands. Yes, the thoughts of Booth flooded my mind, and unpleasant ones they were, filled with hatred and anger.

"What's wrong with this guy?" Kipp muttered, meaning Booth, as he pushed back against my legs as another man stepped a little too close.

I grasped the door frame where we stood, trying not to take a tumble onto the street. "Kipp, we aren't here to try and unravel John Wilkes Booth. It's enough you understand his longstanding resentments beginning with competition against his father and brother. He's an angry man searching for a remedy he'll never find to fix his broken soul."

It was not difficult to follow the thoughts of the men as Dr. Mudd, Booth, and John Surratt discussed what they thought was the state of affairs consuming the nation. While Surratt and Mudd were more controlled and calculating, Booth seemed deranged, barely able to control his agitation, and his energy almost derailed the conversations. Weichmann was quiet, mainly an observer in the discussion. There was a moment when he clearly wished he'd not gone with Surratt that day, since Booth's harangue made it difficult to relax and enjoy the excellent brandy that Booth was providing.

"The discussion has to do with how to disrupt the government," Kipp breathed. "Surratt mentioned that his superiors who oversee the spying for the Confederate government have entertained the thought that if Lincoln could be kidnapped and held, it could force the Union to withdraw and negotiate a peace."

At that minute, a shadowy figure appeared in one of the windows above, and before Kipp said anything, I knew it was Booth, who was staring out the window, his eyes aimlessly searching. It would be only a moment before he found us, skulking, looking obviously guilty, hiding in a doorway where we had no business. It would do better to be bold, I thought instantly. So, with Kipp following, I made as if I was exiting the building where we'd taken refuge and began to walk, my head up high, almost whistling happily as I ambled along, trying to not skip with pretend exuberance.

"Yes, he sees us," Kipp remarked, taking his place at my side. He paused, in his guise of dog, to sniff at something along the sidewalk. "Yuk," he moaned. "I wish I'd chosen something else to smell because that, whatever it is, stinks."

"Kipp, stop it," I whispered. "You're gonna make me laugh, and then I'll look like a crazy woman."

Above, Booth's thoughts were directed at me and took a turn toward the lascivious, as was his nature towards women. He saw the female sex as an object needing conquest and certainly not as a potential equal. Kipp, as always, was fiercely protective of me as his thoughts began to fill my head.

"Let it go, Kipp," I directed. "It is what it is, right?"

We turned the corner, fighting against the crowd of traffic since The National Hotel was an extremely busy location, and walked until we spied Peter and Elani, who were parked across the street, standing beneath a street lantern. Peter's head went up as he motioned for us to join them.

"Well, how did it go?" I asked.

"Elani was able to follow some of their thoughts, but it was difficult due to all the human minds at work," he replied, his shoulders slumping a bit.

"That's good, Elani," Kipp said, giving her a muzzle fist bump. "I think the more you practice, the better you'll get." Elani almost danced on tiptoes with the complement.

"The bad thing is that Booth saw us," I said. "But he wasn't suspicious, although I'd have preferred to not have been spotted." We waited for a break in the traffic before turning for home. The overlapping clouds had reassembled overhead, appearing as if they were ready to burst with rain, and I had a cup of hot tea and a chess game on my mind.

TWENTY-TWO

"How is your tea, Mrs. Holmes?" Mary Surratt allowed a polite smile to cross her normally grave countenance. Having been impressed by my pretty tea service, she dusted off her best set in a subtle ladies' competition. As she leaned forward to pour my second cup, I murmured compliments over the loveliness of the patterned teapot as well as the shape of the delicate cups as the delicate fragrance of jasmine tea wafted through the air. Mary's face flushed with pleasure at my words. She was probably what would have been thought of as a handsome woman, since her features were too strong and not soft enough to be conventionally pretty. There was little to no spontaneity in her as she managed an admirable control over her thoughts as well as her mannerisms. I could see how others might be suspicious of her due to her deliberate nature.

Kipp and I were hopeful we might inadvertently gather more information about the looming conspiracy and still were basking in the flush of triumph at having stalked John Wilkes Booth to his lair the previous afternoon. No, it didn't directly involve Mary Surratt, but we certainly didn't hear any thoughts from her son, John, that might have implicated her. Anna sat quietly, her hands folded in her lap, her eyes darting occasionally towards Kipp, who pretended to be sleeping.

"Why does she keep staring at me?" he grumbled. "I know she doesn't like dogs, but I'm not a dog, and all I'm doing is being quiet, minding my own business."

"Kipp," I said, meaning it as a warning. Was he trying to break my concentration, I wondered?

"I mean, I could really raise a ruckus if I wanted to."

"Kipp," I said again.

"Okay," he replied with a big dog-sounding sigh.

Mary Surratt's thoughts were bruised, almost painfully sensitive, since she and her son, John, had another rather serious altercation that morning. Anna, who was protective of her mother, looked at her frequently, worried over the dark stains beneath Mary's eyes. Her nights of late had been sleepless and marred by disturbing dreams.

"And how are you and your brother settling in?" Mary asked. Peter and Elani had headed out to the Soldiers' Home for another grueling session with Tad. Prior to their departure, Peter had remarked that it was understandable why Tad had run off past tutors with such ruthless efficiency. He was, in modern-day parlance, a piece of work.

"Quite well," I replied, smiling. "We are so grateful to you for your hospitality and helping us secure lodging."

She waved her hand with a delicate laugh. "Only too happy to help another person in need. And the fact you are from the South compelled me to treat you with kindness during this time of war," she added unnecessarily. Her eyes darted to my face, watching for my reaction.

"And there is your opening," Kipp murmured, his amber eyes alert and on me.

"Yes, Mrs. Surratt, quite honestly I wasn't sure how we would be received in Washington," I said, leaning forward, hoping I was wearing the most earnest facial expression in my extensive repertoire.

"Well, Washington is a town of divided loyalties," she replied cautiously.

"Watch yourself, Petra," Kipp intoned. "John mentioned to her last night that you and Peter seem to be pretty visible in town for strangers. After Booth remarked on having spied you from the window of his hotel room, John became concerned thinking that you and Peter might be Union spies. His business, after all, makes him overly cautious and lacking in trust. He told his mother to be careful around you."

I managed to change the tone of the conversation to something light and frivolous. And although after John Surratt met with Booth, the history was that Confederate sympathizers began to use Mary Surratt's house as a gathering place, I didn't know it would happen at that moment. But after hearing the street-level door slam, the murmur of male voices began to drift up from the first floor of the townhouse. John Surratt, Booth, and another man were downstairs! I could only hope they would not make an appearance in the parlor, given John Surratt's suspicious nature. For a moment, my anxiety diverted my attention from Mary, as her words formed a question in my mind.

"Is everything to your liking, Mrs. Holmes?" she asked, a frown wrinkling her forehead.

"Oh, yes, yes, and thank you," I stuttered, trying to regain my footing in the conversation. I'd let Kipp work on what was happening downstairs.

"Booth is here with John Surratt, and I believe the other man is David Herold," Kipp said, taking a deep breath.

Mary's thoughts became as diverted as mine as her worry over John's activities filled her mind. It was almost as difficult for her to continue to talk with me as it was for me to listen and respond. Anna, too, was becoming restless, curious as to what was happening downstairs as we prattled on about nonsense and sipped tea. The words spoken in the kitchen were not decipherable, but there were occasional emotional outbursts of a tone rather than actual spoken phrases I could hear. With effort, I calmed myself; Kipp had shut himself off from me so as to not divert my focus.

The tea finally struggled to an awkward conclusion, and I rose to depart. As I did the courteous leave-taking, murmuring words over how pleasant the afternoon had been, I realized I would have to exit out the front with a high probability I would be seen leaving the house. Given Booth's apparent notice of my frequency of appearances around town, it was not something I desired, but there was no other way around the moment. The tea was finished, and I was being ushered to the door. Kipp pushed against my legs, looking up at me, his tail wagging briefly.

"We'll deal with it," Kipp said, his warmth against my body supplying its usual comfort. With Kipp at my side, all adversity could be met and conquered, or so I chose to think.

The weather, which seemed variable to a high degree, had changed during the time I'd been sipping tea, and once again the sky overhead was turning prematurely dark, the clouds lying low over the city. Although it was cold, I didn't think it was below freezing, and we might be in for another rain event. A warning rumble of thunder caused the iron railing along the stairs to tremble beneath my fingers. I descended carefully, as women had to do in those times due to the voluminous skirts that could hobble one quite suddenly, hoping I would be able to make my departure unseen. As I made it to the street level, two large wagons were rumbling past, the drivers shouting encouraging words to the weary teams of mules, which were overworked and ready for the day to end. With my inhaled breath, I caught the odor of the sweaty animals, the stench from the drivers' unwashed bodies, as well as a more pungent fragrance from one of the nearby waterways which was polluted with human waste. The latter brought a sting to my eyes, which watered. Deeply humid days seemed to capture odors in the air, unwilling to release them, and I prayed for a wind to kick up and blow it all away.

"Booth is watching us," Kipp murmured. "Act, uh, casual," he suggested.

"And how do I do that?" I hissed, irritated at such a silly directive.

"You could whistle or something," he replied, trying to bring levity to the moment.

Even though I'd grown completely lazy and dependent upon Kipp's amazing talents, the thoughts of Booth were as easily accessible to me as they were to Kipp. Yes, he noticed, and instead of his appreciation of my female figure, I followed a trail of suspicion clouding his thoughts. For the first time, he truly wondered if I was who I'd claimed to be. After all, there were female spies on both sides of the Mason Dixon line. Having a dog at my side could be a clever act to appear innocent, since no spy usually traveled with two dogs and a brother. I didn't have to see his handsome face to imagine the changes in his features as a series of emotions and thoughts crossed his mind.

As we entered the townhouse, the rain began to fall, first as a gentle pattering which quickly escalated into a deluge. I glanced back at Mary Surratt's house where the lights from the windows glowed soft amber as the conspirators huddled in the warmth of the ground-level kitchen. Telepaths recognize one another immediately, so I knew that Peter and Elani were already back, upstairs in the parlor. A minute later, they clambered down the staircase, Elani's nails ticking softly against the scarred wood surface. Peter took one look at my face, my flesh showing the chill from the air, and wordlessly put the kettle on the still warm stove.

"Well?" Elani asked, glancing at Kipp.

"Booth, Surratt, and Herold gathered for the first time in the Surratt townhouse," he began. "Wait," he said, taking a deep breath. "John is introducing Booth to his mother and sister right now, and they are both suitably impressed to meet a famous actor." Kipp began to pant with effort. "Booth, as is his talent, is being seductively charming, leading them both to think he is a fine gentleman to know and to entertain. Mary doesn't realize at this point that he is trying to form a conspiracy to act against Lincoln. As much as she despises the Union, and as much concern as she has over John's activities, she is not engaged yet."

Peter saw to my needs, pouring me a cup of tea he'd brewed, as Kipp unraveled all he'd learned. Booth brought Herold, who would later be hanged for his part in the assassination of Lincoln, to meet John Surratt for the first time. It was more of a gripe session, with Booth hogging the stage, which was his nature, due to his extreme political views as well as the consuming hatred that ignited his body like a wildfire. John viewed Booth as a tool he could use, and Booth felt the same about John. Both men were cautious, with the natural suspiciousness of men who wish to bring down a government. For the first time, the notion of kidnapping Lincoln was raised. What

Kipp had overheard appeared to match with what we knew of recorded history.

"And how did your day go?" I asked, glancing at Peter, who had removed his boots and was sitting in his stocking feet, slouched back in his chair from fatigue.

"It was a bust. We drove out there, and for some reason, Tad never showed. After a bit, we just came home." Peter looked unsettled.

"And?" I prompted.

"There were men obviously lurking in the woods, watching us this time, more boldly than before. At some point we will need to confront that issue, I believe." Peter's dark eyes met mine. "They are Confederate spies who watch that road intermittently due to Lincoln and other members of the government who travel that route."

"Well, great," I muttered. "We have spies watching us, and Booth is suspicious of us. I'm worried we may disrupt the timeline unless we are very careful."

"What do you recommend?" Elani asked.

There were a few remedies open to symbionts who were in the midst of a mire of quicksand with potentially dire outcomes. The easiest was to put an end to the time-shift and return home posthaste. My suggestion was met with intense disappointment from my companions, who stared at me as if I'd grown another head.

"My other thought," I added, rushing my words, "is that we create a story to feed the spies who watch the road to the Soldiers' Home, knowing it will get back to Surratt and Booth. I suggest, other than the times we go there, let's stay inside during the day and keep our prowling to after dark when we will be less conspicuous."

We were to have an opportunity to test out our story a few days later, when the rain had cleared, and a warming trend was being encouraged by the winds from the southeast driven by a storm swirling in the turbulent Gulf. I think the few days we'd spent huddling in our townhouse helped us fall off the radar of the conspirators, if our surveillance of Booth and Surratt's thoughts was any measure. Out of sight, out of mind, it seemed. Peter made arrangements for a boy to meet us on the next street corner with a carriage, and after coins exchanged hands, we were on our way, heading north out of the crowded city. Thankfully, we were leaving the stench and congestion behind us. Dusk was falling, and the western sky was making the conversion from blue to pink and deep violet as long, wispy clouds cluttered the horizon. A v-shaped wedge of geese moved overhead, honking noisily as they either fled something or sought something.

Peter had become increasingly comfortable driving the horse, the reins held limply in his hands. I glanced down and approved of the calluses he was developing on his formerly soft flesh. He caught my eyes staring and smiled.

"I guess I'm losing my office hands," he remarked, lifting his dark brows. The wind blew a little harder, stirring the hair that had grown long over his collar where it curled against the stiff white fabric.

"Well, that's a good thing, right?" I said, poking him in the side with my elbow.

On either side of the road, the trees loomed, the twilight making the woods appears more alien than during the familiar light of day. The golden leaves of the American beeches chattered as we passed, their rest disrupted by the breeze, the sound noticeable in the otherwise quiet countryside. For an instant the forest seemed animated, a living thing that was somehow threatening to us. Shaking my head, I reprimanded myself for letting my imagination go wild. Inhaling deeply, I caught the scent of wood smoke from some distant fire.

"There are men up ahead, hiding just within the edge of the trees," Kipp murmured, poking his nose up against the back of my neck. I felt it quiver, moist and cool, against my flesh. Reaching back with my hand, I curled my fingers into the dense fur of his throat as he pressed against me.

"It will be fine," I said, feeling the need to install some comfort into my friends.

The horse, seemingly anxious to arrive at a final destination, picked up the pace, almost breaking out of a meandering trot into a canter. Peter eased back on the reins, since we didn't wish to appear as if we were in a hurry or frightened. After about a hundred yards, four men burst out of concealment from the tree line and galloped towards us, angling so as to cut off our path. Peter pulled up our horse, which began shaking its bay-colored head in annoyance at the unexpected interruption.

"Hello, friends," the lead man said, smiling as he leaned down to peer into the carriage. "What's your business on this road?" Even though he was smiling and his tone was pleasant, his intent was not a good one. He'd been told by his superiors, fed information by John Surratt, to interrogate us. Although his face was partially hidden by the brim of a slouch hat, his thoughts were clear to all of us.

"And why would you ask?" I spoke up, feeling the need to navigate this tricky road. My female status would give me some cover considering the times and the social mores.

The man, as I expected, removed his hat, revealing a greasy pate of hair that fell to his shoulders. He was dressed in a heavy overcoat concealing weapons that were strapped to his waist. The other men were similarly clothed, their faces shrouded in darkness beneath the brims of their hats.

"Well, ma'am," he replied, "there have been reports of highwaymen in these parts, and we're just making sure that people who are traveling have business here abouts." He smiled again, the expression not making it to his dark eyes. A small stain of tobacco juice marked the corners of his mouth, almost causing an artificial frown to appear as if on a clown's painted face.

"My goodness!" I exclaimed, my eyes growing wide. With a dramatic flair, I grasped Peter's arm. "These roads are not safe. I told you that, brother!"

"We are on our way to the Soldiers' Home," Peter said, after patting my hand in what seemed to be a comforting gesture. "A friend of our father is an invalid there, and he's lost his eyesight. We, as a gesture of kindness, sometimes visit to read to him and give him comfort." Peter blinked like an owl as he traded glances with the rider.

"Brother, if these roads are not safe, we shouldn't come anymore," I said, taking the opportunity to look at the surrounding woods, pretending to be anxious. Behind me, Kipp snickered at my performance, clearly amused at my Tallulah Bankhead drama style.

The man relaxed, and as we followed his thoughts, it was clear he believed us and thought we were no danger. After all I was a female, and Peter didn't carry the appearance of a potential combatant. All of this served us well, since he would dutifully report back to Surratt and company, who would hopefully mark us off their list of concerns. Kipp, behind me, had been tensed, prepared to intervene and manipulate the man's notions if needed, but it seemed he was ready to take our explanation and run with it.

I thought I'd sweeten the deal a little. "Sir, since we are strangers to these parts and a long way from Tennessee, do you have advice for us on how to avoid these highwaymen of whom you speak?"

"I'd not carry anything of value," he replied after stumbling a moment.

Peter laughed softly. "No concerns there, my friend. And we appreciate your cautioning us."

As the men road off, their destination clearly Washington, we breathed a collective sigh of relief. That moment could have gone good or bad, but it seemed those men were eager to receive a positive message that they could relay.

"They are intermittently sent out to monitor several of the roads that serve as main highways into and out of Washington," Kipp said. "The weather is cold, and they'd prefer to be at the tavern, drinking whiskey in a warm building versus sitting out here in the woods. In other words, they wanted to hear just what you had to say, and they can go home."

"Petra, you handled that well," Elani said, her eyes glowing bright from the rear of the carriage.

As I nodded my head at the compliment, I realized none of us should clap ourselves on the back with too many congratulations. The times were dangerous, and our need to keep a low profile and a soft footprint was even more necessary than ever.

TWENTY-THREE

I was surprised to find Mary Lincoln in residence at the cottage, as a servant opened the door to greet us. She, apparently, had insisted she meet Tad's tutor. Mary was a protective mother and wanted to approve—or disapprove—of the new player in the life of her child. She was a notoriously jealous woman, I recalled, thinking of her yet to come disastrous encounter with the wife of General Ord and the subsequent humiliation felt by Lincoln when Mary caused an embarrassing scene. I would have to play my cards cautiously.

"Oh, I am so glad I came with my brother today," I gushed, giving an unnecessary curtsey to Mary. I realized she had the need to be treated like royalty. "I typically remain in Washington," I added, "but it is so pretty here in the country." It was important she didn't get the notion I was lying in wait for her husband to show up. "I heard so much about your fashion and style sense, and I see it in play here in this lovely cottage." I tried to not simper but realized I was doing so, despite my druthers. "I must believe it was your gracious hand that brought this to fruition."

"Okay," Kipp grumbled, "that's enough of that!"

But it wasn't, and Mary melted at my words. I think history was unkind to her in so many ways. She was raised in wealth and comfort but married a man who had little to nothing in their early days. What they shared was a fierce ambition for his political success, and she was sufficiently educated to debate the issues of the day with her husband. Their beginnings as a couple were humble, to say the least. She sewed the curtains, made their clothes, and labored about her house, not complaining over the lack of luxuries from what was recorded at the time. Maybe if she had not lost three of her four children, as well as being at her husband's side when he was ruthlessly shot in the head, she would have evolved a bit differently? But in any case, Lincoln was completely devoted to her, and it was rare he lost patience or took a harsh tone. And maybe historians, who found his need to cater to her erratic whims and accumulate debt due to her out of control spending, just didn't appreciate the fragile balance of their lives. I personally thought Stanton's having her removed when she was distraught at the side of a dying Lincoln was cruel. In my mind, if she was good enough for Lincoln, then it was really no one else's business. And who amongst us understands the way of the heart?

But I did read her correctly, and she appreciated my subservient, fawning tone, and it immediately defused any twinge of jealousy she might have harbored. In fact, she seemed to need a female confidant, and she had few in her orbit—most women could not tolerate her unpredictable behaviors and sharp, gossipy tongue—so I was not surprised when she took me by the arm to give me the grand tour of the cottage, explaining all her efforts to beautify the interior.

"You see here, my dear, where I chose these soft colors—almost like a watercolor—to make use of the subtle lighting from that transom," Mary Lincoln said, lifting her hand towards the wall. As we walked from room to room, all fourteen of them, she grasped my hand, and we were like two girlhood friends as we ambled along, Kipp trailing in our wake.

"She's lonely," he remarked.

And she was, indeed, lonely. With the exception of Mary Keckley, there were only a few women in Washington who sought her counsel. Again, I felt a sting of compassion. I glanced at her, noticing how her once pretty features had become blurred with age, although her blue eyes still held the spark of intelligence that had once attracted Lincoln. Some people thought she was stupid, basing this assessment on her erratic behaviors and more than occasional unkind outbursts. But she was really bright and had been articulate in politics and current events when she and Lincoln were young and courting. No doubt, he enjoyed the fact she was a bit unusual, as she was not a conventional woman of the times. Grief and stress had changed her, as can happen to any human being. Perhaps the fact I, too, had lost a child, made me see her in a little different view than some others.

We finally rejoined Lincoln, who was sitting in front of the fireplace, his face a mask of concentration as he stared at the fire. Not only was he dealing with the ongoing war, but also Mary had scheduled a series of White House receptions for the months of January and February. And although he was a garrulous man, he had no true desire to dress in his finest suit and shake hands all afternoon. His health, due to stress, was deteriorating, and the already slender Lincoln was losing weight, making him appear cadaverous. For a man as ambitious as was he, I was a little surprised to find he had a private longing to return to his former life, sharing a small law practice and living a quieter existence. After all, this was what he had worked for, this life of leadership. I suppose humans often find the "getting" is not always what it was thought to be.

Lincoln's face turned towards us as his eyes rested on Mary; his features softened as a smile pulled at his lips. "And did you enjoy showing the cottage, Mother?"

As Mary took a seat in the flanking wing chair, I chose the loveseat and watched their interplay. Mary sat slightly forward in the chair, her eyes eagerly on his face. There was some level of anxiety there, as always. Lincoln's thoughts revealed the dreams that haunted him, dreams of death. In short, Lincoln thought he would die before he left office. Mary, too, had similar beliefs, and she constantly worried that Lincoln would be killed. For a woman plagued by loss, her overwhelming anxiety had tipped her too far over the edge of reason. I glanced at Kipp, finding his amber eyes on me.

"I love you," he said, having followed my thoughts.

"I'm not going anywhere," I replied. The loss of Kipp's mother had left him with some of the same anxieties that plagued the Lincolns.

"How can you, or anyone, make such a promise?" he asked, his voice soft in my mind.

"I can and do," I answered. "Let your mind be still, Kipp." And it was true that both symbionts and humans might make such promises, ones of comfort, but ones with no way to be assured. These were words of love, not reason.

We relaxed and listened to Mary Lincoln's idle chit chat about Washington gossip. Lincoln would smile and nod, even when her comments were sharp and critical. I followed his thoughts as they returned to the war, while Mary chattered on about meaningless things and supposed offenses taken. The fireplace was a focal point of the room for me, the wavering flames dulling my senses, the sounds of the crackling fire and crumbling logs soft against Mary's voice. With effort, I struggled to stay awake and focused.

The rest of the evening passed pleasantly—at least for me, while Peter was in the next room struggling against a headstrong Tad Lincoln. After murmuring our goodbyes, we let the horse amble his way home, finding his way to the stable without being coaxed. During the ride, I hatched an idea, but decided to announce it over breakfast the following morning. Kipp, after we'd gone to bed, was a restless sleeper, and I followed his dreams carefully. Like Kipp, I could telepathically manipulate his dreams but always hesitated since I felt he must need to work through some things lingering like cobwebs in his subconscious mind. He whimpered a few times, paddling his legs, as he dreamt of worry after his mother left him alone to survive, if he could. His puppy heart ached in loneliness and fear at that moment. I took a deep breath and counted to ten, thinking if the dream was still plaguing him at eleven, I'd intervene. Thankfully, it passed, and he relaxed, his sides rising and falling with rhythmic breathing, the soft sound filling our tiny bedroom.

The morning brought the return of the sun and a sky the color of an unblemished robin's egg. The few clouds visible were just wispy, drifting pieces of lace against the blue palette. I was hungry, and while the others feasted on some dried meat that Peter warmed in the heavy iron skillet, I sawed off another piece of our Irish friend's wonderful bread, slathering it with fresh butter and home-made pear preserves. Yes, I could eat like that all the time.

"I want to go to the general store and buy a large brim hat as well as some trousers and a coat," I began. As the others glanced my way, I added, "I think it is time to do a little nighttime prowling, and I will move better and be less conspicuous dressed as a man."

It was a fact that, uh, decent women didn't flit about a city after dark without an escort, and Kipp didn't count. The time had come for us to split up in order to cover more avenues, and the need to do so and not be conspicuous was critical. We'd decided to remain at the townhouse for the most part after the last time we'd fallen under the inspection of Booth, and noted in the month of January an uptick in the gathering of men at the Surratt house. While the Lincolns were busy attending the many receptions being held at the White House, the conspirators were busy planning. We postponed our chess game, focusing instead on activity across the street that seemed to be intensifying. Kipp took the lead, although the rest of us had our radar set and were collecting any thoughts that might available.

"Booth, John Surratt, George Atzerodt, and David Herold are there today," Kipp intoned, settling down in front of the iron stove, sighing in comfort. It was so effortless for him while the rest of us were straining to the point that my head began to hurt. The active thoughts and busy minds of other humans between us and our targets made such focus complicated, and it was easy to follow the wrong rabbit down a hole.

"They're in the dining room downstairs, I think, and Mary has arrived to prepare some food for them." Kipp paused. "She has deliberately sent Maureen from the house on errands and has banned Anna from the room." He glanced at us. "This is the first time she has been involved; it's clear she doesn't want a witness in Maureen, and she needs Anna to remain ignorant in case things go badly. And for all Booth's charm offensive, he is, after all, an actor, and Mary thinks he is an unsuitable person to be around Anna."

He closed his eyes and grunted, trying to remain focused. "The discussion is focused on the technical aspects of kidnapping Lincoln and having the Confederacy hold him for ransom, the deal being that all Confederate prisoners will be released, the war will end, and the South will be allowed to secede."

"This is our first evidence that Mary Surratt knew of the plan," I remarked, taking a deep breath. "We wanted to find this, if it existed, and it does."

"So that makes her a conspirator," Peter said. Leaning forward, he took a sip of the coffee he'd brewed on the stovetop. It was pretty rough stuff…cowboy coffee from my way of thinking. He'd tried to tempt me with it, even added a dollop of fresh cream, but I stuck to my tea instead.

"Yes, but only to kidnapping." Kipp was silent for a few moments. "But she doesn't like it. She's only involved because she thinks John is about to get into trouble, and she wants to know what he's planning. Mary doesn't care for Booth and thinks he is a braggart. She particularly didn't care for the way he kissed Anna's hand one day, since she has him correctly pegged as a womanizer. As much as she supports the South, she is only doing this because of John, not because of her own feelings about the Confederacy."

"So, as usual, it is about protecting her child," Elani remarked. "Ironic, isn't it, that if he'd come back during her trial, he could have testified and taken responsibility, and perhaps she would not have been executed."

"While she was willing to die for him, he was not for her. I think her loyalties were sadly misplaced," Peter said. He replaced his mug to the battered table, sloshing some coffee over the side of the mug as he did so. "Oops," he remarked sheepishly.

I rousted up my companions. "Remember, I have some shopping to do," I reminded them. As much information as we could obtain from listening in to the activities in the Surratt household, we could gather other facts from following the thoughts of the men who seemed to have hatched the notion, courtesy of some prompting by the Confederate government which bankrolled both Booth and Surratt. We decided to choose fairly, as I held the black queen chess piece behind my back in my right hand, the white in my left. If Peter chose the black queen, he would follow Surratt and I would take Booth. And that's exactly what happened. Both men, being actively in the employment of the Confederacy, would have minds full of thoughts involving the people in their orbits. We could determine their impressions of Mary Surratt by actively monitoring them, as well as her.

So, as darkness fell the next evening, I donned my menswear, tucking my long hair up under the slouch brim hat I'd purchased. With a bulky coat that almost brushed my knees, the hat and a muffler wound around my throat and chin, it would be hard to determine my sex or identity after dark. The challenge would be keeping the lupines hidden as we traveled about the streets in covert surveillance of our targets.

Across the street, another brief meeting had been held at the Surratt townhouse, but this time Mary Surratt was not present. She and Anna had left to go to church and were not due back until later. This time, Booth brought the thuggish and savage Lewis Powell, a man who would terrify the household of the Seward family in just a few weeks. He was probably a sociopath, I thought darkly. Anyone who could viciously attack a helpless man, as he had Secretary of State Seward, had issues.

Peter and I waited at the door of our street-level kitchen, the lanterns unlit, as we stood in darkness. Beside me, I felt Kipp bristling with tension, coiled like a spring ready to pop. Elani was his opposite, relaxed, and I fancy I heard her yawn as we waited. Peter's dark eyes met mine and a smile twitched at the corners of his mouth.

"You must enjoy dressing like a man," he quipped. "You seem to try to take every opportunity to go in costume."

"Well, next time you can dress like a woman and see how it feels to wear corsets and hooped skirts...don't forget the bustle," I replied spiritedly. "Try sitting comfortably with a bustle hanging on your fanny."

"Hush, you two," Kipp breathed. "They are leaving."

The door across the street opened, and for a moment we saw figures outlined in the soft yellow glow of a lit lantern in the Surratt kitchen. A man stepped out, sweeping a hat on his head as he did so. As he paused to light a cigar, the flash of the match illuminated his face. It was Booth, ready to leave, Lewis Powell at his side. After a few words and laughter, Booth swaggered away, Powell's large body hulking next to him, as the two men headed west on H Street. A second later, the smaller form of Surratt with a man we'd not identified headed east.

"Good luck," Peter said, squeezing my arm. After looking carefully both ways, he slipped out, making certain to hug the sidewalks and streets as close to the hovering buildings as was possible. Elani kept between him and the walls so as to be less apparent.

"Kipp, are you ready?"

He blinked his amber eyes in response and nuzzled my hand.

We shut the door silently behind us. The chill in the air struck my face; a very fine mist was falling, coating the street with dampness, and I was grateful not to contend with bulky skirts tangling around my ankles. A low lying bank of fog had consumed Washington, and I strained to catch a fleeting glimpse of Peter and Elani glide out of sight around a corner. Booth and Powell were a block ahead of us, making a shadowy outline as they paused under a gas light. Powell, tall and powerfully built, overshadowed the slighter form of Booth, but it was clear who the leader was, and it was Booth. Even from our distance, his toxic thoughts floated back to us on the cool night air. Yes, Powell shared Booth's hatred of Lincoln and the Union, but his thoughts didn't have the rabid, impenetrable focus of Booth. Powell was clearly a man in search of a leader.

"I'm almost surprised Booth can have a coherent discussion with anyone," Kipp murmured to me. "He has the same feelings of derangement that I've followed in other obsessed people."

"He's not deranged to the point he can't control himself when needed," I replied. A man wearing a heavy coat approached and pretended to stumble upon a rough patch in the road, falling against me. It's difficult for humans to surprise us symbionts, and I realized before his hand reached into my inner coat pocket, that he was a skilled pickpocket, one of those who could lift a wallet without breaking a sweat or causing alarm to the victim. What he didn't count on was Kipp, who was concealed in the shadows. I felt the man's hand freeze against my rib cage as Kipp's massive head rose, his lips pulling back to display his impressive teeth.

The man's eyes opened wide as he began to backpedal, stumbling again as he did so. The last we saw, he was running down the street, gaining momentum with every step.

"Hee hee," Kipp giggled, looking up at me. "Reckon he won't grab anyone's wallet for a while."

"You're so bad," I replied softly, tweaking his ear. "Okay, let's get back to work."

We trailed behind Booth and Powell, dropping back by another block, since the two men had a pattern of walking determinedly before stopping to talk. I feared each time they stopped that they would look around to see if anyone was close enough to listen. Once, as they paused, Booth almost whipped around, and I literally fell over Kipp into an alleyway.

"Hey, watch it," Kipp complained. "You stepped on my toe."

I wasn't too happy either, since I managed to fall into a pile of horse poo, fairly fresh but not quite steamy. As I finally got back on my feet, I glared at Kipp, daring him to laugh. "Remind me to tell Peter that this work is not all glamour," I finally managed to say. I have to give Kipp high marks for pretending to be worried about me when what he wanted to do was to laugh.

I peeked around the corner of the alley and was dismayed to find that Booth and Powell had disappeared. We would have to proceed with caution. Placing my hand lightly along Kipp's back, we walked slowly, Kipp turning his head, maximizing his ability to almost throw out sonar to pick up the now familiar thoughts of the men. He paused, once, and I felt his hair rise beneath my palm, before continuing in a slow, cautious, prowling gait. After we'd gone two blocks, he paused again and motioned me into a dark recessed area that led to the doorway of a small shop that was closed for the night.

"They are in there," Kipp breathed, using his long nose as a pointer.

I hadn't really been paying attention to the route we'd been taking, but it seemed we'd arrived at Ford's Theatre, and Booth and Powell were inside Taltavul's Star Saloon, where they were ordering whiskey. It would be a good time to listen in on their thoughts with their tongues loosened by alcohol.

"Booth has found in Powell someone who matches his viciousness as well as his thoughts of violence. The other conspirators might agree to be agents in a kidnapping, but already Booth is beginning to think that a mere theft and confinement of Lincoln will not suffice. Powell actually shares his thoughts," Kipp said.

As we stood in the dark and the cold air surrounded us, I rubbed my arms with my hands, trying to keep warm. I figured Booth and Powell would be in the saloon for quite some time. The fog and dampness was closing in, clinging to my woolen clothes like a shroud.

"Booth is calculating, and although kidnapping is the current plan on the table, he thinks it doesn't go far enough. He would like to see Lincoln injured, abused while in custody. He places all his rage over what he can't control, all his pent up anger, on one man, and that is Abraham Lincoln."

We waited longer until I felt the lingering cold begin to work its way past my heavy greatcoat, and despite trying not to show it, I began to shiver. Kipp's heavy pelt kept him insulated against the elements. He looked up at me and nuzzled my thigh.

"Let's go. They aren't thinking about Mary Surratt, and as you aptly reminded us, that is the focus of our trip."

I knew he was just being a gentleman in consideration for my discomfort, but he was also correct, so, after hesitating for a moment, I began walking back towards our townhouse. I was tired and sleep beckoned.

TWENTY-FOUR

"What are you doing?" Peter asked. It was yet early, and his dark hair was standing on end, badly in need of a vigorous combing.

I sighed deeply, staring at him, while trying to keep the irritation from my response. After all, his query was perfectly reasonable. "I had to clean my britches because I fell in a pile of horse manure," I replied, daring him to laugh. My eyes narrowed as his lips twitched.

I was in the kitchen, which smelled of wood smoke and apples— I was trying my hand, long out of use, at baking some apples with cinnamon and cloves --having come inside from the back alley where I used a stiff bar of lye soap and water to launder my pants. After a valiant effort to reshape the wool, I hung the pants on a wooden drying rack I'd found in a closet and placed the contraption in front of the stove. Hopefully, I didn't stretch the damp wool to the degree that the seat of my pants would sag to my knees. Peter could have sniggered at my predicament but controlled his reaction and instead went to the warm stove to place the large kettle on top.

"You need some tea," he remarked, turning to glance at me, his expression a mask.

His hair was getting too long, and his beard was looking a little scruffy, I thought unkindly. Unlike Peter, I still tried to maintain my grooming, I sniffed to myself, and was not responsible for the vague stench of horse manure that filled the kitchen as the soggy wool dried from the warmth of the stove. My less than charitable thoughts were interrupted by a scratch at the back door; Peter paused to open the door, and the lupines hurried inside, almost shoving each other against the door frame in their rush to escape the cold.

"I miss our backyard at home," Kipp remarked wistfully. "These alleys are rough, filled with debris and trash." He yawned, still tired from a night plagued by dreams of which I'd been the primary focus. In one, Booth kidnapped me, and as he raced off with me as a prisoner, Kipp tried in vain to pursue as we disappeared into the night. I still keenly felt his despair at having lost me. "There was something dead, too, decomposed to the point I could no longer identify its origin."

It was clear the dreams had left him morose, a condition rarely seen in my normally ebullient and optimistic Kipp. Being enmeshed in the thoughts of disturbed men, such as Booth, as well as the sad, melancholy thoughts of Lincoln and Mary Lincoln, the latter of whom seemed to be clinging precariously to sanity, had brought him to his current state. Unfortunately, I could not soothe his worries, and Kipp would have to use this time-shift as a personal growth experience.

However, in contrast to Kipp, Elani seemed energetic and bristling with excitement. "I was listening in to the Surratt house," she began, claiming a spot in front of the kitchen stove. It was early in the morning yet, with few humans traveling between us and the object of our focus, enabling Elani to eavesdrop successfully. I was proud of her initiative.

"Mary just concluded another serious talk with John, trying to persuade him to give up his connection with Booth. Frankly, she doesn't trust Booth, nor does she like him. His manner towards Anna, though carefully polite, is just a mask, and Mary deduces his true seductive intentions. Anna, of course, is young, and Booth is handsome and famous, so she is a little starstruck." Elani glanced at me, shaking her head from side to side. "It seems, in retrospect, that Mary's lack of trust is well-founded since he ends up coercing the others by basically entrapping them to be a part of his scheme to assassinate the President."

It was a fact that Booth had written a letter to the press that basically took credit for the assassination and named the people involved. So even if the other men backed out, the letter implicated them, and no one would believe their innocence. It was a diabolical plot on the part of Booth and demonstrated his obsessive hatred of Lincoln eclipsed any pretended loyalty to his men.

"And John's response to his mother?" Peter asked.

"Consistent with history in that he will continue on with his spying activities and meeting with Booth. He, under direction of the Confederate government, supports a kidnapping as long as he doesn't have to actually do any of the dirty hands-on work himself." She paused, thinking of the right words. "He is slippery, like an eel, self-serving, and very careful."

Washington, in January and February of 1865, was cold and often rainy, but despite that, it was a time of accelerated activity in the city. The country decided to reelect Lincoln for another four years, and on February 8th, 1865, the votes were tallied, and his new term would begin on March 4th. Mary, true to form as the first lady, filled the early winter months with receptions at the White House. Though society was polite with her, mostly out of consideration for Lincoln, Mary's ostentatious displays and her outlandish expenditures on her clothing were the subject of quiet scorn and ridicule.

Lincoln's health continued to suffer, and he'd lost thirty-five pounds from his already slender frame. He could not get warm, no matter what he did, his hands and feet aching from poor circulation, the flesh pale and almost cyanotic at times. On the rare instances I encountered him at the Soldiers' Home, he would sit in front of the fireplace, desperately trying to absorb the warmth emitted from the crackling flames. He never complained, however, and smiled, asking as to my comfort as well as that of Peter. It was a point with Lincoln, despite his inherent melancholic nature, to put on an affable face.

On one particularly cold evening in February, I was with Lincoln in the library, as Tad was arguing with Peter over some ridiculous, non-debatable point in basic mathematics. I enjoyed those times, lured like a seaman to the rocks, drawn by the sirens' seductive call.

Yes, I realized those small encounters threatened the established timeline, but I couldn't stop myself. Kipp, in other circumstances, might have been the voice of reason, but he was as captivated as I by the moment and opportunity. Mary was not present that night, and I was glad. Her mind was so filled with agitation that it was impossible for a telepath to relax in the swirling maelstrom of thoughts, most of which dealt with the loss of her two sons and her anxiety over Lincoln. She was often angry and volatile, I found.

"May I get you some buttermilk?" I asked Lincoln.

He normally wore his personable mask with me, the one he'd learned as a part and parcel of his role as politician. But on that night, he allowed himself to be genuine, and his bearded chin sank deeper and deeper on his chest, as his gray eyes stared, as if hypnotized, at the fire.

"Yes, Mrs. Holmes, that would be very kind of you." Perhaps, knowing Mary's penchant for jealousy, Lincoln remained very formal in his address of me.

I heard a loud, childish voice wail in protest and wondered if Tad's progress as a student would change the historical record, but I didn't think it would make much of a dent. Apparently, he didn't really apply himself until he was in his mid-teens, and tragically he died before he turned twenty, so his footprint was small and overshadowed by having been the child of one of the most famous men in history.

Kipp, in front of the fireplace, giggled, listening to Peter struggle with the willful lad. "Tad is putting Peter's patience to the test tonight," he said. Yawning, he blinked sleepily at the fire, which cracked and popped as a log collapsed, the sparks traveling up the chimney with a soft whoosh.

As I rose to get the buttermilk, I returned to Lincoln, placing the glass on a small side table next to his chair. I had picked up a woolen throw and placed it in his lap, stretching the ends to cover his chilled feet. Lincoln smiled up at me in appreciation.

"Do you know what a doppelganger is, Mrs. Holmes?" His voice rushed on. "And do you believe in the portents of such events?"

"Yes, I know the reference, and, no, I do not believe in a supernatural relation," I added firmly.

There was a reported time in March when he would see what he thought to be his doppelganger in a mirror, finding the moment disturbing. Apparently, it had happened earlier, too. He was also pursued by the many death threats made, almost on a daily basis by then. Previously, he'd brushed them off as the work of unstable minds. But increasingly, with the dreams he was having that seemed to foreshadow his death as well as the doppelganger staring back at him from the mirror, he was forced to face the fragile grasp he had on life. Mary's anxiety was not helping to stabilize his worries, and she clung to him obsessively, waiting for the other shoe to drop. She'd lost two sons and Lincoln was next, she feared. She'd even taken to wearing mourning clothing when it was not appropriate. I noticed she recently wore a particular piece of jewelry made of jet, commonly known in Victorian times as a mourning brooch.

After a pause, Lincoln replied. "I'd like to say that I am a man swayed more by letters written by learned man than the unseen things, but I confess a bad dream can leave me restless and unsettled."

I was amazed he would make such a confession to a relative stranger. But maybe that was exactly why he did so. My opinion, as a woman who would pass from his life, would not be of consequence. He spoke to relieve the burden from his soul.

Kipp glanced up at me. "I know exactly how he feels," he snorted, flaring his nostrils.

"Dreams, Mr. Lincoln, have that effect on all of us," I replied cautiously. "We awaken, not certain of our reality, remaining that way until the sun rises to cast illumination on the darkness. At that point, reason returns to a clouded mind." Sitting primly was getting on my nerves; I readjusted my skirts and surreptitiously managed to tuck one leg beneath me, quasi yoga pose. Maybe there was one good outcome of the big skirts in that the ample folds of fabric could cover many lapses in manners and decorum.

"Are you comfortable?" Kipp sniggered at me.

"I have many detractors, Mrs. Holmes, as you can imagine. Perhaps, as I try to sleep, those thoughts become nightmares, ones of my own making." Lincoln smiled. "And, perhaps, I can make them disappear just as easily."

I hesitated, not certain how personal I should become with him, considering the times. But he was an unusual man and one who had married an outspoken, politically savvy wife, which was not the typical choice. Taking a deep breath, I plunged further into the unknown.

"Mr. Lincoln, I believe the more control we have over our thoughts, the more control we have over our feelings. Hopefully, we can think away many of our fears and anxieties. That's not to say that we shouldn't be cautious of negating actual threats, but we can't allow ourselves to be overburdened by our worries."

Kipp took that opportunity to stand, stretch and walk over to rest his head on Lincoln's lap. His amber eyes closed as he enjoyed the gentle tug of Lincoln's long, slender fingers through his dense pelt of fur. A smile pulled at the corner of Lincoln's mouth.

"I wish I could be as relaxed and carefree as your dog, Mrs. Holmes. His main concern is whether or not he will get enough to eat." Lincoln laughed softly. "That is the natural life of the beasts, and we have made our human lives much too complicated."

"War and strife tends to do that," I replied.

Lincoln's thin chest rose and fell, his breaths deep and steady. I realized he was trying intentionally to breathe away his worries.

That night will always remain fixed in my memories, as I sat with a fascinating man, one who had the burdens of the future of a country and all her citizens on his thin shoulders. As Peter and I drove off into the night, I glanced back, once, to see Lincoln and Tad framed in the light of the doorway of the cottage, their hands lifted in goodbye waves.

"He managed to get his son, Robert, enlisted in the army," I remarked. Elani had stuck her head in between Peter and me to rest it lightly on my shoulder. I'm not sure why, but she seemed to think I needed some comfort. Maybe I did and hadn't realized it yet. "Lincoln is aware that he is subject to great criticism because his son isn't serving when so many have been injured or killed. Of course, Grant will put him in a protected position on his personal staff, so Robert will be safe." I sighed. "I guess I can't blame him after having lost two other sons."

There would be more action in February, 1865, too. We were

back in our hidey-hole monitoring the Surratt house. George Atzerodt had managed to take a room there, but despite his being part of John Surratt's inner circle with Booth, his use of alcohol was offensive to Mary Surratt. Her husband had been an alcoholic, and she'd had to tolerate it in him…but not in a boarder. So, after more than one episode of drunkenness, Atzerodt was evicted in a flurry of noisy, agitated activity. John had pleaded with his mother to let the man remain but, for once, she was firm in her convictions.

The re-election of Lincoln only served to whip Booth into a bigger frenzy, and his meetings at the Surratt household became more frequent. Usually, he was accompanied by Herold, Atzerodt, and Powell, as they huddled with John Surratt in the dining room. If Lincoln had lost the election, then all the plans would change, and the future of the Confederacy might be different. Swirling always, in Booth's toxic mind, was his hatred for Lincoln, which was obsessive in nature, as well as his vile thoughts about slavery, the freeing of slaves and making them citizens of a united county. Although the other men supported the plans to kidnap Lincoln, Booth's unhinged ranting and raving threatened to derail any meeting they held. While the other men could discuss the plans calmly, Booth would typically go off on another lengthy, emotionally laden harangue. It was clear he was escalating, and I found it curious that increasingly John Surratt tried to take the pose of calm reason with the man. Mary had insinuated herself into the meetings, always sending Maureen out, and working to prepare food for the men herself.

"She doesn't trust Booth," Elani said. "She may support the Confederacy, but she still thinks that the plan to kidnap Lincoln will put her son at risk. I think the best way to describe it is to say she is playing along with all of the conspiracy talk so that she will know what is going on. She is still, in her way, trying to protect John."

Kipp looked up at me. "And her protection of her son will ultimately cost her life."

We had another opportunity for a little nighttime sleuthing during the last week of February, having decided to once again follow the men after they left the boarding house. Looking back, I question my motives, since Mary Surratt was the target of our surveillance, and she was not with them. We talked ourselves into believing that it was important to review the men's thoughts, if any, about Mary to help us further determine her intent. But I don't think that was the real reason. I think we were just nosey and curious about history. That penchant for nosiness has gotten many a symbiont, including myself, into serious trouble. And so it would be again, on that rainy, cold night in February.

Kipp and I took Booth and Powell, noticing they often left together. Booth knew Powell was probably his most solid recruit, a brutish man with no scruples about savagery...Herold and Atzerodt, less so. Peter squeezed my arm, wishing me good luck as he darted after John Surratt, who was accompanied by Herold that night. Peter would return with superior intelligence than my own, since he and Elani were sifting through John's fresh thoughts following his interactions with his mother.

I was once again dressed like a man, my long hair pinned up under the slouch hat, my face covered with a muffler. The rain had lessened, turning into a fine mist that hung in the cold air like a frozen fog bank. My wool britches, dampened by the elements, tangled uncomfortably around my legs, chafing my flesh as I walked. And although I'd never say it to Kipp because the words offended him, he smelled more than a little like a wet dog. A big, wet dog. Booth and Powell had turned south, moving towards the general direction of the National Hotel as well as Pumphrey's stable. Kipp remained in the shadows between me and the building fronts. In any event, it was effortless to follow the men since we knew their thoughts before any words were spoken. As they paused beneath a street lamp, Powell turned to glance in our direction. His thoughts betrayed concern the men were being followed, but at least he didn't see Kipp and had no worries it was one Petra Holmes with her loyal dog tailing him.

At that point, the men separated, Booth leaving the misty rain to duck inside the National, seeking the warmth and comfort of his room, while Powell moved on towards the stable. Cautiously, I drew closer, Kipp huddling at my side. The cold air made it more difficult to breathe, and my chest hurt with each inhalation. Symbionts often display questionable judgment, I suppose, as I reflected on my choice to be following a really nasty guy in the dark streets of Washington. Sometimes I'm kind of stupid, I guess, and that's another factor to consider.

"Let's get out of here," Kipp breathed. He, as well as I, honed in on the thoughts of an invisible Powell after he disappeared into the stable. Powell was waiting to accost me, certain now, that he was being followed.

"You go ahead, quick, and get out of sight," I said.

"I'm not leaving you," Kipp replied.

"Kipp, if he sees you, our anonymity is gone. If he sees me, dressed like this, in the dark, he won't be able to identify us."

Kipp stared at me, a flash of fire caught in his eyes. "If anything happens, I will be back in a flash." It was clear he didn't want to leave me, but he realized the wisdom of my words. Turning, he raced up the street, turning at the next block, lost from sight.

I began to follow, my footsteps rapid. The sounds of someone walking behind me, his pace increasing to match mine, filled the otherwise empty street. It was Powell, his thoughts curious, not alarmed, since he was confident in his ability to equal and subdue any other man. I wanted to run but knew that would be a giveaway, so instead, I slowed my steps, hoping Powell would mirror me. I had calculated correctly, and he did, too, not wishing to overplay his hand. My mind was working in concert with Kipp's, who was ahead, lurking in the dark. I could feel my heart pounding in my chest; my breathing became ragged, and I forced myself to take slow, deep breaths. If Powell rushed me, could Kipp come to my aid in time? I knew there was no way for me to protect myself from Powell, who was a large, powerful man. Despite the chill in the air, I felt a bead of sweat trickle between my shoulder blades and down my back.

It was past time to do some quick, creative thinking, and I had a sudden flash of inspiration as I passed a small tavern, filled with men, smoke, and raucous laughter. Pulling my hat brim down to obscure my features, I wandered inside and approached the bar. The tender, who was an overweight man sporting a dark handlebar mustache, glanced at me.

"A bottle of whiskey," I said, lowering my voice, trying to grind out the words.

He lifted his brows, smiling, and waited to see the currency on the bar before giving me the amber-colored bottle, which was more like a flattened flask. Powell was watching me from the window, and I followed as his thoughts turned from suspicion to amusement. I wandered from the tavern, the bottle in my hand, making a big display of uncorking it and pretending to take a swig.

Powell, left behind in the shadows, laughed softly, as he watched me trail up the damp street, pausing to pretend to take another deep swallow. Just another drunkard, he thought, going to find a place to drink and stay out of the elements. He turned, going to join Booth at the National, seeking his own comfort in the hospitality Booth always offered.

I didn't realize it until I reached the next corner where Kipp waited, that my legs were trembling. It had been a tense moment for many reasons. If I'd blown our cover, the trip would be over, as well as the possibility that we would inadvertently change the timeline of events. And for such a notable event, our negative impact would be devastating to symbiont activities with a ripple effect over what trips were approved and which ones would be limited. My days of traveling might be over, and while I could live with that, I didn't want to damage the futures of Kipp, Peter, and Elani. As my fingers gratefully found the top of Kipp's broad head, I determined there would be no more nighttime excursions where we crept around the streets of Washington in pursuit of evil.

TWENTY-FIVE

March arrived, and with it came the typically unpredictable weather filled with highs and lows. A brisk wind pushing its way down from the north arrived to torment us, making the chill seem even more intense. The rain and cold, which had been largely persistent for the majority of our trip, stubbornly settled in, and a gloom hovered over the city. The days were filled with misty, drifting rain; fog cluttered the darkened hollows and valleys, hopeful the sun might arrive briefly to burn it away for flashes of brightness and color to return to the land. The war was dragging on, and even though Lincoln and his generals could smell victory in the air, it had not yet landed in the palms of their hands, and the ever present worry over the fate of the nation lingered, casting a pall over the people. I had not seen Lincoln since that evening when we spoke of prophetic dreams and doppelgangers, and I was grateful for the separation, considering what would occur in about six weeks. It was almost like withdrawing off of a forbidden and dangerous substance, craving it but knowing it would lead to my destruction. My fascination for Lincoln was just that way. He presented a conflicted face, which, for symbionts, made the investigation of his mind even more interesting. There was the melancholy underpinning which was frequently upstaged by his folksy, personable way with people. Also, there was a stubbornness to the man that served him well when surrounded by other equally strong personalities, as well as the piece of his structure that was politically calculating. All of that conflicted with his obvious soft, overly indulgent spot for his wife and children.

In terms of Mary Surratt, she kept busy with her townhouse that was full of boarders, but we felt the vibrations of her agitation and the ever-present conflict between her and John Surratt. Yes, she was "going along" but only for the purpose of keeping knowledge-able about John's activities. So as to not antagonize Booth, she played nice and friendly, while inwardly she chafed with worry. One thing was clear, however—at that point in time, the plan still revolved around a kidnapping of Lincoln. Booth might idly comment on how the country would be greatly improved if Lincoln was dead, but he had not proposed an assassination. I think at that time, only Powell would have wholeheartedly supported such a drastic move.

So, in the eyes of history, was Mary Surratt guilty? Yes, I suppose, in that she knew of a plot, and she did nothing to obstruct it. But she was still innocent of a more diabolical plan, and it was for the assassination that she was hanged. An even more interesting question to ponder would be to examine Mary's involvement in Confederate spying activities had it not been for her son. The answer to that question will never be known, and even Kipp, with his amazing investigative abilities, couldn't tweak out those facts. She was pro-Confederate, that much was apparent, but would she have stayed safely on the sidelines, keeping her opinions to herself?

There was a soft, polite tap on the kitchen entrance door early on the morning of March 1st. I was a little surprised, since callers typically would present themselves to the main entrance, and tradesmen and servants used the kitchen door. Mary Surratt peeked in through the rippled window, squinting and turning her head a little to try and see if anyone was in residence. It was the soft glow of the lantern that had drawn her to the window, much like a moth seeking a flickering flame. I was sitting at the kitchen table, sipping a cup of tea, Kipp relaxing in front of the stove. Peter and Elani had gone exploring about the city. I had declined going with them, although I'd urged Kipp. As it were, I was tired and indulging my lazy side, and the provocative lure of the warm stove was significantly stronger than my curiosity. Kipp chose to stay with me, as was his preference, even if there was something more exciting in the offing.

"Why Mrs. Surratt!" I exclaimed, glad she was visiting since reading her thoughts was much easier when I was staring at her across the room. "Please, come in and make yourself warm. I've just made a pot of tea," I added, hoping to entice her. As she passed me, I caught the ladylike lavender scent that I'd detected before.

She smiled and nodded her head. In proper circumstances, we would meet in the parlor, preferably in the afternoon when callers arrived. And if one was really upscale, one would present a calling card to be presented by a servant to the mistress of the house. The closest I might come to that particular etiquette would be to scribble my name on a napkin, I suppose. But since it was early, we broke protocol and remained in the kitchen, where the warmth surrounded us with an amber glow. I brought another of the daffodil teacups from the sideboard and set it before her with a little crockery pot containing honey and a plate of tea cakes. We'd not been able to find any sugar, and if we had, the price would have been exorbitant, so we did without just as did everyone else. It was no problem for me as I preferred honey in my tea and was content.

Mary's face looked careworn; the circles beneath her eyes were dark and shadowed, revealing a night of restless sleep due to worry and anxiety. Her usually neatly coiffed hair seemed a little askew, with a few long hairs escaping from the side rolls. Her hands, when she reached for the cup, had a fine tremor. She wore a simple silver brooch at her neck, and I noticed it was pinned just a wee bit crooked.

"She had a terrible argument with John this morning," Kipp remarked. His whiskey-colored eyes softened. "He said cruel things to her that injured her heart."

"Mrs. Holmes," Mary began, her voice soft at first before she seemed to rouse herself and strengthen. "I don't mean to be personal, but have you ever had children?"

"Yes, I had a son, George, but he passed many years ago. And please call me Petra," I added.

"And I'm Mary," she replied, nodding her head. "Children are such a blessing and bring both great joy and heartache, do they not?" Mary glanced down at her hands and frowned before she clasped them in her lap to subdue the noticeable tremor.

I realized she needed to ventilate and sought a woman in whom she could confide. "George died so young that I didn't experience the heartache associated with growing, but, yes, having to raise children and have them do right and develop into good adults is not easy. Many children, as they get older, want to oppose the wisdom of their parents and then the former pleasure becomes strained."

"I'm sorry for your loss," she murmured, dipping her head politely. Her thoughts were clear that she was embarrassed to find she'd wished to discuss the difficulties of motherhood and brought her distress to the table of a mother who had lost a son.

"As I said, it was a long time ago, and I don't feel the pain as much as I once did." I knew I'd have to give her permission to talk. "Your children seem very pleasant and bright," I remarked.

"My Anna is such an effortless child, with kind ways and a loving heart. John is more spirited, wanting to make his own way in the world."

"Well, maybe that is to be expected with a male child, don't you think?" I tried to put a positive spin on it since I was not in a position to tell her what I really thought.

"Yes, I suppose." She seemed to relax and took a deep, shuddering breath, once, then twice, before smiling at me. "This tea blend is very nice, Petra."

We went on to chat about tea, and she made a few comments about living in Washington versus living in the country at the old tavern she and her husband once operated. Her eyes rested on Kipp, who glanced up at her. "And I'm growing fond of dogs," she remarked. "Yours are so well behaved." Leaning forward, she held out her hands to Kipp, who rose, and padded across the room to lay his head in her lap. "His fur is warm from the stove. I can see the comfort you draw from his presence. Perhaps, when this terrible winter passes, I may look for a dog of my own."

It was a sad comment. Mary Surratt would not enjoy the company of a dog or, for that matter, other humans, for a long time. When the winter cleared and spring arrived, she would be placed in prison and not leave there until the day she would be executed. As she left the comfort of my warm kitchen, I pressed a canister of the tea blend in her hand, folding my hands over hers as she tried to demure. Her hands, despite the cold chill in the air, were warm and strong. She would need that strength.

The morning of March 4th arrived, and I was excited, since we planned to join the throngs of people who would be present for Lincoln's second inauguration, which would take place on the steps of the Capitol building. As I looked outside, I registered that written history was unfortunately correct, and we were facing another cold, rainy day. At least we had acquired a couple of umbrellas, and the truth of the matter was that we were just going to get soaked.

"Petra, I swear if you make any wet dog smell comments, I'm outta here," Kipp warned, lowering his head at me.

"I promise, Kipp," I replied as I tried valiantly to keep the smile from my face. Kipp had very few detectable Achilles' heels, but that was it.

Finding a carriage on that day was not in the cards, so we just decided to brave it and walk. Peter and I took positions on the outside with the lupines between us, since the streets were so crowded, we feared they'd get their feet trampled. Peter glanced at me with a mock grimace and pulled his collar up closer around his neck and face. I have to give it to him, he was game and never a complainer. A cold breeze tumbled down Pennsylvania Avenue, blasting us in the face as if we were in a wind tunnel. Reaching up, I grabbed for my hat, which, despite the hat pins, threatened to go air born. Tucking my chin to my chest, I placed my hand onto Kipp's back, and we pressed forward, with me taking advantage of his strength. The other benefit was that he and Elani kind of acted like snowplows, and people just got out of their way.

Historians speculated that at least fifty thousand people were present for the inauguration. I didn't pause for a headcount, but it might have been a few more. Well dressed men and women mingled with people clothed in rags and tattered clothing. The area reeked of a combination of damp wool, aftershave, perfume, and unwashed bodies. I almost felt a little dizzy.

Andrew Johnson, the Vice President, spoke first and seemed to have trouble focusing on his speech, which rambled on for longer than necessary. Kipp glanced up at me and nodded his head. It seemed Mr. Johnson had indulged in a little liquid courage before the speech, and the result was a loosening of his controls that was both embarrassing and unfortunate. As the crowds pressed in, I felt suffocated and had to swallow a couple of times to try and forestall that sense of drowning that engulfed me. Kipp pushed hard against my legs, almost making me lose my balance with the ferocity of his contact.

Lincoln approached the podium. In concert, the four of us found John Wilkes Booth in the crowd, his fiancée, Lucy Hale, at his side. That relationship, in itself, was complicated. The engagement had not been made public, and Lucy's father did not approve of Booth. Lucy knew Booth had political notions, but he had kept from her some of his more extreme views. He had the actor's ability to play many parts depending upon the situation and people involved. Lucy was a conquest he'd made mainly to stoke his vanity. She was highly sought-after as a companion, and Booth had her in his pocket. Such an arrangement served the part of him that was narcissistic, and that was more than fifty percent. Kipp focused briefly on Lucy, since she was unknown to us. Booth's thoughts, now familiar, spread out over the crowd to us like a dark storm cloud covering a meadow, casting shadows where none had been.

As Lincoln passed on his way to the podium, Booth lunged at him, even though he was not armed, and a policeman grabbed his arm to shove him back. I registered the alarm of the policeman, who was on guard for possible assassination attempts. Booth, using his actor's agile tongue, managed to give a convincing story to the man who released him. Meanwhile, Booth struggled to regain his composure. It would not serve his purpose to prematurely play his hand before all the pieces of his plan were in place. Booth's hatred for the cheering crowds felt like a wall, as I pressed my mind up against his. I must have worn a facial expression of dismay and dislike, because Peter gently squeezed my arm as if to remind me where I was.

Lincoln's speech, which was memorable and poetic to my way of thinking, floated over the crowds. His voice, which was oddly high pitched for such a tall man, seemed to get even higher in tone as he strained to project his words to reach all the people who were assembled. As he leaned forward, placing his hands on the podium, the misting rain ceased, and the clouds parted to reveal the golden disc of the sun as rays of brilliant light struck the earth in wavering streams of pale yellow and silver. All of us who inhabit the earth have been honored to view such a beautiful moment given to us by nature. The romantic part of my mind thought, just for a second, that Lincoln's dark head had been illuminated by a halo of golden light.

Booth's eyes were canvassing the crowd, looking for familiar faces. I drew back, hoping he would not see us, and I managed to pull Peter so that we were partially concealed behind a couple of very tall, broad men. It worked, and I followed Booth's thoughts as he registered people with whom he associated, both as a spy for the Confederacy as well as an actor. He was enraged to see freed slaves in attendance, such was his hatred for, as Kipp had noted, people with dark skin. From my place of concealment, I shuddered, thinking of those dark eyes of Booth's and what might happen if he saw us present on that day.

Lincoln fell ill a week or so later, and Peter received communication that Tad would be sent, accompanied by a staffer, to the cottage. It followed, towards the middle of the month, that the ill-fated plan of Booth to kidnap Lincoln went awry when he and Mike O'Laughlen laid in wait for Lincoln to pass on his way to the Soldiers' Home. But because of his illness, Lincoln had curtailed his trips from the White House to his refuge in the country. Booth stormed into the kitchen of the Surratt house, where he railed against John for what he believed to be poor intelligence that had sent him out on a fool's errand. Surratt, for once, lost his temper with Booth, and we waited to see if the two men would come to blows before Mary arrived to order them both to sit down while she made coffee. In the midst of a situation with no humor, that particular moment was rather amusing because she was talking to them as if they were two schoolboys out in the yard having a fight over a game. But it worked, and both men cooled their tempers and shook hands. After all, Booth needed Surratt, who was the man who kept the operations funded.

It was later that month that John Surratt, accompanied by Atzerodt and David Herold, took guns to the family's tavern in Surrattsville. We overheard the discussions from the kitchen of the Surratt boarding house. And that was not the only stockpiling of guns that was going on in the vicinity. Apparently, the Confederate spy network was doing so in the event a pivotal moment might occur, such as the successful kidnapping and detention of Abraham Lincoln. I was curious to note that Mary's agitation seemed to subside, and I believed she had given in to her strong-willed son.

In fairness to history, I realize that Mary Surratt actively involved herself with the men and their spy ring during the month of March. Not only was she made aware of the guns going to her tavern in the county, but also she acted as a courier of information between her son and John Wilkes Booth. But as Kipp sifted through her thoughts, he was not under the impression that her involvement spoke of her passion for a cause but more for her concern for her son. And there was some degree of her just having been worn down to the point of being convinced by a charismatic actor as well as John Surratt, whose believe in cause surpassed his loyalty for his own mother.

"So, although she supports the Confederacy, if her son had not pushed this scenario, she probably would have limited her support to talking to other people, and it would have stopped there." Elani took a deep breath. She was stretched out in front of the stove in the parlor, where we gathered after finishing another game of chess. I had partnered with Elani and we had been completely devastated by a triumphant Peter and a regretful Kipp.

"I think that is correct up to this point," Kipp replied. He darted his mournful eyes at me, hanging on to the bad feeling he acquired when besting me in anything. I winked at him, smiling. I had that type of love for him that enabled me to welcome his triumphs, even when they came at a cost to me.

The latter part of March would be quiet for us, since Lincoln would be traveling to Grant's headquarters in Virginia. Mary and Tad accompanied him, so Peter's temporary assignment as tutor to Tad Lincoln was on hold. Peter didn't dislike Tad by any measure, but working with him was tiring, and I don't think Peter minded the respite one little bit. And although the war was grinding to a halt with Lincoln serving as commander in chief over the victorious federal army, his moroseness grew incrementally as the days passed. April, and all it would bring, was next on the horizon.

TWENTY-SIX

I awoke slowly, reluctantly; the rain was falling heavily outside the house, the noise of the storm easily heard in the small, dark bedroom with no windows. As I lay there, I heard Kipp's breathing, slow and steady. In a moment he would awaken and fill my mind with his thoughts. But he was still sleeping, dreamless and at peace. Another soft roll of thunder trembled as I recalled a conversation Peter and I had the previous evening when Elani was outside with Kipp. I'd broached, carefully, the progress of his deepening connection with Elani. He'd shared that it was difficult for him to relax and engage since being so enmeshed was an unusual state for our contemporary brethren.

"But I'm trying, Petra," he said, his face earnest. "I think it is important, and not just because Elani wants to. It's important because it's natural, and I want to maximize my abilities."

I felt, in that moment, some worry in him that he was lagging behind the rest of us, and he most certainly wasn't. That particular concern made him push too hard. And pushing too hard often led to mistakes and lapses in judgment.

"Peter," I began, choosing my words with care, "you really need to remember that our lupine partners have skills that we lack just as we have abilities they lack. You can't compare yourself to Elani."

His dark eyes met mine as he smiled. "Thanks, Petra. I know that but sometimes forget it. I need a reminder and a kick in the butt occasionally."

"And that's why I'm here," I replied, laughing. I liked his honesty and the fact he probably could take more criticism than I did at his age. Our exchange summed up my relationship with Peter. We danced around the margins to occasionally connect on a deeper level. At times, as would be true in the human world, we annoyed one another, those times contrasting with moments of pure and total understanding and compassion. As I continued to replay the conversation, Kipp began to slowly awaken, his breath warm on my cheek as he unconsciously moved closer to press his jaw against my chest until it almost was painful. He nestled, almost like a pup, seeking the closeness of a cherished one. Reaching up, I gently scratched between his ears, the touch of his fur soft against my fingers.

"Wake up," I whispered, placing my cheek against his fur. He stirred in response.

"I think I could stay in bed and snooze all day," he replied. "The sound of that rain is like a sleeping pill."

I knew for a fact that Kipp had not taken a sleeping pill in his life, but the analogy was sound, nonetheless.

While we stayed in town, waiting for Lincoln to come back to Washington and face his destiny, we kept at our eavesdropping and watched carefully as Booth and the others continued to gently pull Mary Surratt into the web they built. And although it was impossible, I would have loved to have been a fly on the wall while the Lincolns were traveling. It was rare that Lincoln was furious with Mary, but the scandalous incident during which she embarrassed hardened men of war over her jealous exchange with General Ord's wife had left everyone in the party flabbergasted. The sight of Mrs. Ord, who was attractive and vibrant, riding a horse, while an over-weight and aging Mary Lincoln followed along in a carriage, had challenged the fragile ego of Mary. But that entire period of Lincoln's life was difficult, despite his having won the re-election. He once again saw his doppelganger lurking in the mirror as well as having a vividly disturbing dream where he'd been assassinated.

Mary, convinced his time was limited, brought mourning clothes as a part of her ensemble for the trip to Grant's headquarters in Virginia. Other than reviewing Grant's successes, the trip was an emotionally difficult one for Lincoln. While Lincoln struggled with the dark side of his psyche, he likewise toiled to keep Mary's emotions in balance and her behaviors in check. Tad went with his parents and got to experience a journey on the steamboat River Queen.

We caught up with Tad after being notified he was back in town and that John Hay would bring him to the cottage for a session one evening. Hay left as soon as we arrived, always feeling pressed to be back at work at the White House, where his workload accumulated even in his short absence. Tad, after hugging Kipp and Elani, plopped down on the floor in front of the library fireplace, lying back to rest his head on Elani, as if she was a pillow.

"How did you like the River Queen?" I asked, smiling at him. He was kicking one leg in the air in his typically energetic and rest-less manner.

"Oh, it was okay, I guess," he said. "Papa had some kind of bad dream, so mama brought me home."

"Does he have a lot of bad dreams?" I asked.

"Yeah, I think so, but I'm not sure. I don't think they want me to know, but I hear things."

I bet he did. He was a busy body, and since there were no controls on him, he barged into cabinet meetings as well as war councils. Tad Lincoln probably overheard most of the top-secret planning of the Civil War. He'd just turned twelve on April 4th, so we'd planned a little impromptu party with a cake baked by Maureen's skilled mother. Tad, because the attention was on him, was delighted. He was not narcissistic, just a boy who enjoyed being loved. Peter, despite his grumbling over his task of tutor, had become attached due to his contact with Tad; me, perhaps some, but less so. It would be hard for Peter to leave him.

Sometimes, while on a time-shift, the niceties could get lost, and Peter had, for the most part, neglected his hair and beard. He was looking really shaggy, so I made him sit in the kitchen in one of the uncomfortable wooden chairs, while I draped a towel over his shoulders. After checking the sharpness of my scissors, I aimed at his neckline, angling the shears.

"Whoa!" Peter shouted, standing up suddenly. He was lucky I didn't stab him accidentally. "Do you know what you're doing?"

"I think so," I replied tartly. "I've cut many a head of hair, and in case you didn't know, I give Fitzhugh his trims." I neglected to add I could wield a straight razor with the best of them but considered he'd probably take off running.

"Well, that doesn't make me feel any better." Peter pulled the towel a little closer to cover his exposed flesh, no doubt thinking I would draw blood in any minute.

As we grumbled back and forth like a couple of argumentative siblings, Kipp and Elani both stood simultaneously and walked towards the door to the kitchen. Although they had no need, they stared out the window at the Surratt townhouse. I saw them glance at one another before returning their gaze to the dwelling.

"Some events are falling into place," Elani finally said, turning to us. "Questions about historical facts are being answered."

"Like what?" I asked.

"Do you remember that at Mary's trial, a tenant testified she made a comment about 'getting the shooting irons ' in reference to her tavern in Surrattsville?"

I nodded. I'd rested my hand on Peter's shoulder and removed it before he complained. It wouldn't do for him to think I was too familiar.

"John Surratt and David Herold—and she is a little more impressed with him over the other of Booth's renegades because he's an educated man—have told her that Lincoln is going to have the army confiscate the firearms of all citizens who have not made a loyalty pledge. They've convinced her that people in Washington with any faint loyalty to the Confederacy are going to be locked up." Elani and Kipp exchanged glances. "She has become fearful of her safety and that of her family. They also told her that personal property will be confiscated, and she thinks the family will have to flee to Surratsville at some point."

"So that explains the reference about the shooting irons," Peter mused. "During her trial, it appeared that she was purposely stockpiling guns to assist in the assassination, while, in truth, it was related to the story she'd been told by her son and Herold."

"And the reason she said nothing to defend herself goes back to her intense need to protect her son," I concluded.

I tilted Peter's head to the side and began to trim the hair that was almost covering his ears. He looked like one of the Beatles or maybe a Monkee, but without the hip clothing.

It was April 11th, the day Lincoln would make an impromptu appearance and speech from the second-floor center window of the White House. And despite the fact we knew Booth would be there, all four of us felt the need to go. The crowds were as described, with many of the people drunk and rowdy after a day of celebration. The war, for the most part, was over and Lee's Army of Northern Virginia had surrendered. Yes, there were others still involved in skirmishes, but that would soon end, too. Without supplies and financing, there was no way in which the remaining rebel forces could continue the battle. We'd dressed in our warm clothing, since it was still chilly despite the fact we were in the second week of April. We kept to the margins of the crowd, within whose ranks there was more than a little pushing and shoving as people jockeyed for positions. The lawn and flower beds, which were already compromised by constant foot traffic, had turned into a large tract of mud, and the once lovely daffodils had been trampled into the dirt. There was no way my skirts would avoid the debris, but then, I thought with some sadness, our job would be done in a few short days and there was no need for an extensive wardrobe.

With all the human minds at work, many of them agitated and more than a few inebriated, it took quite a bit of effort to locate Booth. I knew he was beneath a tree, so each of us took a quadrant and began searching. Much of the crowd was seething with the conclusion of the war, wanting Lincoln to make the pronouncement that I knew Lincoln would not give. He would not serve the South up to the people for punishment; his way was reconciliation.

Peter, to his credit, found Booth before the rest of us, and his face glowed with the accomplishment. Before we could be seen, we moved to an angle where we would be less conspicuous, taking advantage of some battered hedges to help block us from view.

Kipp's eyes closed in concentration as he tilted his head towards Booth, who was there with Powell and David Herold.

"Booth has made the shift, the one which has teased at the edge of his brain, and now is firmly planning the assassination," Kipp murmured softly. "And he hopes to get Herold and Powell equally agitated so that they will follow his lead without question."

I had turned to the side, using veiled glances to peek at Booth, hoping we could stay hidden. It helped that the lupines were pretty well concealed behind the shrubs. Peter, likewise, turned to the side and put his arm around my back as if he was protecting me from the surging, agitated crowds.

There was a hush followed by cheers as Lincoln appeared in the center window on the second floor of the White House. After he allowed the initial, frenetic energy to dispel, he began his speech, which by some was welcomed while others were disappointed at the content. The latter group began to leave since they were not getting the excitement they desired, slowly drifting away in small groups to find happiness in taverns and elsewhere.

Booth, however, remained, his agitated and vitriolic hatred of Lincoln flowing out to our minds as we stayed engaged with him. Powell had a navy Colt revolver on his hip; Booth glanced down at it and almost pulled the gun, but resisted, knowing the chances of a kill were remote. He told Powell to try and shoot Lincoln, but Powell, who was accustomed to taking orders from Booth, knew a mob would kill him in return and refused.

It was at that precise moment when one of those issues of poor timing and the chance of fate occurred. And I suppose those things are just a part and parcel of our species inserting itself into a past time event and hoping beyond hope that everything proceeds naturally. But when I think of it, going back to Whitechapel, Kipp's chasing Jack the Ripper forced an accident that most likely caused a premature end for the man. As far as anyone knows, his reign of terror had already ended, but what if it hadn't, and he lived many more years to harm other people? It was the risk we took with our job.

"Peter!"

It was Tad's voice! He'd obviously spied us from a window and was racing across the muddied ground towards us. It would be unheard of today, but the thought of the president's son running around, unprotected, was not unusual. Tad had done it before, wearing a soldier's uniform, much to the amusement of the crowds.

Peter looked at me, stricken, hoping Booth would not witness the exchange. Sometimes luck was with us, but not on that day. I purposely didn't look towards Booth, but my thoughts locked with his to register first his amazement, followed by interest, then a growing suspicion. Yes, he'd wondered about us with our much too visible face. Now he speculated if we were Union spies, somehow aware of his plans. This had become dangerous and such events could turn just that quickly.

We managed to clumsily deflect Tad and send him home as the four of us turned back towards the townhouse. Kipp's worried thoughts tangled with mine, although none of us spoke during the journey through the congested streets. In my hurry, I managed to twist my right ankle on a large rock, the pain shooting up my leg. Kipp paused, pressing his nose against my leg with concern.

"I can make it," I said, welcoming Peter, who put his arm around my waist. It was with a sigh of relief that I shut the kitchen door behind us, happy to be back in the warmth of the kitchen. We weren't any safer, but it felt so.

"So, what do we do now?" Elani asked.

I took a seat at the table, nodding at Peter, who put a kettle on the warm stove. Maybe a cup of tea would help me think and ignore the throbbing in my ankle. And why, I wondered, were my three companions all staring at me? Feeling the pressure, I rolled my head from side to side, easing out the tension in my neck. Glancing at Kipp, I saw only trust in his amber eyes; his tail thumped the floor as he waited. I hoped I could be worthy of that trust.

"We don't know yet if we affected the timeline," I began, hesitantly. "So, leaving now or staying a few more days really makes no difference. I would opt for laying low and remaining in the event there is some recovery that needs to be made." I hoped I was thinking clearly and not just from motivation to see the event to the end since it was our task.

"You are thinking clearly," Kipp spoke confidently. "You actually don't want to be present when Lincoln is killed, when you are honest with yourself." He settled himself on the floor next to Elani. "I think we should finish this job." He sounded definitive in his vote.

"And the rest of you?" I asked.

"Let's see it out," Peter said, nodding at Elani, who blinked.

We all had restless sleep before awakening to a sunny April 12th. Peter wanted to walk to the National and have our meal delivery stopped in a few days. After all, we wouldn't need it after April 17th, unless we left earlier. With my now swollen ankle, I needed to rest, and Kipp and I stayed home.

"Be back soon," Peter said, taking his hat and coat as he and Elani disappeared out the door. He promised, on the way home, to visit an apothecary and bring me some liniment for my ankle.

I was relaxing in the parlor, enjoying the splash of sunlight that found me in my chair, foot propped up on a pillow, when there was a knock at the door. Kipp, who had been dozing, awoke, immediately stood, and I saw the hackles of fur go up on his neck.

"It's Booth and Powell," he breathed, turning to stare at me.

I could access their thoughts, too, and their suspicions of me and my party were evident. They wanted to question us and make a determination as to our intentions.

We had the choice not to answer the door, but then maybe this was the time to recover the time-shift, which had gone astray since the first moment we landed. Kipp had the same thought and nodded his head. I limped to the door and paused to take a deep breath while smoothing out my skirt, which was rumpled from sitting all morning. As I opened the door, I tried to act surprised and then pleased.

"Why, Mr. Booth! How pleasant to see you," I added, smiling at him. "May I help you?"

He actually whipped the hat off his dark head in spontaneous courtesy, as did Lewis Powell, who hulked behind him, a large, malignant presence. I glanced at Powell's once handsome face that had been injured in a long ago accident; his mind was that of a killer, one who enjoyed such acts. Booth stumbled for a moment, trying to decide how to proceed, since he didn't want to reveal his true intentions and loyalties.

"Is your brother here?" he asked.

"Why, no, Mr. Booth. He actually has gone to the train depot to check on tickets for us," I replied, thinking quickly.

"Are you leaving town?" he purred as his dark eyes examined my face.

"Yes, relatively soon. We are headed west to set up a home," I replied.

He moved forward a step, and it was all I could do not to retreat. Kipp pushed up beside me, giving me support.

"I came to tell you that I think it is time you and your brother leave town," Booth said. His face darkened a little as he frowned at me. "This town is a dangerous place for outsiders. It's really not a healthy environment for some people," he added. "And you and your brother seem to be in a lot of people's business, and that's not healthy, either." The part of the man that was enraged was starting to simmer, and he took another step forward. Although he was not a man given to violence against women, the thought flashed through his mind to strike me as if to convince me I needed to get out of town, and quickly. I think, more than anything, the aggressive impulse towards me was another indicator of his increasing instability. He wasn't sure of our intentions, but he wanted us gone so that our presence wouldn't annoy and distract him from his purpose. Behind him, Powell was grinning at me, enjoying the spectacle.

Kipp, in response to Booth's veiled verbal threat as well as his thoughts, began to growl, and I realized it was completely involuntary on his part. When Booth heard the sound, he retreated a step, and Powell's hand found the butt of his navy Colt revolver. They both saw my eyes drift to the gun.

"Kipp, stop it," I hissed, realizing Powell was on the edge of shooting him.

The rumbling stopped, but Powell, just for meanness and to frighten me, began to slowly pull the gun. Killing a dog to make a point with me didn't bother him at all; in fact, he enjoyed the temporary power he felt he had over me.

"You will not shoot my dog," I said, moving slightly to give Kipp cover behind me. "He will not hurt you." They would have to shoot me to get to Kipp, I thought grimly.

Booth's hand moved as if to stay Powell, and I saw the gun slowly slide back in the holster. "How is it your brother knows the son of the president?" he asked. Booth's dark eyes were boring into my face, hoping to intimidate me. He didn't realize he'd led me just where I wanted to go.

"Mr. Booth, that is by way of an odd coincidence, and nothing more than that. My brother and I have been going to the Soldiers' Home to read to a friend of my father. While there, we accidentally met the boy, and my brother was asked by Mr. John Hay to help him learn his ciphering and letters." I changed the expression on my face to one of fake vulnerability. "We, quite honestly, needed the money, and work is difficult to find in such an overcrowded city."

"Good job," Kipp breathed. "He's starting to relax a little." Kipp was preparing to intervene and manipulate Booth's thoughts if needed, but it appeared the looming disaster was abating on its own.

"Mr. Booth, I injured my ankle yesterday, and I hate to be rude, but I fear my ankle is painful and throbbing, so if there is nothing else with which I can help you, I truly need to rest." I was done with the man and his henchman, Powell, since Powell still had his fingers on the handle of the revolver. True, he'd stopped thinking of shooting Kipp, but that could change in an instant. One thing symbionts couldn't foresee was impulsivity.

"I'm sorry to hear of your injury, Mrs. Holmes," Booth remarked insincerely as he replaced his hat on his head. "And I hope you and your brother enjoy your exploration of new territory." He smiled, the expression fake and, he hoped, intimidating. "I think this city is too crowded for you to remain here and be content and," he paused dramatically for a moment before adding, "safe."

"And I agree, sir."

As they walked down the steps, I almost collapsed with relief, as I limped back to my chair.

"And what was that stunt of getting in front of me?" Kipp demanded.

"Do you really need to ask?" I replied.

TWENTY-SEVEN

Peter and Elani were disappointed they'd missed the visit by Booth, although I think it could have gone badly if Peter had been there. Booth had brought Powell to, well, rough up Peter if needed. And even though Booth had a sudden notion to slap me, he hadn't, and I was not really their target on that day. But Kipp and I both believed we'd done all we could to preserve the timeline. And we would stay out of Booth's way, for certain.

On that day he visited Kipp and me, April 12th, he'd finalized the plan he'd been nursing privately, and that was to move from kidnapping to assassination. Booth had been cleverly grooming the others for such a shift, mentioning his hatred of Lincoln and his fervent wish that Lincoln would die, but he'd not actually proposed the murder of the man. General Ulysses Grant was also in Washington, and Booth hoped to catch both men together and kill them in one action. Although I was busy navigating rough waters while engaged with a staredown with Booth, I was able to trace some of his stray thoughts that included the simultaneous killings of the secretary of state as well as the vice president. Such an action would cause chaos in the government and, Booth hoped, give the crumbling Confederacy time to reform and plan. He also envisioned himself become a hero of the Confederacy, and he would enjoy the fame he'd sought for years.

"One thing saddens me," Peter remarked, as he sipped at a cup of tea after blowing carefully on the rim.

"What?" I asked. It was a fact we left things accumulated behind, and I had the frivolous thought that I would miss my pretty daffodil tea set. Fitzhugh would have enjoyed serving from it during his morning tea.

"I won't have a chance to say goodbye to Tad," he said.

At that moment, there was a tap on the downstairs door; Peter raced down the staircase, his footsteps loud and echoing. As he returned to the room, he wore an expression of amazement.

"It's a message from Lincoln, asking if I can be at the Soldiers' Home this afternoon to work with Tad." Peter's eyes rounded. "Is that a coincidence or what?"

"Well, not from Lincoln's perspective," I replied. "With their trip to Virginia and everything going on with the end of the war, it's been a while since Tad had a lesson. Lincoln is just being a good parent and seeing to his son." Pausing, I waited for Peter to tell us his reply to the summons.

"I said yes." He lowered his head as if he feared I might disapprove.

"That is probably a good thing," I remarked, trying not to smile at the expression on his face. "If you can arrange a carriage so we can surreptitiously leave town, it will be a good day to do so. Tomorrow is when everything heats up."

"I know we aren't supposed to get emotionally involved, and I don't think I have to a great degree, but it seems unkind to disappear and not say goodbye to Tad." Peter's dark eyes found mine. "After all, he is about to lose his father, who he adores, tomorrow."

Kipp and Elani were lying close together in front of the stove. I'd noticed more of that since Elani practiced some of her physical empathic skills with him. Purposely, he kept the part of his mind that dealt with his feelings about Elani blocked from me, and I didn't push the issue. I couldn't help but wonder if there was a future love connection between the two, and I also wondered if I'd be the last to know. Kipp knew I was thinking about him and shot me a big mental frown across the room. Hastily, I sipped my tea.

"Let's get ready." I stood and retreated to my room to get dressed.

The message stated that Tad would be at the cottage by four o'clock that afternoon. Peter paid a boy to go fetch a carriage and have it delivered a couple of blocks from the townhouse. As we were leaving, I heard a voice call my name. It was Mary Surratt, accompanied by Louis Weichmann, and we saw she had a buggy waiting in front of her townhouse.

"Why, Mrs. Holmes," she began before correcting herself. "I mean, Petra," she said with a smile. "And, Mr. Keaton, how nice to see you, too." She seemed relaxed as she glanced up at the sunny sky, smiling, and squinting slightly as the brightness of the sun overwhelmed her afflicted eyes. "Mr. Weichmann and I are planning on enjoying a nice ride to the country," she added.

Her planned journey fell exactly where it was supposed to on the timeline. On April 11th, she had gone to the tavern to allegedly check on the guns that were being stockpiled. The lupines determined that she'd been manipulated into thinking that her family could be at risk due to their confederate sympathies and that arming themselves was a must. As we delved into her thoughts, it was clear as of that day, April 13th, she was aware that Booth and his sympathizers were working on a plan to kidnap Lincoln. Booth had gone out of his way, in her presence, to emphasize that Lincoln would not be harmed. But she was not being completely truthful with us, and why should she? Coming closer, she pressed my hand between her two. She had not yet donned her gloves, and her flesh felt warm and dry against mine. We stepped closer to the edge of the road as a lumber dray passed; the smell of sweaty horses overwhelmed the soft scent of lavender that seemed to be a part of Mary Surratt. She winced, just a mite, as the driver of the wagon shouted some ribald comment to the backside of his horses. Mary Surratt was not one to appreciate vulgarities.

"I truly hope you enjoy this lovely weather," Mary said, regaining her composure.

I realized after our talk about children she felt kindly towards me despite the fact our connections had been few and far between. John had warned her against any alliances with strangers, but what was the risk of a woman and her dog, Mary had wondered. And she'd been careful to conceal the inner workings of the household.

"Perhaps we can enjoy tea again, next week?" she asked.

"Yes, please, let's do," I responded, forcing an artificial smile on my face. No, we wouldn't share tea. Mary would be imprisoned by the next week, and she'd be executed by summer. Her blinding loyalty to her son and her manipulation at the hands of a clever, cunning John Wilkes Booth had led her to this point. Yes, she had confederate sympathies, but she was no assassin and would not have supported such an act. But she would pay for it with her life while her son failed to come to her defense and remained hidden away. Kipp pushed close to me, using his body as a physical link, although symbionts didn't need such a thing with our telepathic abilities. Nevertheless, it felt good.

Elani stepped forward, gently bumping Mary with her broad head, inviting a caress. Her fur was warmed by the afternoon sun, and Mary smiled as her fingers combed the dense fur, enjoying the sensation against her skin. Elani used the moment for another brief flash of insight into the woman.

"I told you, Petra, I do intend to get a dog of my own. You've made me into a convert with your well-behaved doggies." Mary laughed politely.

Weichmann helped her into her carriage, and they disappeared down the crowded street, their horse moving slowly against the flow of traffic. I glanced at Elani and realized she felt the same as did I. An injustice was about to take place, and it was difficult to sit back and let it happen. Mary Surratt might be guilty of many things, but she did not conspire to assassinate the president. But sitting back and allowing history to unfold was what we did and would always do.

As Peter drove the carriage out to the cottage for the last time, I relaxed, happy he'd learned how to guide a horse and buggy so I could sightsee. The trees, which had been naked and starkly gray all winter, were budding with bright green foliage, the new growth of spring. There was a wind brushing along the edge of the tree line, and I detected the faint fragrance of some flowering plant; there was a sweetness in the air that I could taste on my tongue. Our passage startled a large flock of birds feeding amongst the grass, and they took flight, their wings causing a great rushing sound in the air. Momentarily, they blocked the light, causing a shadow against the blue sky.

As usual, when we arrived, a worker had laid out some cold refreshment, an obvious gesture of thoughtfulness by Lincoln. One would have thought he had too many things on his crowded plate to worry about our comfort, but apparently not. I spied the pitcher of buttermilk, an added kind touch, since he knew I enjoyed it so much. Odd, the buttermilk almost unhinged me, and I felt the sting of tears behind my eyes.

"What's wrong?" Peter asked. The wind had disturbed his thick hair, which fell in strands across his brow. His hands found the watch chain across his chest as he fingered the links, his face searching mine.

"Just a little sad, I think," I replied, patting his arm. My hand went to his brow where I smoothed his hair into submission.

Tad was already in residence, and he raced outside with Elani and Kipp to play before he'd be forced to settle down and focus. The weather was exceptional, cool but not cold, and a stand of wild dogwoods in bloom stood silent watch on the grounds of the Soldiers' Home. Close to the cottage, lilac bushes, ancient and towering, were covered with pale lavender blooms, the scent billowing inside as Peter closed the door.

"It's going to always be like this, isn't it?" Peter asked. He'd followed me to the library.

I deciphered his meaning as I removed my green wool wrap and draped it on the back of a chair. "Yes, Peter. The engagement and the subsequent leaving are almost like a personal loss. No matter how unpleasant certain aspects will be during a time-shift, you will make connections that will be missed when you return home."

"It feels like a rollercoaster," he remarked.

"An apt analogy," I replied, lifting a dark eyebrow.

My ankle was still sore from having turned it, so I chose my favorite chair in the library and sat. Peter thoughtfully pulled up a padded ottoman and helped me to elevate the limb. He poured me a glass of buttermilk and, at my direction, pulled *Othello* from the bookshelf. I felt like a queen.

Even though the temperatures outside were becoming more tolerable, the library at the cottage remained cold and drafty, and the servant who'd supplied the refreshments had also laid a fire. Maybe there is something about the crackling sound and radiating warmth as well as the smell of wood smoke, but I just fell asleep, despite my attempts to rouse myself. Kipp was stretched out on the floor, tired after Tad's antics, and Peter and Elani had herded the child into the makeshift classroom.

"And I knew I'd find her reading, or trying to read," a voice tinged with amusement woke me from my dreamless slumbers.

Kipp was sitting up, wagging his tail, which brushed a semi-circle on the wooden floor. He slowly closed one eye at me.

"Kipp, you could have warned me," I grumbled at him. I started to stand, but Lincoln waved me to stay where I was.

"I just came out to retrieve Tad," he said. The man had lost weight from our first meeting and looked wasted and thin. One would think that the Union victory would have energized him, but he seemed more fatigued and preoccupied than ever. His thoughts revealed his ongoing worry on how to heal a fractured populace. He took his usual seat, angled in front of the fireplace. I knew, from recorded history, that he'd spent the day with Grant and was, well, curious.

"Has your day been pleasant?" I asked, hoping to tease him into an exchange.

"Very much so," he replied, nodding his head. His hair had grown long again, brushing against his white collar. His black suit was rumpled, and I noticed that a fallen cluster of blossoms from one of the lilacs was clinging to his lapel. Lincoln saw the flowers, too, and gently plucked them free and laid them on the table. "I spent the day with General Grant," he added. I'm not certain why, but he seemed to want to talk. "A very talented man, in terms of war," he added. Lincoln's head tilted to the side. "You might think such a man to be extroverted, but General Grant is very quiet and into his own thoughts." He laughed. "So, I have to pull those thoughts from him."

I smiled. "I'm certain the general is relieved that he can return home, just as all warriors when the battle is done." From my own reading of the man, I knew him to be close to his wife and always despising his separations from his beloved Julia.

"Yes, Mrs. Holmes. It is past time for our people to be home, living their lives and caring for their families." Lincoln's head dipped. For all his political ambitions, he had tired of the life and yearned to return to a simple existence. Just he, Mary, and Tad. That was all that was left of his family, since Robert had become an adult and would forge his own way. As I followed his thoughts, I realized he was still haunted by the disturbing dream he'd had a couple of days earlier where he saw himself in a coffin, the president dead as result of an assassination. He'd told Mary, who predictably became upset. The prophecy of dreams was a debatable subject for many, but it was a fact that Lincoln appeared to have many experiences and dreams that foreshadowed his own doom.

Peter emerged from the back of the cottage, his hand resting lightly on Tad's shoulder. "He did very well today, Mr. Lincoln," Peter said, lightly ruffling Tad's hair in an affectionate gesture. Tad, wanting to please his papa, began to recite a multiplication table. Lincoln's eyes widened.

"You have been a godsend," he said, smiling at Peter. "But I wonder how much credit goes to your pretty doggie, who seems to captivate my boy."

Elani stepped up to Lincoln and rested her head on his knee. For a moment, the two of them made eye contact, his gray eyes staring into her brown ones. Her ears dropped down flat as his slender fingers scratched the top of her head. As she explored him, I realized her talent was the direct opposite of Kipp's. When Kipp was boring into someone's psyche, he was intrusive and active in his pursuit. Elani, however, relaxed and was almost like an open vessel, and parts of the other individual just entered her while she remained passive. Completely opposite talents by two lupines. I couldn't wait to get back and talk with Fitzhugh.

It was to be our last time spent with Lincoln as well as young

Tad. As I prepared to leave, I collected the tiny lilac blossoms and carefully folded my handkerchief around the flowers. That little item would return home with me, an accidental gift from Abraham Lincoln.

For four symbionts who, by our nature, have eternally curious and busy minds, the ride back to Washington was unusually quiet. Even Kipp's active thoughts, which were usually bouncing around inside my head like a ping pong ball, were still, as if frozen into inactivity. The woods, as we passed, were thankfully absent of spies, highwaymen, or anyone else, and we were free to examine the birds flying to their early spring nests as well as the odd sprinkling of young wildflowers that were tempting fate, since the weather was by no means certain.

As we entered our townhouse, I glanced at the Surratt home. The soft glow of lamps illuminated the windows; a shadowy figure passed in front of one of the apertures. I sought out Mary Surratt and found her, peaceful, her home empty of conspirators, as she and Anna sat in the parlor chatting about a gown Anna had seen and coveted. Mary had returned from the country tavern on business related to Booth and now she spoke of frivolities.

I wanted desperately to make another covert trip into the city to eavesdrop on Booth at the Herndon House, but it would be a poor choice to make, and I wasn't ready to tempt fate once again. Forcing down the thought, I turned to the cold dinner we'd set out, having no appetite. As I stared at a slice of bread made with wheat and honey, the sweetness of it was lost to me, and it was as dry and tasteless as cardboard. Glancing across the room, I caught Kipp's eyes on me, his thoughts private.

"What?" I asked, tilting my head.

"You're in a mood," he replied, sharing his thoughts with Peter and Elani. "And you shouldn't be," he added.

"And why not?"

"Because we've done what we came to do, and we avoided disrupting a very complicated and important timeline. So, you've done your job and done it well." He leaned his massive head forward to lick daintily at his forepaw.

I bit back my response, which would have involved asking him who elected him the king of everything and that I had a right to feel however I wanted to feel.

"And, no, I'm not the king of everything," he replied tartly, "but you know I'm right."

And he was. I hated to admit it, but he was.

TWENTY-EIGHT

I t was the morning of the assassination, April 14ᵗʰ, and again we remained out of sight while Booth went about the city putting together all the pieces of his carefully constructed puzzle. He'd given the letter, which named the other assassins, to a fellow actor to be delivered and made public, thus ensuring no one would back out of his grand coup at the last minute. Just so we wouldn't go stir crazy, we took a walk, enjoying the temperature after what seemed to be the permanent chill left behind after winter. We were careful to avoid running into Booth, who was, at that time, engaged in his threatening stare down of Grant and his wife, Julia, who were in a carriage leaving town. It was impossible to wonder what would have happened if Grant had gone to the theatre with Lincoln, as Lincoln had wished. But Julia could not tolerate Mary Lincoln, and Julia was no meek, subservient woman. She wanted them to leave town and in doing so avoid the theatre and social time spent with a notorious gossip and sharp-tongued woman whom she despised. Grant, a man who'd led men to battle and many to their deaths, acquiesced to his wife and was probably saved from Booth's attack. We circled our block a few times so the lupines could stretch their legs.

"Petra, I'm looking forward to getting home so that we can start running again," Kipp remarked, tilting his head to glance up at me hopefully. My ankle was still sore, but the liniment Peter had obtained seemed to be a miracle cure. It smelled like turpentine and burned like the dickens, but it helped ease the pain and swelling. The label on the amber-colored bottle didn't list ingredients, and that was probably a good thing.

"Me, too, Kipp," I replied, my hand finding the top of his head.

"You know we have to go to Ford's Theatre tonight and wait outside, don't you?" he asked.

I looked at him, stricken, before realizing he'd had the conversation with Elani and, after all, it was her time-shift.

"You guys may have to make that trip without me," I stuttered, feeling my face flush.

"You cannot back out of this," Kipp replied, getting bossy. "I didn't think you were a coward."

I stopped walking, staring at him as I struggled to control my reaction. A glance at Peter and Elani revealed their startled, then embarrassed expressions. Peter's cheeks turned red as he looked down at his feet before staring across the street at a passing vendor trying to sell meat pies. But Kipp wasn't as clever as he thought, and I just as quickly realized he had used the provocative word purposely but not because he thought it of me.

"Stinker," I replied. "And I think I am a coward where this is concerned."

"But you'll go," he pushed, his amber eyes on mine.

"I'll think about it," I said reluctantly.

We resumed our walk, which had disintegrated from a brisk pace to a meandering stroll as the four of us realized what we had in store for later that evening. Unless some odd twist of fate prevented it, we would be outside Ford's Theatre when a dying Lincoln would be carried out. I didn't want to go, but it did seem cowardly, to use Kipp's word, to hide out in the townhouse while my companions finished the job. In looking back with a critical eye, I think my years of observing the occasional tragedy had worn on me more than my friends, who were still relatively new at the game.

As we returned to the town house, I glanced at Mary's home, which was quieter since her son, John, had departed. She gave voice to missing him, but privately there was a part of her that was happy he'd taken his malcontent and chaos with him. But she'd never admit to that. We set up our chessboard but paused in the afternoon to watch out the window as Booth arrived, dashing and handsome as ever, to converse with her. He was there to give her a package containing binoculars to deliver to the tavern in Surrattsville where the guns were hidden. She was delivering goods at the direction of Booth. And Weichmann, who would later testify against her, was present, although his actual knowledge of events was fractured. I guess he wanted to save his hide since conspirators were most likely going to be executed. It was not much later when Weichmann arrived in the buggy, and we saw Mary departing with him to the tavern.

I sighed, turning away from the window. Glancing up, my companions were watching me. Kipp's ears flattened.

"Come on, Petra. We're getting our butts whipped by these two youngsters. Get your head in the game." He growled at me from across the room.

I returned to the table and made a boneheaded move with my white knight. Peter really had no mercy in chess and proceeded to capitalize on my stupidity. Kipp glared at me, intolerant of my care-lessness.

"I'm not playing with you anymore," he complained.

"There's something we've never really discussed in any depth," I began, ignoring Kipp while taking a deep breath and glancing at my companions. I guess the serious tone of my voice broke the other prevailing moods and my friends stared at my face. "If we are still present when Lincoln actually dies, you need to cut off any connection you have with his thoughts."

"Why?" Kipp asked, turning his head slightly.

"It is the place we just don't need to go," I said, realizing my reason sounded weak, feeble and inadequate.

"But, why?" he asked again.

"There isn't a specific rule, but I've known symbionts who made that journey, and they were changed by it, and sometimes not in a good way. I just need you to trust me and break contact with him before he actually dies." I sighed. "And I realize the questions about the afterlife are some of the most compelling, but you just need to trust me. I don't think any of you are mature enough yet to go that far; I know, for certain, I'm not." I looked at Kipp, because he concerned me the most due to his bottomless well of curiosity. "Kipp, you must promise."

"But I've been in the presence of humans who died..." he began before I cut him off.

"It's different, Kipp, when you spend time with a human and become involved with the person on an emotional level. There is the temptation to follow that individual due to the connection you've had. I think, in general, we have some innate protection, an inner instinct, which keeps us from going too far. But with that emotional connection, our protection fails and curiosity and emotion take over."

He took a deep breath and looked away for a moment. Then his eyes met mine. "Okay, Petra, I promise."

The others did, too, and I relaxed. How was it we'd not really talked about this compelling issue? In any case, I was ready for a nap, since we had a long evening ahead of us, and my focus and concentration was not what it needed to be. The others reluctantly agreed, and we retired to our rooms. Wanting comfort, I stripped down to my chemise and climbed in the bed which was narrow and the mattress stiff, but it felt as if I'd sunk down into a cloud. This time-shift had been exhausting, mentally. Kipp climbed up and curved as close as possible to me, resting his head on my chest.

"I was just kidding, you know. I always want to be your partner, even when you can't play worth a dime," he added.

"I know, Kipp. Go to sleep."

And sleep all four of us did, until darkness fell. I awoke first and tentatively peeked into the quiescent minds of Peter and Elani, who were resting, dreamless, their bodies at ease. Kipp was dreaming of Booth, and in his dreams he was part of the pursuit party chasing Booth after Lincoln was shot. Kipp's legs were paddling in the bed, tangled in the sheets, as he ran in his dream state. I put my hand on his side to gently waken him.

"What?" He sat up awkwardly, confused.

"Time to get up," I whispered, tweaking his ear. "It's okay; you were dreaming."

"Whew! And I am worn out," he complained. "I've been running for hours it seems."

To fortify ourselves, we ate some cold leftovers, but none of us had an appetite. Peter checked his watch, and it was 9:30 in the evening. The assassination would occur in forty-five minutes. As we left the townhouse, I glanced across the street. Mary's home was quiet, the kitchen dark. She had probably put her day to bed and was resting. Searching, I found her, probably in her room, trying to darn a sock despite her visual problems, straining to see with the feeble light of an oil lamp.

The streets lacked the business of commerce as seen during the day, but the evening was an active time in the city, with people going to the theatre, seeking dining, or enjoying the company of friends. We took our time, sticking to the darkness as much as possible. It was our plan to find a hidden corner where we'd not risk being seen by anyone who could recognize us and watch the event. We took H Street until it intersected with 7th Street and turned south, walking slowly. The front of Ford's Theatre was lit by lanterns, the flickering lights cascading upward to illuminate the entrance. Boards had been placed, since the streets were muddy, so that women could leave their carriages and not have their gowns soiled. Quickly the four of us did a mental sweep and didn't find Booth in the immediate vicinity, so we hurried past Ford's and passed the row house where Lincoln would be taken and found refuge on the other side of a porch where a steep set of steps angled to meet the level surface.

Kipp closed his eyes and focused, turning his head back and forth slowly. I knew he was looking for Booth.

"He's behind Ford's," Kipp whispered. "He's giving his horse to Ned Spangler to hold for him."

As we waited, huddled in the darkness, the occasional carriage or man on horseback would pass us. I fancied I could hear laughter from inside the theatre, as the crowd appreciated the comedy being presented, *Our American Cousin*. John Parker, Lincoln's worthless bodyguard, had already left the doorway where he was supposed to be protecting the president, and was in Taltavul's getting blasted with his daily allotment of whiskey. It was time to solve another little mystery that had haunted me.

"Kipp, find Parker and determine if he was part of the conspiracy." Although he'd been found not implicated, I'd always wondered. It was very convenient for him to be absent at the exact time Booth arrived. Since we'd briefly met Parker, Kipp could do as I asked, although it was a bit of a push, and he was panting but victorious when he found him amongst unfamiliar minds.

"He's had too much to drink, so his thoughts are all jumbled up," Kipp said. "But I get nothing at all that would make me think he is a part of the assassination plot. I think it was just fate that he was absent when Booth arrived."

I glanced at Elani. "A side mystery solved," I said, nodding at her.

The street lights were flickering; a mild wind stirred the leaves in the few trees that had been left for decoration along the street. A couple passed us, strolling, as we sank back into the shadows even further. Inhaling, I caught the smell of his cologne—dusky like autumn's fallen leaves—as well as her perfume. Two nicely dressed individuals out for the evening, thinking nothing at all exciting would happen on that particular day. Since we all knew Booth quite well by then, he was easy to spot as he turned the corner to go to Taltavul's for a shot of whiskey, finding amusement that Lincoln's bodyguard was there, drinking, too. There were so many people inside Ford's that I could not find Lincoln amongst the dense web of swirling emotions and thoughts. Kipp could and did.

"He's enjoying himself," Kipp said, looking up at me. "He feels very close to Mary, almost playful as if they are courting one another again."

Cautiously, I peered around the barricade of steps and watched as Booth left the tavern, almost swaggering as he walked to Ford's. The flickering street lamps cast their light, and his moving shadow was caught against the wall of the theatre. Of course, he was a well-known figure there, and his admittance was not questioned. I knew everything would turn, and it did, in that moment. It was almost as if a tsunami hit us all in the face as the happiness inside the building turned to confusion and then horror. Kipp physically flinched as Booth's bullet struck Lincoln. And since I was connected with Kipp, I realized, too, Lincoln's flash of confusion, and then the thoughts numbed and went dark, almost as if a candle had been blown out. There was no fear, just startled confusion, and then nothing coherent. Yes, he had awareness of those around him and the chaos and emotion, but he lacked the ability to put it into any type of organized thought process. He could hear Mary's anguished wailing and wanted to reach out and comfort her but couldn't.

And I give credit to Peter, who was trying to find Booth, and he did so, noting Booth's triumphant exit on horseback as he galloped away into the darkness on F Street. People began to boil out of the theatre in mass, and crowds such as that can be dangerous. We pulled back even deeper into the corner where we huddled against the row house. It was not long before militia arrived to restore order, and four soldiers carried Lincoln's prostrate body on a board across the street to the Peterson house. Mary followed in his wake, her sobbing heard over the noise of the crowd. The four of us had to detach from her, so painful was her grief and fear. It was simply not bearable.

We'd had the debate as to how long to stay with the cautionary advice I'd given to separate from Lincoln before he actually died. And Mary Surratt would not be immediately arrested, so we didn't have to rush back to the townhouse. But the crowd's agitation escalated more than we anticipated, and one man was almost killed as people looked for someone to blame. Neither I nor my companions had any wish to risk injury at the hands of the mob. As the soldiers struggled to restore some order, even resorting to fists and drawn swords, we realized it was time to go. We'd learned all we could, and it was time to return to the townhouse to observe what was to happen with Mary Surratt in a few short hours.

As one would expect in a small town, which Washington was in those days, the word of the attempt on Lincoln's life was spreading like wildfire, and small groups of people were huddled, their faces filled with a multitude of emotions. For those who opposed him, there was quiet relief and even happiness since he was viewed by them as a tyrant. But for those who loved him, there was unimaginable pain. There were even people openly weeping amongst those who were angry and looking for vengeance. We managed to get home safely and, with a collective sigh of relief, closed the kitchen door behind us and locked it. Peter started to light a lantern but I stayed his hand.

"Let's keep it dark and pretend no one is home," I suggested. "We've been seen in the company of Mary Surratt and could be implicated."

We huddled in the parlor, in darkness, and two hours later, we heard the clatter of horses' hooves on the street below. Peeking through the windows, we saw a group of men approaching the Surratt house. A man stepped forward and began to knock on the door; one by one, I could see the windows above illuminated by lantern light. The door opened, and Mary, wearing her dressing gown, stood in the aperture, clearly startled.

"Elani, this is your time-shift," I said. "So, what conclusions do you draw?"

She concentrated, as did we. "Mary Surratt is surprised to learn of the assassination of Lincoln. The men are looking for Booth as well as Mary's son, John. She is anxious, fearful that John has involved himself in something grave and potentially disastrous."

"How did the men know to come to her house?" Peter asked.

"A fellow actor of Booth's was aware of some of his extreme views and had been at a tavern when Booth was meeting with John Surratt when the two men were introduced. After the shooting, the actor mentioned this connection to the militia." Kipp took a breath. That particular bit of information was difficult to come by since he'd had to pry into the brain of the man speaking with Mary. I stroked his furry head. Kipp was and is remarkable.

"She is telling them she's met Booth but that she knows nothing. And she's lying about John, stating he's been out of the country for weeks."

Kipp stood and his posture became rigid. His amber eyes were following a shadowy figure who arrived, standing at the edge of the group of soldiers. As I watched, the figure turned and pointed to our townhouse, where we lurked, hidden out of sight. Two of the soldiers turned, too, their heads tilted in curiosity.

"Uh oh," Kipp muttered. "That man is a neighbor on this street who has mentioned that we seem to be cozy with Mary Surratt and also said he saw Booth visit this home."

As he spoke, a small group of the soldiers broke off and began walking rapidly across the muddy street to the street-level door. They began to pound on the door, the sound resonating up the stairs to where we hid in the parlor. As the sounds intensified, we could hear the door began to splinter.

"Uh, guys, I think it's time to leave." I stood and rushed the others to the small room I'd shared with Kipp, closing the door behind us.

I had the handkerchief with the lilac blooms Lincoln had discarded tucked into my bodice. Other than that, we made certain we had the essentials, which would, for me, be Harrow's pearls resting cool against my neck, and Peter's grandfather's watch, which he was wearing. Everything else was expendable...even the daffodil tea set.

I sat on the floor, Kipp's head in my lap, while Peter and Elani took a similar stance. Footsteps sounded on the wooden stairs, approaching the parlor landing, as I felt the surroundings melt, and the sound of rushing air filled my ears as we fell into blackness.

TWENTY-NINE

"So, did you all just get bored while I was away?" I asked, standing next to Fitzhugh in the doorway of my house. It was good to be back home in North Carolina. In some ways, it seemed we'd been gone for years, but in others, I felt I'd just left and returned after a day trip to the country. But we had remained gone for the entire period that surrounded events before and after Lincoln's assassination, and during that time, my friends had been busy. As I watched, a large rental moving truck parked awkwardly two houses away across my street. Since it was April in the piedmont, the trees' limbs were heavy with fresh growth, the vividness of the green leaves filtering the bright sunlight which struck the ground in an uneven pattern of gold. The door of the truck opened with a groan that caused the birds to flee in alarm, and a figure well known to me hopped out. It was Philo, who seemed to have rediscovered his energy following the demise of his marriage to Claire. Through years of close association, I appreciated the vitality and snap that seemed to be in his walk. He was clearly feeling good again. Turning, he spied Fitzhugh and me and waved, a smile on his face.

"How do you feel about so many of your associates crowding in?" Fitzhugh asked. His shoulder brushed mine as he turned to go to the kitchen to retrieve the whistling kettle of water. In Fitzhugh's world, it was tea time.

It seemed Philo had pounced on an available house that happened to be on my street and sold his large, cavernous one during our absence. I think the echoes of the empty halls and years of accumulated memories had finally weighed too heavily upon him. He would live in the newly acquired home with Vashti, who seemed very content to be a non-traveling companion for a change. And, to make things even more interesting, there was a small basement apartment, and Philo was renting that to Peter and Elani. My street, typically overrun with humans, would now be overrun with symbionts.

Kipp was not with me at that moment, since he'd rushed across the street to monitor and, with his characteristic bossiness, direct all the activity. I wasn't sure how he felt about Elani living in such close proximity, but he seemed a little too excited...in a deliberately nonchalant way. Following Fitzhugh to the kitchen, I dropped into a chair and watched him make tea while ignoring his question. "Fitzhugh, there was this lovely tea service we bought and used, and I wish I could have brought it home to you." I began to describe it, realizing my words didn't do it justice.

"And you are avoiding my question," he replied, smiling.

"While you are at it, Kipp needs some information retrieved about past symbionts and how they navigated the issue of being in contact with a human who is dying. He wants to add that topic to the ethics class." I nodded as he placed a teacup in front of me; the distinctive smell of bergamot filled the kitchen.

"Okay, don't answer me." Fitzhugh set the steeping pot on the table and sat opposite me. "What is your impression of Victor?" he asked. In my absence, Philo had brought on a new assistant to work with Fitzhugh in the library. "I could be wrong, of course, but I think he will get on splendidly with you," he finished in a rush of words. It was clear he hoped to please me. Since historically he'd not cared one way or the other about my feelings, the fact he did now was a sign of our evolving relationship.

"Well, I hope so. I'm ready for some peace and quiet." Even as I said it, I realized I probably wasn't, since it wasn't really in our nature to remain quiescent for long. Maybe a few weeks would be nice? Victor and his symbiont, Fyre, were former travelers until Fyre was badly injured—oddly, not during one of our dangerous time-shifts but as result of a car accident. With his leg broken in several places, he'd lost the confidence as well as agility needed to time-shift, and the two remained earthbound. I didn't get the impression Victor minded, but in Fyre there was an underlying restlessness that was undeniable. He didn't care for being stuck in a single dimension, but such was his life unless he regained his willingness to engage in life-threatening work. Philo was looking for a good employment fit for him at Technicorps, which would be difficult since he lacked some of the advanced skills that made Kipp, Elani and Juno more flexible. He might not have thought so, because of his bad leg, but Fyre was a very attractive lupine, still relatively young and very bright. Is it not so that we often see qualities in others that they cannot see in themselves?

Kipp distracted me from my thoughts as he arrived at the back door, demanding entrance. "Wow, this is gonna be great!" he exclaimed, walking up to place his large chin on the edge of the table. "We'll all be together." His back end swayed with the vigorous wagging of his tail. "And Philo said something about grilling out, whatever that means, but it involves food. Why don't you grill out?" he asked.

I started to make some negative comment before I realized that for Kipp, who lost his family so young, this was a recreation of a family and, therefore, important. Smiling at him, I ruffled the fur on top of his head. "Tell Philo I'll be over in a minute to help, okay?" It was with effort I restrained myself from teasing him once again about Elani.

Kipp dashed out the door again, disappearing around the corner of the house. I wondered what my neighbors thought of all the large dogs racing around, but since my symbiont partners had never posed any issues, there had been no complaints. And as long as one's "dog" stayed on one's property, there was no violation of any ordinances. So we were good.

"This is a bit of a change, Petra, you must admit." Juno's soft voice entered my mind. I could be a little avoidant and sassy with

Fitzhugh, but not Juno. "You were accustomed to living a quiet life, just you and your symbiont. Now you have me and Fitzhugh, as well as Lily," she said, nodding to the striped feline who stalked into the room looking for food. Finding her bowl empty, Lily sat and glared at me, wrapping her tail tightly around her feet.

Sighing, I went to the cabinet and found a little can of something horribly smelly; the stinky food seemed to be her favorite. Lily danced on tiptoes, doing figure eights through my legs as I spooned the contents into her bowl. Fitzhugh was smiling at me.

"What?"

"You're all domesticated," he said, laughing.

"I'm going to help Philo," I replied, not liking to be caught in a trap of words. Following Kipp's path, I exited out the kitchen door and wandered around the side of my house. Some shrubs were getting too large, I thought critically, fed by the spring rains and ample sunlight. Maybe I needed to hang around for a change and get some work done on my home. There were a couple of symbionts I recognized from Technicorps helping lift the heavier objects, while Philo and Peter struggled with a love seat.

"Get the door, will you?" Philo grunted. The sweat was beaded on his forehead, and his face was flushed, but he was clearly enjoying himself.

"Glad I can help," I replied, ignoring his glare. Curious, I entered the house, which seemed like a good mama bear choice… not too big, not too small. Since I was nosey, I wandered to the stairs and found the basement apartment that would be Peter's new digs. Elani followed me, the excitement glowing in her dark eyes.

"Won't this be wonderful?" she said, her tail wagging with happiness. "We'll all be close by and can spend more time together."

I hoped it would be wonderful. Sometimes too much time spent in the company of friends and loved ones could get strained. It was good Elani had brushed past her initial discomfort being around Vashti, and they now seemed to get along splendidly. But I realized, in her love-struck heart of hearts, she could see Kipp more often and not appear as if she was making an effort. It would be a simple thing to come over to my house to borrow, let's say, a cup of sugar, just to be able to say hello to Kipp. I went back to the kitchen, which was nice and spacious with lots of windows overlooking a small garden in the rear. The yard was a little neglected, but I figured Philo and Peter could whip it into shape. There was a large box labeled "dishes", and I began to unpack them. Philo walked by, holding the other side of a large table. "Just put them up, please, anywhere that looks reasonable and logical."

It was nice to have free reign, and I began to whistle a little as I worked. Without being conscious of it, I picked a well-known song, and before long, I could hear Elani singing the words, audible in my head. Yes, I figured this closeness could be okay. Maybe.

As I scouted out the prime locations for the dishes, I thought back to our return from 1865 Washington. Elani had led the debriefing of our trip, and it was a difficult one, simply because she was so honest. I'd learned, over time, to breeze past moments that might cause the Twelve to wrinkle their collective brows and frown at me. No, I wouldn't say I actually lied to that august body, I just minimized the rough spots. In my way of thinking, why did they need to worry about the process if the outcome was okay? Elani pulled out every detail in a painstaking manner, not omitting any possible flubs that we made. In the end, however, the Twelve felt we'd recovered as much of the original timeline as was possible and averted a potential disaster. It was not my easiest time-shift, nor was it my most difficult. If I were forced to choose, I think it would be a tossup between Titanic and Whitechapel.

I heard voices in the hallway and glanced up to see Victor arrive, laughing at something Philo said. Why would a new guy help someone move unless he wanted something in return, I thought cynically? Then, I felt bad because I realized, as I listened, that Philo had helped Victor when he moved to our collective, and Victor was returning the favor. Fyre ambled into the kitchen, his limp pronounced. And a moment later, Vashti followed him, her eyes meeting mine as she gave a wag of her tail.

"Petra, have you seen my water bowl? Everyone is getting a little thirsty...I think Philo packed it in that box over there," she said, using her long nose to point.

Yes, it was there, or I had completely lost my touch. She was making veiled glances at Fyre, who was trying not to look back at her. I felt like I was at an adolescent dance party where everyone is a little awkward at first, waiting for someone else to make the first move. Well, I age myself. Adolescent dance parties used to be such, and I had no idea what on earth was going on with humans in the contemporary age, but I suspected it was a little more freewheeling than it once was. I wanted to groan. First there was Kipp and Elani; now we had Fyre and Vashti. I felt old.

Filling the water bowl to the rim, I stepped back and placed it on the floor and watched the dance of courtesy between Vashti and Fyre. As I watched him limp forward at her insistence as hostess, I registered how badly his right foreleg must have been shattered to leave him with such a pronounced limp. He was an unusual color of brown and just starting to get the tiniest fringe of gray on his muzzle. Fyre made me think of a distinguished middle-aged man who was acquiring gray at the temples, just enough to make him look learned and dependable. Yes, it was there, subtle but present. Vashti had a crush on Fyre. Great, I thought. All the love waves circling in the air would give me a headache.

Philo rushed past, whistling, having picked up the tune I'd been humming. He squeezed my arm and kissed me on top of my head before pulling his wallet out of his back pocket and throwing it on the table.

"Hey, call the pizza guy and order us some food," he ordered before disappearing. "And no onions, since Kipp doesn't like them."

I personally refused to have a cell phone, but Peter did and made the call. Thirty minutes, the pizza guy promised. Oddly, I needed to see Fitzhugh again and walked back over to my house. He was still sitting at the dinette, sipping tea. Nodding, as if he expected me, he poured me a cup and thoughtfully added a spoonful of honey to mine.

"What is bothering you?" he asked, glancing up at me. The room was empty, save him. Juno was in my front parlor room, snoozing in a patch of sunlight. "You are more restless and unsettled than usual."

"Fitzhugh, what exactly do you know from your experience about travelers who have stayed telepathically connected to a human who is dying?" I clasped my hands in my lap as I sat across from him. "The idea is disturbing to me."

"Why is that?"

"Well, for symbionts as well as humans, there is curiosity about the afterlife, and we have developed belief systems to help us cope with the unknown. Some of us choose faith, others choose science or nature, and then there are those who believe there is no afterlife. The fact that it is technically an unknown until one makes that final journey means that one's belief system could be challenged." I sighed deeply.

He nodded. "And that is one reason we don't advocate symbionts maintain that connection. Any particular symbiont's belief system could be challenged and cause a life-changing moment." Fitzhugh smiled. "But I think more importantly, that final journey for any of us is deeply personal, and I know I would prefer to take it without others monitoring me out of curiosity. I would have to think it is the same for most humans."

"Maybe that is more of the issue," I replied, glad we were talking. "It feels morbid to glom onto someone's personal spiritual journey. Or even if that human—or symbiont—is not particularly spiritual, there is the departing of life that is emotional." I sighed again. "Kipp may need more help with the explanation than I can give him." I lifted my eyebrows and smiled. "You know how he is."

"I'll talk with him," Fitzhugh promised. "And it is a good topic to introduce to the ethics class. People, as well as symbionts tend to avoid discussing death, but it is just another part of our life cycle."

Fitzhugh had already had a couple of heart attacks, and even though he seemed pretty vigorous, one never could know. And then there was Juno, who was aged.

"Fitzhugh, do you think we sometimes avoid deeper connections for fear of losing one another?"

"Are you speaking in generalities or are you speaking of yourself?"

I glanced at him and laughed. "It seems a little unreal to me, our journey, I mean. I can't envision in the past having this type of meaningful discussion with you. And I doubt you thought you'd see yourself sitting across the table from me talking as we are right now."

"And we have, despite our earlier rough start, developed a close relationship. Petra, I never had a daughter, but if I had, I would like to think she would be more than a little like you. And I would hope we would be able to touch one another's hearts and minds." He smiled through his beard and mustache as I felt my heart squeeze at his words. "I think I see so many of your qualities that mirror mine, and that has made for some past quarrels as well as personal growth."

I glanced at the back door; Kipp stood there, his sides heaving with exertion. He purposely was staying out of my head but returned with a vengeance, demanding I open the door.

"Philo needs you," he said, taking a few deep breaths. "The pizza guy is about to show up."

"If there is pizza, count me in, too," Fitzhugh said, standing. Reaching down, he held out his hand, which I took. "Let's go eat."

It seemed a good thing to do. I wasn't exactly unwilling to have a deep, purpose-driven discussion with Fitzhugh, but at the same time, it was sometimes nice to share some pizza, laughs with friends, and good times. Before we left, I peeked in on Juno, who was in a deep, comforting sleep. Not wanting to awaken her, I determined I'd save her a slice. As Fitzhugh and I rounded the corner of my house, I saw the bright sunlight strike Kipp's broad back, the ruddy fur looking like burnished copper. There was a mild breeze angling through the trees, and Kipp turned into the wind, lifting his head as he took in the scents of the neighborhood. He could have remained wild and untouched, but he had chosen life with me. I reminded myself of his choice and the degree of responsibility I felt to be a good partner to him. He had such capacity for growth and knowledge, and I hoped I could be up to the task. Kipp turned to glance at me, and his thoughts flooded my mind.

"I love you," he said.

"Ditto, kid," I replied.

ROBIN HOOD, 1192

THE SYMBIONT TIME TRAVEL ADVENTURE SERIES, BOOK SEVEN

It all began with a novel, *Ivanhoe*, written by Sir Walter Scott. Who would have thought Kipp's fascination with the story would escalate into one of the most challenging adventures to date for an intrepid and endlessly curious quartet of time travelers?

Was Robin Hood based on the life of a real man, or were the adventures, which lasted over centuries, just fables created to entertain the populace? Petra and her partner Kipp intend to find out, traveling back to medieval England posing as a young woman and her dog. They are accompanied by the duo of Peter and Elani, who are young learners trying to master a complicated craft.

The culture itself poses challenges as does the political intrigue of the times, when Richard the Lion Heart is absent, and his brother, Prince John, schemes to take control of the country. The sheriff of Nottingham dominates the lands that encompass Sherwood Forest, and strangers traveling in his domain are immediately under suspicion as he struggles to control lawlessness. Somehow, a group of contemporary time travelers must use their telepathic gifts to avoid detection as they search for the real Robin Hood.

Available in Paperback and eBook from Your Favorite Bookstore or Online Retailer

ALSO BY T.L.B. WOOD

The Symbiont Time Travel Adventures Series

The Symbiont

Tombstone, 1881

Whitechapel, 1888

The Great Locomotive Chase, 1862

Titanic, 1912

A Conspiracy to Murder, 1865

Robin Hood, 1192

ABOUT THE AUTHOR

T.L.B. Wood began her love of liter-
ature at an early age, encouraged by
her mother who was an English
teacher. She and her husband share
a love of nature and animals, and
more than one rescued dog or cat
has found a forever home with the
Wood family.

T.L.B. is an author in many
genres: the inspirational romance *In
the Eye of Hugo*, a paranormal history
The Way of Telitha, the science fiction
novels *The Last Child of Tole* and *The
Ambassador from Tole*, and the epic fantasy *The Eagles of Arundell*.

She is best known for her young adult Symbiont Time Travel
Adventure Series, which includes the books *The Symbiont*, *Tombstone,
1881*, *Whitechapel, 1888*, *The Great Locomotive Chase, 1862*, *Titanic,
1912.* and the forthcoming *A Conspiracy To Murder, 1865*.

In that series, time travelers with an eye for detail and a nose for
trouble travel from the present era to investigate history's great
mysteries. Humans think Petra is one of their own, a young woman
accompanied by Kipp, her seemingly canine companion. But the
reality is that Kipp and Petra are a bonded pair of telepaths in
search of adventure.

T.L.B. has been described by reviewers as writing characters that
"feel like old friends" with her "intelligent writing and research,"
and "improves with every book she writes."

Join the adventure!

www.ingramcontent.com/pod-product-compliance
Lightning Source LLC
Chambersburg PA
CBHW030959260626
47169CB00002B/619